THE WHOLE WORLD'S CRAZY

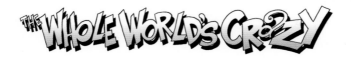

Jimmy Gownley's

AMELIA RULES!™

THE WHOLE WORLD'S CRAZY

Atheneum Books for Young Readers
New York London Toronto Sydney

· Special thanks to Michael Cohen ·

Atheneum Books for Young Readers
An imprint of Simon & Schuster Children's Publishing Division
1230 Avenue of the Americas, New York, New York 10020
Book design by Jimmy Gownley and Sonia Chaghatzbanian
Manufactured in China
0311 WGL
First Atheneum Books for Young Readers paperback edition May 2009
6 8 10 9 7 5
ISBN 978-1-4169-8604-1

These comics were originally published individually by Renaissance Press.

With Love and Thanks
to Mom and Dad...

With appreciation for
the Vision and Faith of
Joe, John, Jerry, and Bill...

And with gratitude for
the Patience and Friendship
of Michael...

This book is dedicated with love...
for Karen.

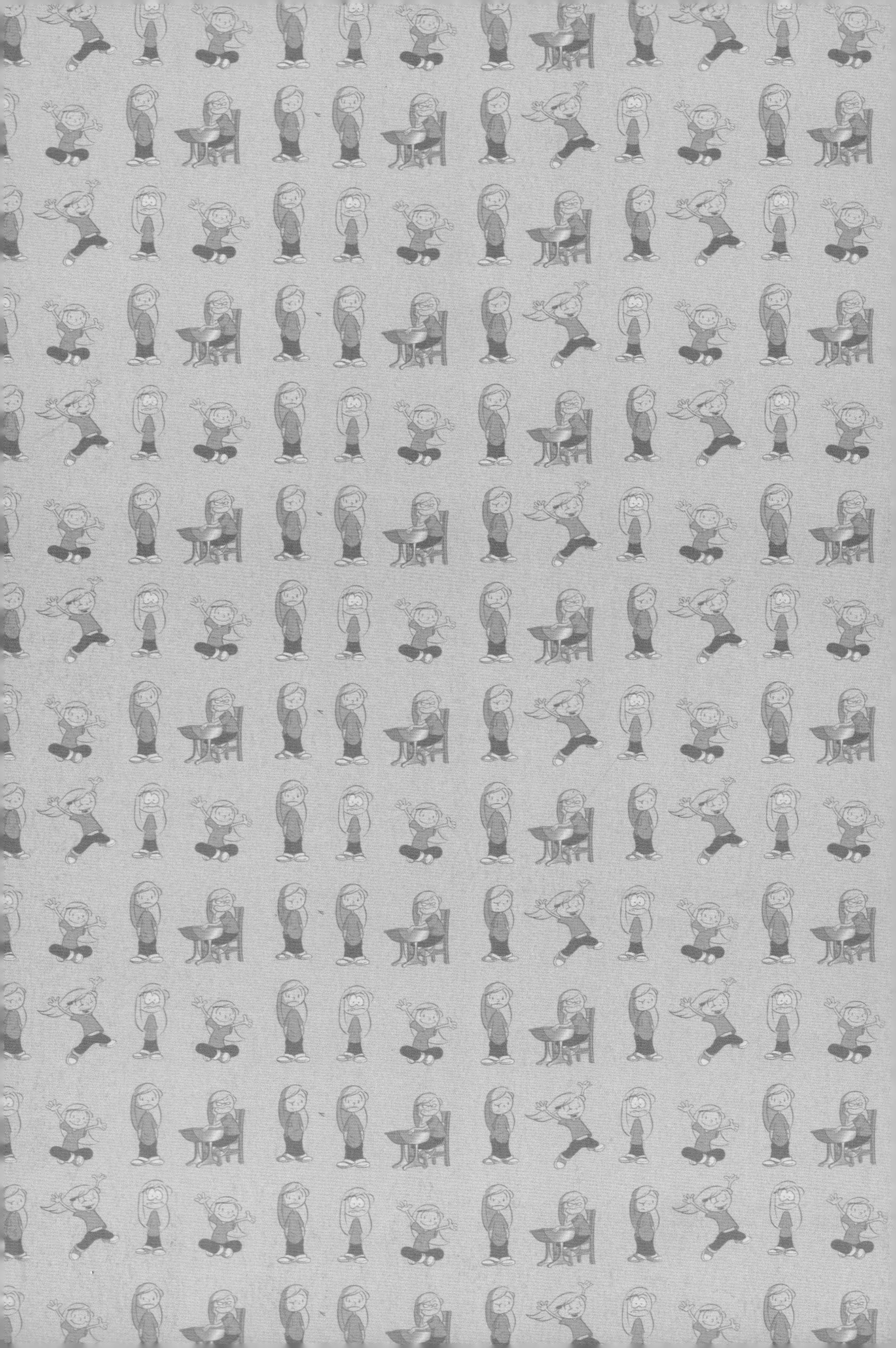

Amelia vs. the Sneeze Barf

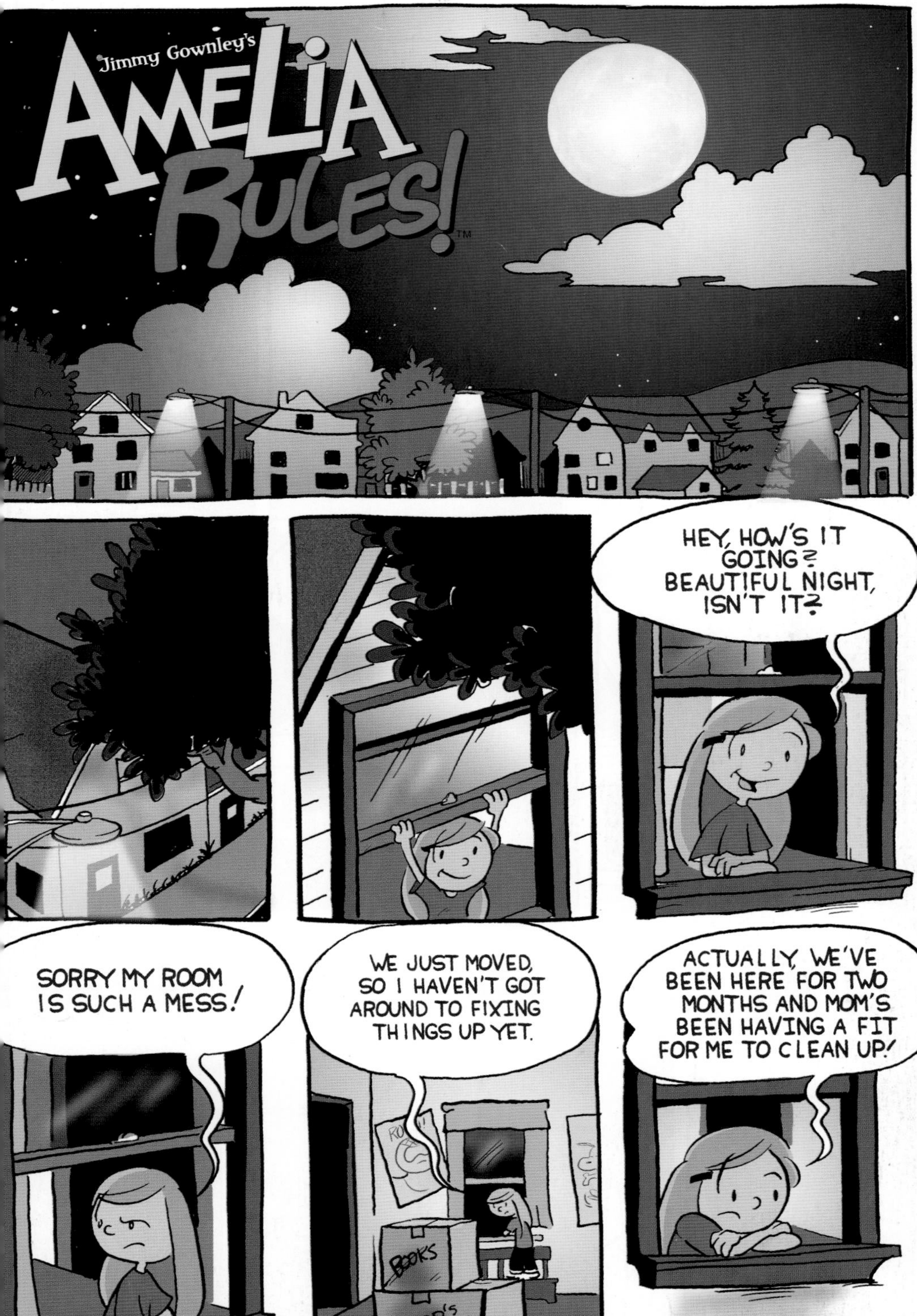
Jimmy Gownley's
AMELIA RULES!
TM
HEY, HOW'S IT GOING? BEAUTIFUL NIGHT, ISN'T IT?
SORRY MY ROOM IS SUCH A MESS!
WE JUST MOVED, SO I HAVEN'T GOT AROUND TO FIXING THINGS UP YET.
BOOKS
CD'S + COMICS
FRAGILE
ACTUALLY, WE'VE BEEN HERE FOR TWO MONTHS AND MOM'S BEEN HAVING A FIT FOR ME TO CLEAN UP!

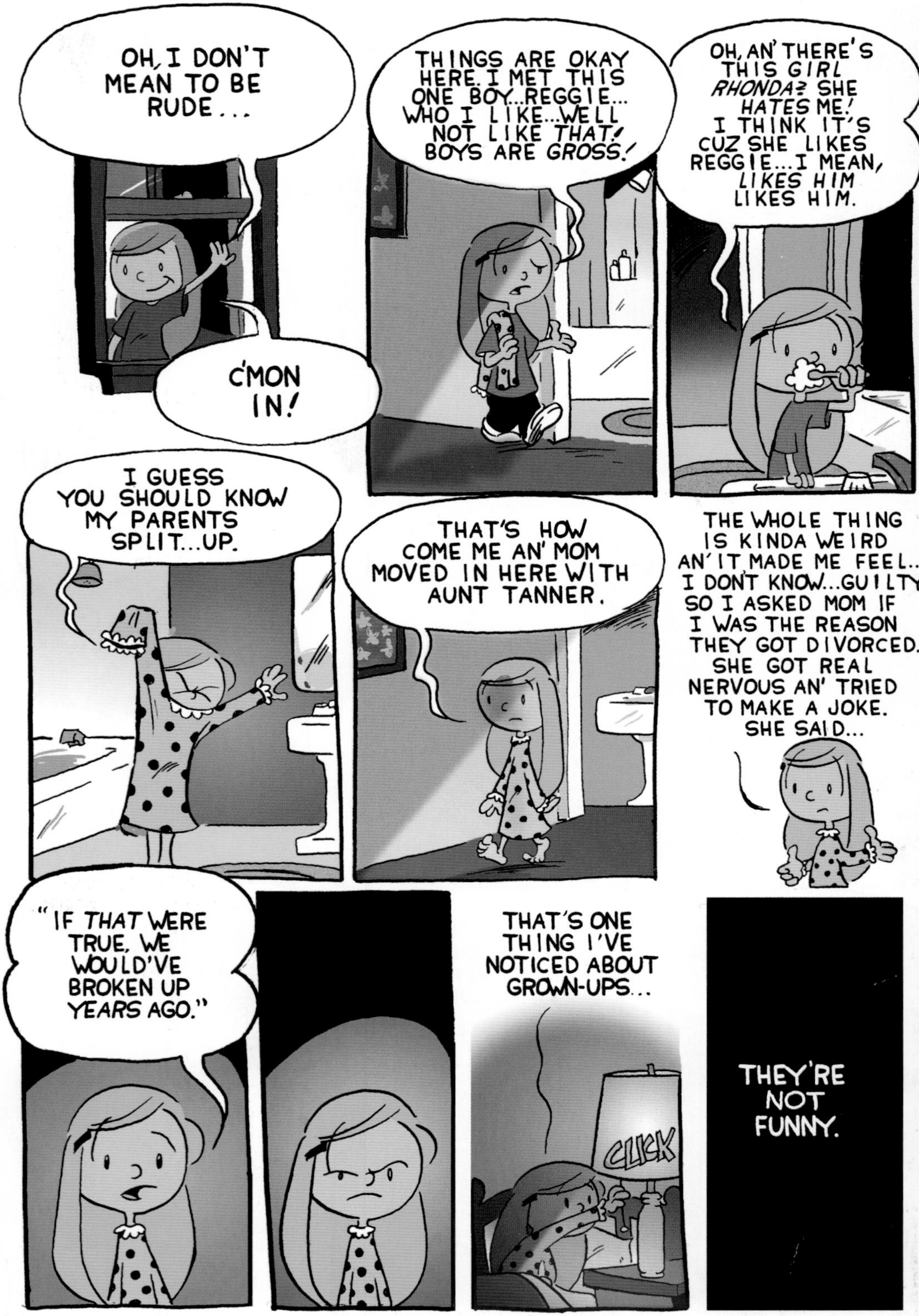
OH, I DON'T MEAN TO BE RUDE...
C'MON IN!
THINGS ARE OKAY HERE. I MET THIS ONE BOY...REGGIE... WHO I LIKE...WELL NOT LIKE *THAT!* BOYS ARE *GROSS!*
OH, AN' THERE'S THIS *GIRL RHONDA?* SHE *HATES* ME! I THINK IT'S CUZ SHE LIKES REGGIE...I MEAN, *LIKES HIM* LIKES HIM.
I GUESS YOU SHOULD KNOW MY PARENTS SPLIT...UP.
THAT'S HOW COME ME AN' MOM MOVED IN HERE WITH AUNT TANNER.
THE WHOLE THING IS KINDA WEIRD AN' IT MADE ME FEEL... I DON'T KNOW...GUILTY SO I ASKED MOM IF I WAS THE REASON THEY GOT DIVORCED. SHE GOT REAL NERVOUS AN' TRIED TO MAKE A JOKE. SHE SAID...
"IF *THAT* WERE TRUE, WE WOULD'VE BROKEN UP *YEARS* AGO."
THAT'S ONE THING I'VE NOTICED ABOUT GROWN-UPS...
CLICK
THEY'RE NOT FUNNY.

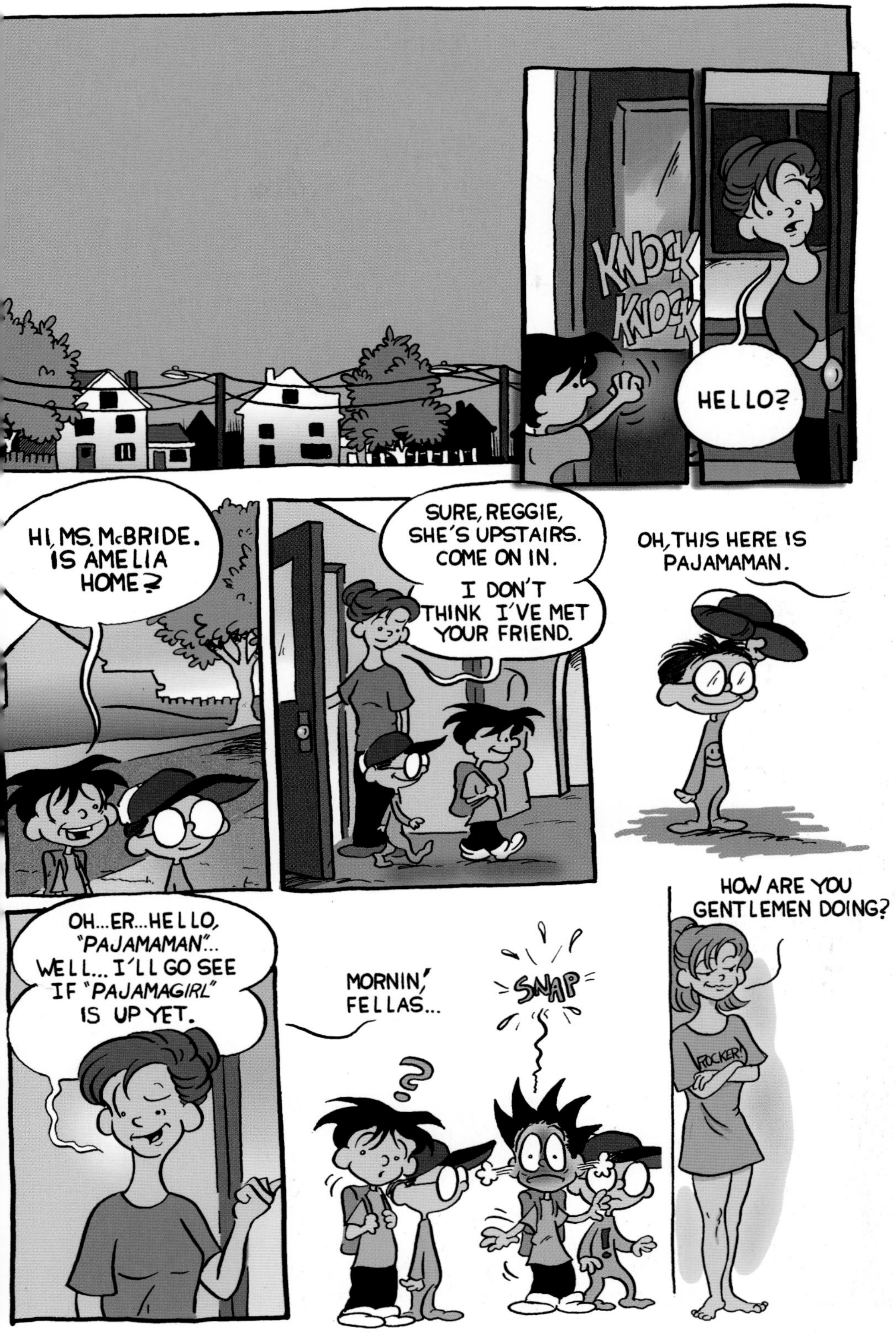
KNOCK KNOCK
HELLO?
HI, MS. McBRIDE. IS AMELIA HOME?
SURE, REGGIE, SHE'S UPSTAIRS. COME ON IN.
I DON'T THINK I'VE MET YOUR FRIEND.
OH, THIS HERE IS PAJAMAMAN.
OH...ER...HELLO, "PAJAMAMAN"... WELL... I'LL GO SEE IF "PAJAMAGIRL" IS UP YET.
MORNIN', FELLAS...
SNAP
?
HOW ARE YOU GENTLEMEN DOING?
ROCKER!

GULP

HHHHHHH HI, T-TANNER!

POUND POUND POUND

SO, WHAT ARE YOU BOYS DOING HERE SO EARLY?

Doing umm...

¡pəp! ON əʌɐɥ I ···yn I

ha ha ha THAT'S CUTE, REGGIE...! YOU GOOFBALL!

Cute? Did YOU say cute?

MILK EGGS CEREAL C.D

ROCKER!

WELL, LET'S SEE IF I CAN HELP. ARE YOU SELLING SOMETHING TO PAY YOUR WAY THROUGH COLLEGE? OR ARE YOU HERE TO VISIT AMELIA?

umm...

THUD

Who's Amelia?

ROCK

AHEM!

CRASH!

6

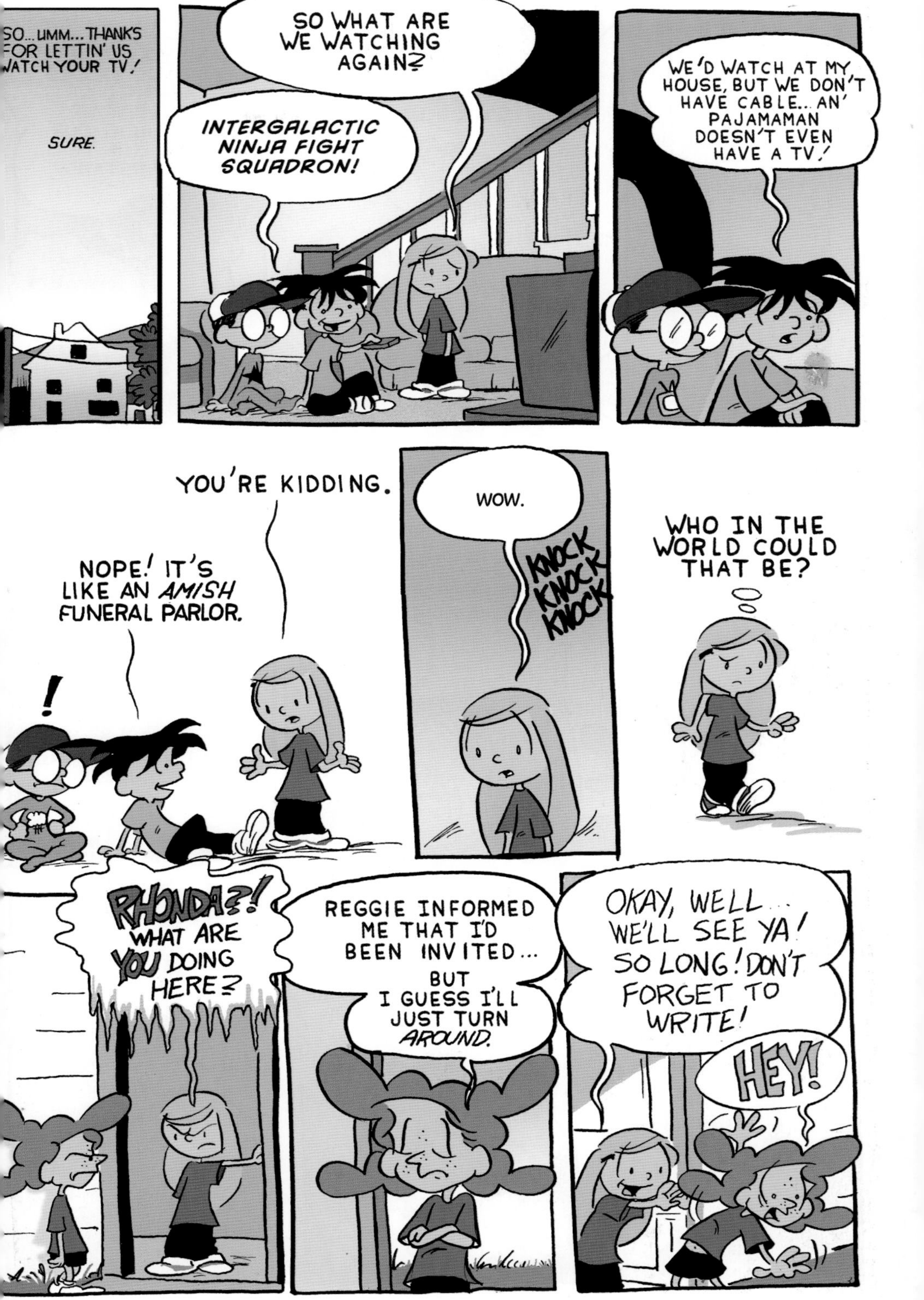
SO... UMM... THANKS FOR LETTIN' US WATCH YOUR TV!
SURE.
SO WHAT ARE WE WATCHING AGAIN?
INTERGALACTIC NINJA FIGHT SQUADRON!
WE'D WATCH AT MY HOUSE, BUT WE DON'T HAVE CABLE... AN' PAJAMAMAN DOESN'T EVEN HAVE A TV!
YOU'RE KIDDING.
NOPE! IT'S LIKE AN AMISH FUNERAL PARLOR.
!
WOW.
KNOCK KNOCK KNOCK
WHO IN THE WORLD COULD THAT BE?
RHONDA?! WHAT ARE YOU DOING HERE?
REGGIE INFORMED ME THAT I'D BEEN INVITED...
BUT I GUESS I'LL JUST TURN AROUND.
OKAY, WELL... WE'LL SEE YA! SO LONG! DON'T FORGET TO WRITE!
HEY!

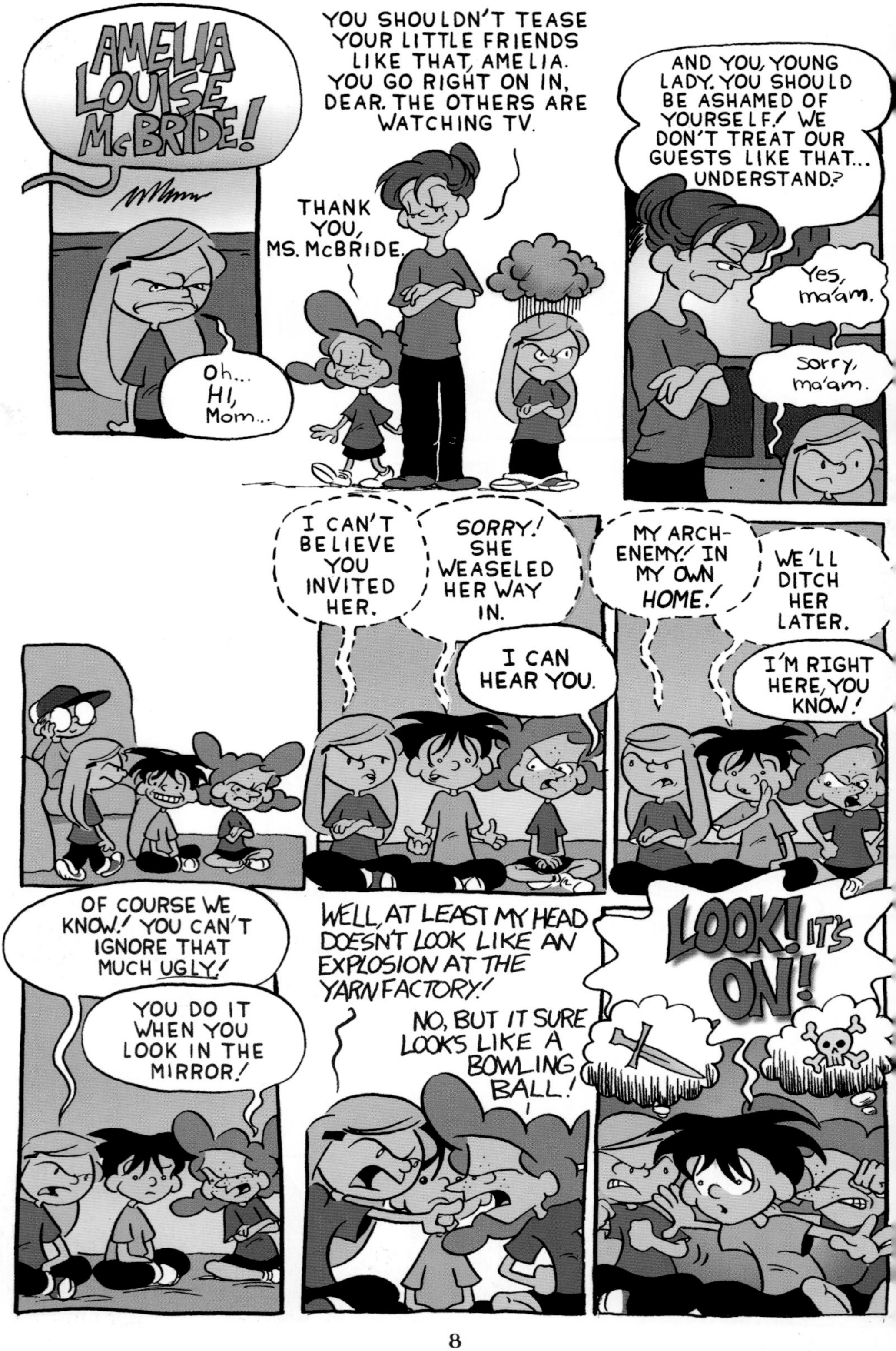

AMELIA LOUISE McBRIDE!
Oh... HI, Mom...
YOU SHOULDN'T TEASE YOUR LITTLE FRIENDS LIKE THAT, AMELIA. YOU GO RIGHT ON IN, DEAR. THE OTHERS ARE WATCHING TV.
THANK YOU, MS. McBRIDE.
AND YOU, YOUNG LADY. YOU SHOULD BE ASHAMED OF YOURSELF! WE DON'T TREAT OUR GUESTS LIKE THAT... UNDERSTAND?
Yes, ma'am.
Sorry, ma'am.
I CAN'T BELIEVE YOU INVITED HER.
SORRY! SHE WEASELED HER WAY IN.
I CAN HEAR YOU.
MY ARCH-ENEMY! IN MY OWN HOME!
WE'LL DITCH HER LATER.
I'M RIGHT HERE, YOU KNOW!
OF COURSE WE KNOW! YOU CAN'T IGNORE THAT MUCH UGLY!
YOU DO IT WHEN YOU LOOK IN THE MIRROR!
WELL, AT LEAST MY HEAD DOESN'T LOOK LIKE AN EXPLOSION AT THE YARN FACTORY!
NO, BUT IT SURE LOOKS LIKE A BOWLING BALL!
LOOK! IT'S ON!

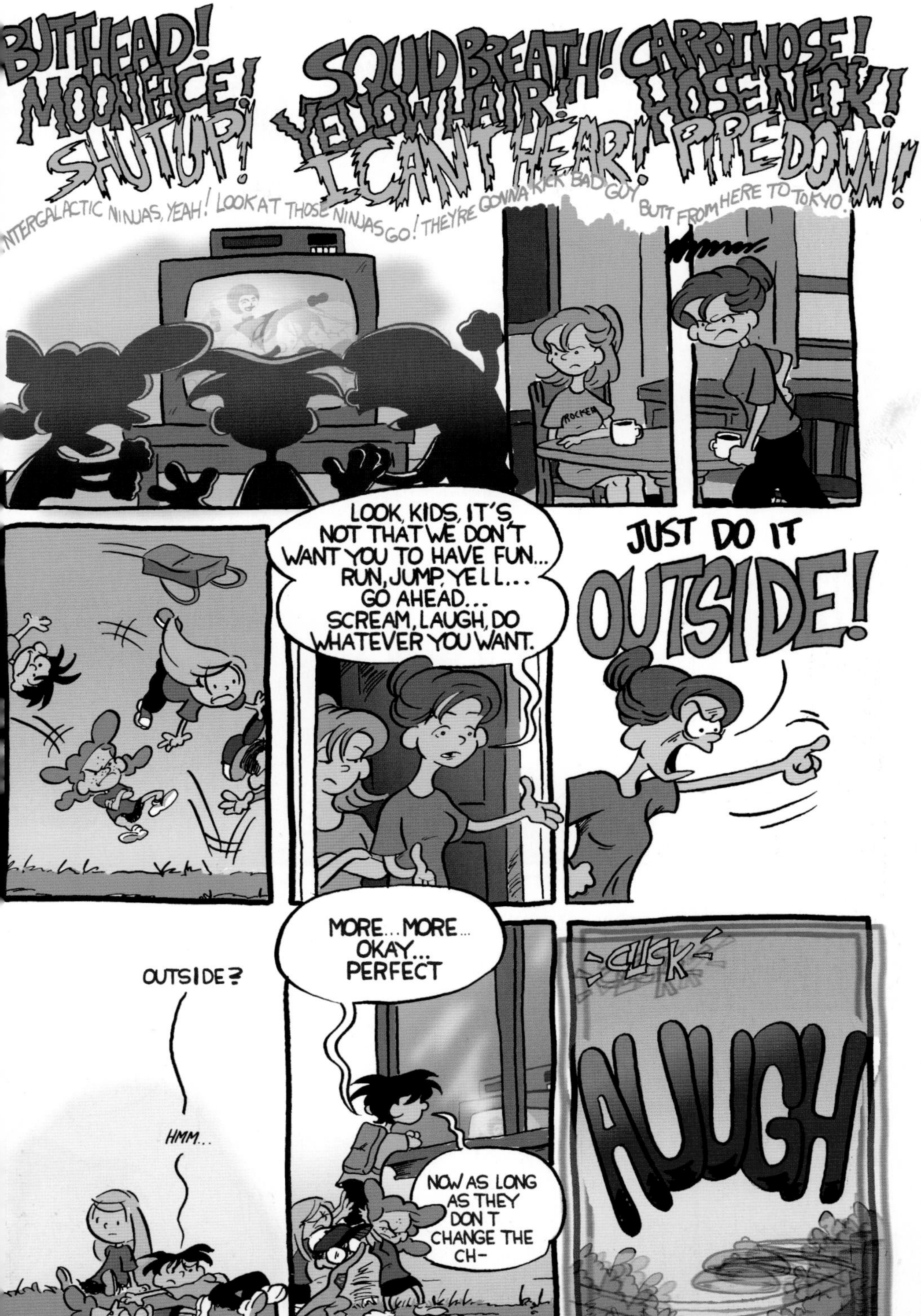
BUTTHEAD! MOONFACE! SHUTUP!
SQUIDBREATH! YELLOWHAIR! I CAN'T HEAR! CARROTNOSE! HOSENECK! PIPEDOWN!
INTERGALACTIC NINJAS, YEAH! LOOK AT THOSE NINJAS GO! THEY'RE GONNA KICK BAD GUY BUTT FROM HERE TO TOKYO!
ROCKER
LOOK, KIDS, IT'S NOT THAT WE DON'T WANT YOU TO HAVE FUN... RUN, JUMP, YELL... GO AHEAD... SCREAM, LAUGH, DO WHATEVER YOU WANT.
JUST DO IT OUTSIDE!
OUTSIDE?
HMM...
MORE... MORE... OKAY... PERFECT
NOW AS LONG AS THEY DON'T CHANGE THE CH-
CLICK
AUUGH!

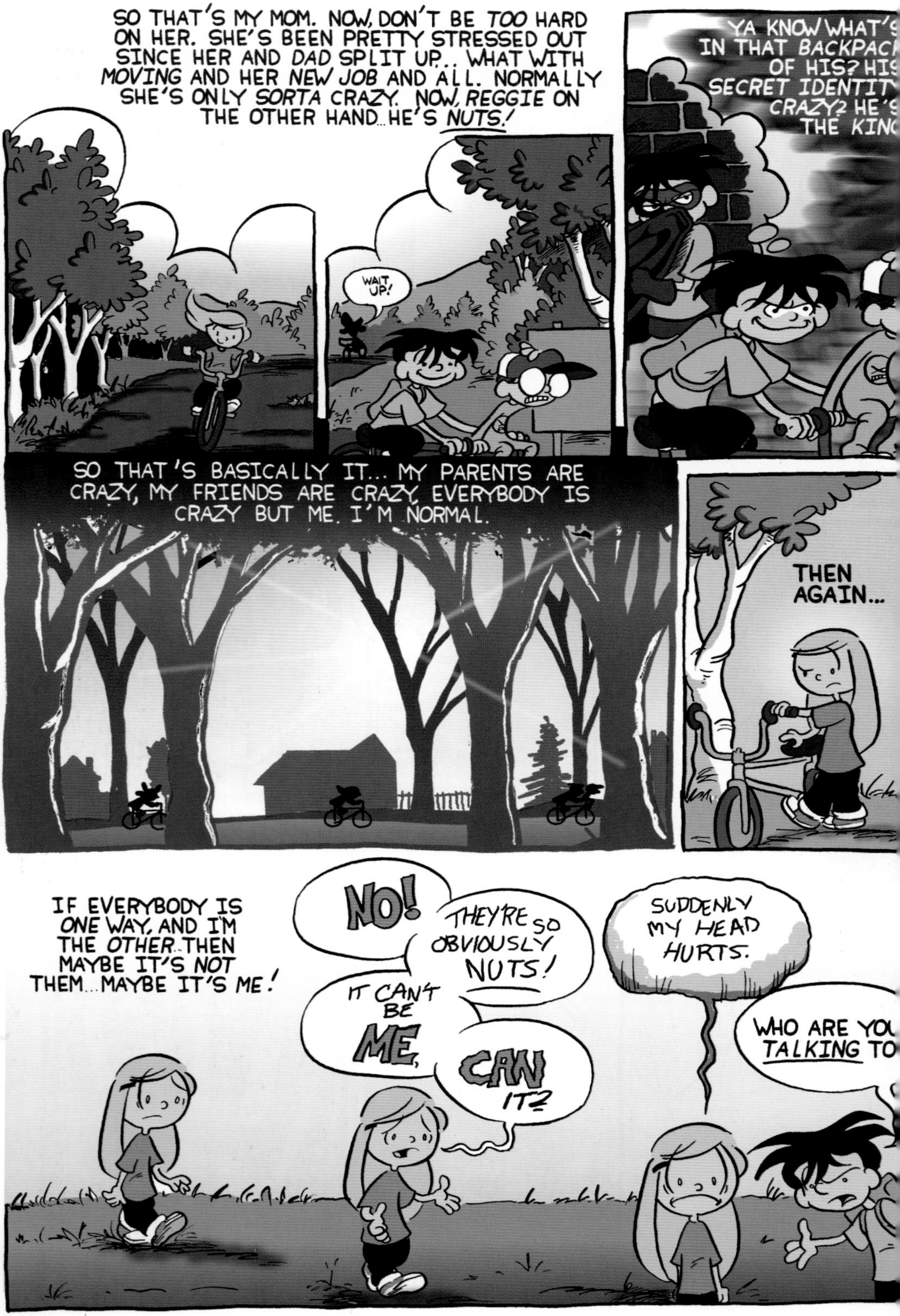
SO THAT'S MY MOM. NOW, DON'T BE TOO HARD ON HER. SHE'S BEEN PRETTY STRESSED OUT SINCE HER AND DAD SPLIT UP.. WHAT WITH MOVING AND HER NEW JOB AND ALL. NORMALLY SHE'S ONLY SORTA CRAZY. NOW, REGGIE ON THE OTHER HAND... HE'S NUTS!
WAIT UP!
YA KNOW WHAT'S IN THAT BACKPACK OF HIS? HIS SECRET IDENTITY. CRAZY? HE'S THE KING
SO THAT'S BASICALLY IT... MY PARENTS ARE CRAZY, MY FRIENDS ARE CRAZY, EVERYBODY IS CRAZY BUT ME. I'M NORMAL.
THEN AGAIN...
IF EVERYBODY IS ONE WAY, AND I'M THE OTHER... THEN MAYBE IT'S NOT THEM... MAYBE IT'S ME!
NO!
THEY'RE SO OBVIOUSLY NUTS!
IT CAN'T BE ME, CAN IT?
SUDDENLY MY HEAD HURTS.
WHO ARE YOU TALKING TO

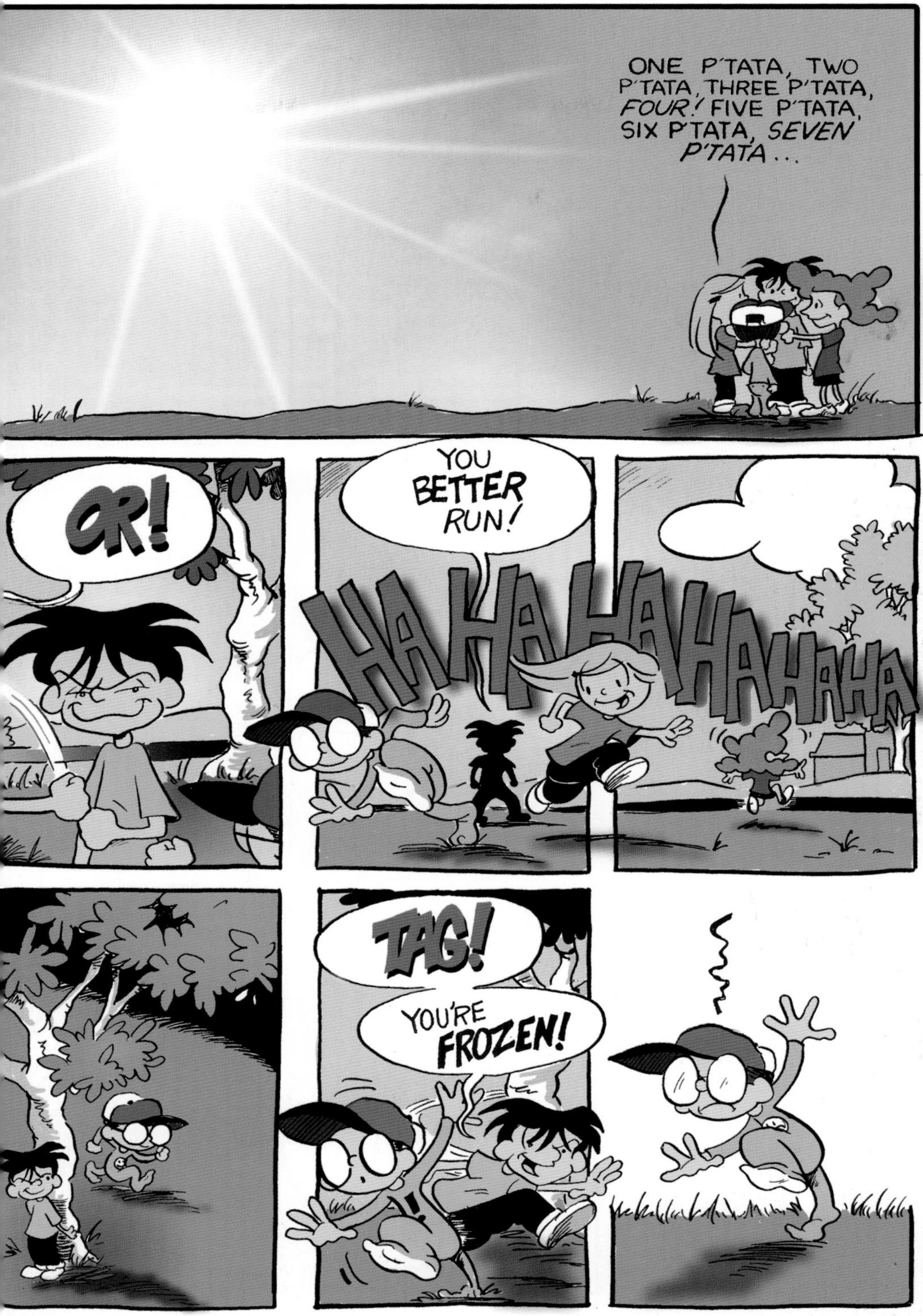
ONE P'TATA, TWO P'TATA, THREE P'TATA, FOUR! FIVE P'TATA, SIX P'TATA, SEVEN P'TATA...
OR!
YOU BETTER RUN!
HA HA HA HAHAHAHA
TAG!
YOU'RE FROZEN!

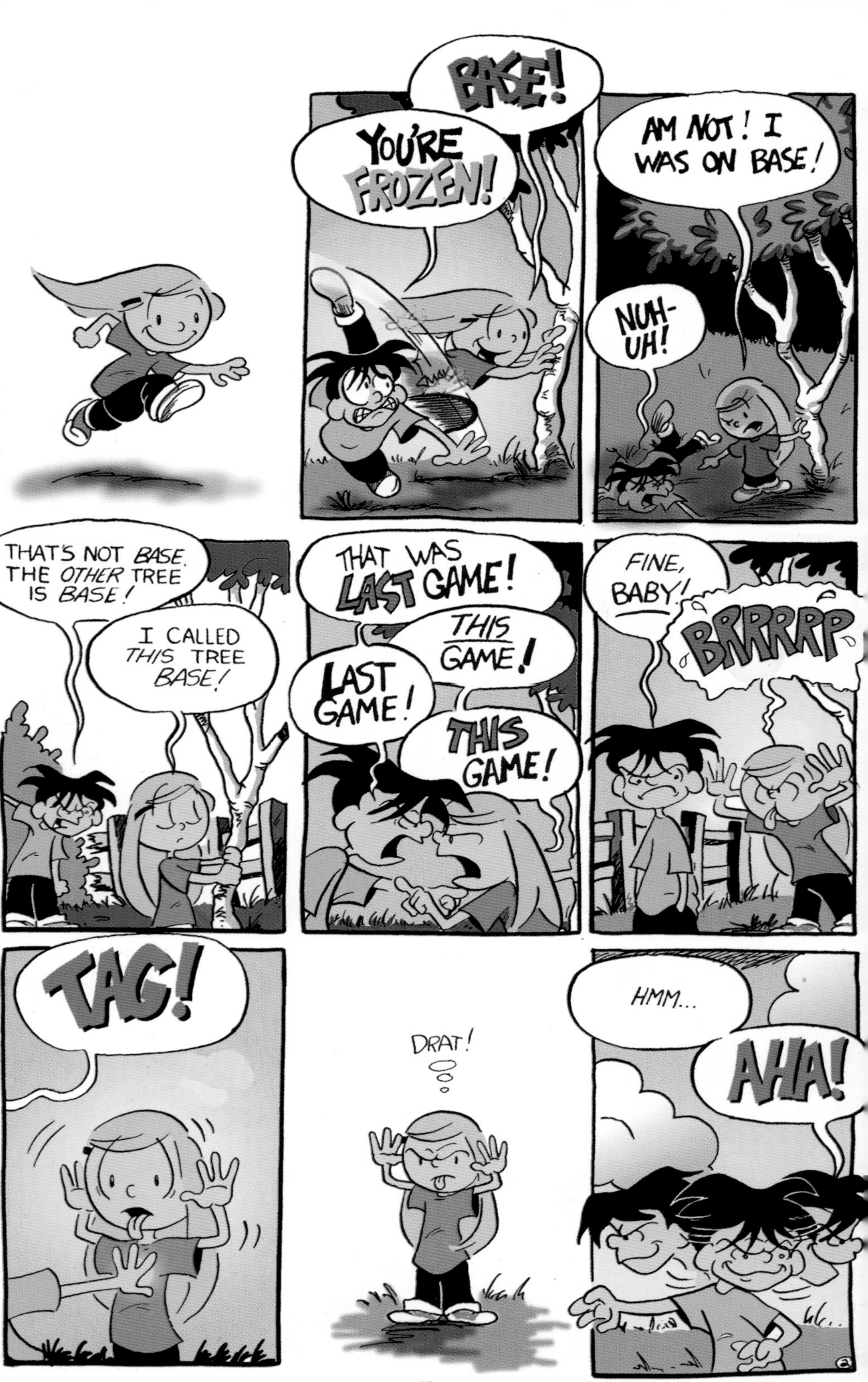
BASE!
YOU'RE FROZEN!
AM NOT! I WAS ON BASE!
NUH-UH!
THAT'S NOT BASE. THE OTHER TREE IS BASE!
I CALLED THIS TREE BASE!
THAT WAS LAST GAME!
THIS GAME!
LAST GAME!
THIS GAME!
FINE, BABY!
BRRRRP
TAG!
DRAT!
HMM...
AHA!

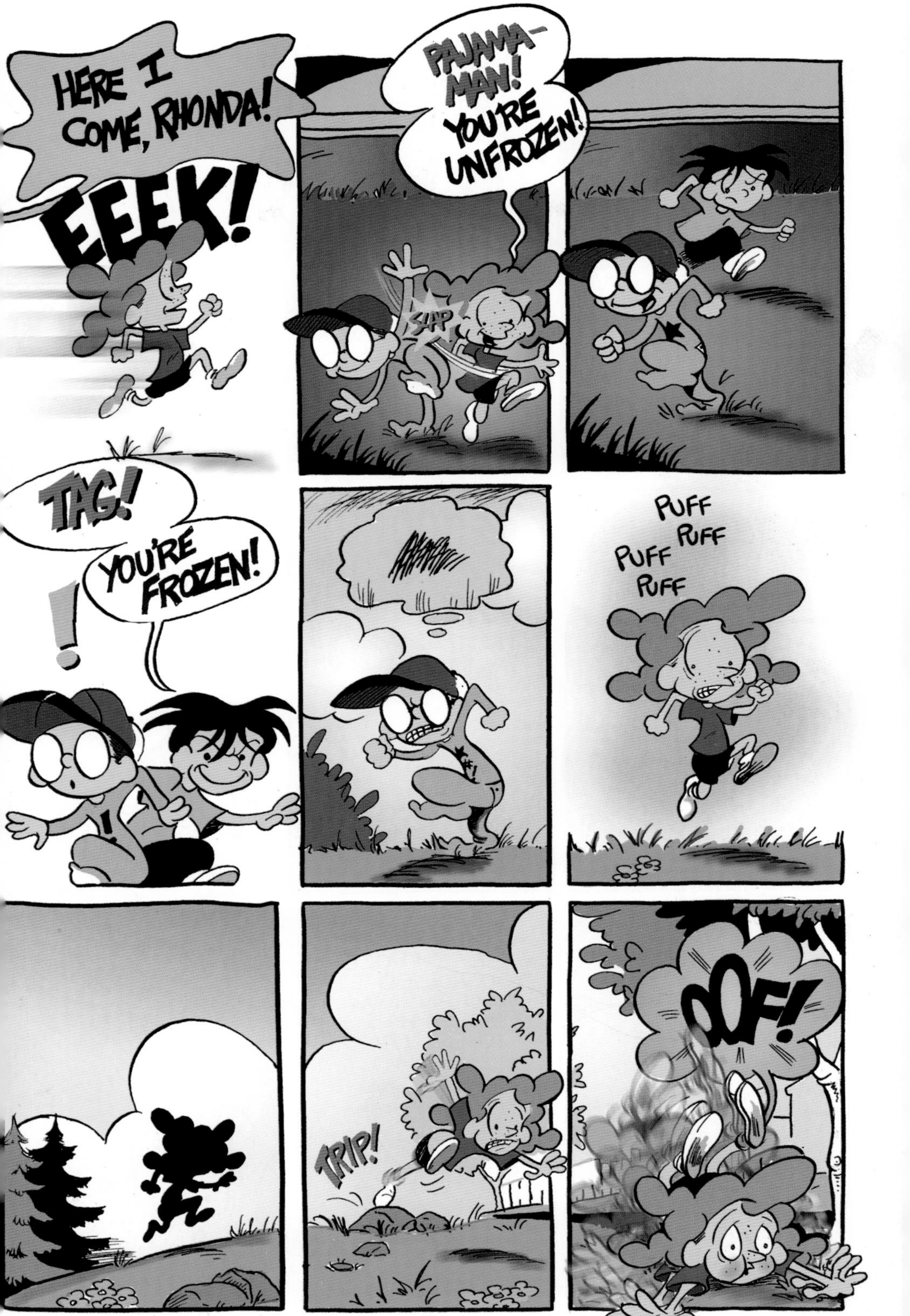
HERE I COME, RHONDA!
EEEK!
PAJAMA-MAN! YOU'RE UNFROZEN!
SLAP!
TAG!
YOU'RE FROZEN!
!
PUFF PUFF PUFF PUFF
TRIP!
OOF!

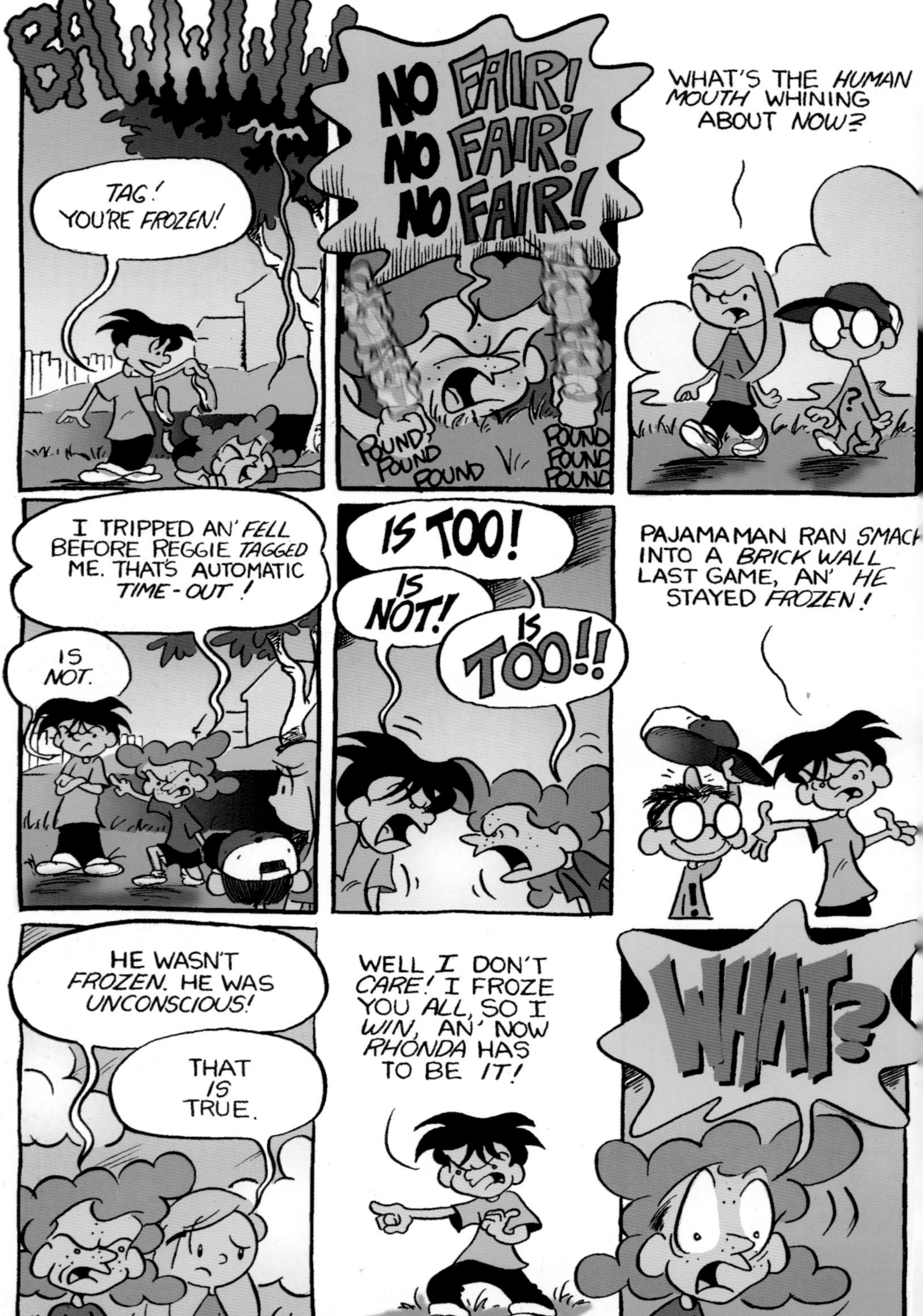
BAWWW
TAG! YOU'RE FROZEN!
NO FAIR! NO FAIR! NO FAIR!
POUND POUND POUND
POUND POUND POUND
WHAT'S THE HUMAN MOUTH WHINING ABOUT NOW?
I TRIPPED AN' FELL BEFORE REGGIE TAGGED ME. THAT'S AUTOMATIC TIME-OUT!
IS NOT.
IS TOO!
IS NOT!
IS TOO!!
PAJAMAMAN RAN SMACK INTO A BRICK WALL LAST GAME, AN' HE STAYED FROZEN!
HE WASN'T FROZEN. HE WAS UNCONSCIOUS!
THAT IS TRUE.
WELL I DON'T CARE! I FROZE YOU ALL, SO I WIN, AN' NOW RHONDA HAS TO BE IT!
WHAT?

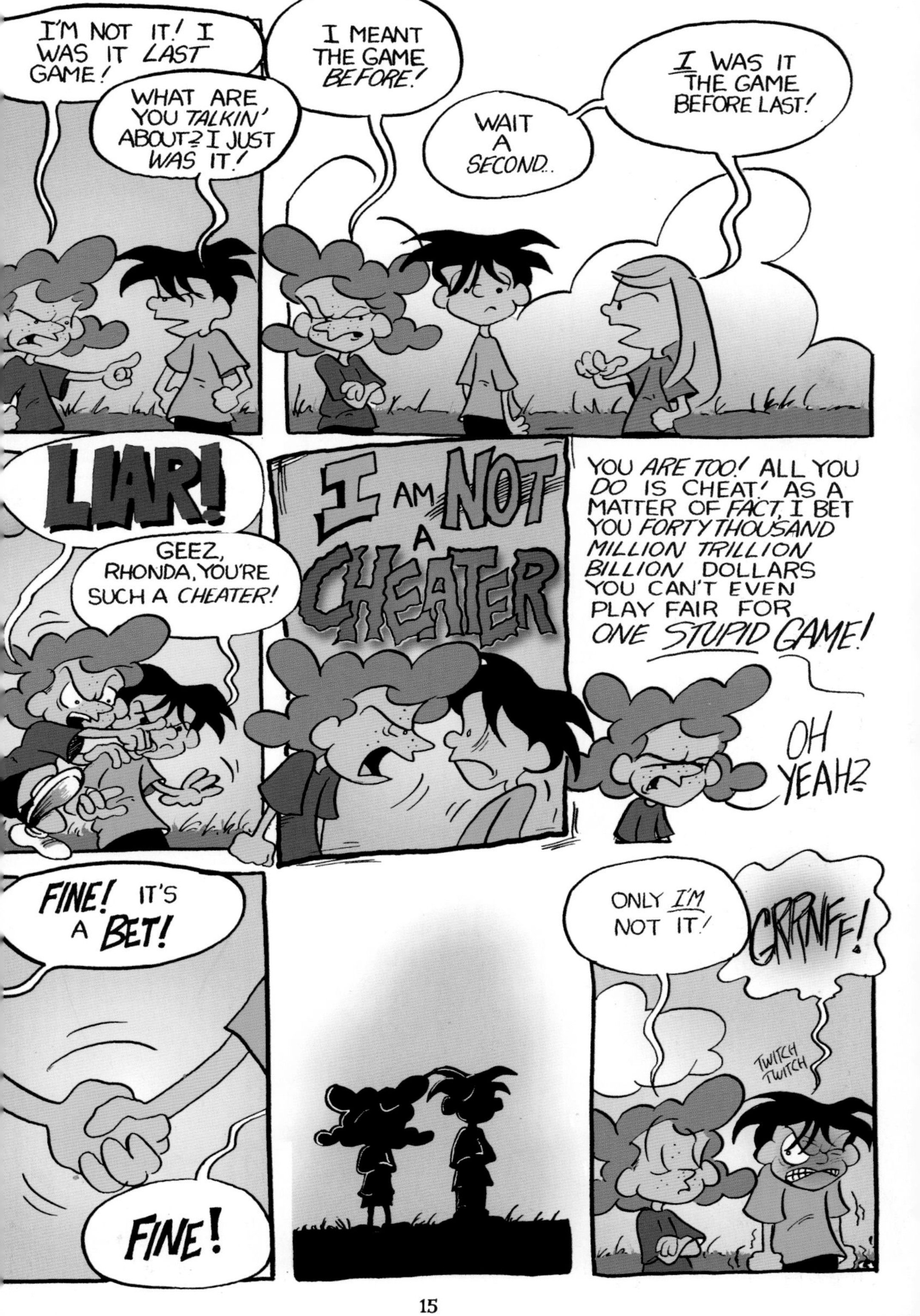
I'M NOT IT! I WAS IT *LAST* GAME!
WHAT ARE YOU *TALKIN'* ABOUT? I JUST *WAS* IT!
I MEANT THE GAME *BEFORE!*
WAIT A *SECOND*...
I WAS IT THE GAME BEFORE LAST!
LIAR!
GEEZ, RHONDA, YOU'RE SUCH A *CHEATER!*
I AM NOT A CHEATER
YOU *ARE TOO!* ALL YOU *DO* IS CHEAT! AS A MATTER OF *FACT*, I BET YOU *FORTY THOUSAND MILLION TRILLION BILLION* DOLLARS YOU CAN'T EVEN PLAY FAIR FOR *ONE STUPID GAME!*
OH YEAH?
FINE! IT'S A *BET!*
FINE!
ONLY *I'M* NOT IT!
GRRNFF!
TWITCH TWITCH

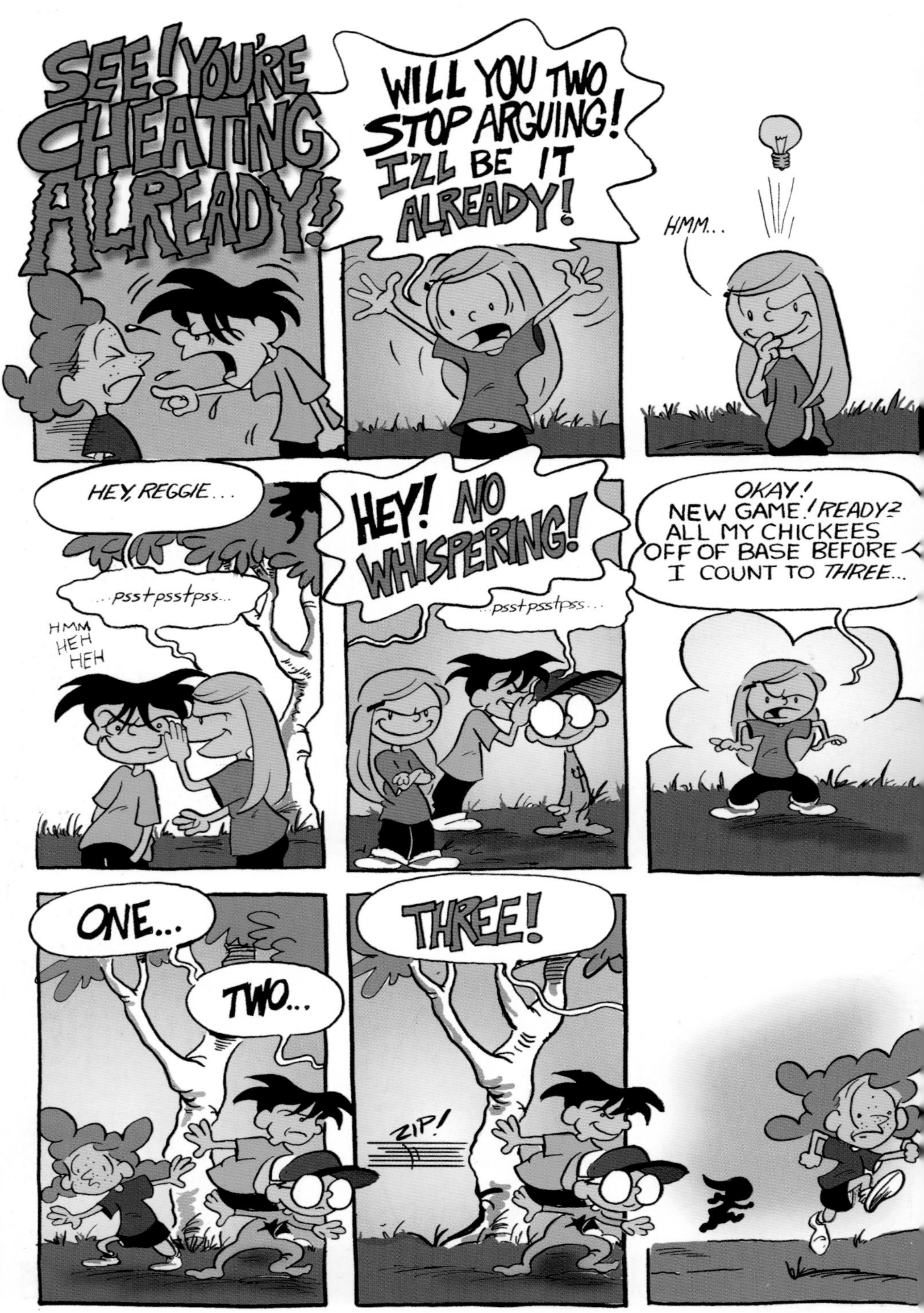

SEE! YOU'RE CHEATING ALREADY!
WILL YOU TWO STOP ARGUING! I'LL BE IT ALREADY!
HMM...
HEY, REGGIE...
...psst psst pss...
HMM HEH HEH
HEY! NO WHISPERING!
...psst psst pss...
OKAY! NEW GAME! READY? ALL MY CHICKEES OFF OF BASE BEFORE I COUNT TO THREE...
ONE...
TWO...
THREE!
ZIP!

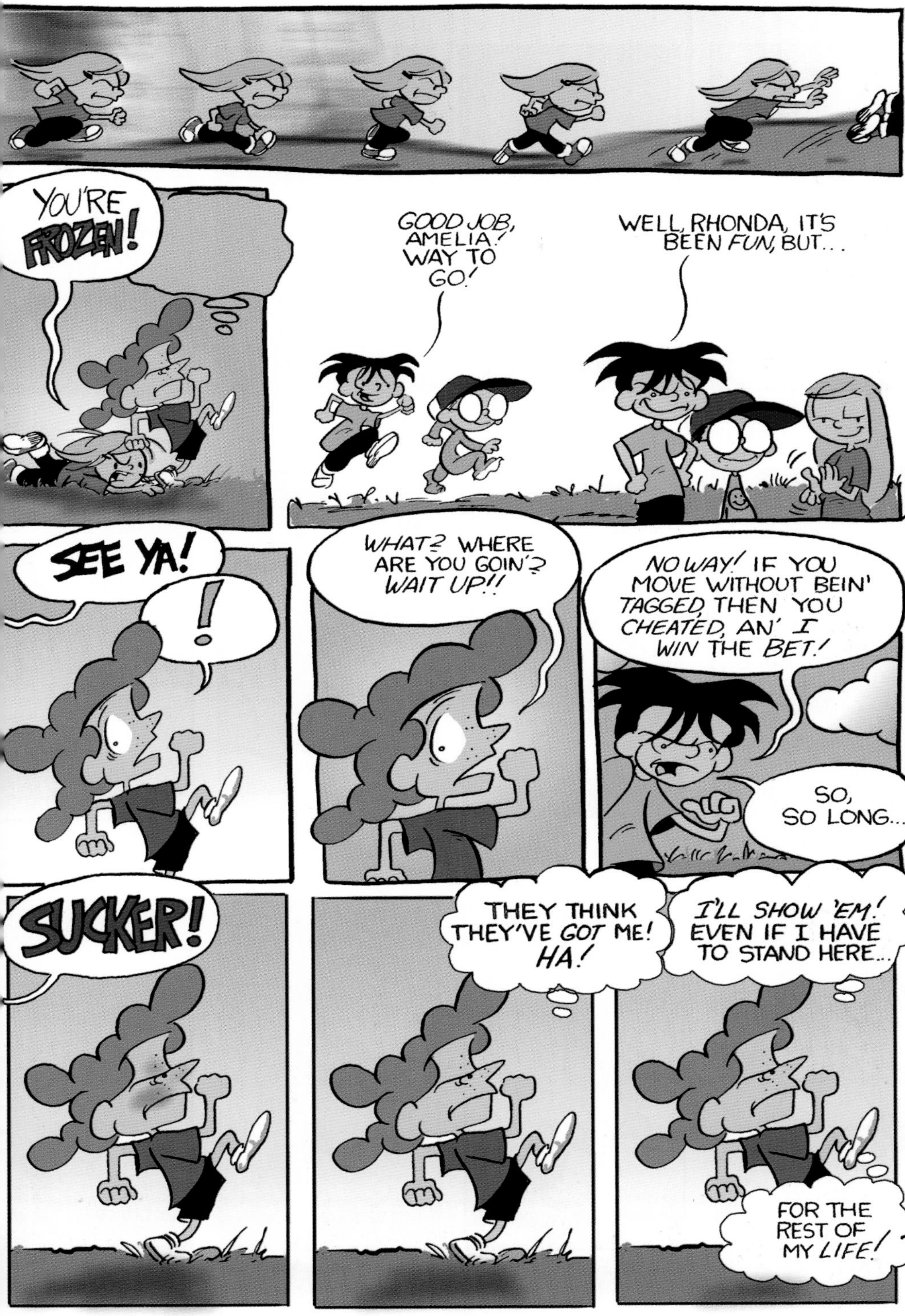
YOU'RE FROZEN!
GOOD JOB, AMELIA! WAY TO GO!
WELL, RHONDA, IT'S BEEN FUN, BUT...
SEE YA!
!
WHAT? WHERE ARE YOU GOIN'? WAIT UP!!
NO WAY! IF YOU MOVE WITHOUT BEIN' TAGGED, THEN YOU CHEATED, AN' I WIN THE BET!
SO, SO LONG...
SUCKER!
THEY THINK THEY'VE GOT ME! HA!
I'LL SHOW 'EM! EVEN IF I HAVE TO STAND HERE...
FOR THE REST OF MY LIFE!

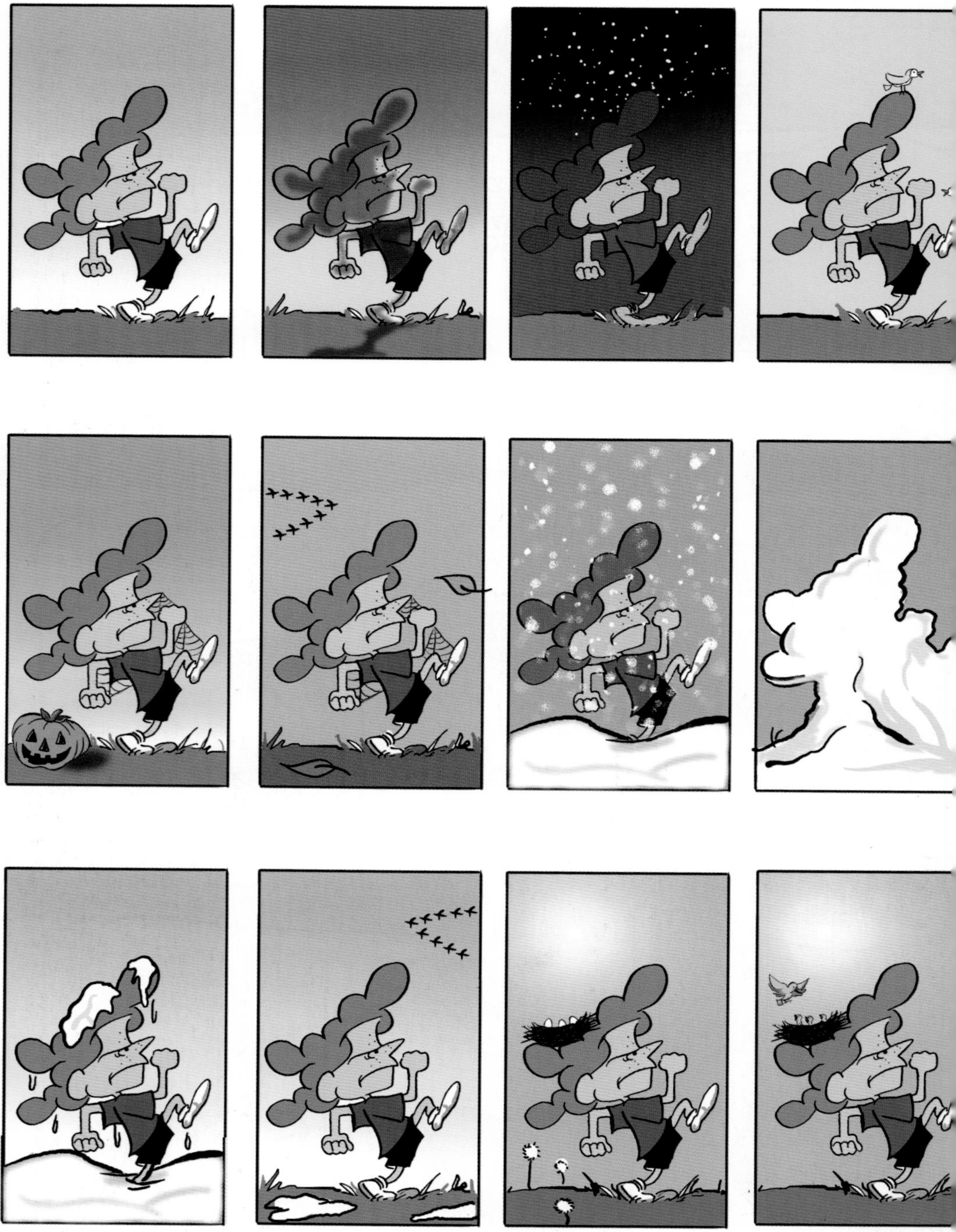

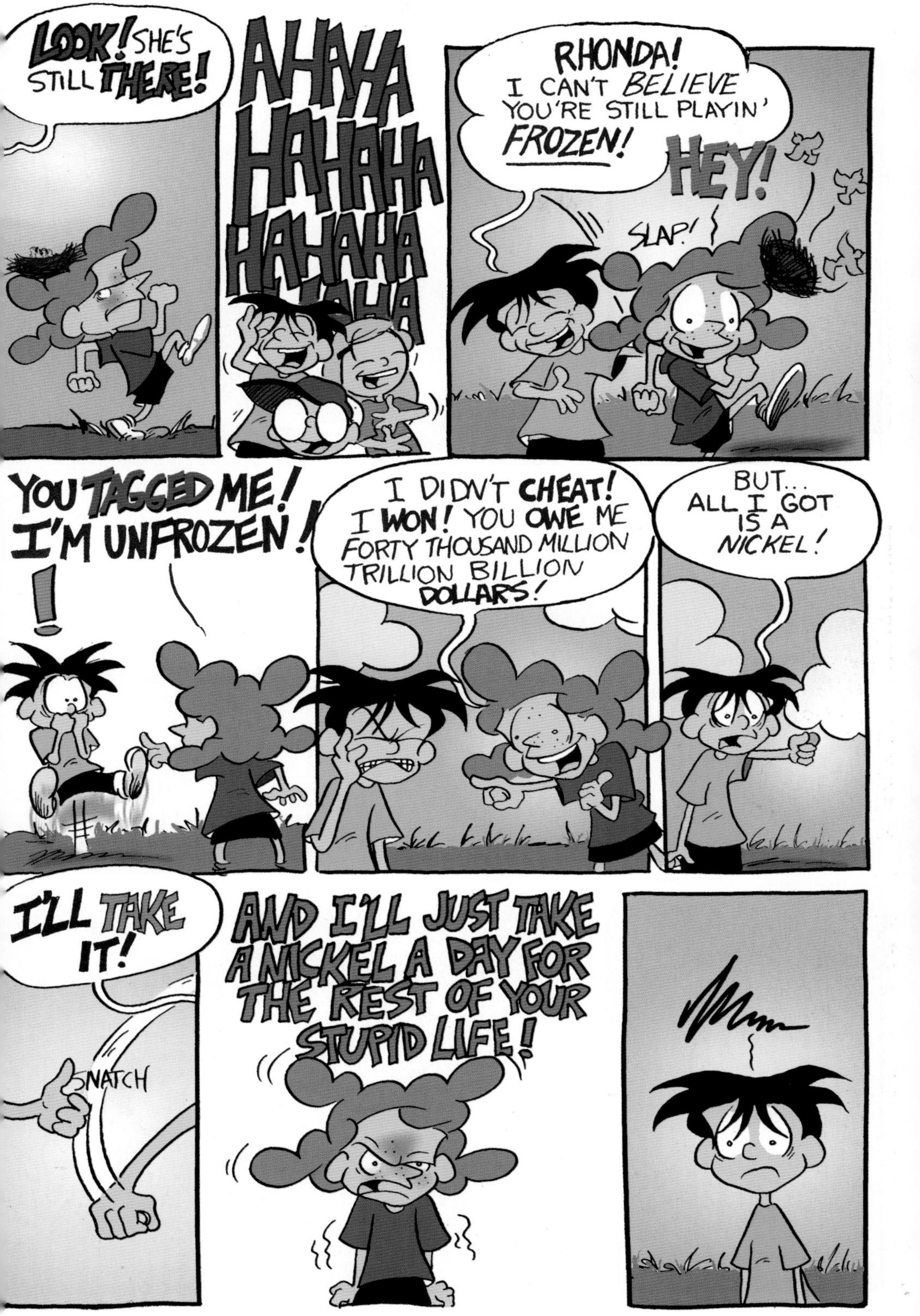
LOOK! SHE'S STILL THERE!
AHAHA HAHAHA HAHAHA HAHA
RHONDA! I CAN'T BELIEVE YOU'RE STILL PLAYIN' FROZEN!
HEY!
SLAP!
YOU TAGGED ME! I'M UNFROZEN!
!
I DIDN'T CHEAT! I WON! YOU OWE ME FORTY THOUSAND MILLION TRILLION BILLION DOLLARS!
BUT... ALL I GOT IS A NICKEL!
I'LL TAKE IT!
SNATCH
AND I'LL JUST TAKE A NICKEL A DAY FOR THE REST OF YOUR STUPID LIFE!

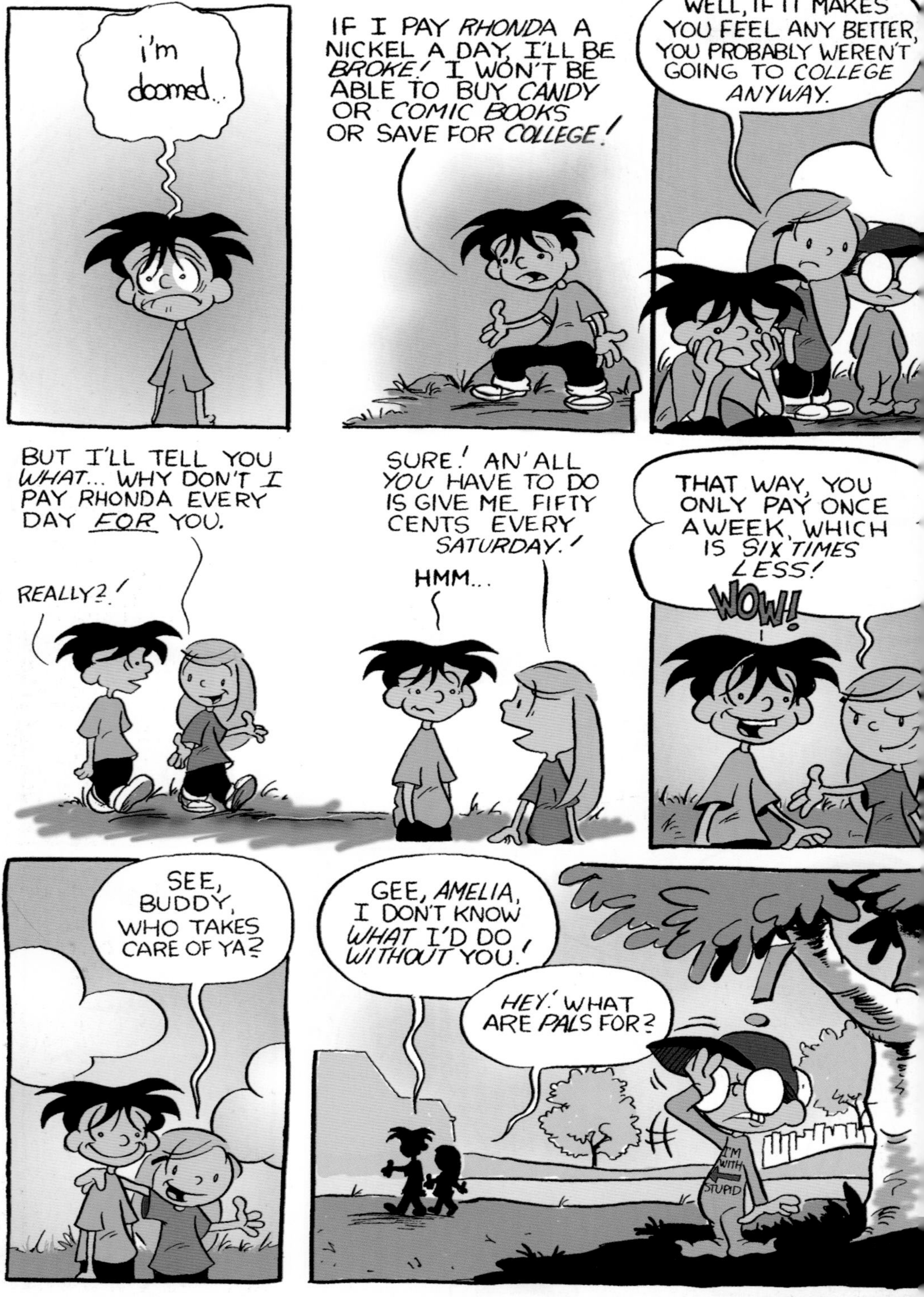
i'm doomed...
IF I PAY RHONDA A NICKEL A DAY, I'LL BE BROKE! I WON'T BE ABLE TO BUY CANDY OR COMIC BOOKS OR SAVE FOR COLLEGE!
WELL, IF IT MAKES YOU FEEL ANY BETTER, YOU PROBABLY WEREN'T GOING TO COLLEGE ANYWAY.
BUT I'LL TELL YOU WHAT... WHY DON'T I PAY RHONDA EVERY DAY FOR YOU.
REALLY?!
SURE! AN' ALL YOU HAVE TO DO IS GIVE ME FIFTY CENTS EVERY SATURDAY!
HMM...
THAT WAY, YOU ONLY PAY ONCE A WEEK, WHICH IS SIX TIMES LESS!
WOW!
SEE, BUDDY, WHO TAKES CARE OF YA?
GEE, AMELIA, I DON'T KNOW WHAT I'D DO WITHOUT YOU!
HEY! WHAT ARE PALS FOR?
I'M WITH STUPID

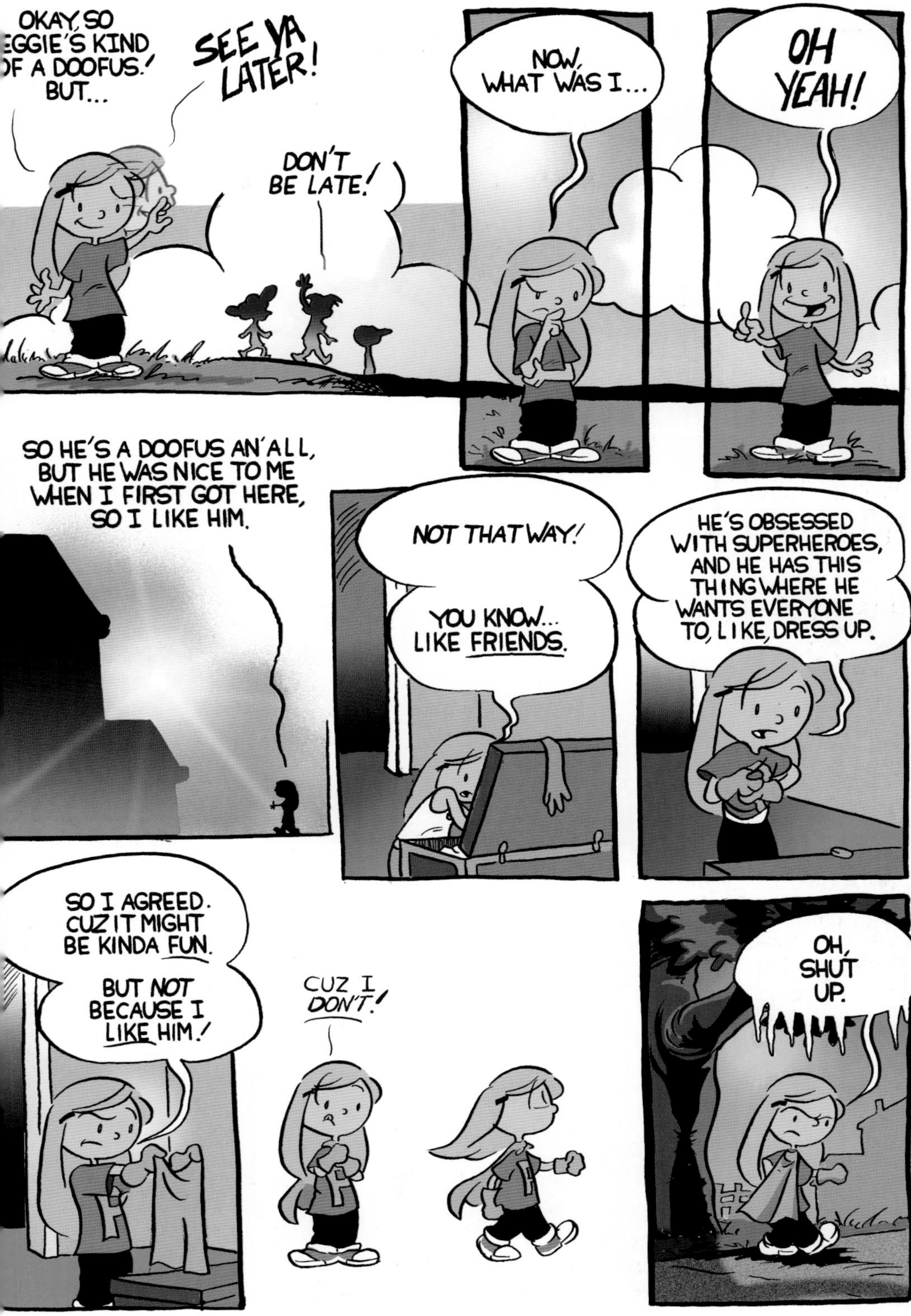
OKAY, SO
EGGIE'S KIND
OF A DOOFUS.
BUT...
SEE YA LATER!
DON'T BE LATE!
NOW, WHAT WAS I...
OH YEAH!
SO HE'S A DOOFUS AN' ALL, BUT HE WAS NICE TO ME WHEN I FIRST GOT HERE, SO I LIKE HIM.
NOT THAT WAY!
YOU KNOW... LIKE FRIENDS.
HE'S OBSESSED WITH SUPERHEROES, AND HE HAS THIS THING WHERE HE WANTS EVERYONE TO, LIKE, DRESS UP.
SO I AGREED. CUZ IT MIGHT BE KINDA FUN.
BUT NOT BECAUSE I LIKE HIM!
CUZ I DON'T!
OH, SHUT UP.

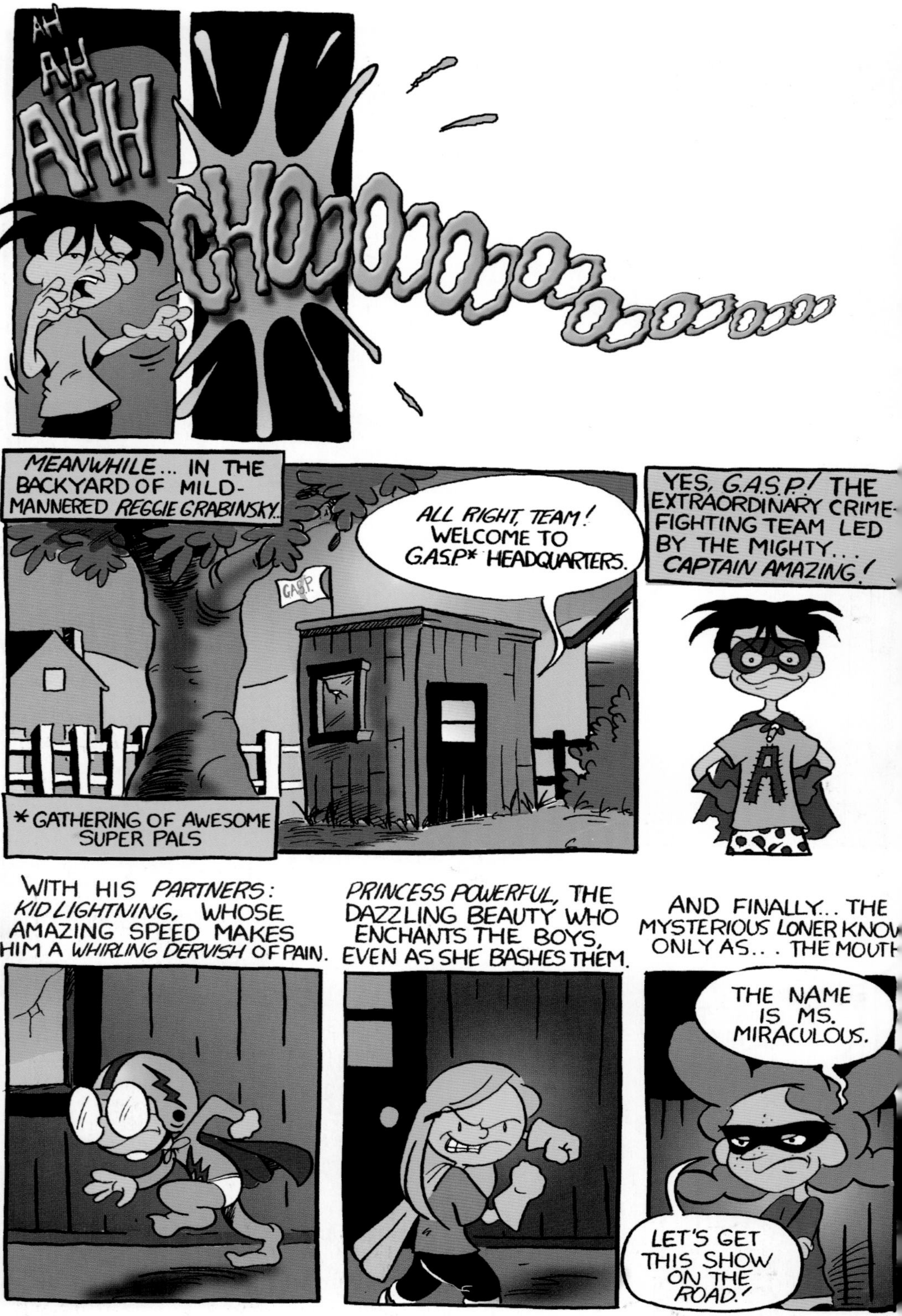
AH
AH
AHH
CHOOOOOOOOOOOOOOOO
MEANWHILE... IN THE BACKYARD OF MILD-MANNERED REGGIE GRABINSKY...
ALL RIGHT, TEAM! WELCOME TO G.A.S.P.* HEADQUARTERS.
G.A.S.P.
* GATHERING OF AWESOME SUPER PALS
YES, G.A.S.P.! THE EXTRAORDINARY CRIME-FIGHTING TEAM LED BY THE MIGHTY... CAPTAIN AMAZING!
A
WITH HIS PARTNERS: KID LIGHTNING, WHOSE AMAZING SPEED MAKES HIM A WHIRLING DERVISH OF PAIN.
PRINCESS POWERFUL, THE DAZZLING BEAUTY WHO ENCHANTS THE BOYS, EVEN AS SHE BASHES THEM.
AND FINALLY... THE MYSTERIOUS LONER KNOW ONLY AS... THE MOUTH
THE NAME IS MS. MIRACULOUS.
LET'S GET THIS SHOW ON THE ROAD!

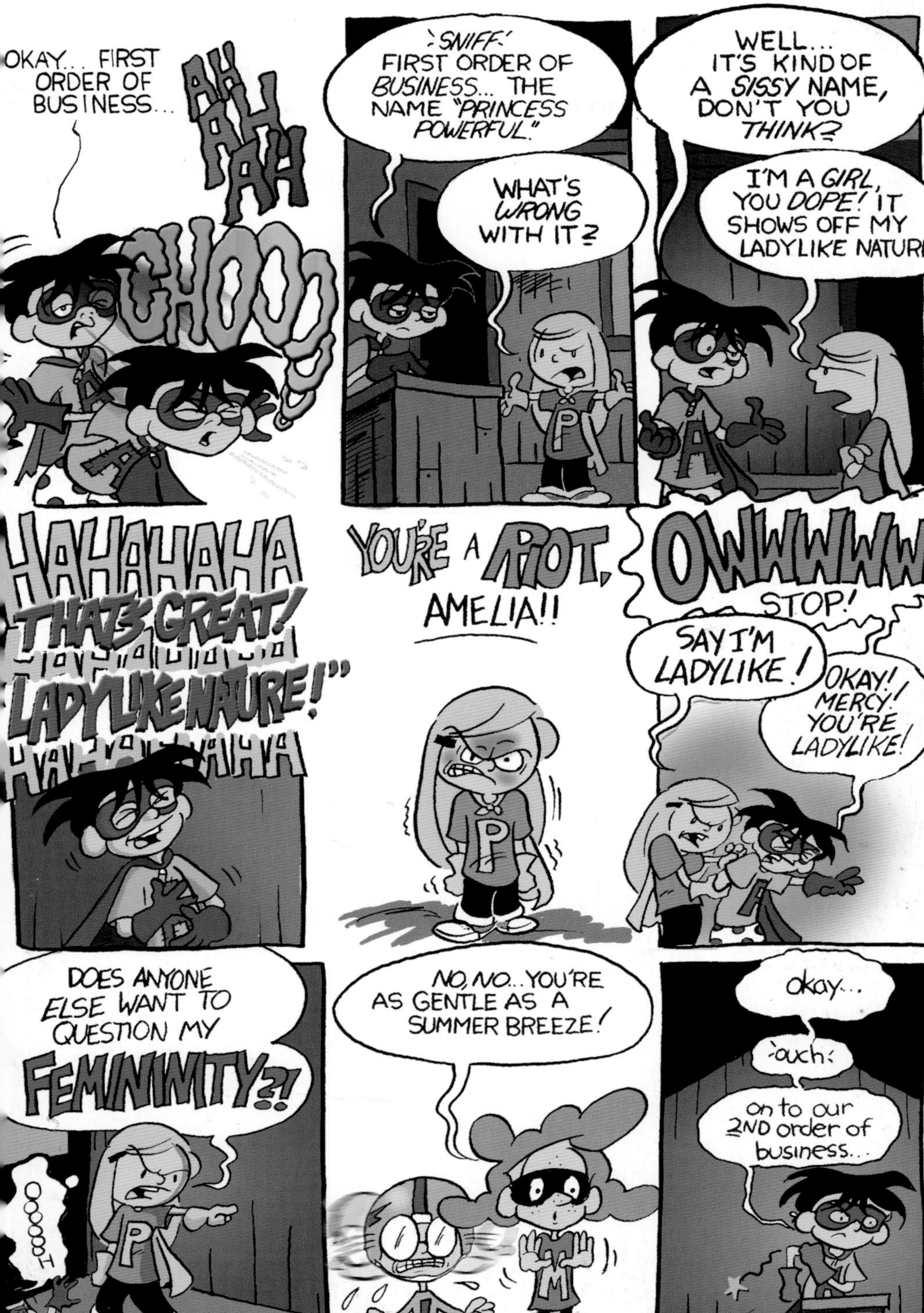

OKAY... FIRST ORDER OF BUSINESS...
AH AH AH AH
CHOOO
:SNIFF: FIRST ORDER OF BUSINESS... THE NAME "PRINCESS POWERFUL."
WHAT'S WRONG WITH IT?
WELL... IT'S KIND OF A SISSY NAME, DON'T YOU THINK?
I'M A GIRL, YOU DOPE! IT SHOWS OFF MY LADYLIKE NATURE!
HAHAHAHA
THAT'S GREAT!
"LADYLIKE NATURE!"
HAHAHAHA
YOU'RE A RIOT, AMELIA!!
OWWWWW
STOP!
SAY I'M LADYLIKE!
OKAY! MERCY! YOU'RE LADYLIKE!
DOES ANYONE ELSE WANT TO QUESTION MY FEMININITY?!
OOOOOH
NO, NO... YOU'RE AS GENTLE AS A SUMMER BREEZE!
okay...
:ouch:
on to our 2ND order of business...

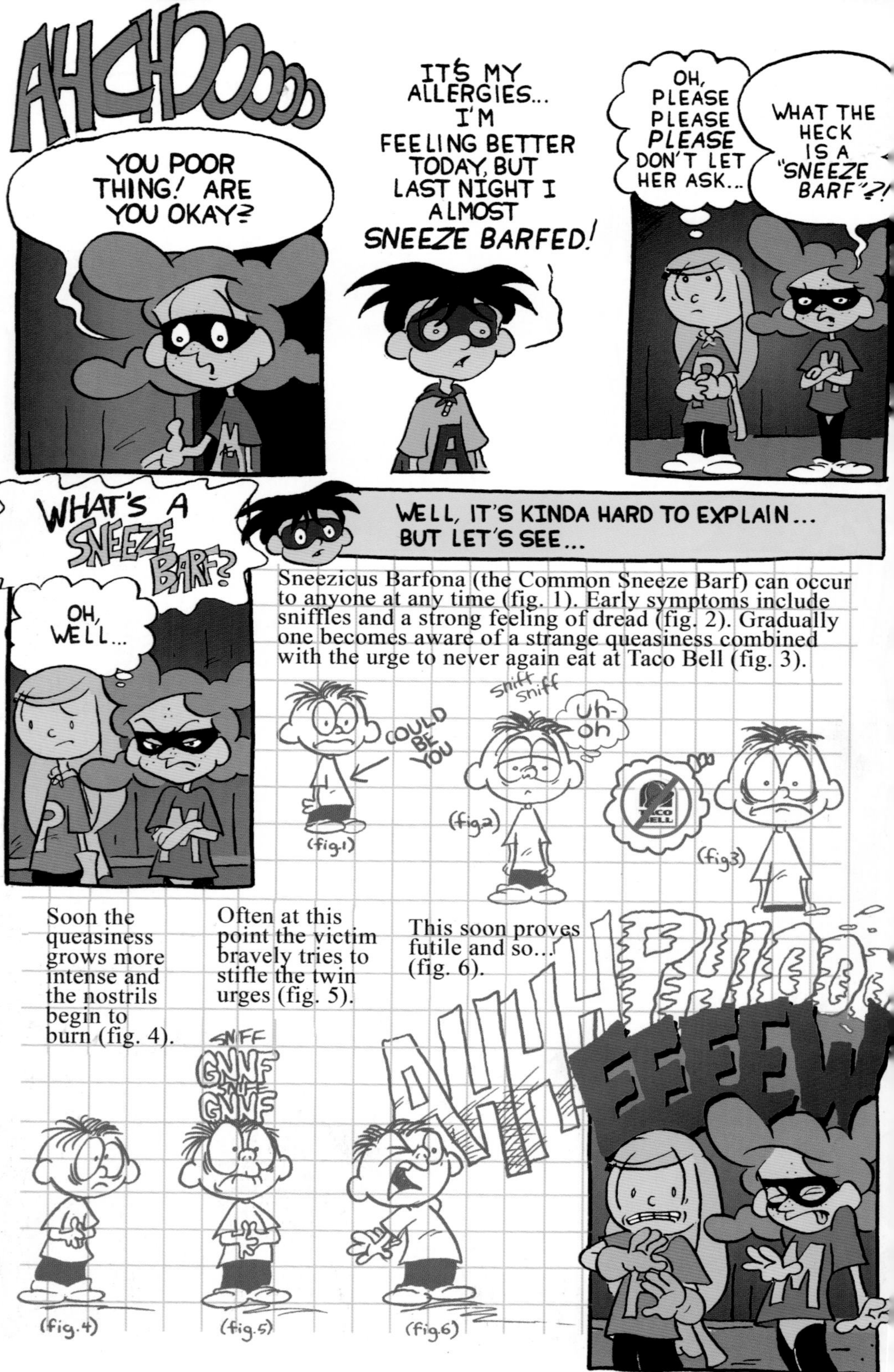

AHCHOOOOO
YOU POOR THING! ARE YOU OKAY?
IT'S MY ALLERGIES... I'M FEELING BETTER TODAY, BUT LAST NIGHT I ALMOST SNEEZE BARFED!
OH, PLEASE PLEASE PLEASE DON'T LET HER ASK...
WHAT THE HECK IS A "SNEEZE BARF"?!
WHAT'S A SNEEZE BARF?
OH, WELL...
WELL, IT'S KINDA HARD TO EXPLAIN... BUT LET'S SEE...
Sneezicus Barfona (the Common Sneeze Barf) can occur to anyone at any time (fig. 1). Early symptoms include sniffles and a strong feeling of dread (fig. 2). Gradually one becomes aware of a strange queasiness combined with the urge to never again eat at Taco Bell (fig. 3).
COULD BE YOU
(fig.1)
sniff sniff
uh-oh
(fig.2)
TACO BELL
(fig.3)
Soon the queasiness grows more intense and the nostrils begin to burn (fig. 4).
Often at this point the victim bravely tries to stifle the twin urges (fig. 5).
This soon proves futile and so... (fig. 6).
SNIFF
GNNF
SNIFF
GNNF
(fig.4)
(fig.5)
(fig.6)
AHHHPHOOO
EEEEW

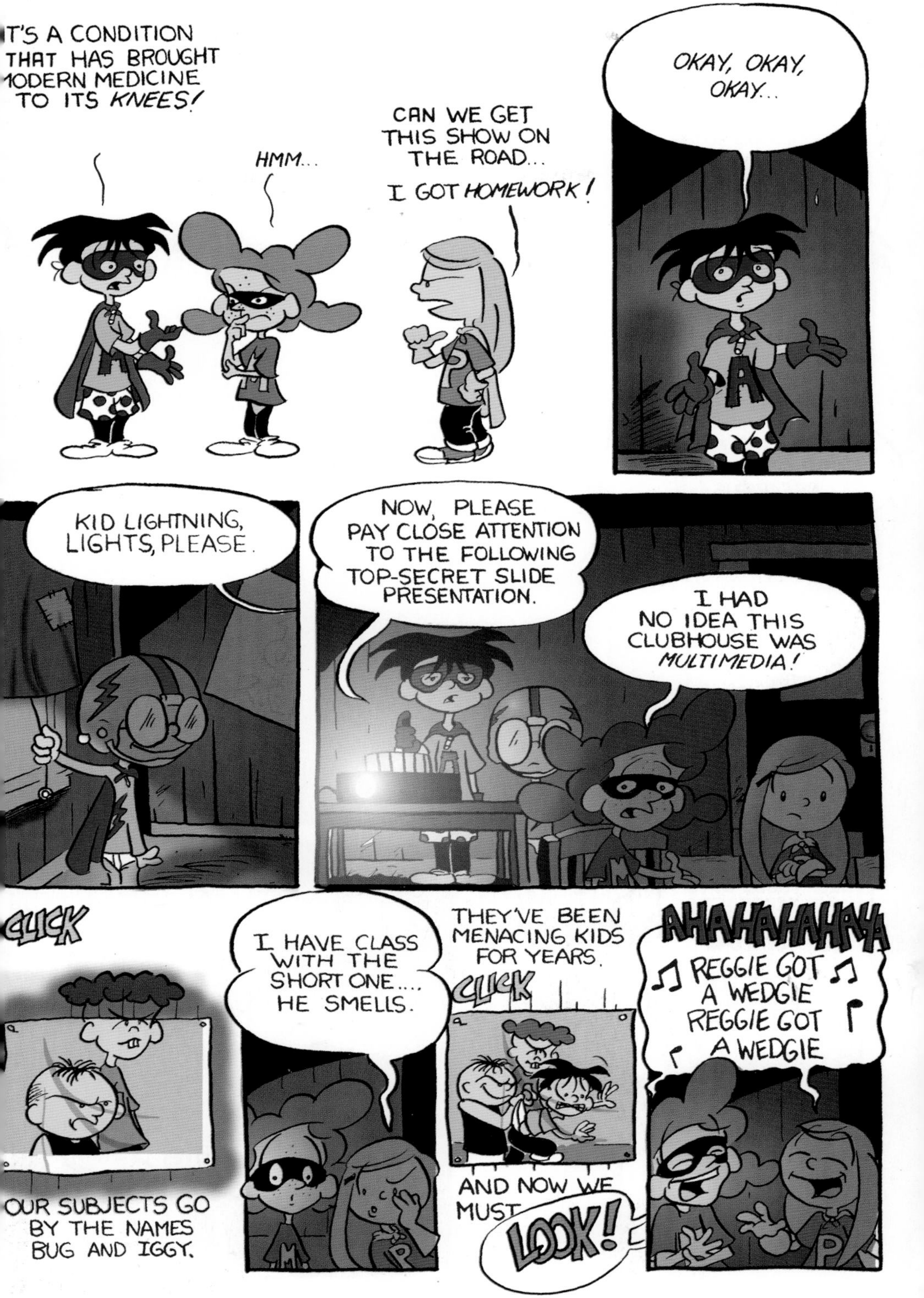

T'S A CONDITION THAT HAS BROUGHT 1ODERN MEDICINE TO ITS *KNEES!*
HMM...
CAN WE GET THIS SHOW ON THE ROAD...
I GOT *HOMEWORK!*
OKAY, OKAY, OKAY...
KID LIGHTNING, LIGHTS, PLEASE.
NOW, PLEASE PAY CLOSE ATTENTION TO THE FOLLOWING TOP-SECRET SLIDE PRESENTATION.
I HAD NO IDEA THIS CLUBHOUSE WAS *MULTIMEDIA!*
CLICK
OUR SUBJECTS GO BY THE NAMES BUG AND IGGY.
I HAVE CLASS WITH THE SHORT ONE.... HE SMELLS.
THEY'VE BEEN MENACING KIDS FOR YEARS.
CLICK
AND NOW WE MUST
LOOK!
AHAHAHAHAHAHA
REGGIE GOT A WEDGIE REGGIE GOT A WEDGIE

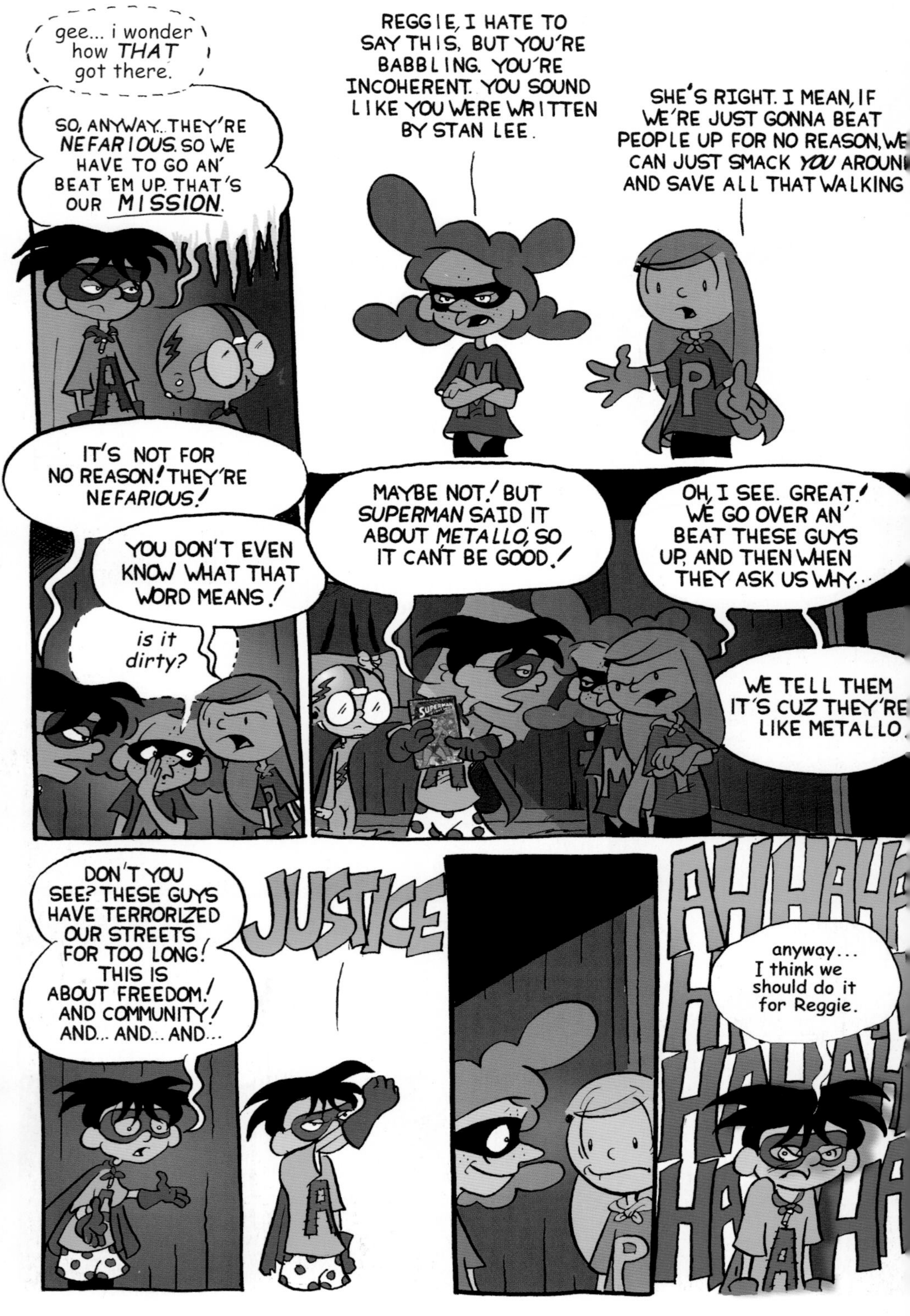

gee... i wonder how THAT got there.
SO, ANYWAY... THEY'RE NEFARIOUS. SO WE HAVE TO GO AN' BEAT 'EM UP. THAT'S OUR MISSION.
REGGIE, I HATE TO SAY THIS, BUT YOU'RE BABBLING. YOU'RE INCOHERENT. YOU SOUND LIKE YOU WERE WRITTEN BY STAN LEE.
SHE'S RIGHT. I MEAN, IF WE'RE JUST GONNA BEAT PEOPLE UP FOR NO REASON, WE CAN JUST SMACK YOU AROUN AND SAVE ALL THAT WALKING
IT'S NOT FOR NO REASON! THEY'RE NEFARIOUS!
YOU DON'T EVEN KNOW WHAT THAT WORD MEANS!
is it dirty?
MAYBE NOT! BUT SUPERMAN SAID IT ABOUT METALLO, SO IT CAN'T BE GOOD!
SUPERMAN
OH, I SEE. GREAT! WE GO OVER AN' BEAT THESE GUYS UP, AND THEN WHEN THEY ASK US WHY...
WE TELL THEM IT'S CUZ THEY'RE LIKE METALLO.
DON'T YOU SEE? THESE GUYS HAVE TERRORIZED OUR STREETS FOR TOO LONG! THIS IS ABOUT FREEDOM! AND COMMUNITY! AND... AND... AND...
JUSTICE
AHHAHA HA HA HA HA HA
anyway... I think we should do it for Reggie.

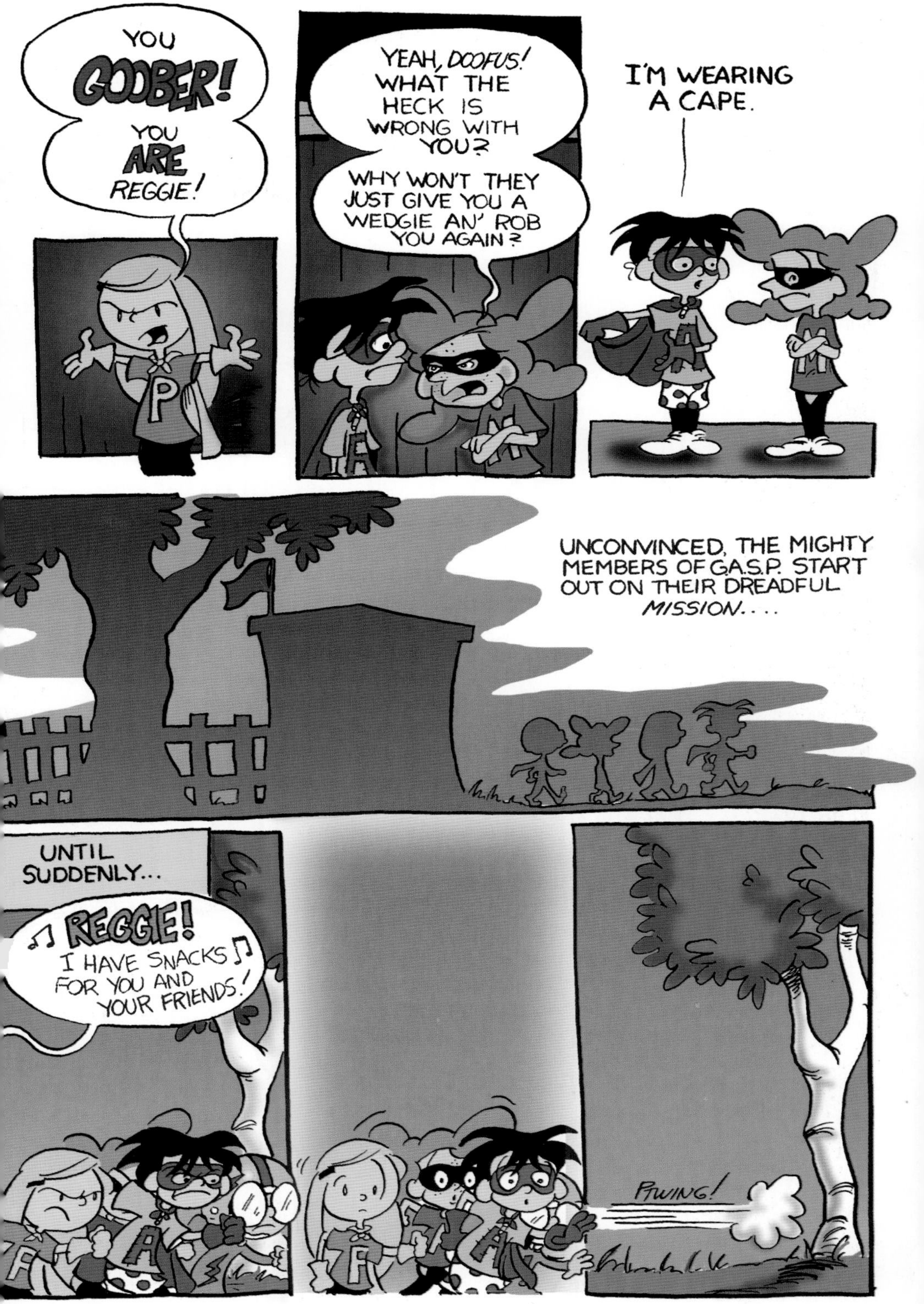
YOU GOOBER! YOU ARE REGGIE!
YEAH, DOOFUS! WHAT THE HECK IS WRONG WITH YOU?
WHY WON'T THEY JUST GIVE YOU A WEDGIE AN' ROB YOU AGAIN?
I'M WEARING A CAPE.
UNCONVINCED, THE MIGHTY MEMBERS OF G.A.S.P. START OUT ON THEIR DREADFUL MISSION. . . .
UNTIL SUDDENLY...
REGGIE! I HAVE SNACKS FOR YOU AND YOUR FRIENDS!
PTWING!

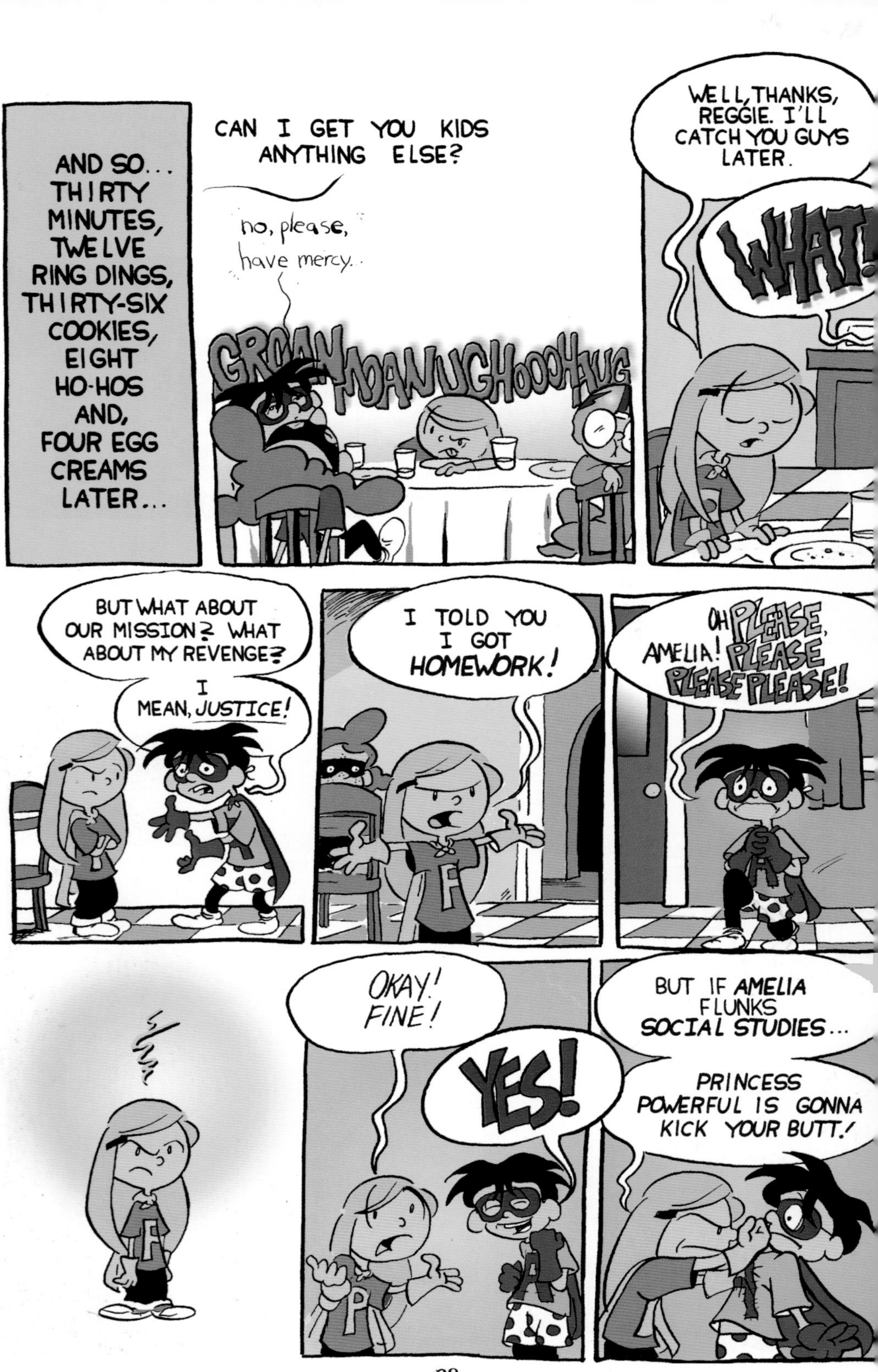

AND SO... THIRTY MINUTES, TWELVE RING DINGS, THIRTY-SIX COOKIES, EIGHT HO-HOS AND, FOUR EGG CREAMS LATER...
CAN I GET YOU KIDS ANYTHING ELSE?
no, please, have mercy...
GROANMOANUGHOOOHAUG
WELL, THANKS, REGGIE. I'LL CATCH YOU GUYS LATER.
WHAT!
BUT WHAT ABOUT OUR MISSION? WHAT ABOUT MY REVENGE?
I MEAN, JUSTICE!
I TOLD YOU I GOT HOMEWORK!
OH PLEASE, AMELIA! PLEASE PLEASE PLEASE!
OKAY! FINE!
YES!
BUT IF AMELIA FLUNKS SOCIAL STUDIES...
PRINCESS POWERFUL IS GONNA KICK YOUR BUTT!

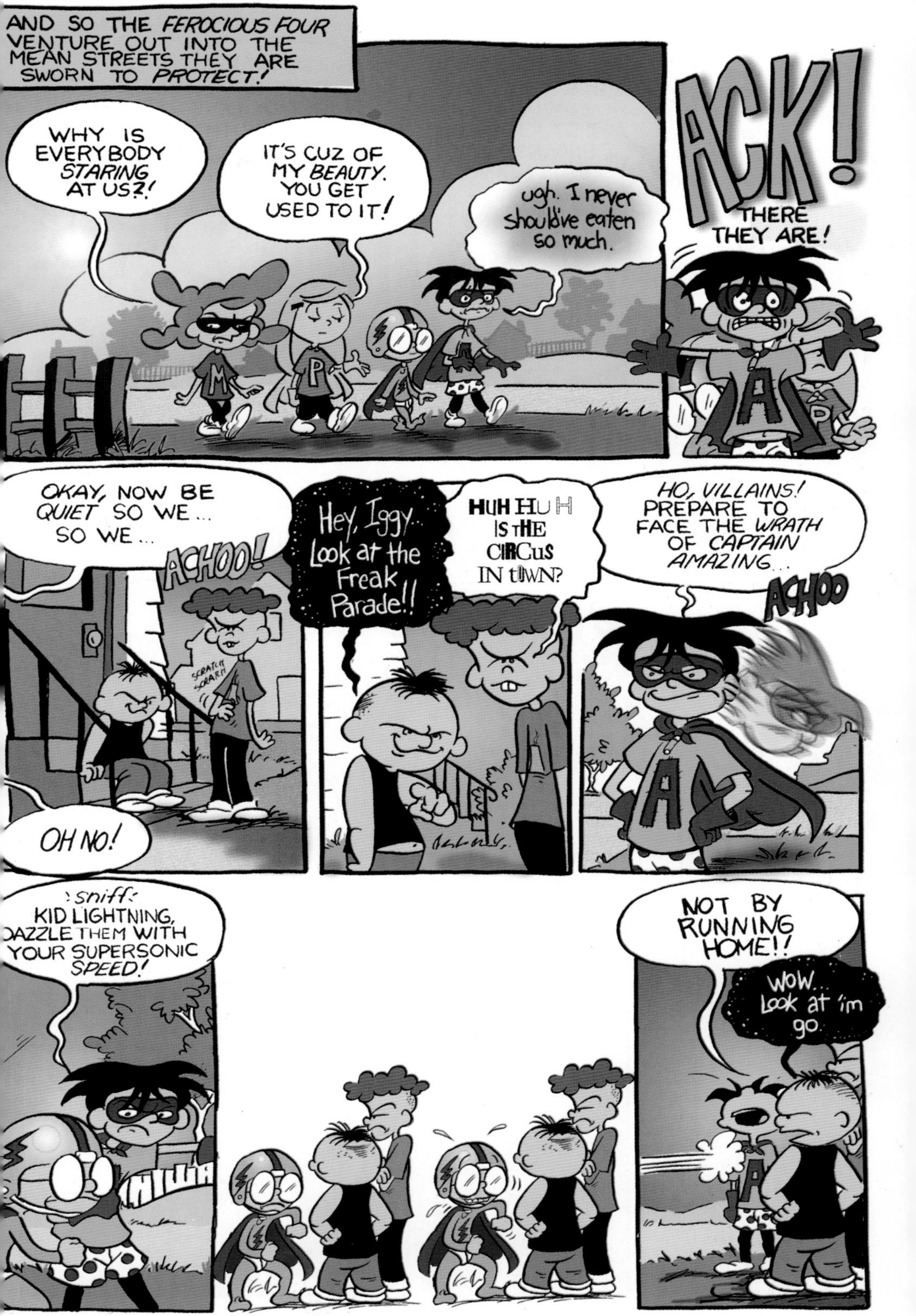
AND SO THE FEROCIOUS FOUR VENTURE OUT INTO THE MEAN STREETS THEY ARE SWORN TO PROTECT!
WHY IS EVERYBODY STARING AT US?!
IT'S CUZ OF MY BEAUTY. YOU GET USED TO IT!
ugh. I never should've eaten so much.
ACK!
THERE THEY ARE!
OKAY, NOW BE QUIET SO WE... SO WE...
ACHOO!
SCRATCH SCRATCH
OH NO!
Hey, Iggy. Look at the Freak Parade!!
HUH HUH IS THE CIRCUS IN TOWN?
HO, VILLAINS! PREPARE TO FACE THE WRATH OF CAPTAIN AMAZING...
ACHOO
:sniff: KID LIGHTNING, DAZZLE THEM WITH YOUR SUPERSONIC SPEED!
NOT BY RUNNING HOME!!
WOW. Look at 'im go.

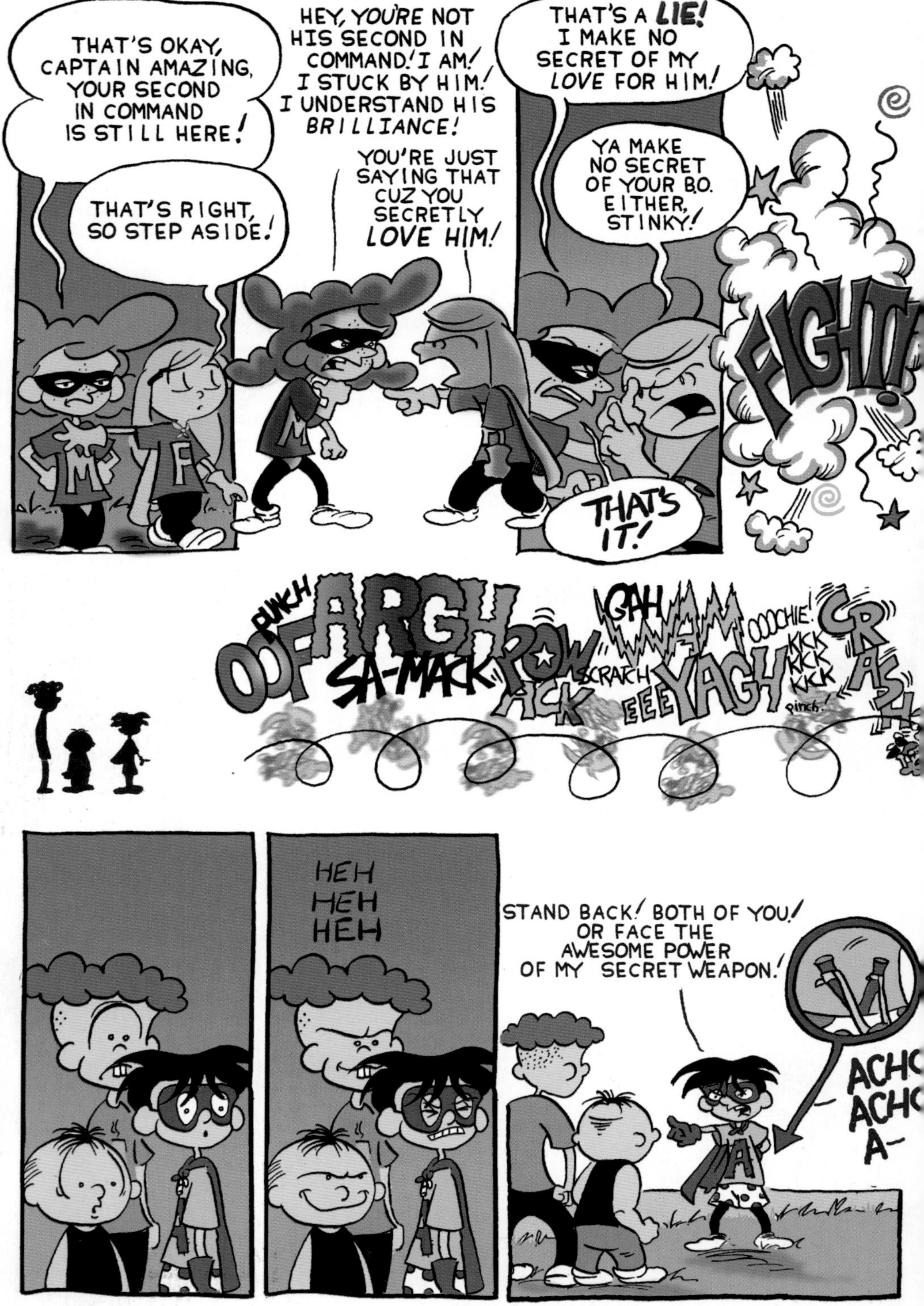
THAT'S OKAY, CAPTAIN AMAZING, YOUR SECOND IN COMMAND IS STILL HERE!
THAT'S RIGHT, SO STEP ASIDE!
HEY, YOU'RE NOT HIS SECOND IN COMMAND! I AM! I STUCK BY HIM! I UNDERSTAND HIS BRILLIANCE!
YOU'RE JUST SAYING THAT CUZ YOU SECRETLY LOVE HIM!
THAT'S A LIE! I MAKE NO SECRET OF MY LOVE FOR HIM!
YA MAKE NO SECRET OF YOUR B.O. EITHER, STINKY!
THAT'S IT!
FIGHT!
PUNCH OOF ARGH SA-MACK POW ACK GAH WAM SCRATCH EEE YAGH OOOCHIE! KKK KKK KKK pinch! CR ASH
HEH HEH HEH
STAND BACK! BOTH OF YOU! OR FACE THE AWESOME POWER OF MY SECRET WEAPON!
ACHO ACHO A-

ONE'S CERTAIN WHAT HAPPENED NEXT. PERHAPS IT WAS THE GLARING LATE AFTERNOON SUN. PERHAPS IT WAS THE ALLERGIES. IT ALMOST CERTAINLY WAS THE SNACK FOOD. REGARDLESS, THE NEXT INSTANT WOULD BE BURNED INTO THESE FIVE YOUNG MINDS ... FOREVER.

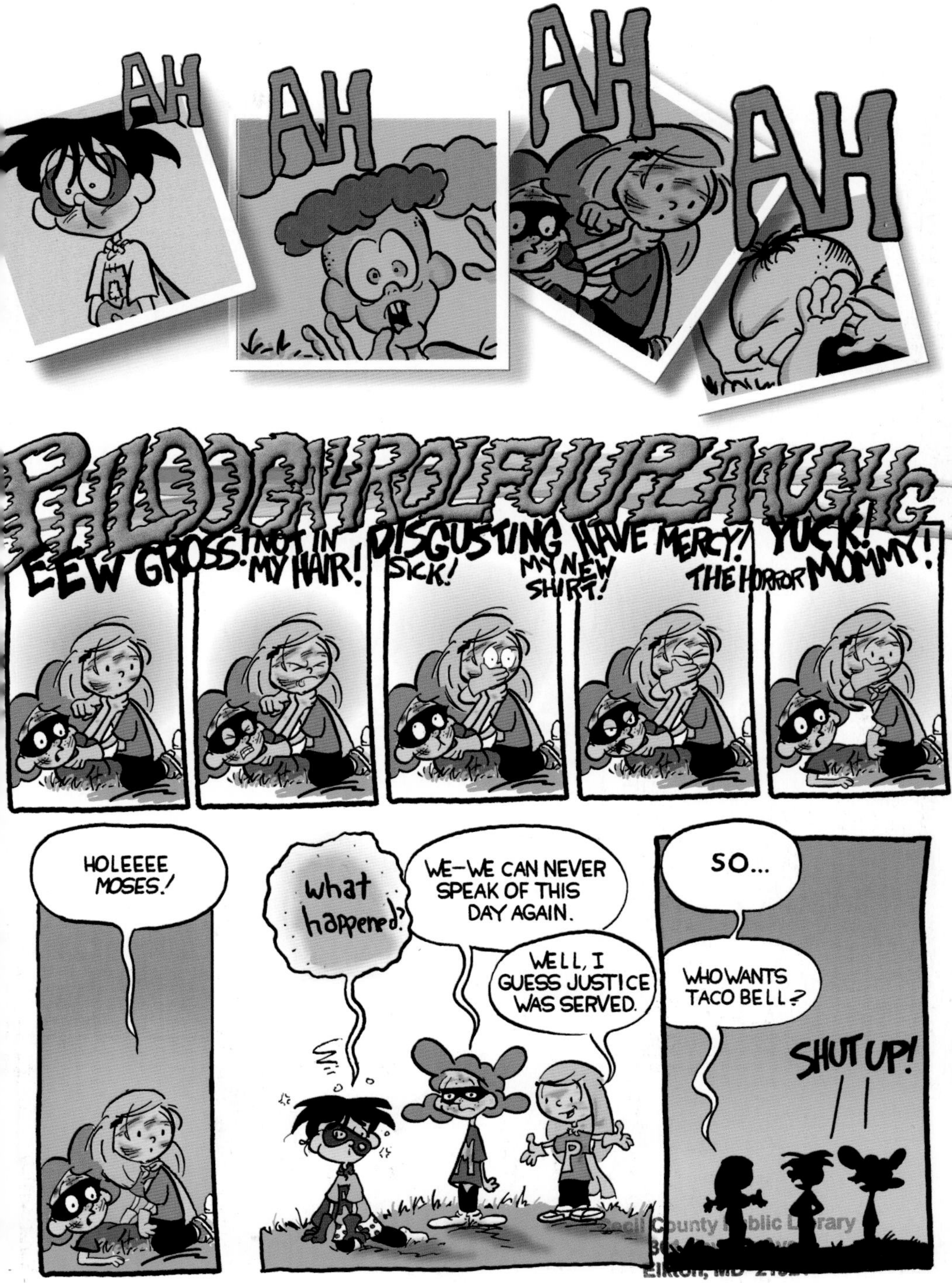
AH
AH
AH
AH
PHLOOGHROLFUUPLAUGHG
EEW GROSS!
NOT IN MY HAIR!
DISGUSTING
SICK!
HAVE MERCY!
MY NEW SHIRT!
YUCK!
THE HORROR
MOMMY!
HOLEEEE MOSES!
what happened?
WE-WE CAN NEVER SPEAK OF THIS DAY AGAIN.
WELL, I GUESS JUSTICE WAS SERVED.
SO...
WHO WANTS TACO BELL?
SHUT UP!

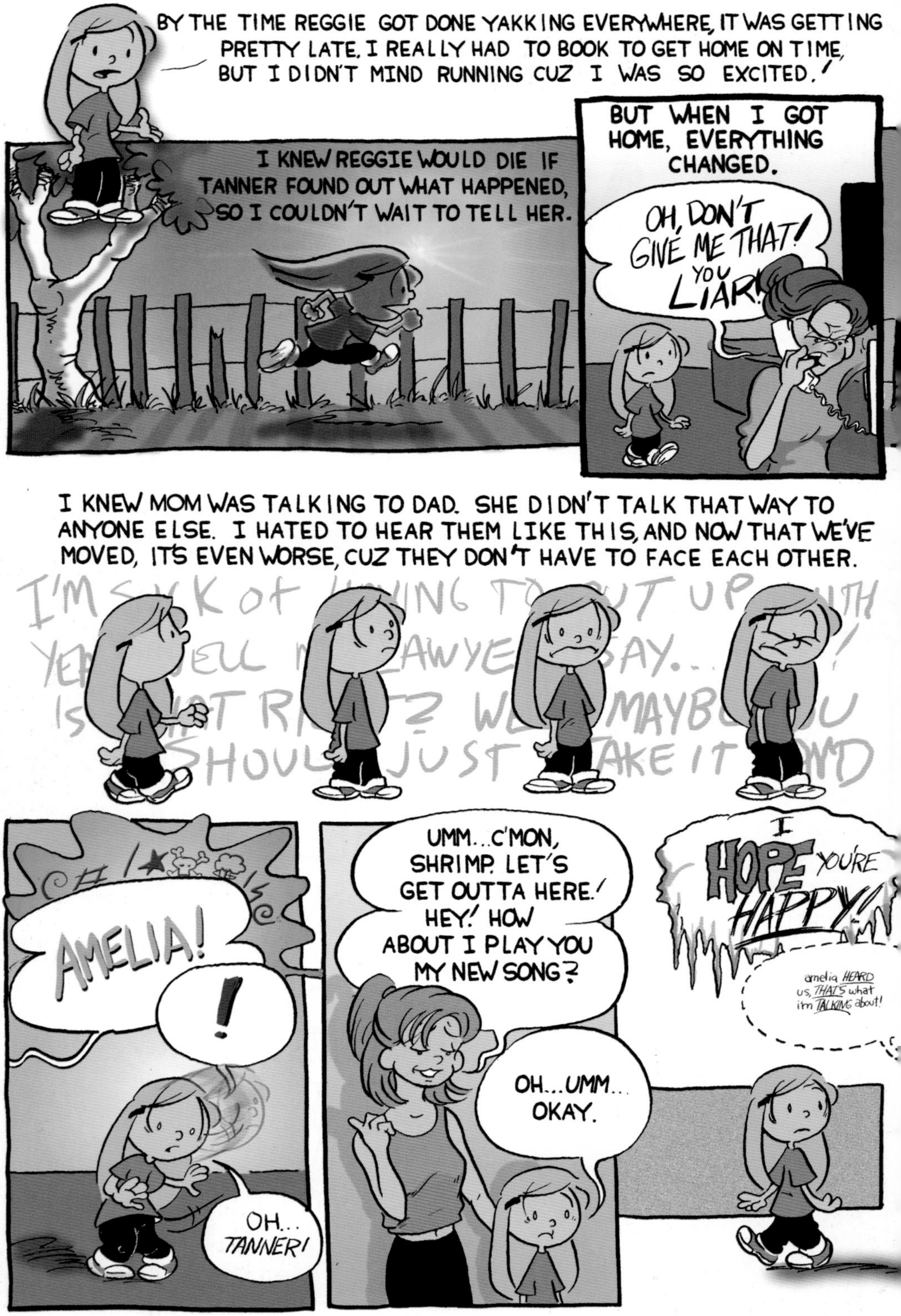

BY THE TIME REGGIE GOT DONE YAKKING EVERYWHERE, IT WAS GETTING PRETTY LATE. I REALLY HAD TO BOOK TO GET HOME ON TIME, BUT I DIDN'T MIND RUNNING CUZ I WAS SO EXCITED.!
I KNEW REGGIE WOULD DIE IF TANNER FOUND OUT WHAT HAPPENED, SO I COULDN'T WAIT TO TELL HER.
BUT WHEN I GOT HOME, EVERYTHING CHANGED.
OH, DON'T GIVE ME THAT! YOU LIAR!
I KNEW MOM WAS TALKING TO DAD. SHE DIDN'T TALK THAT WAY TO ANYONE ELSE. I HATED TO HEAR THEM LIKE THIS, AND NOW THAT WE'VE MOVED, IT'S EVEN WORSE, CUZ THEY DON'T HAVE TO FACE EACH OTHER.
AMELIA!
!
OH... TANNER!
UMM...C'MON, SHRIMP. LET'S GET OUTTA HERE.! HEY! HOW ABOUT I PLAY YOU MY NEW SONG?
OH...UMM... OKAY.
I HOPE YOU'RE HAPPY!
amelia HEARD us, THAT'S what i'm TALKING about!

WE WENT UP TO TANNER'S ROOM AN' SHE STARTED PLAYING FOR ME, BUT I WASN'T LISTENING. I COULDN'T STOP THINKING ABOUT WHAT I HEARD...WHAT WAS GOING ON.

BUT TANNER DIDN'T LET ME MOPE FOR LONG.

≥SIGH≤

"I USED TO BE DISGUSTED, NOW I TRY TO BE AMUSED."

WHAT?

ELVIS COSTELLO... FIRST ALBUM.

YOU KNOW, AMELIA, JUST BECAUSE YOUR HOME IS BROKEN...

THAT DOESN'T MEAN YOU HAVE TO BE.

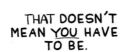

UMM... TH-THANKS.

THANKS, TANNER.

DON'T MENTION IT. NOW DO YOU WANNA HEAR THIS SONG?

SURE.

YOU'LL LIKE IT. IT'S GOT LYRICS YOU'RE TOO YOUNG TO HEAR.

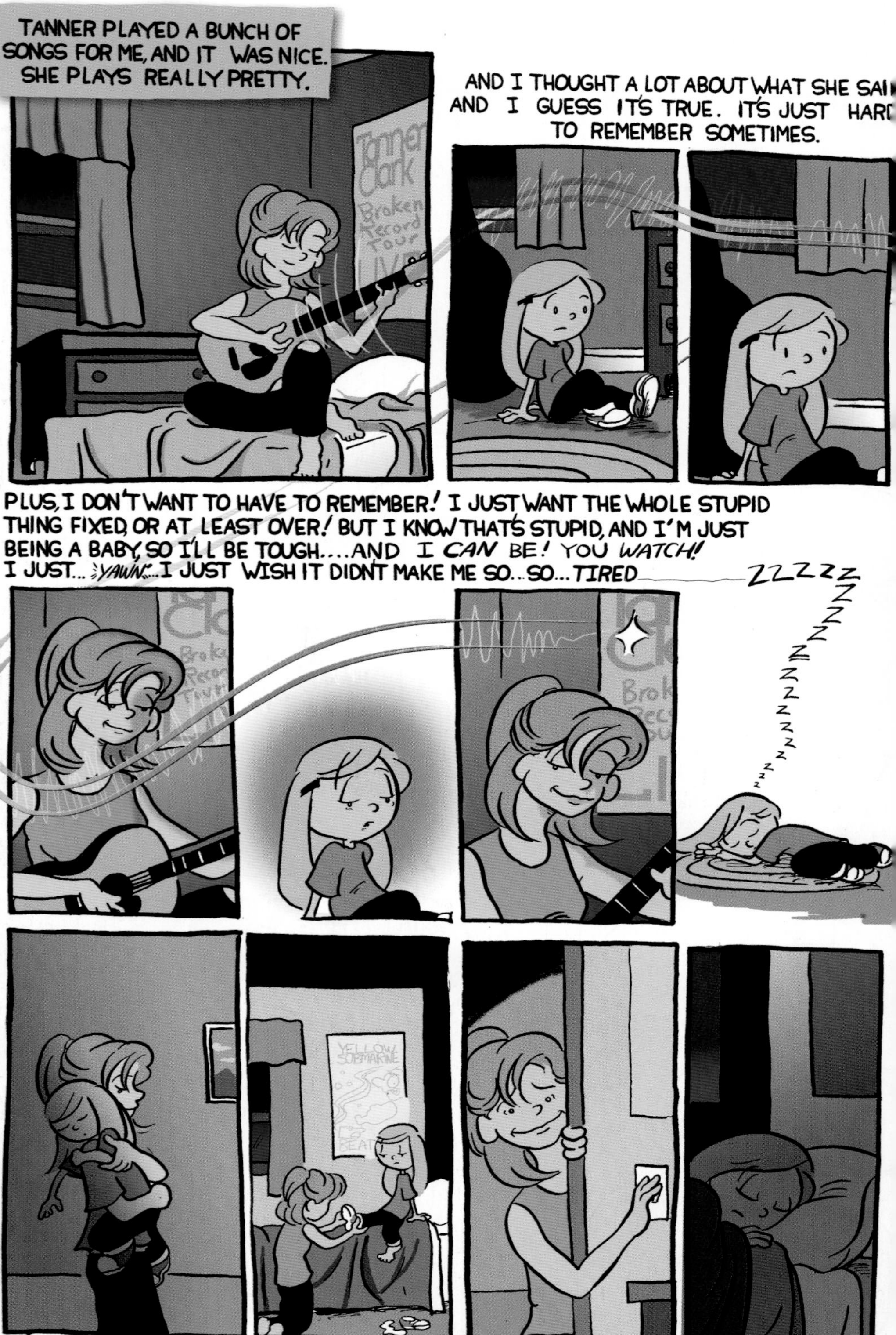
TANNER PLAYED A BUNCH OF SONGS FOR ME, AND IT WAS NICE. SHE PLAYS REALLY PRETTY.
Tanner Clark Broken Record Tour LIVE
AND I THOUGHT A LOT ABOUT WHAT SHE SAI
AND I GUESS IT'S TRUE. IT'S JUST HARD
TO REMEMBER SOMETIMES.
PLUS, I DON'T WANT TO HAVE TO REMEMBER! I JUST WANT THE WHOLE STUPID THING FIXED, OR AT LEAST OVER! BUT I KNOW THAT'S STUPID, AND I'M JUST BEING A BABY, SO I'LL BE TOUGH....AND I CAN BE! YOU WATCH!
I JUST... YAWN... I JUST WISH IT DIDN'T MAKE ME SO...SO...TIRED
ZZZZZ
YELLOW SUBMARINE

The Gym Class System

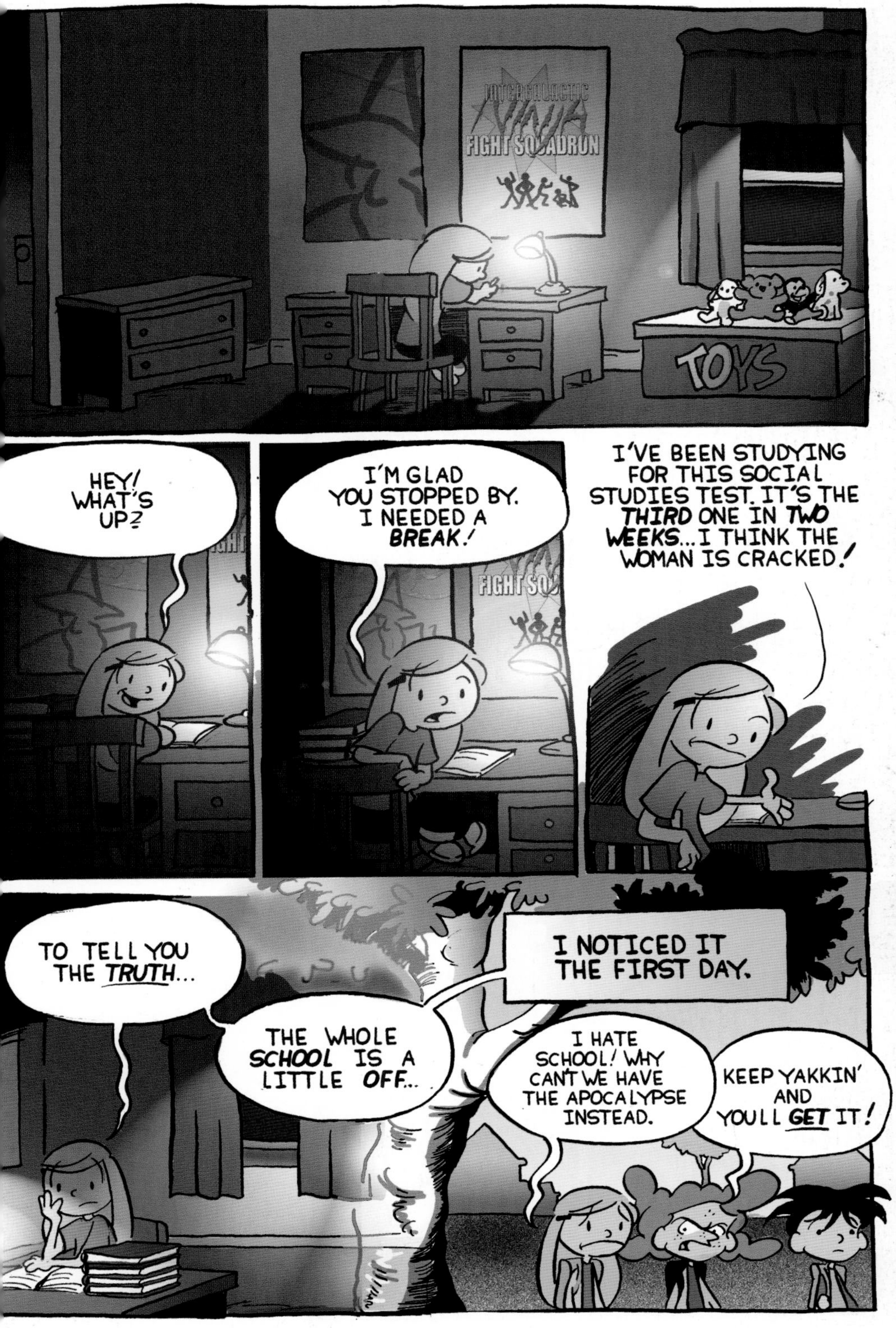
INTERGALACTIC NINJA FIGHT SQUADRON
TOYS
HEY! WHAT'S UP?
I'M GLAD YOU STOPPED BY. I NEEDED A BREAK!
FIGHT SQ
I'VE BEEN STUDYING FOR THIS SOCIAL STUDIES TEST. IT'S THE THIRD ONE IN TWO WEEKS... I THINK THE WOMAN IS CRACKED!
TO TELL YOU THE TRUTH...
THE WHOLE SCHOOL IS A LITTLE OFF...
I NOTICED IT THE FIRST DAY.
I HATE SCHOOL! WHY CAN'T WE HAVE THE APOCALYPSE INSTEAD.
KEEP YAKKIN' AND YOU'LL GET IT!

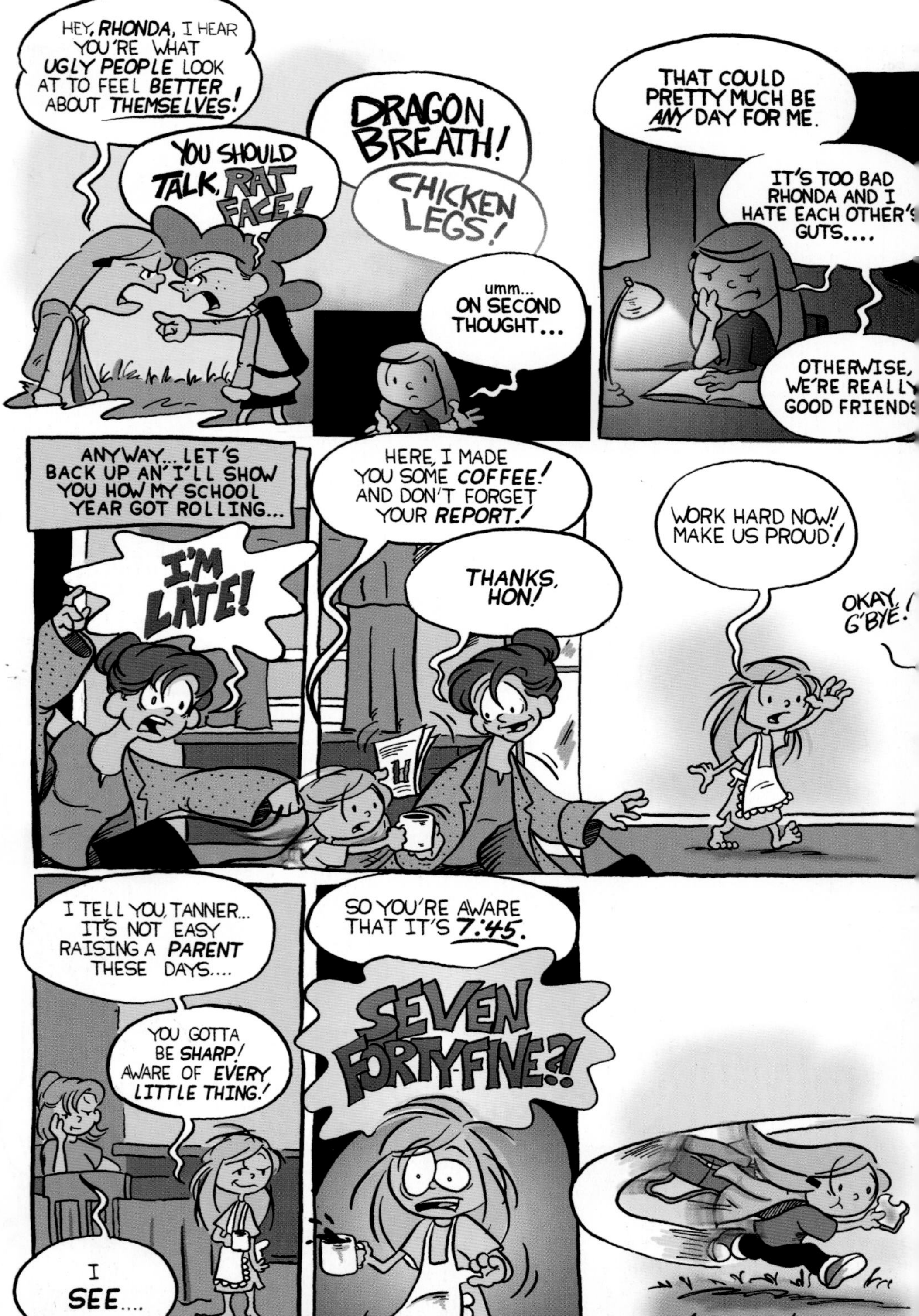
HEY, RHONDA, I HEAR YOU'RE WHAT UGLY PEOPLE LOOK AT TO FEEL BETTER ABOUT THEMSELVES!
YOU SHOULD TALK, RAT FACE!
DRAGON BREATH!
CHICKEN LEGS!
umm... ON SECOND THOUGHT...
THAT COULD PRETTY MUCH BE ANY DAY FOR ME.
IT'S TOO BAD RHONDA AND I HATE EACH OTHER'S GUTS....
OTHERWISE, WE'RE REALLY GOOD FRIENDS
ANYWAY... LET'S BACK UP AN' I'LL SHOW YOU HOW MY SCHOOL YEAR GOT ROLLING...
I'M LATE!
HERE, I MADE YOU SOME COFFEE! AND DON'T FORGET YOUR REPORT!
THANKS, HON!
WORK HARD NOW! MAKE US PROUD!
OKAY, G'BYE!
I TELL YOU, TANNER... IT'S NOT EASY RAISING A PARENT THESE DAYS....
YOU GOTTA BE SHARP! AWARE OF EVERY LITTLE THING!
I SEE....
SO YOU'RE AWARE THAT IT'S 7:45.
SEVEN FORTY-FIVE?!

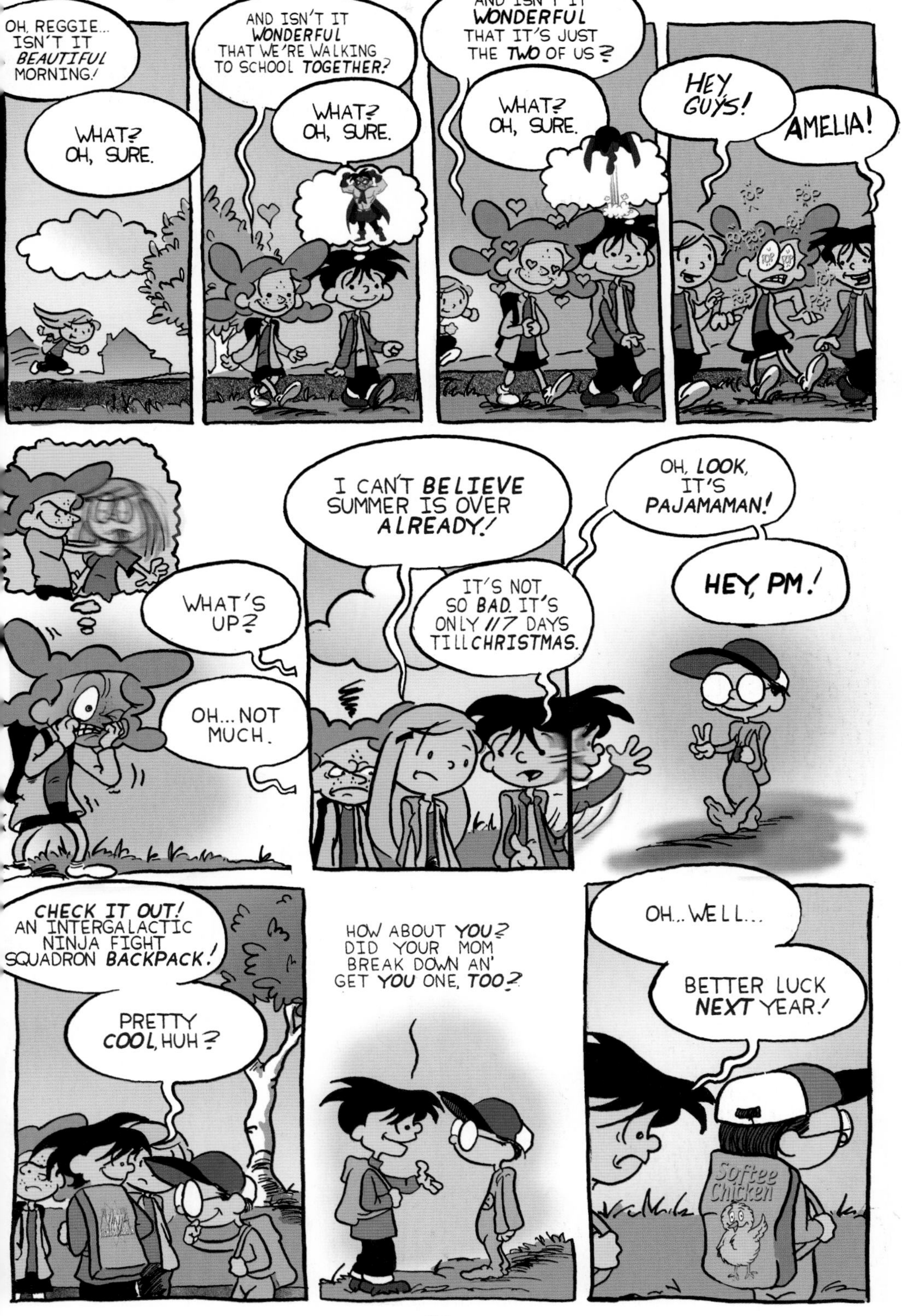
OH, REGGIE... ISN'T IT BEAUTIFUL MORNING!
WHAT? OH, SURE.
AND ISN'T IT WONDERFUL THAT WE'RE WALKING TO SCHOOL TOGETHER?
WHAT? OH, SURE.
AND ISN'T IT WONDERFUL THAT IT'S JUST THE TWO OF US?
WHAT? OH, SURE.
HEY GUYS!
AMELIA!
POP POP POP POP POP POP POP
WHAT'S UP?
OH... NOT MUCH.
I CAN'T BELIEVE SUMMER IS OVER ALREADY!
IT'S NOT SO BAD. IT'S ONLY 117 DAYS TILL CHRISTMAS.
OH, LOOK, IT'S PAJAMAMAN!
HEY, PM!
CHECK IT OUT! AN INTERGALACTIC NINJA FIGHT SQUADRON BACKPACK!
PRETTY COOL, HUH?
HOW ABOUT YOU? DID YOUR MOM BREAK DOWN AN' GET YOU ONE, TOO?
OH... WELL...
BETTER LUCK NEXT YEAR!
Softee Chicken

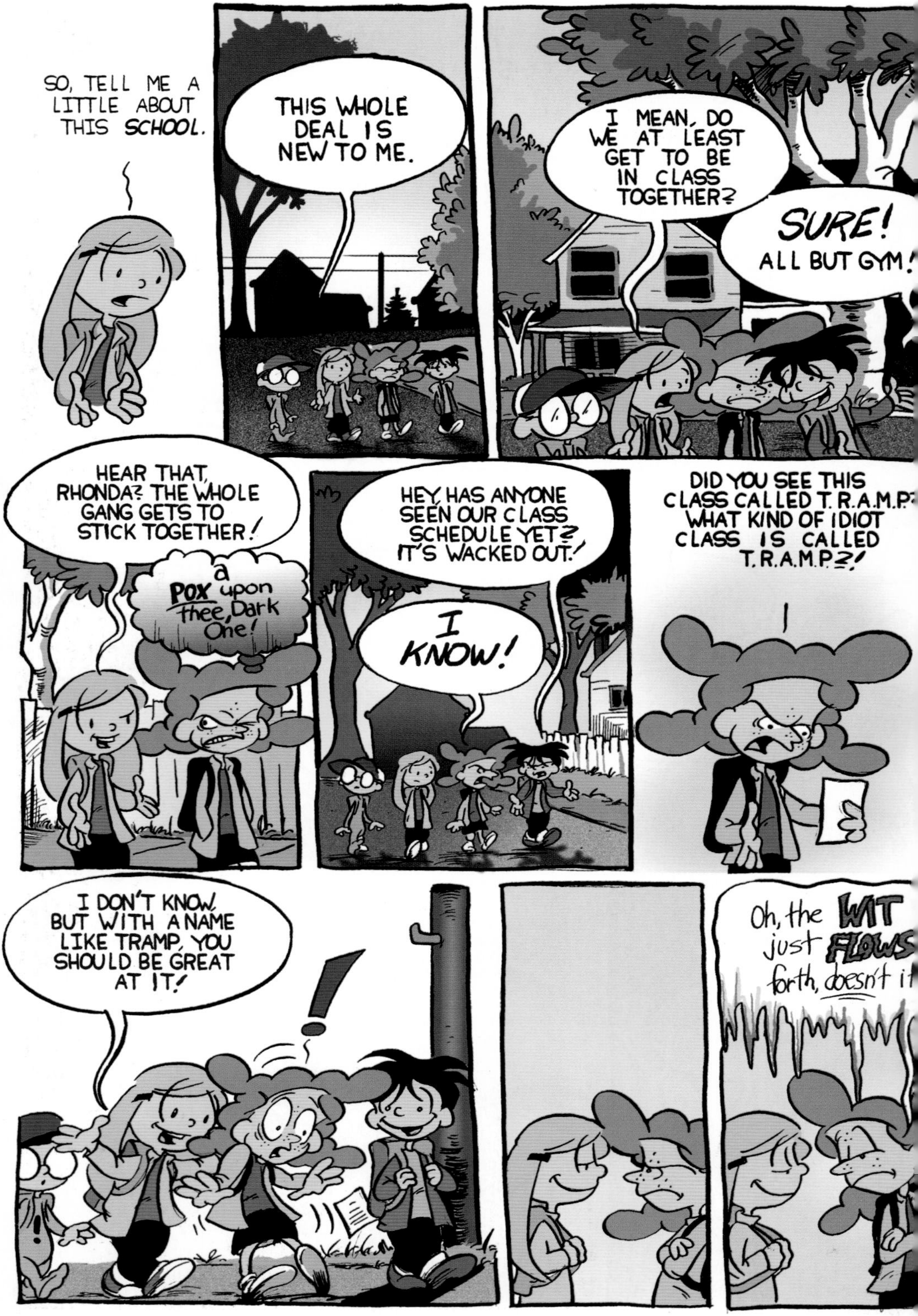
SO, TELL ME A LITTLE ABOUT THIS SCHOOL.
THIS WHOLE DEAL IS NEW TO ME.
I MEAN, DO WE AT LEAST GET TO BE IN CLASS TOGETHER?
SURE! ALL BUT GYM!
HEAR THAT, RHONDA? THE WHOLE GANG GETS TO STICK TOGETHER!
a POX upon thee, Dark One!
HEY, HAS ANYONE SEEN OUR CLASS SCHEDULE YET? IT'S WACKED OUT!
I KNOW!
DID YOU SEE THIS CLASS CALLED T.R.A.M.P.? WHAT KIND OF IDIOT CLASS IS CALLED T.R.A.M.P.?!
I DON'T KNOW. BUT WITH A NAME LIKE TRAMP, YOU SHOULD BE GREAT AT IT!
!
Oh, the WIT just FLOWS forth, doesn't i

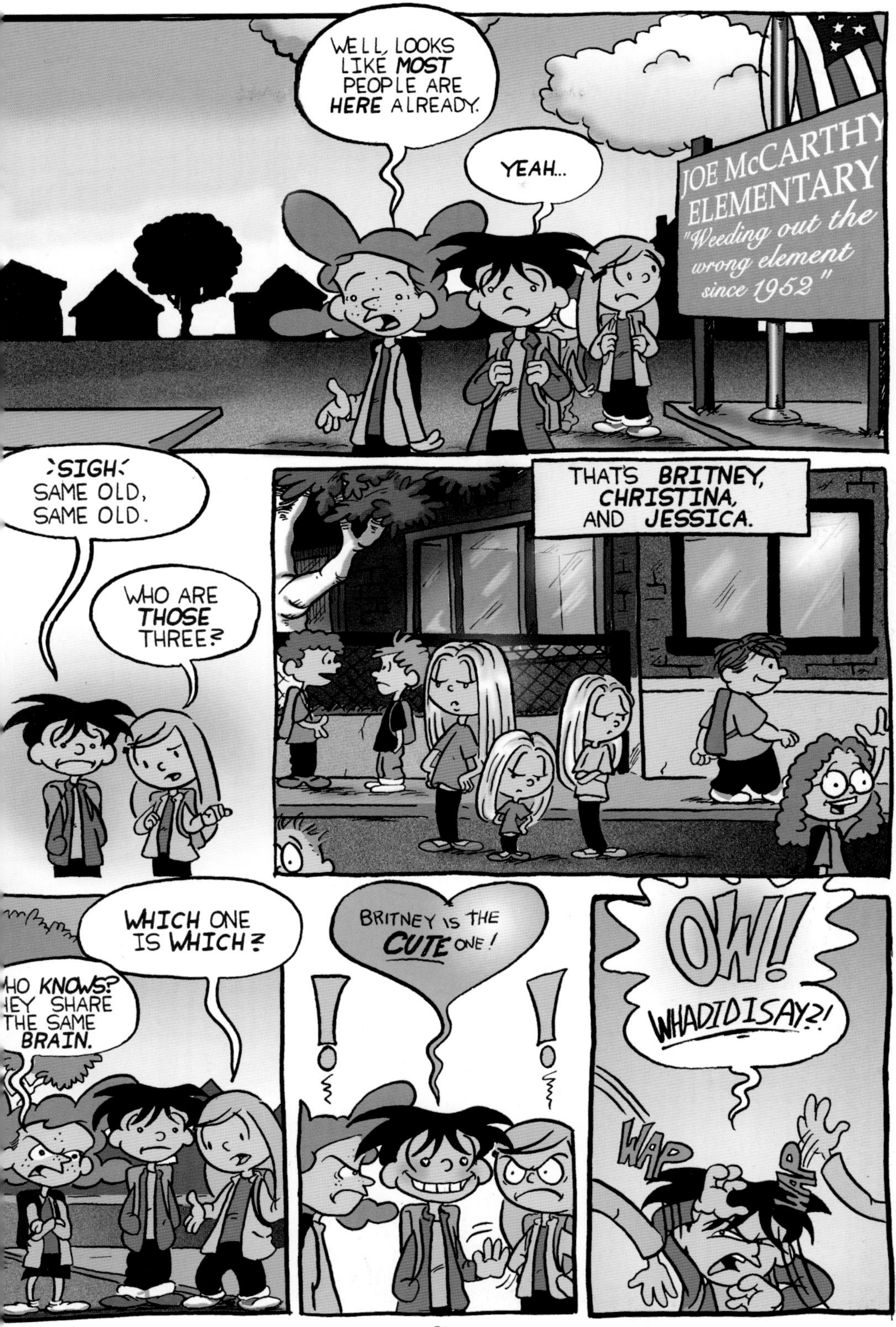
WELL, LOOKS LIKE **MOST** PEOPLE ARE **HERE** ALREADY.
YEAH...
JOE McCARTHY ELEMENTARY "Weeding out the wrong element since 1952"
SIGH SAME OLD, SAME OLD.
WHO ARE **THOSE** THREE?
THAT'S **BRITNEY, CHRISTINA,** AND **JESSICA.**
WHICH ONE IS **WHICH**?
HO **KNOWS?** HEY SHARE THE SAME **BRAIN.**
BRITNEY IS THE **CUTE** ONE!
!
!
OW!
WHADIDISAY?!
WAP
WAP

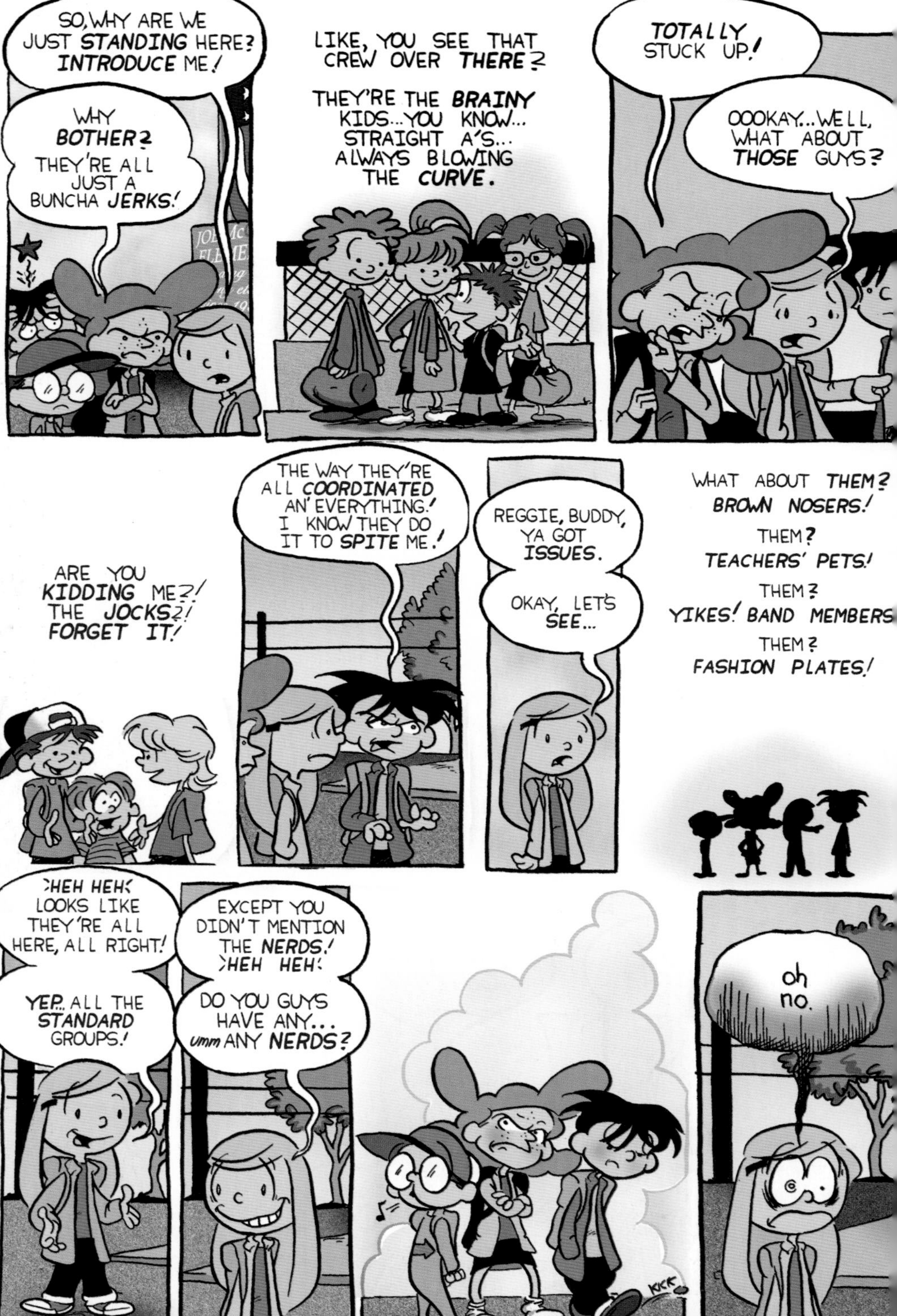

SO, WHY ARE WE JUST STANDING HERE? INTRODUCE ME!
WHY BOTHER? THEY'RE ALL JUST A BUNCHA JERKS!
LIKE, YOU SEE THAT CREW OVER THERE?
THEY'RE THE BRAINY KIDS...YOU KNOW... STRAIGHT A'S... ALWAYS BLOWING THE CURVE.
TOTALLY STUCK UP!
OOOKAY...WELL, WHAT ABOUT THOSE GUYS?
ARE YOU KIDDING ME?! THE JOCKS?! FORGET IT!
THE WAY THEY'RE ALL COORDINATED AN' EVERYTHING! I KNOW THEY DO IT TO SPITE ME.!
REGGIE, BUDDY, YA GOT ISSUES.
OKAY, LET'S SEE...
WHAT ABOUT THEM? BROWN NOSERS!
THEM? TEACHERS' PETS!
THEM? YIKES! BAND MEMBERS
THEM? FASHION PLATES!
>HEH HEH< LOOKS LIKE THEY'RE ALL HERE, ALL RIGHT!
YEP... ALL THE STANDARD GROUPS!
EXCEPT YOU DIDN'T MENTION THE NERDS! >HEH HEH<
DO YOU GUYS HAVE ANY... umm ANY NERDS?
KICK
oh no.

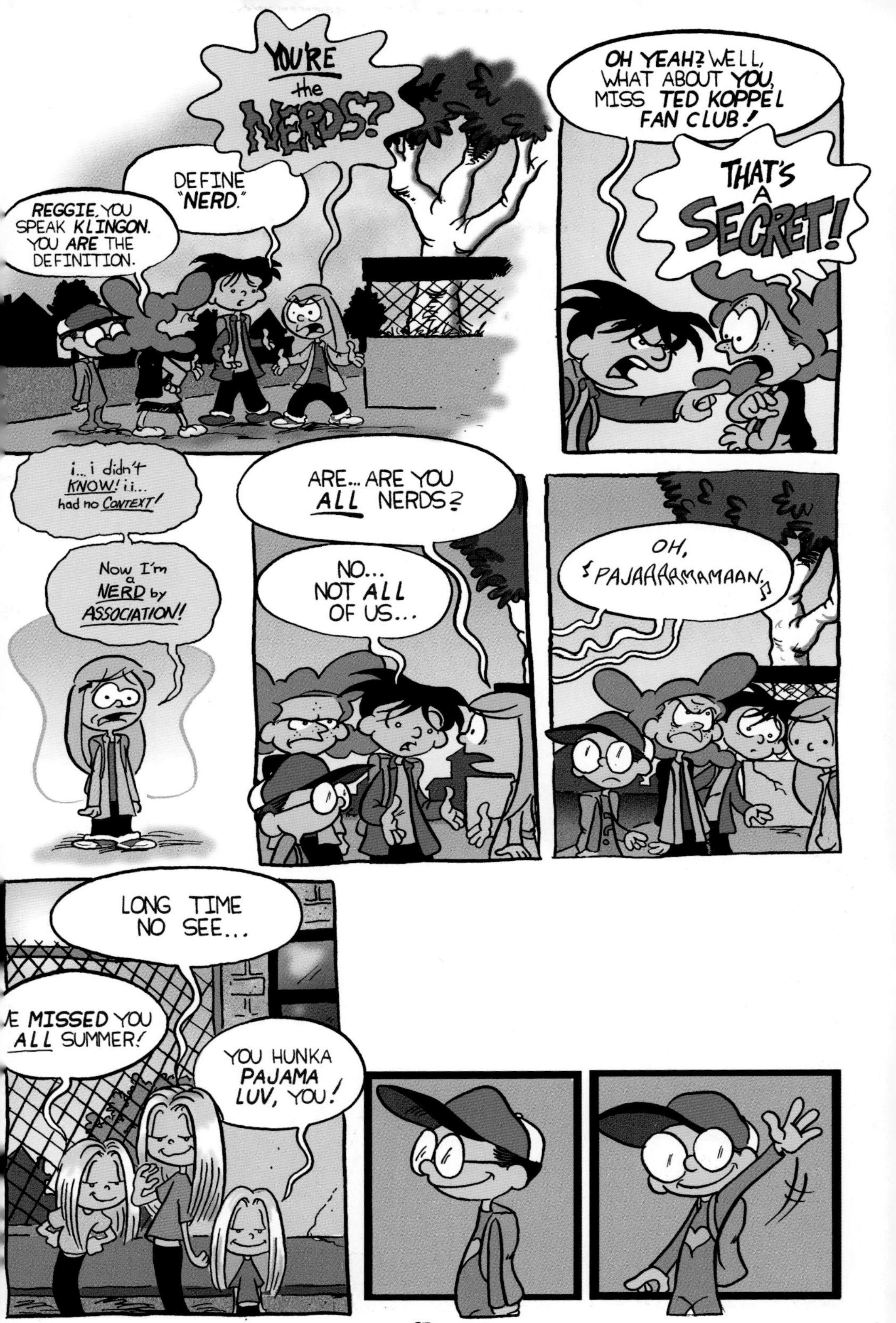

REGGIE, YOU SPEAK KLINGON. YOU ARE THE DEFINITION.
DEFINE "NERD."
YOU'RE the NERDS?
OH YEAH? WELL, WHAT ABOUT YOU, MISS TED KOPPEL FAN CLUB!
THAT'S A SECRET!
i... i didn't KNOW! i.i... had no CONTEXT!
Now I'm a NERD by ASSOCIATION!
ARE... ARE YOU ALL NERDS?
NO... NOT ALL OF US...
OH, PAJARRRAMAMAAN,
LONG TIME NO SEE...
E MISSED YOU ALL SUMMER!
YOU HUNKA PAJAMA LUV, YOU!

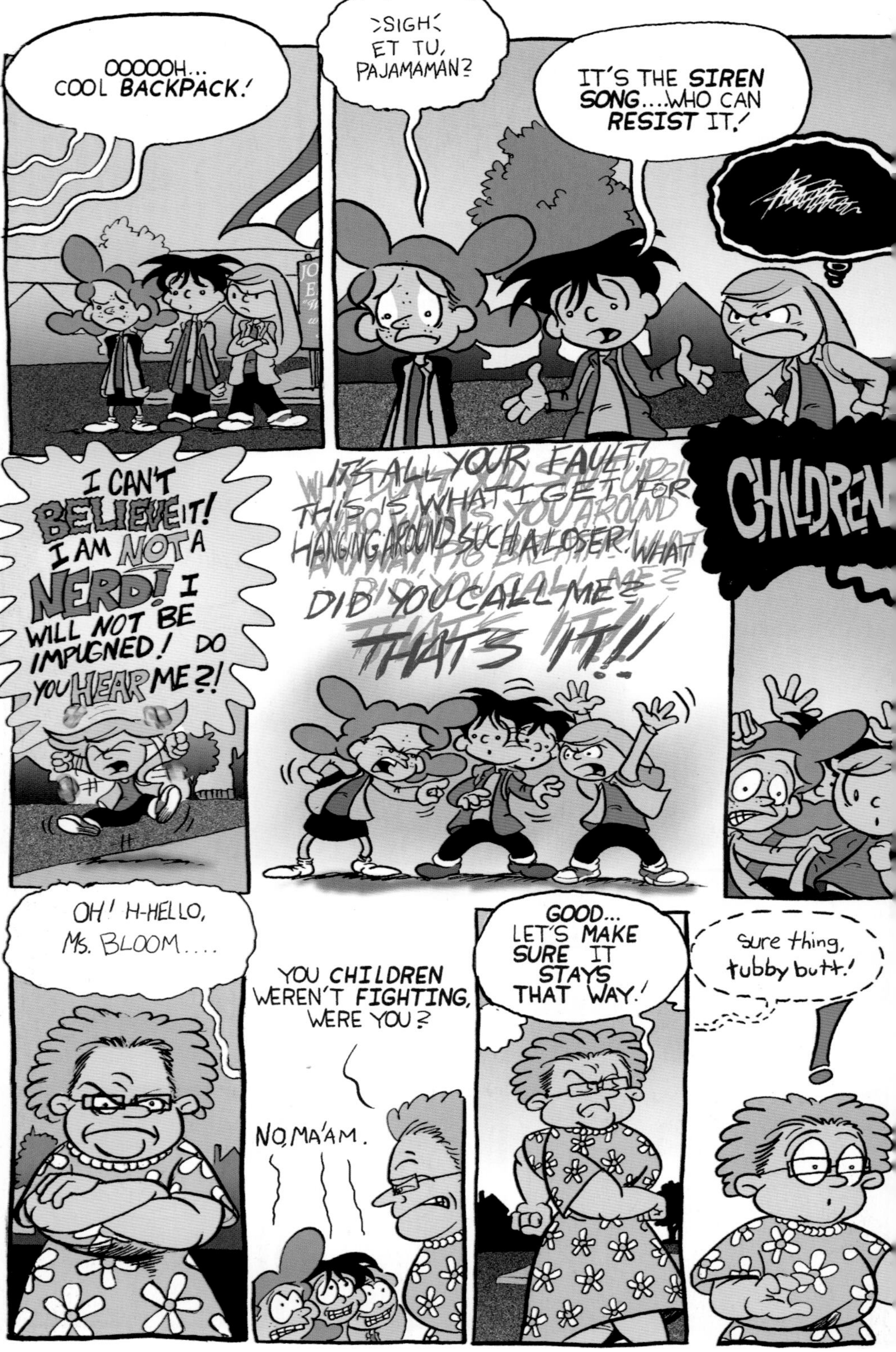

OOOOOH... COOL BACKPACK!
>SIGH< ET TU, PAJAMAMAN?
IT'S THE SIREN SONG....WHO CAN RESIST IT!
I CAN'T BELIEVE IT! I AM NOT A NERD! I WILL NOT BE IMPUGNED! DO YOU HEAR ME?!
IT'S ALL YOUR FAULT! THIS IS WHAT I GET FOR HANGING AROUND SUCH A LOSER! WHAT DID YOU CALL ME? THAT'S IT!!
CHILDREN
OH! H-HELLO, MS. BLOOM....
YOU CHILDREN WEREN'T FIGHTING, WERE YOU?
NO, MA'AM.
GOOD... LET'S MAKE SURE IT STAYS THAT WAY!
Sure thing, tubby butt!
!

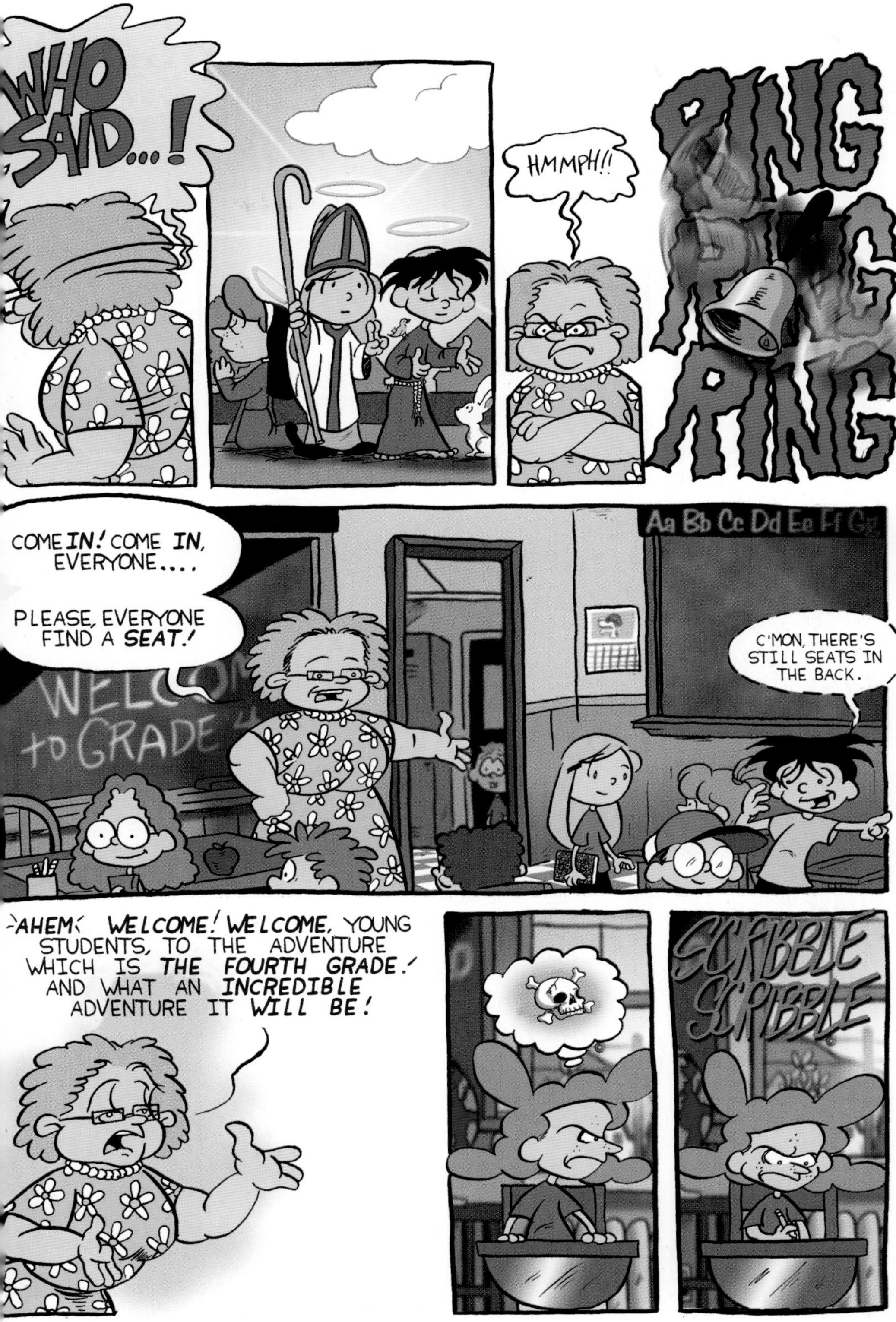
WHO SAID...!
HMMPH!!
RING RING RING
COME IN! COME IN, EVERYONE....
PLEASE, EVERYONE FIND A SEAT!
Aa Bb Cc Dd Ee Ff Gg
WELCOME to GRADE 4
C'MON, THERE'S STILL SEATS IN THE BACK.
-AHEM- WELCOME! WELCOME, YOUNG STUDENTS, TO THE ADVENTURE WHICH IS THE FOURTH GRADE! AND WHAT AN INCREDIBLE ADVENTURE IT WILL BE!
SCRIBBLE SCRIBBLE

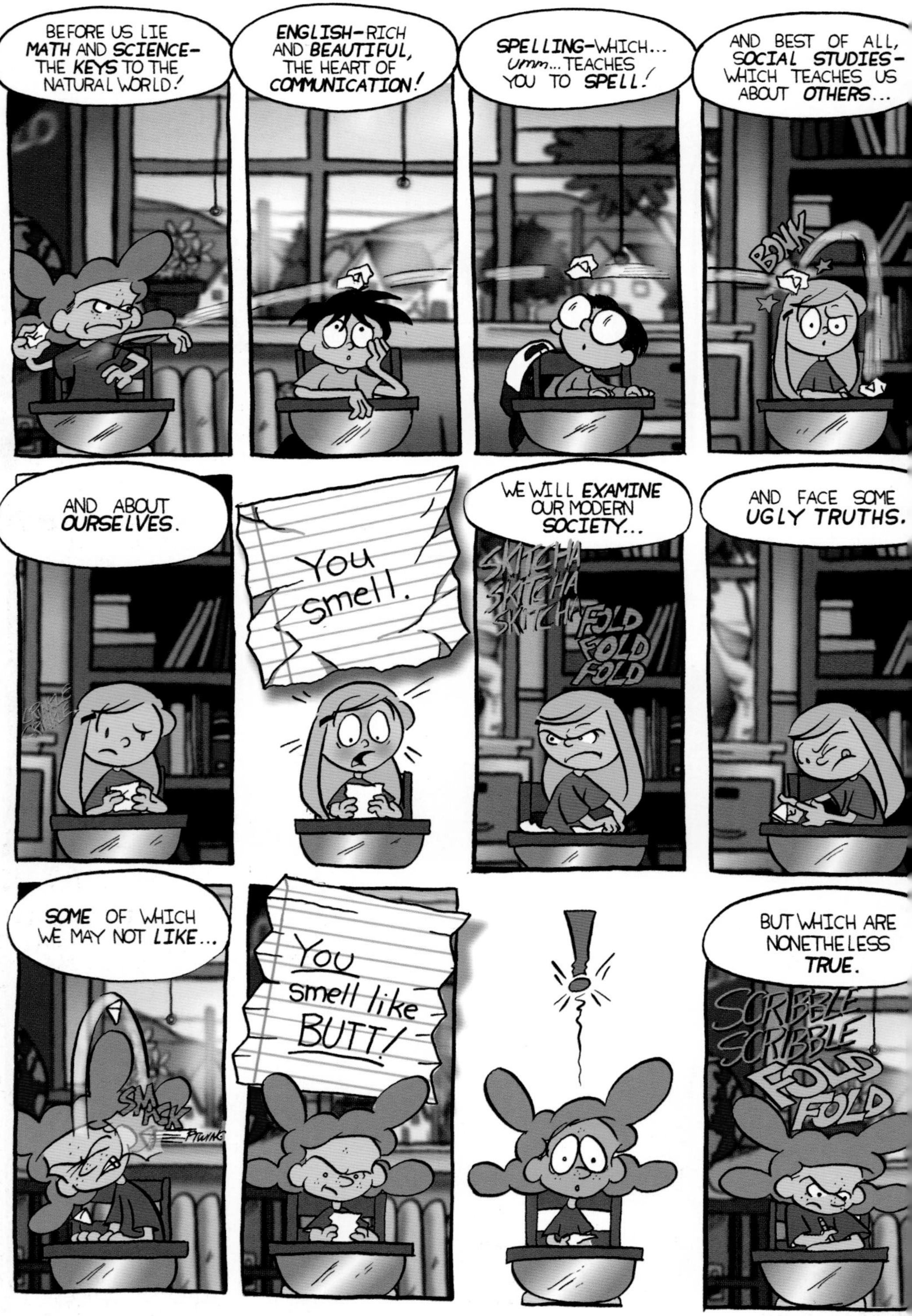
BEFORE US LIE MATH AND SCIENCE– THE KEYS TO THE NATURAL WORLD!
ENGLISH–RICH AND BEAUTIFUL, THE HEART OF COMMUNICATION!
SPELLING–WHICH... UMM... TEACHES YOU TO SPELL!
AND BEST OF ALL, SOCIAL STUDIES– WHICH TEACHES US ABOUT OTHERS...
BONK
AND ABOUT OURSELVES.
You smell.
WE WILL EXAMINE OUR MODERN SOCIETY...
SKITCHA SKITCHA SKITCHA
FOLD FOLD FOLD
AND FACE SOME UGLY TRUTHS.
SOME OF WHICH WE MAY NOT LIKE...
SMACK
PTWING
You smell like BUTT!
!
BUT WHICH ARE NONETHELESS TRUE.
SCRIBBLE SCRIBBLE
FOLD FOLD

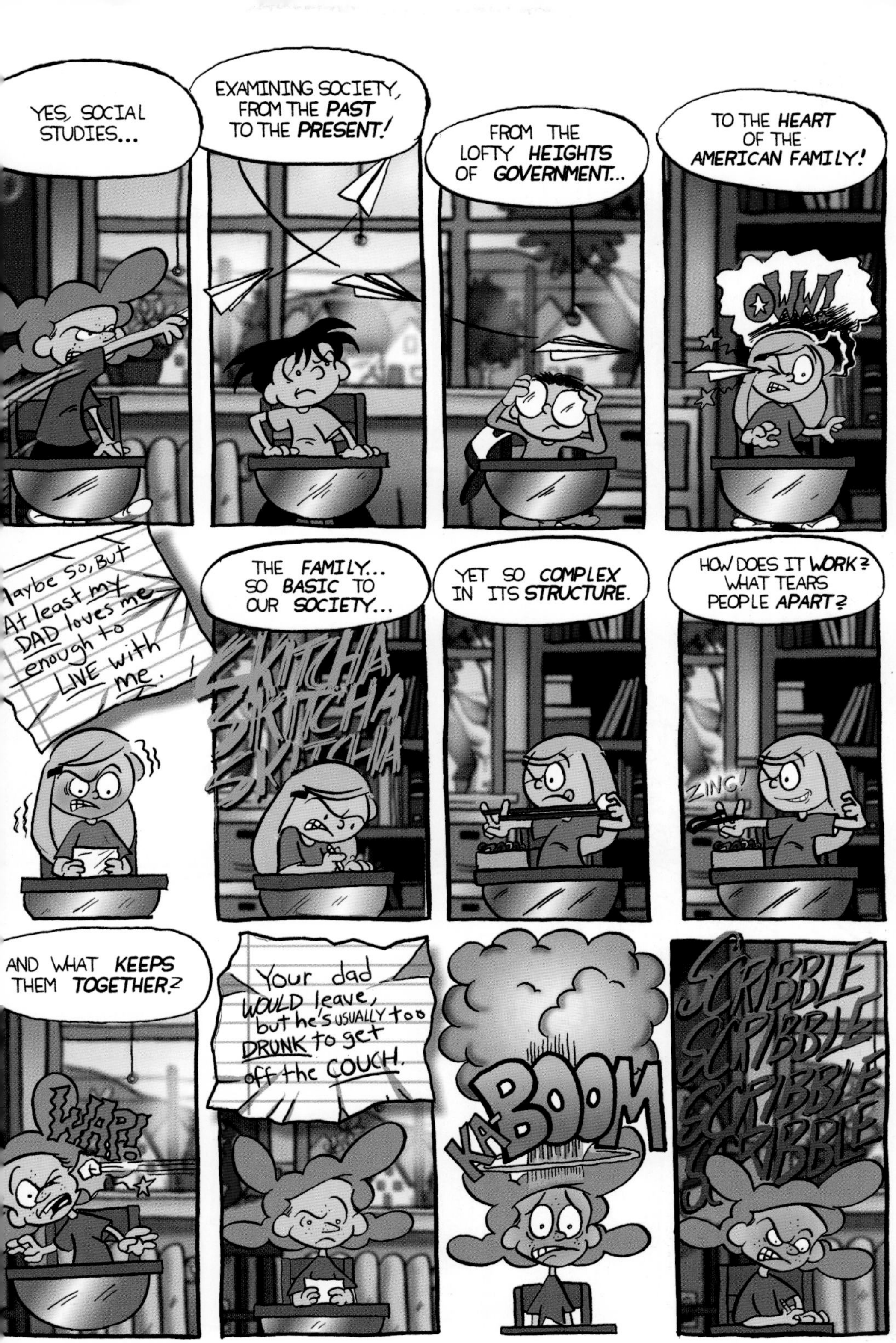
YES, SOCIAL STUDIES...
EXAMINING SOCIETY, FROM THE PAST TO THE PRESENT!
FROM THE LOFTY HEIGHTS OF GOVERNMENT...
TO THE HEART OF THE AMERICAN FAMILY!
OWW!
laybe so, But At least my DAD loves me enough to LIVE with me.
THE FAMILY... SO BASIC TO OUR SOCIETY...
SKITCHA SKITCHA SKITCHA
YET SO COMPLEX IN ITS STRUCTURE.
HOW DOES IT WORK? WHAT TEARS PEOPLE APART?
ZING!
AND WHAT KEEPS THEM TOGETHER?
WAP!
Your dad WOULD leave, but he's USUALLY too DRUNK to get off the COUCH.
KA-BOOM
SCRIBBLE SCRIBBLE SCRIBBLE SCRIBBLE

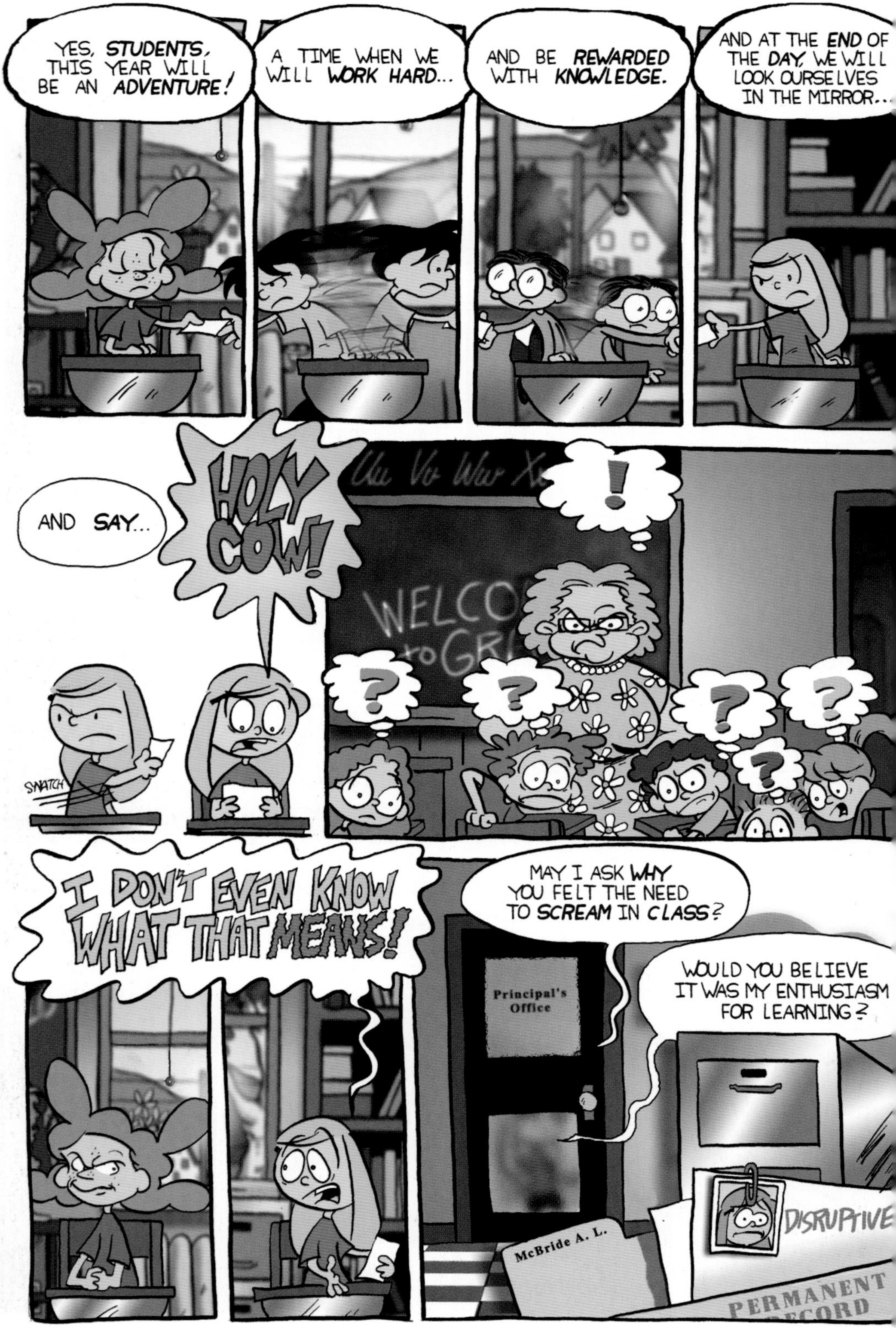
YES, STUDENTS, THIS YEAR WILL BE AN ADVENTURE!
A TIME WHEN WE WILL WORK HARD...
AND BE REWARDED WITH KNOWLEDGE.
AND AT THE END OF THE DAY, WE WILL LOOK OURSELVES IN THE MIRROR...
AND SAY...
HOLY COW!
!
WELCO to GR
?
SNATCH
I DON'T EVEN KNOW WHAT THAT MEANS!
MAY I ASK WHY YOU FELT THE NEED TO SCREAM IN CLASS?
WOULD YOU BELIEVE IT WAS MY ENTHUSIASM FOR LEARNING?
Principal's Office
DISRUPTIVE
McBride A. L.
PERMANENT RECORD

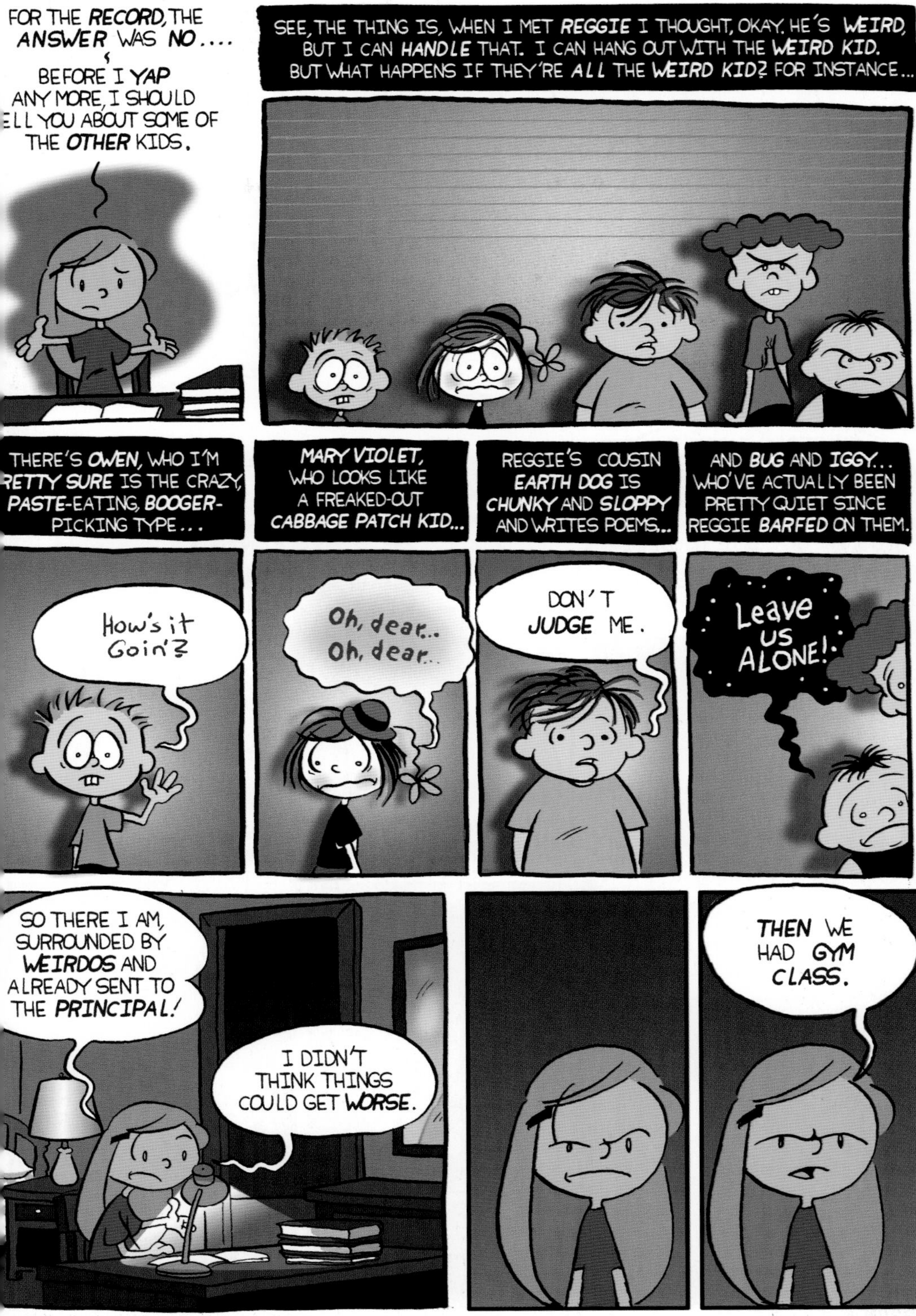
FOR THE RECORD, THE ANSWER WAS NO....
BEFORE I YAP ANY MORE, I SHOULD ELL YOU ABOUT SOME OF THE OTHER KIDS.
SEE, THE THING IS, WHEN I MET REGGIE I THOUGHT, OKAY. HE'S WEIRD, BUT I CAN HANDLE THAT. I CAN HANG OUT WITH THE WEIRD KID. BUT WHAT HAPPENS IF THEY'RE ALL THE WEIRD KID? FOR INSTANCE...
THERE'S OWEN, WHO I'M RETTY SURE IS THE CRAZY, PASTE-EATING, BOOGER-PICKING TYPE...
MARY VIOLET, WHO LOOKS LIKE A FREAKED-OUT CABBAGE PATCH KID...
REGGIE'S COUSIN EARTH DOG IS CHUNKY AND SLOPPY AND WRITES POEMS...
AND BUG AND IGGY... WHO'VE ACTUALLY BEEN PRETTY QUIET SINCE REGGIE BARFED ON THEM.
How's it Goin'?
Oh, dear... Oh, dear...
DON'T JUDGE ME.
Leave us ALONE!
SO THERE I AM, SURROUNDED BY WEIRDOS AND ALREADY SENT TO THE PRINCIPAL!
I DIDN'T THINK THINGS COULD GET WORSE.
THEN WE HAD GYM CLASS.

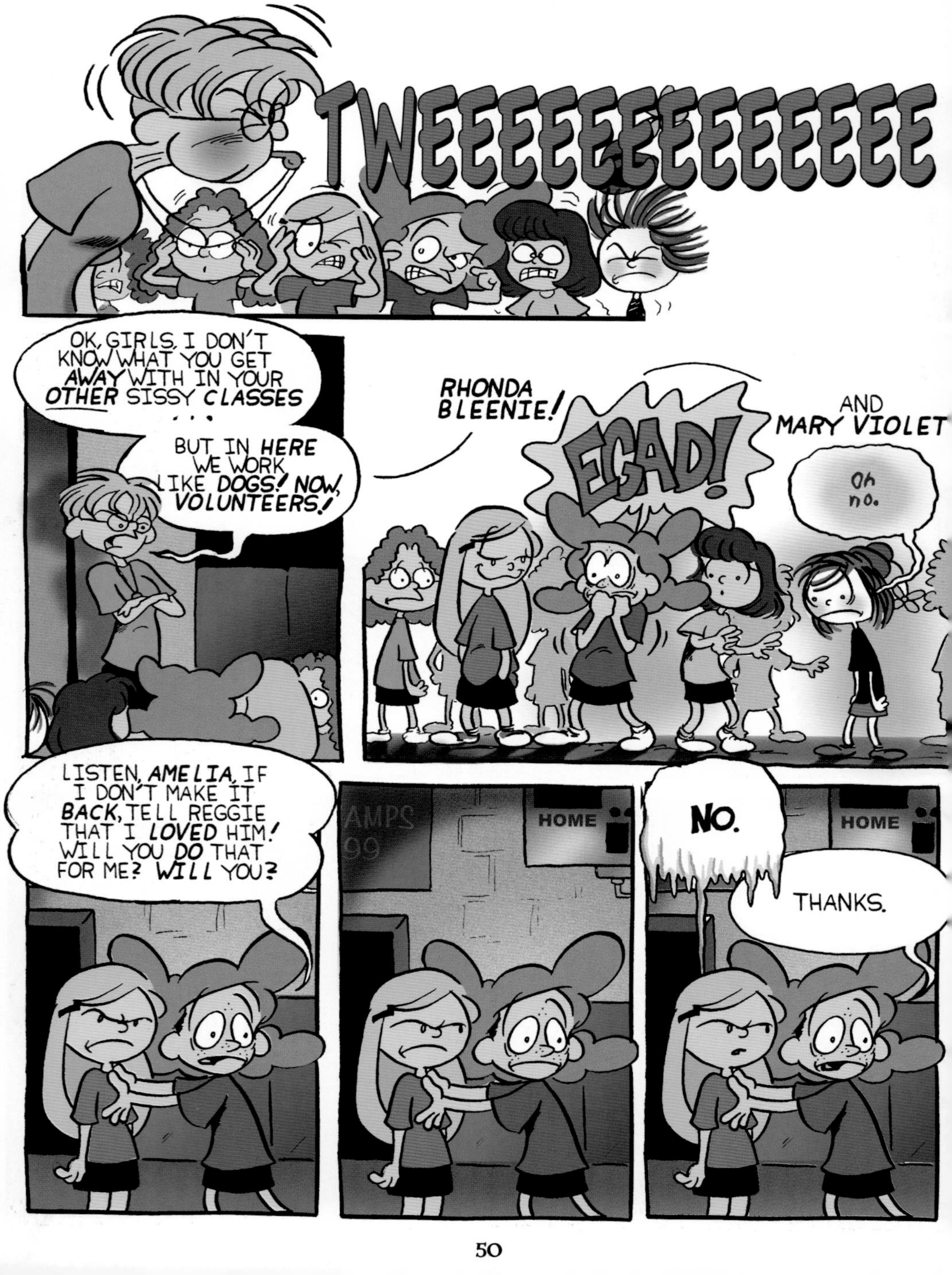
TWEEEEEEEEEEEEEE
OK, GIRLS, I DON'T KNOW WHAT YOU GET AWAY WITH IN YOUR OTHER SISSY CLASSES . . .
BUT IN HERE WE WORK LIKE DOGS! NOW, VOLUNTEERS!
RHONDA BLEENIE!
EGAD!
AND MARY VIOLET
Oh no.
LISTEN, AMELIA, IF I DON'T MAKE IT BACK, TELL REGGIE THAT I LOVED HIM! WILL YOU DO THAT FOR ME? WILL YOU?
HOME
NO.
HOME
THANKS.

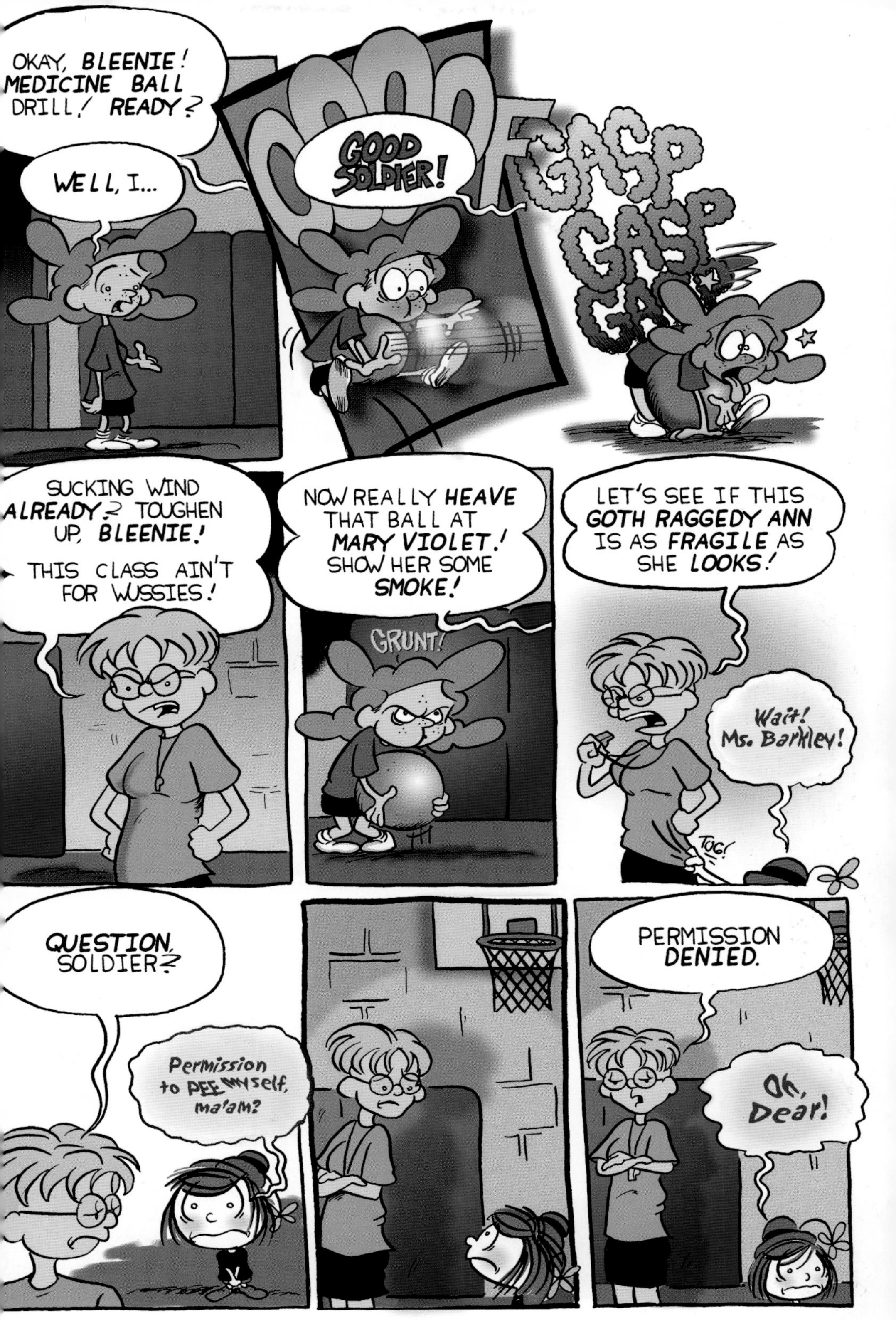
OKAY, BLEENIE! MEDICINE BALL DRILL! READY?
WELL, I...
OOOOF
GOOD SOLDIER!
GASP GASP GASP
SUCKING WIND ALREADY? TOUGHEN UP, BLEENIE!
THIS CLASS AIN'T FOR WUSSIES!
NOW REALLY HEAVE THAT BALL AT MARY VIOLET! SHOW HER SOME SMOKE!
GRUNT!
LET'S SEE IF THIS GOTH RAGGEDY ANN IS AS FRAGILE AS SHE LOOKS!
Wait! Ms. Barkley!
TUG!
QUESTION, SOLDIER?
Permission to PEE myself, ma'am?
PERMISSION DENIED.
Oh, Dear!

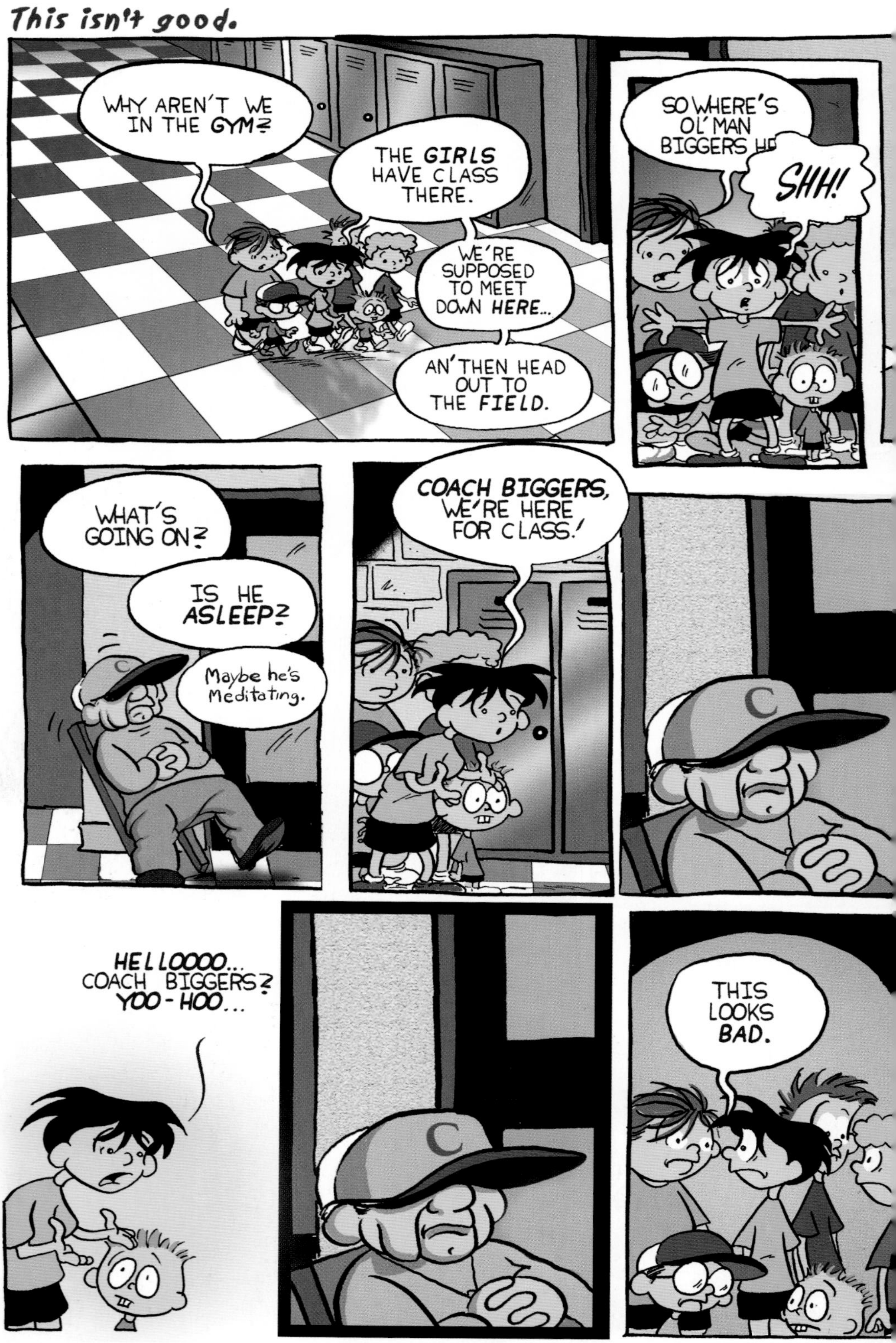
This isn't good.
WHY AREN'T WE IN THE GYM?
THE GIRLS HAVE CLASS THERE.
WE'RE SUPPOSED TO MEET DOWN HERE...
AN' THEN HEAD OUT TO THE FIELD.
SO WHERE'S OL' MAN BIGGERS
SHH!
WHAT'S GOING ON?
IS HE ASLEEP?
Maybe he's Meditating.
COACH BIGGERS, WE'RE HERE FOR CLASS!
HELLOOOO... COACH BIGGERS? YOO-HOO...
THIS LOOKS BAD.

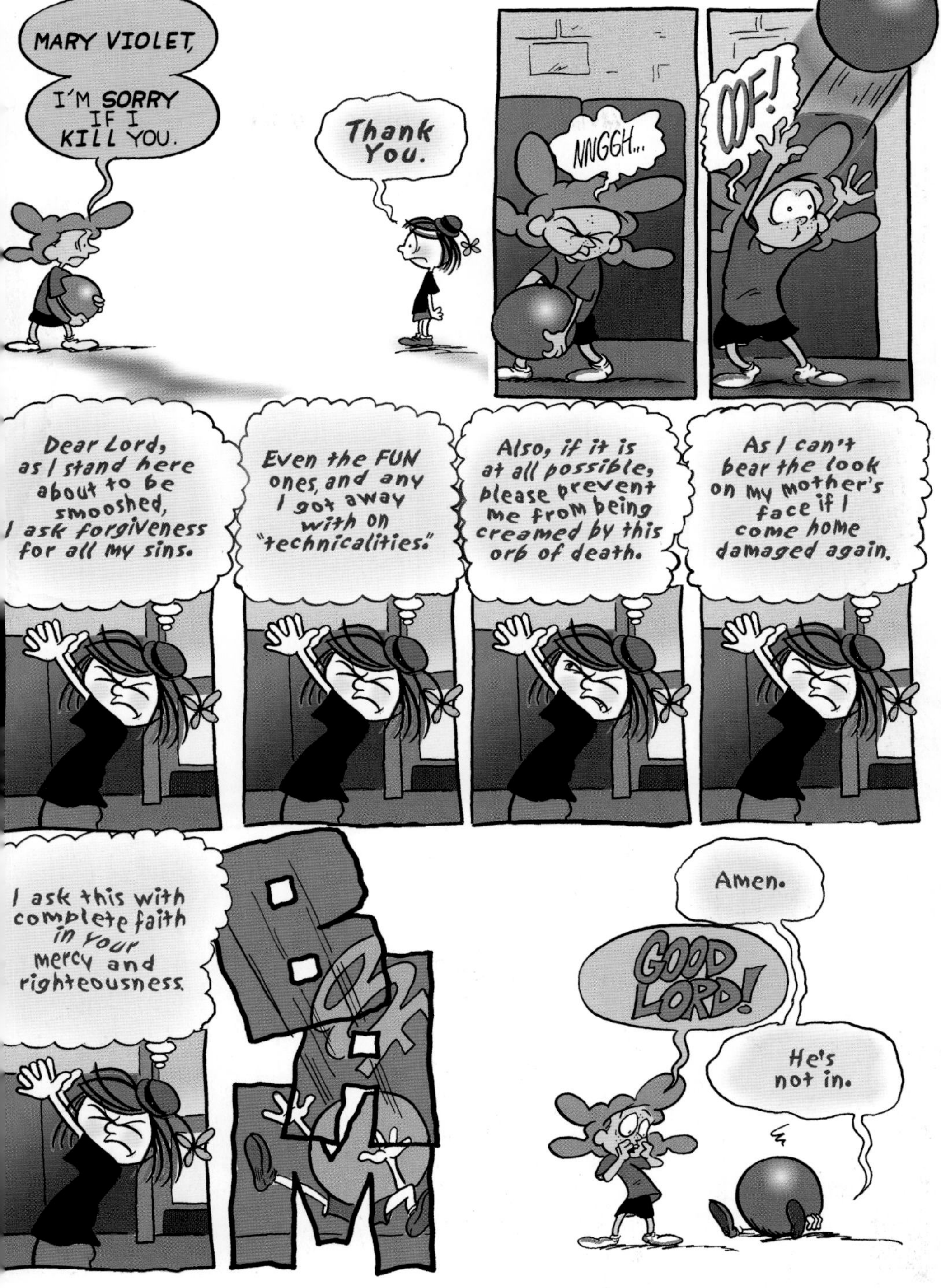
MARY VIOLET, I'M SORRY IF I KILL YOU.
Thank You.
NNGGH...
OOF!
Dear Lord, as I stand here about to be smooshed, I ask forgiveness for all my sins.
Even the FUN ones, and any I got away with on "technicalities."
Also, if it is at all possible, please prevent me from being creamed by this orb of death.
As I can't bear the look on my mother's face if I come home damaged again.
I ask this with complete faith in your mercy and righteousness.
Amen.
GOOD LORD!
He's not in.

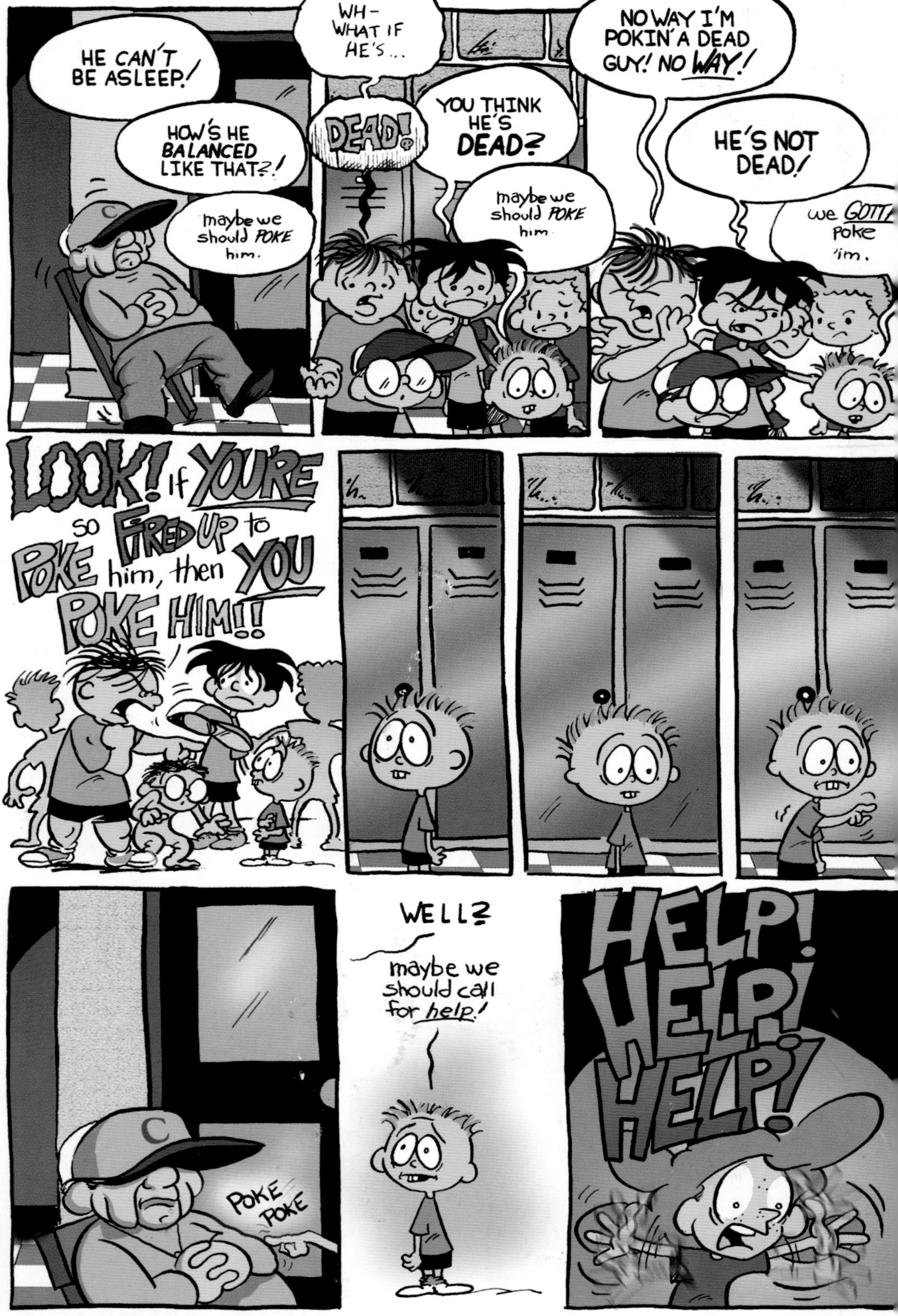
HE CAN'T BE ASLEEP!
HOW'S HE BALANCED LIKE THAT?!
maybe we should POKE him.
WH- WHAT IF HE'S...
DEAD!
YOU THINK HE'S DEAD?
maybe we should POKE him.
NO WAY I'M POKIN' A DEAD GUY! NO WAY!
HE'S NOT DEAD!
we GOTTA poke 'im.
LOOK! If YOU'RE so FIRED UP to POKE him, then YOU POKE HIM!!
POKE POKE
WELL?
maybe we should call for help!
HELP! HELP! HELP!

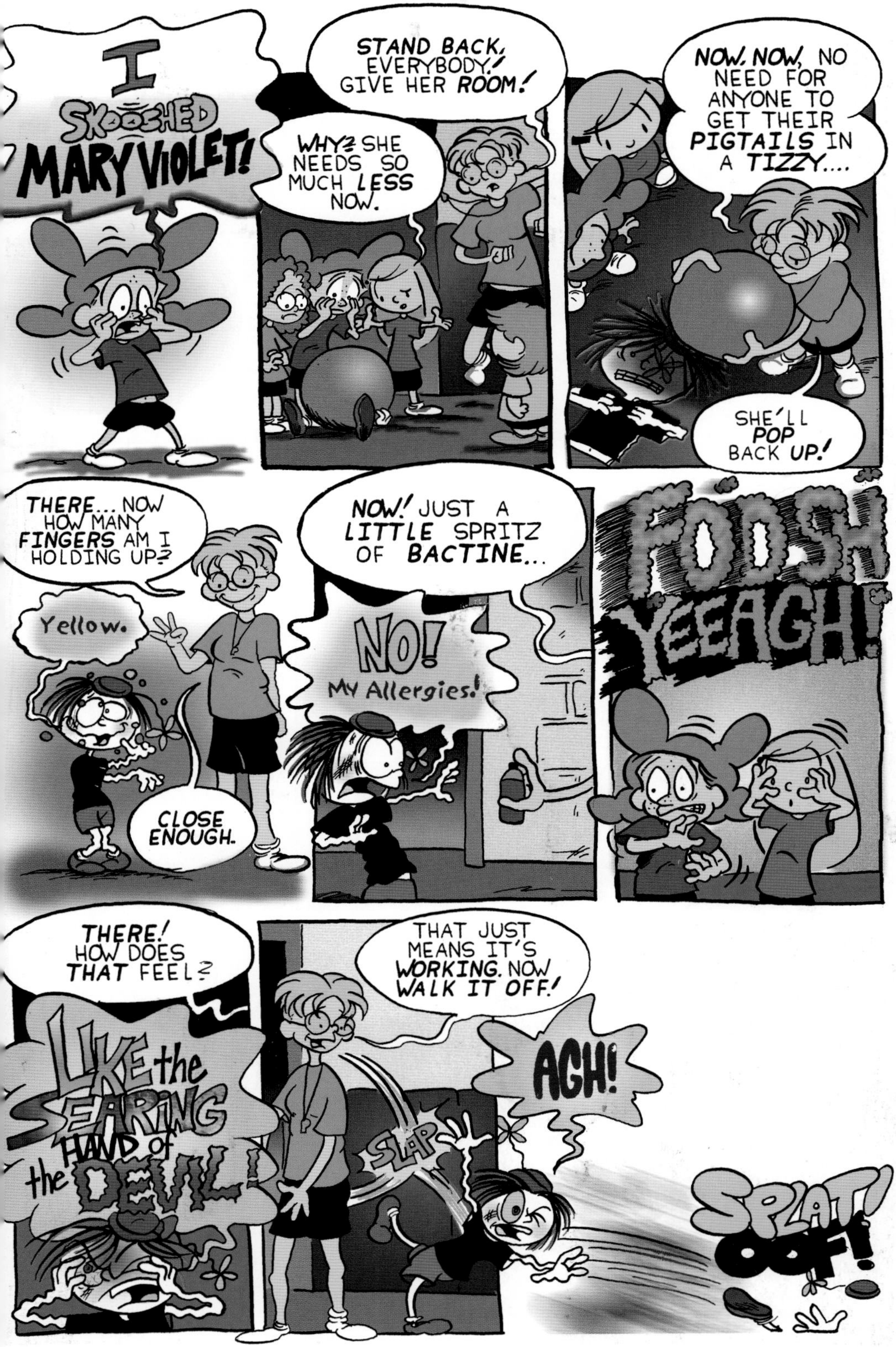
I SKOOSHED MARY VIOLET!
STAND BACK, EVERYBODY! GIVE HER ROOM!
WHY? SHE NEEDS SO MUCH LESS NOW.
NOW, NOW, NO NEED FOR ANYONE TO GET THEIR PIGTAILS IN A TIZZY....
SHE'LL POP BACK UP!
THERE... NOW HOW MANY FINGERS AM I HOLDING UP?
Yellow.
CLOSE ENOUGH.
NOW! JUST A LITTLE SPRITZ OF BACTINE...
NO! My Allergies!
FOOSH
YEEAGH!
THERE! HOW DOES THAT FEEL?
LIKE the SEARING HAND of the DEVIL!
THAT JUST MEANS IT'S WORKING. NOW WALK IT OFF!
AGH!
SLAP
SPLAT!
OOF!

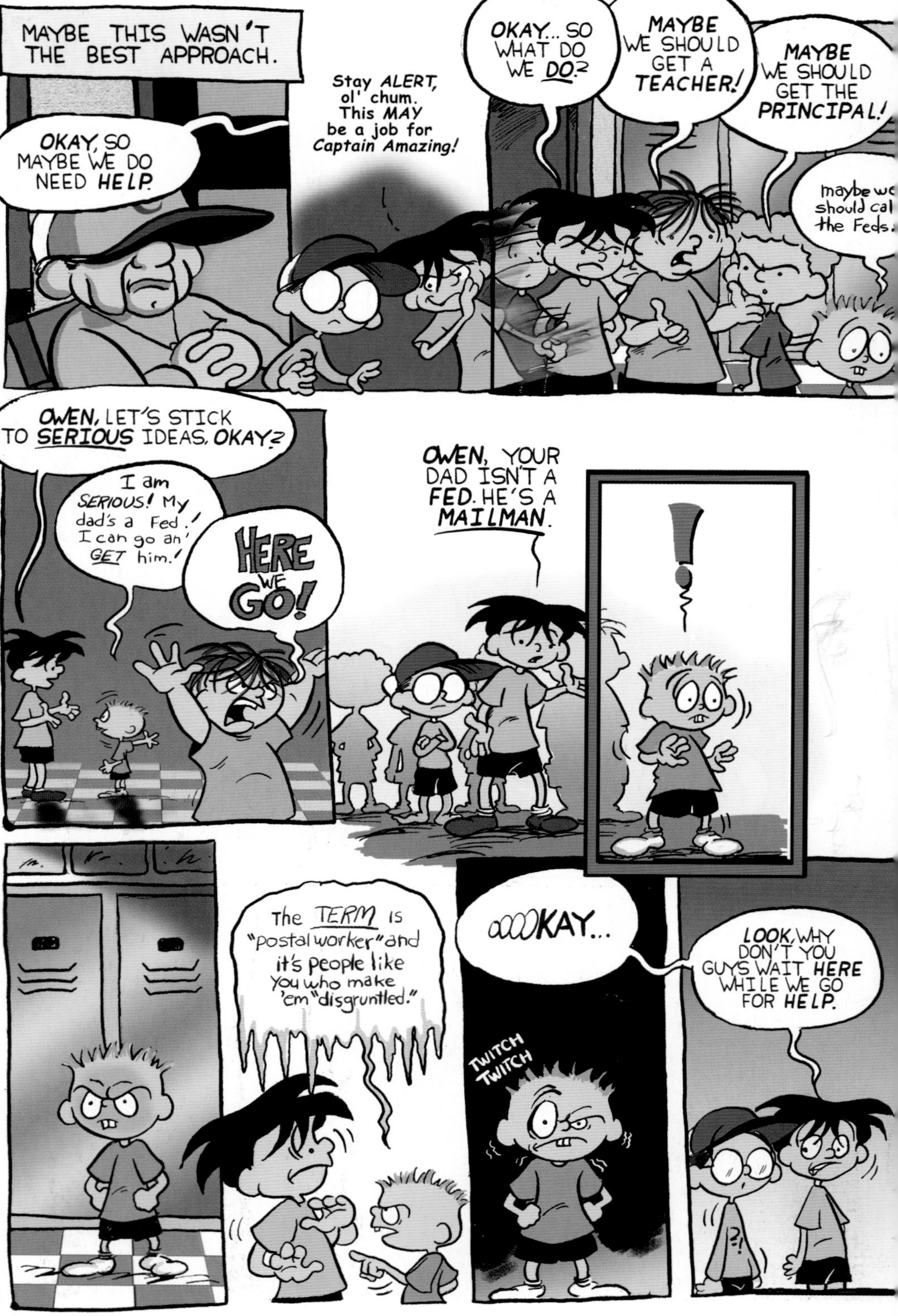
MAYBE THIS WASN'T THE BEST APPROACH.
OKAY, SO MAYBE WE DO NEED HELP.
Stay ALERT, ol' chum. This MAY be a job for Captain Amazing!
OKAY... SO WHAT DO WE DO?
MAYBE WE SHOULD GET A TEACHER!
MAYBE WE SHOULD GET THE PRINCIPAL!
maybe we should cal the Feds.
OWEN, LET'S STICK TO SERIOUS IDEAS, OKAY?
I am SERIOUS! My dad's a Fed! I can go an' GET him!
HERE WE GO!
OWEN, YOUR DAD ISN'T A FED. HE'S A MAILMAN.
!
The TERM is "postal worker" and it's people like you who make 'em "disgruntled."
oooOKAY...
LOOK, WHY DON'T YOU GUYS WAIT HERE WHILE WE GO FOR HELP.
TWITCH TWITCH
?!

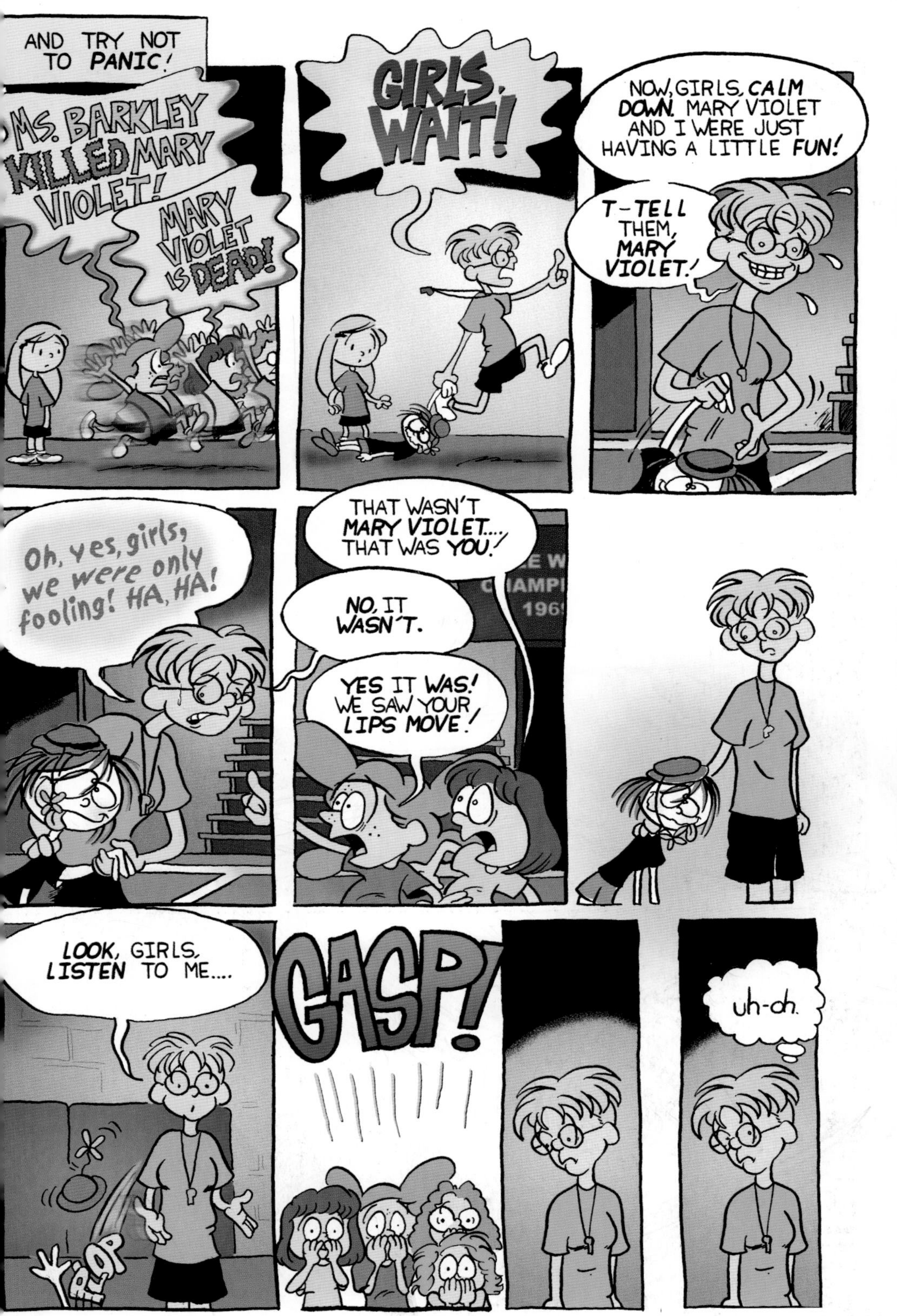
AND TRY NOT TO PANIC!
MS. BARKLEY KILLED MARY VIOLET!
MARY VIOLET IS DEAD!
GIRLS, WAIT!
NOW, GIRLS, CALM DOWN. MARY VIOLET AND I WERE JUST HAVING A LITTLE FUN!
T-TELL THEM, MARY VIOLET!
Oh, yes, girls, we were only fooling! HA, HA!
THAT WASN'T MARY VIOLET.... THAT WAS YOU!
NO, IT WASN'T.
YES IT WAS! WE SAW YOUR LIPS MOVE!
LOOK, GIRLS, LISTEN TO ME....
GASP!
uh-oh.

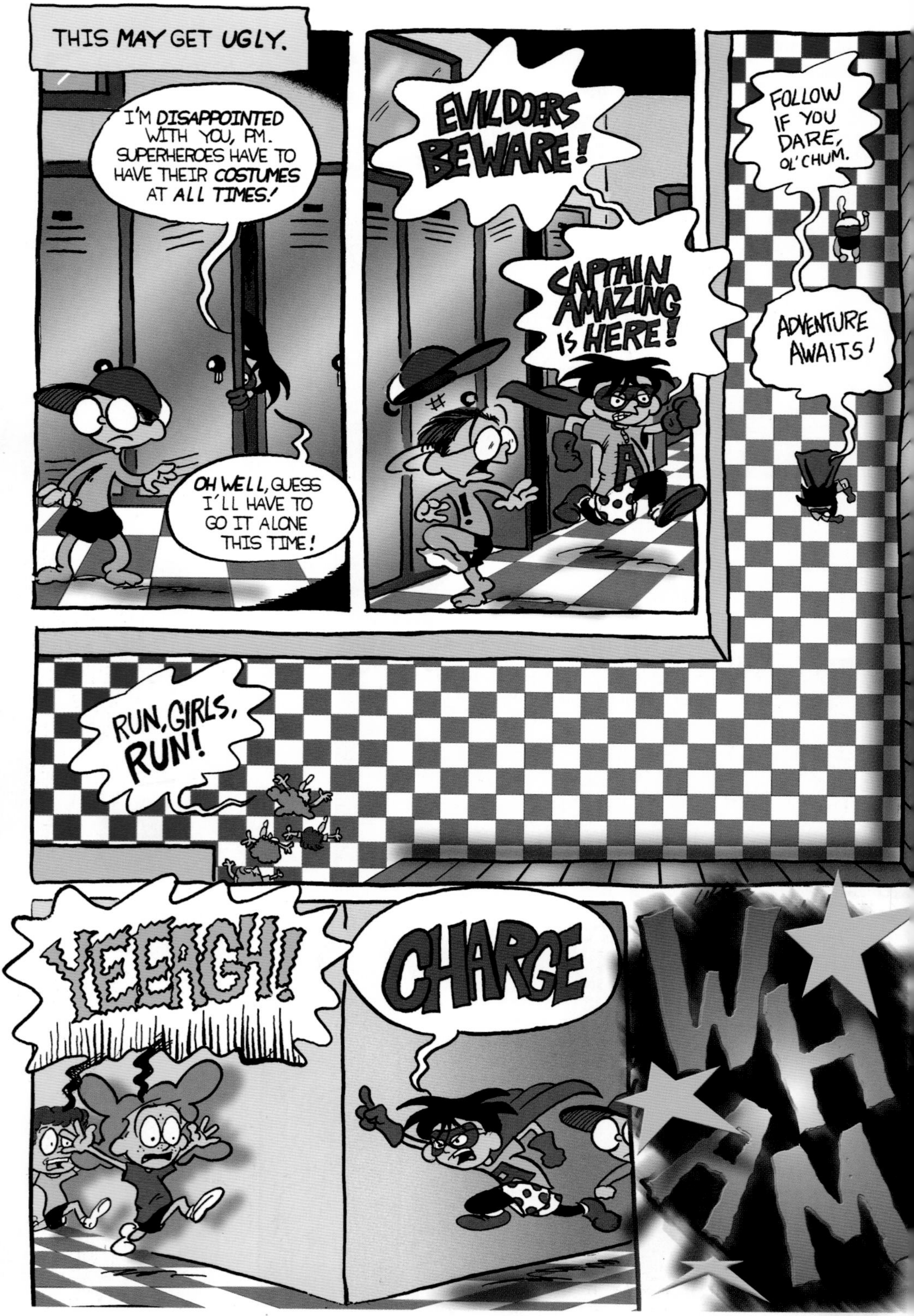
THIS MAY GET UGLY.
I'M DISAPPOINTED WITH YOU, PM. SUPERHEROES HAVE TO HAVE THEIR COSTUMES AT ALL TIMES!
OH WELL, GUESS I'LL HAVE TO GO IT ALONE THIS TIME!
EVILDOERS BEWARE!
CAPTAIN AMAZING IS HERE!
FOLLOW IF YOU DARE, OL' CHUM.
ADVENTURE AWAITS!
RUN, GIRLS, RUN!
YEEAGH!
CHARGE
WHAM

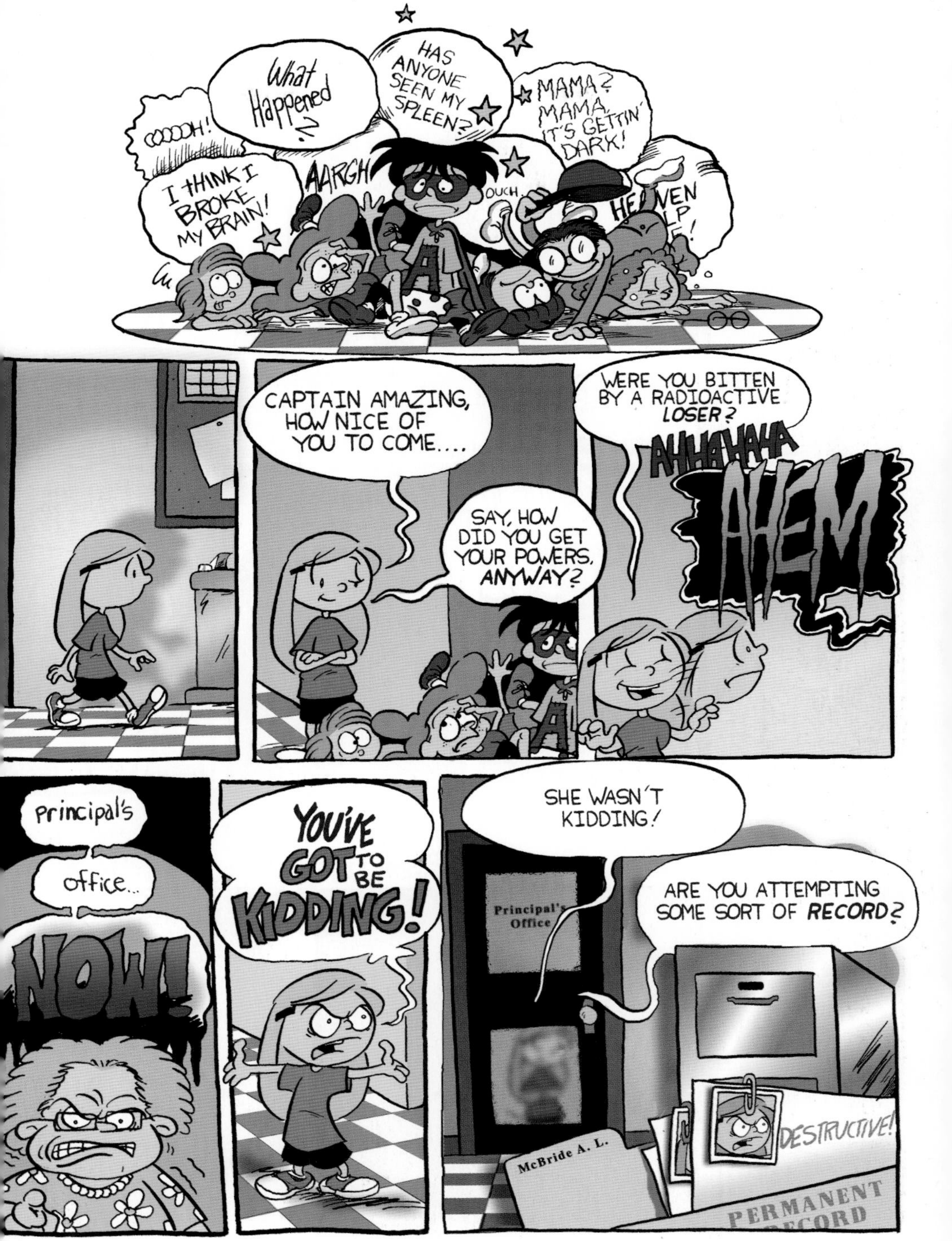

OOOOOH!
What Happened?
HAS ANYONE SEEN MY SPLEEN?
MAMA? MAMA, IT'S GETTIN' DARK!
I THINK I BROKE MY BRAIN!
AARGH
OUCH.
HEAVEN
CAPTAIN AMAZING, HOW NICE OF YOU TO COME....
SAY, HOW DID YOU GET YOUR POWERS, ANYWAY?
WERE YOU BITTEN BY A RADIOACTIVE LOSER?
AHHAHAHA
AHEM
Principal's
office...
NOW!
YOU'VE GOT TO BE KIDDING!
SHE WASN'T KIDDING!
Principal's Office
ARE YOU ATTEMPTING SOME SORT OF RECORD?
McBride A. L.
DESTRUCTIVE!
PERMANENT

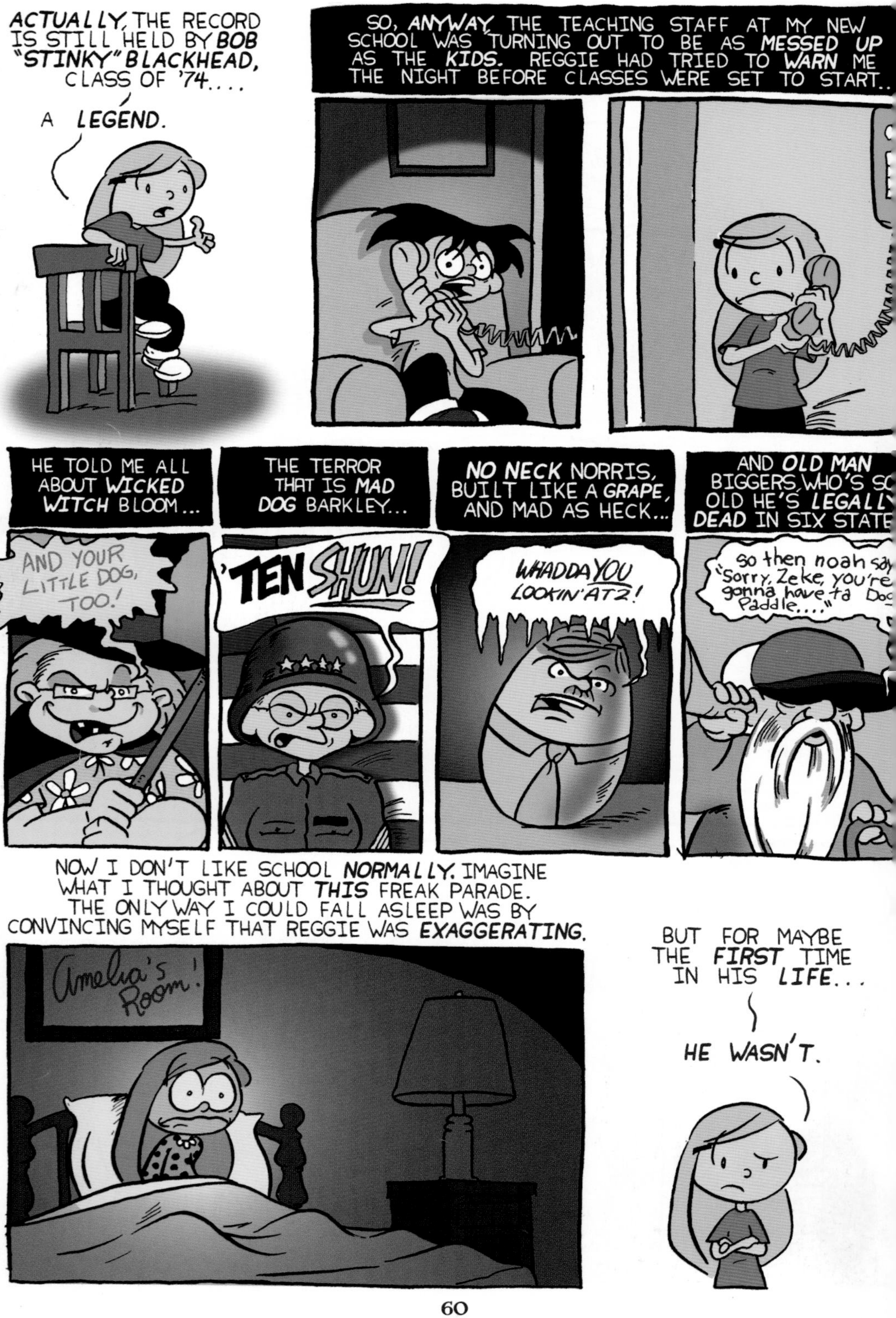

ACTUALLY, THE RECORD IS STILL HELD BY BOB "STINKY" BLACKHEAD, CLASS OF '74....
A LEGEND.
SO, ANYWAY, THE TEACHING STAFF AT MY NEW SCHOOL WAS TURNING OUT TO BE AS MESSED UP AS THE KIDS. REGGIE HAD TRIED TO WARN ME THE NIGHT BEFORE CLASSES WERE SET TO START..
HE TOLD ME ALL ABOUT WICKED WITCH BLOOM...
AND YOUR LITTLE DOG, TOO!
THE TERROR THAT IS MAD DOG BARKLEY...
'TEN SHUN!
NO NECK NORRIS, BUILT LIKE A GRAPE, AND MAD AS HECK...
WHADDA YOU LOOKIN' AT?!
AND OLD MAN BIGGERS, WHO'S S
OLD HE'S LEGALL
DEAD IN SIX STATE
so then noah say
"Sorry, Zeke, you're
gonna have ta Do
Paddle...."
NOW I DON'T LIKE SCHOOL NORMALLY. IMAGINE WHAT I THOUGHT ABOUT THIS FREAK PARADE. THE ONLY WAY I COULD FALL ASLEEP WAS BY CONVINCING MYSELF THAT REGGIE WAS EXAGGERATING.
Amelia's Room!
BUT FOR MAYBE THE FIRST TIME IN HIS LIFE...
HE WASN'T.

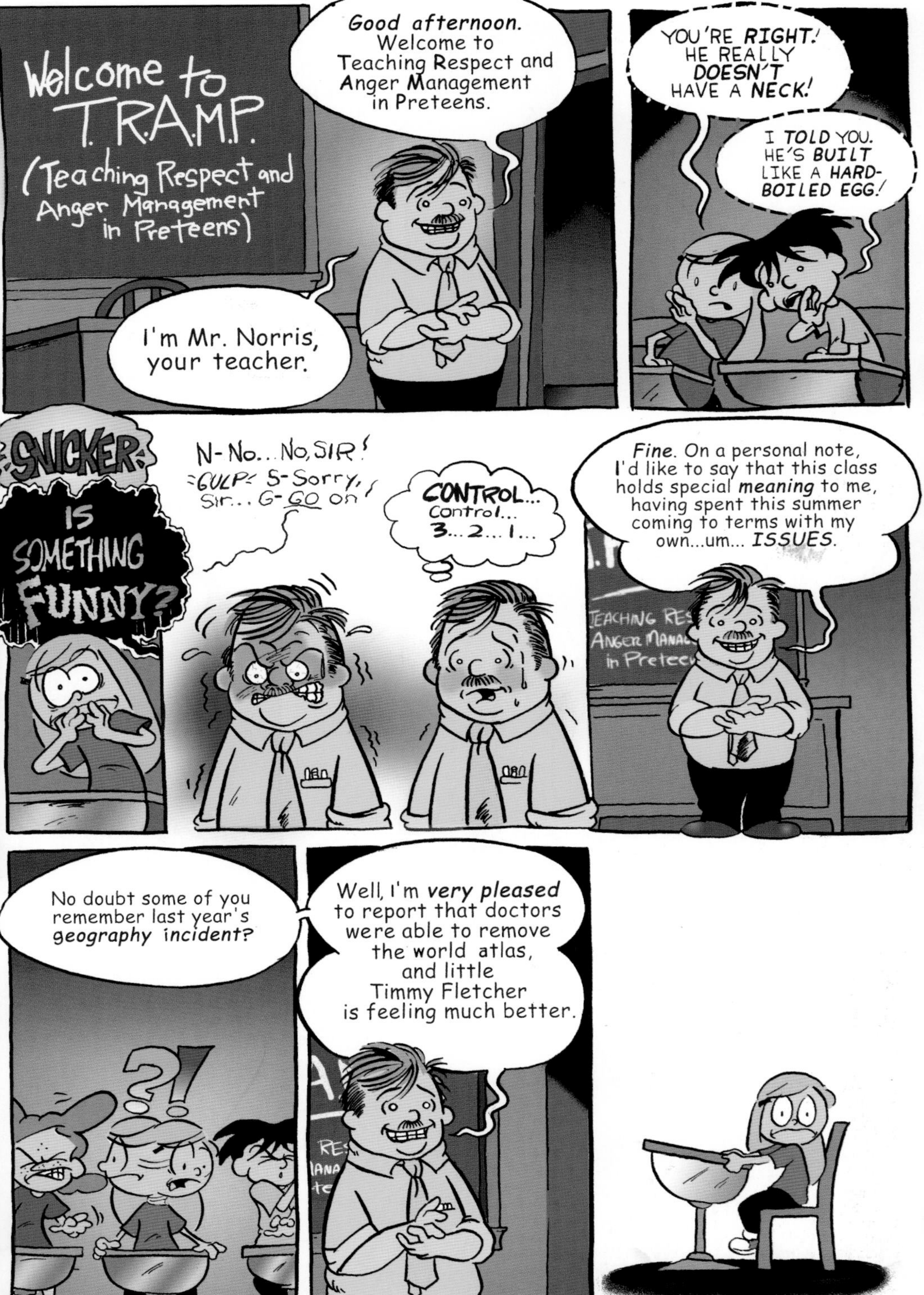
Welcome to T.R.A.M.P. (Teaching Respect and Anger Management in Preteens)
Good afternoon. Welcome to Teaching Respect and Anger Management in Preteens.
I'm Mr. Norris, your teacher.
YOU'RE RIGHT! HE REALLY DOESN'T HAVE A NECK!
I TOLD YOU. HE'S BUILT LIKE A HARD-BOILED EGG!
SNICKER
IS SOMETHING FUNNY?
N-No... No, SIR!
GULP! S-Sorry, Sir... G-GO on
CONTROL... Control... 3... 2... 1...
Fine. On a personal note, I'd like to say that this class holds special meaning to me, having spent this summer coming to terms with my own...um... ISSUES.
TEACHING RES
ANGER MANAG
in Preteen
No doubt some of you remember last year's geography incident?
Well, I'm very pleased to report that doctors were able to remove the world atlas, and little Timmy Fletcher is feeling much better.
?!

Well, anyway, let's just put all of that **behind** us.

Umm... no **pun** intended.

To get started, I thought we'd take a little **"personality test"** to get the feel of the group.

Show of hands... If caught in a disagreement with another, how many of you would...

A. Seek resolution by expressing your opinion verbally yet forcefully.

Hmm...interesting... interesting...

B. Keep silent and attempt to avoid any conflict whatsoever.

Yes, yes... fascinating.

Simply fascinating.

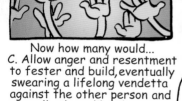

Now how many would... C. Allow anger and resentment to fester and build, eventually swearing a lifelong vendetta against the other person and all others like them.

Very good, I...

!?!

Aa Bb Cc Dd Ee Ff Gg Hh

62

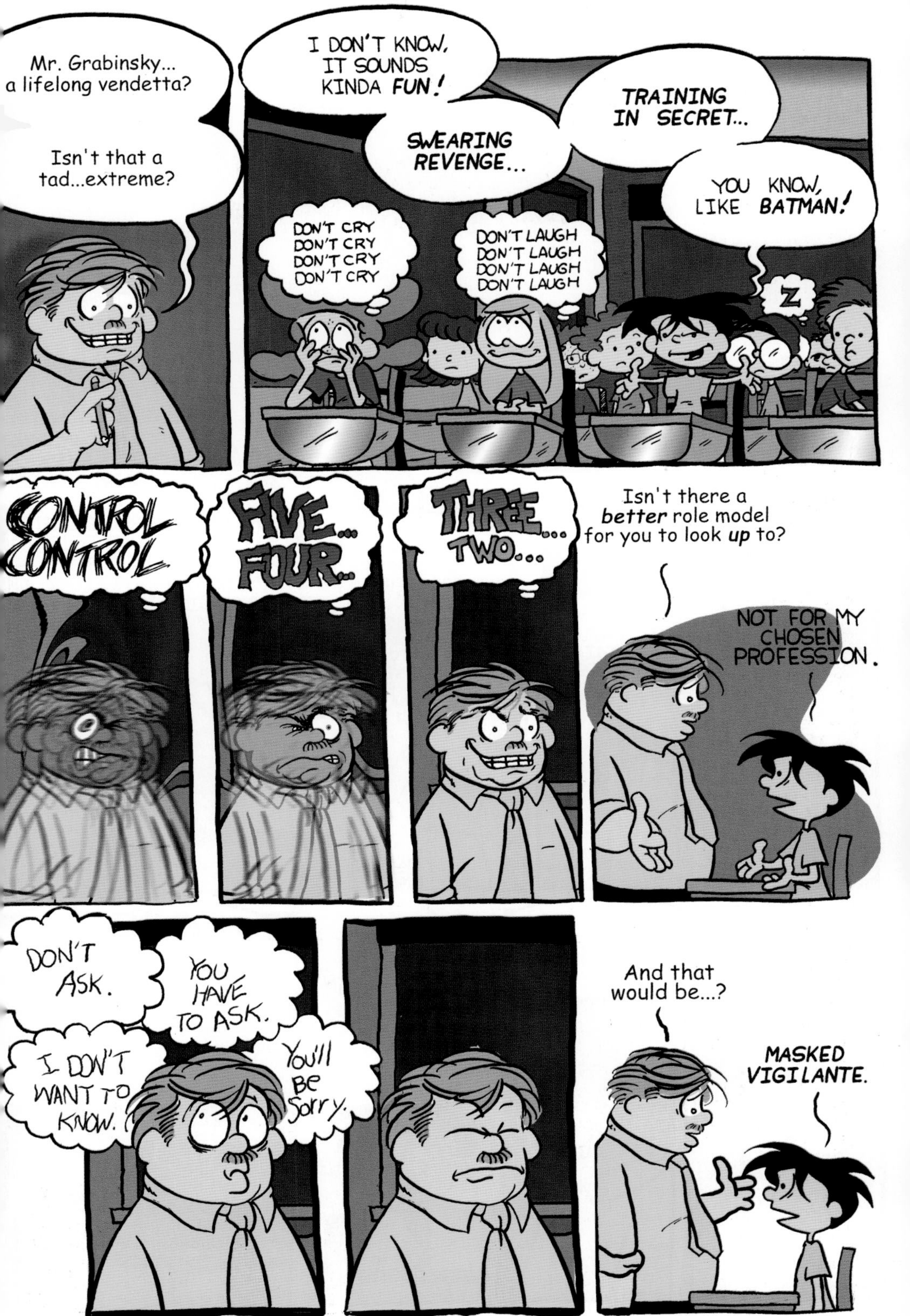
Mr. Grabinsky...
a lifelong vendetta?
Isn't that a
tad...extreme?
I DON'T KNOW,
IT SOUNDS
KINDA FUN!
SWEARING
REVENGE...
TRAINING
IN SECRET...
YOU KNOW,
LIKE BATMAN!
DON'T CRY DON'T CRY DON'T CRY DON'T CRY
DON'T LAUGH DON'T LAUGH DON'T LAUGH DON'T LAUGH
Z
CONTROL CONTROL
FIVE... FOUR...
THREE... TWO...
Isn't there a
better role model
for you to look up to?
NOT FOR MY
CHOSEN
PROFESSION.
DON'T ASK.
YOU HAVE TO ASK.
I DON'T WANT TO KNOW.
You'll Be Sorry.
And that
would be...?
MASKED
VIGILANTE.

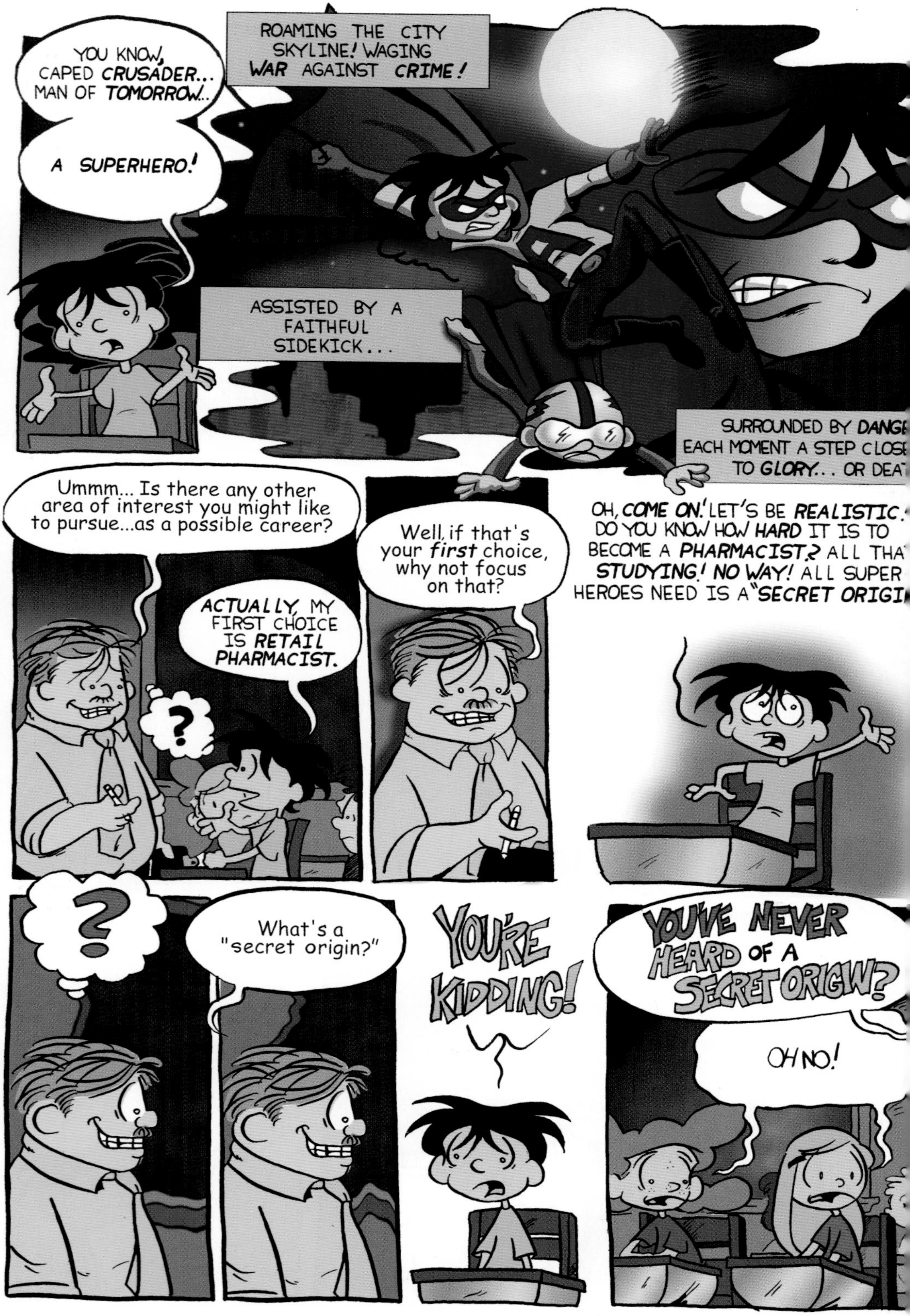
YOU KNOW, CAPED CRUSADER... MAN OF TOMORROW...
A SUPERHERO!
ROAMING THE CITY SKYLINE! WAGING WAR AGAINST CRIME!
ASSISTED BY A FAITHFUL SIDEKICK...
SURROUNDED BY DANG
EACH MOMENT A STEP CLOS
TO GLORY... OR DEA
Ummm... Is there any other area of interest you might like to pursue...as a possible career?
ACTUALLY, MY FIRST CHOICE IS RETAIL PHARMACIST.
?
Well, if that's your first choice, why not focus on that?
OH, COME ON! LET'S BE REALISTIC. DO YOU KNOW HOW HARD IT IS TO BECOME A PHARMACIST? ALL THA STUDYING! NO WAY! ALL SUPER HEROES NEED IS A "SECRET ORIGI
?
What's a "secret origin?"
YOU'RE KIDDING!
YOU'VE NEVER HEARD OF A SECRET ORIGIN?
OH NO!

Secretariat Orangejulius (The Common Secret Origin) can occur to anyone at anytime (fig. 1). While going about one's daily business, something out of the ordinary occurs, for example, finding a radioactive ladybug (fig. 2). Usually at this point some unforseen incident takes place, e.g., the ladybug vicously attacks (fig. 3).

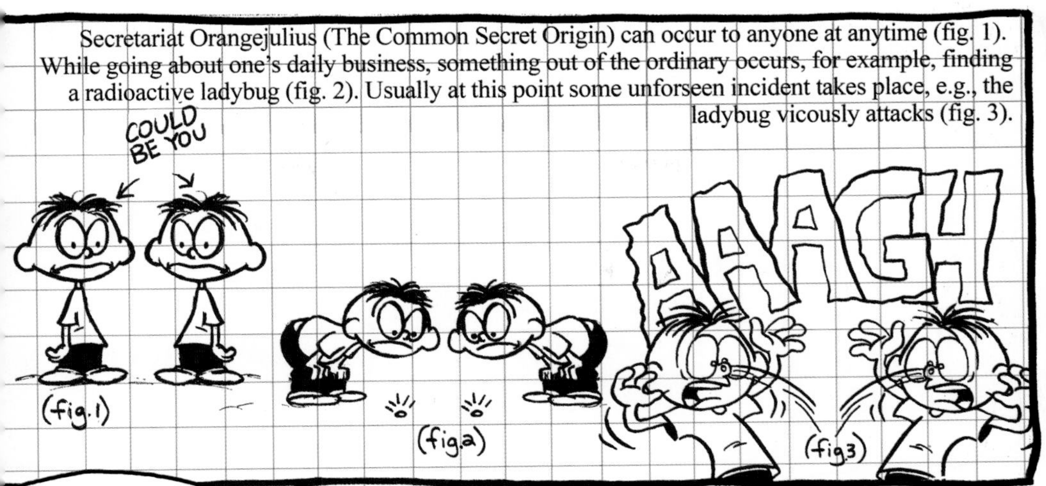

COULD BE YOU
(fig. 1)
(fig. 2)
AAGH
(fig 3)

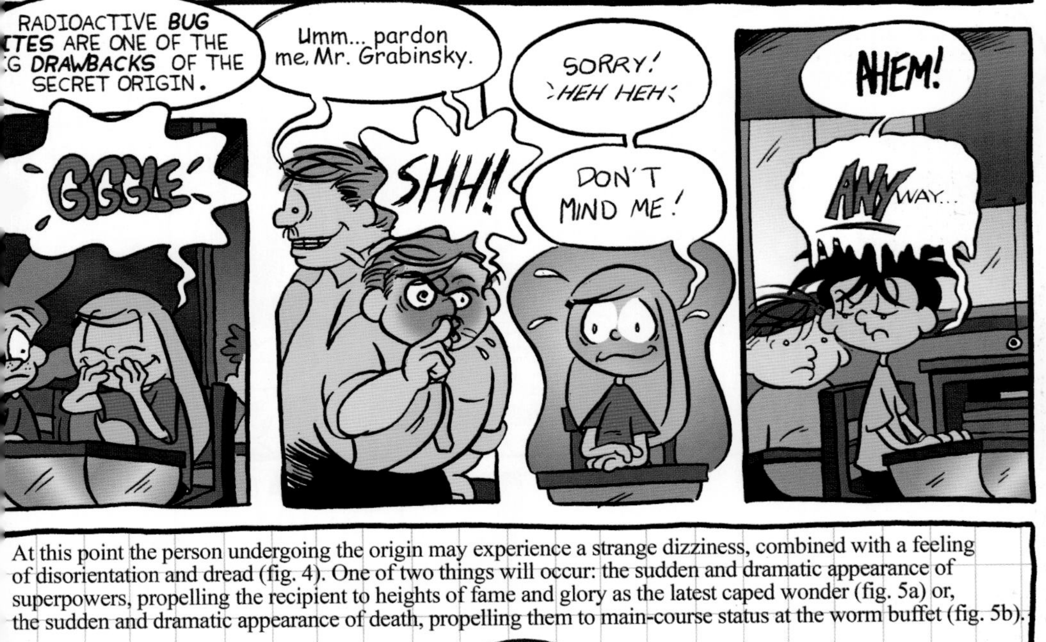

RADIOACTIVE BUG
TES ARE ONE OF THE
G DRAWBACKS OF THE
SECRET ORIGIN.
GIGGLE
Umm... pardon me, Mr. Grabinsky.
SHH!
SORRY! HEH HEH
DON'T MIND ME!
AHEM!
ANYWAY...

At this point the person undergoing the origin may experience a strange dizziness, combined with a feeling of disorientation and dread (fig. 4). One of two things will occur: the sudden and dramatic appearance of superpowers, propelling the recipient to heights of fame and glory as the latest caped wonder (fig. 5a) or, the sudden and dramatic appearance of death, propelling them to main-course status at the worm buffet (fig. 5b).

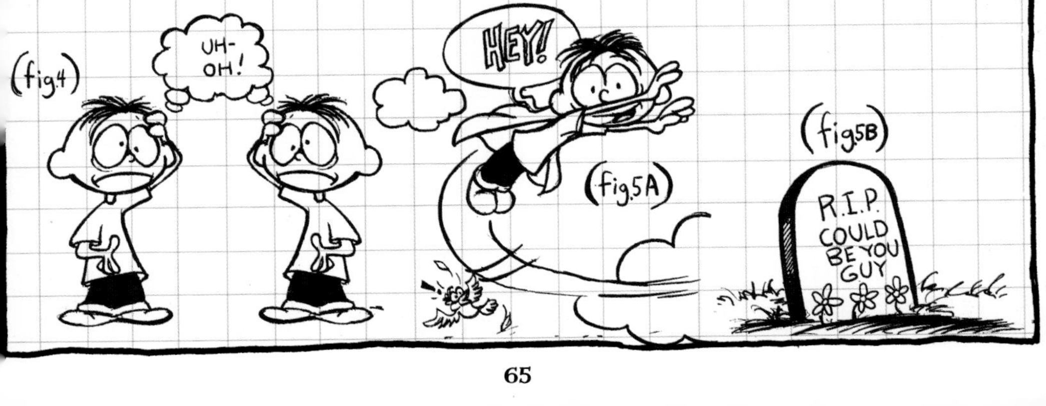

(fig 4)
UH-OH!
HEY!
(fig 5A)
(fig 5B)
R.I.P.
COULD BE YOU GUY

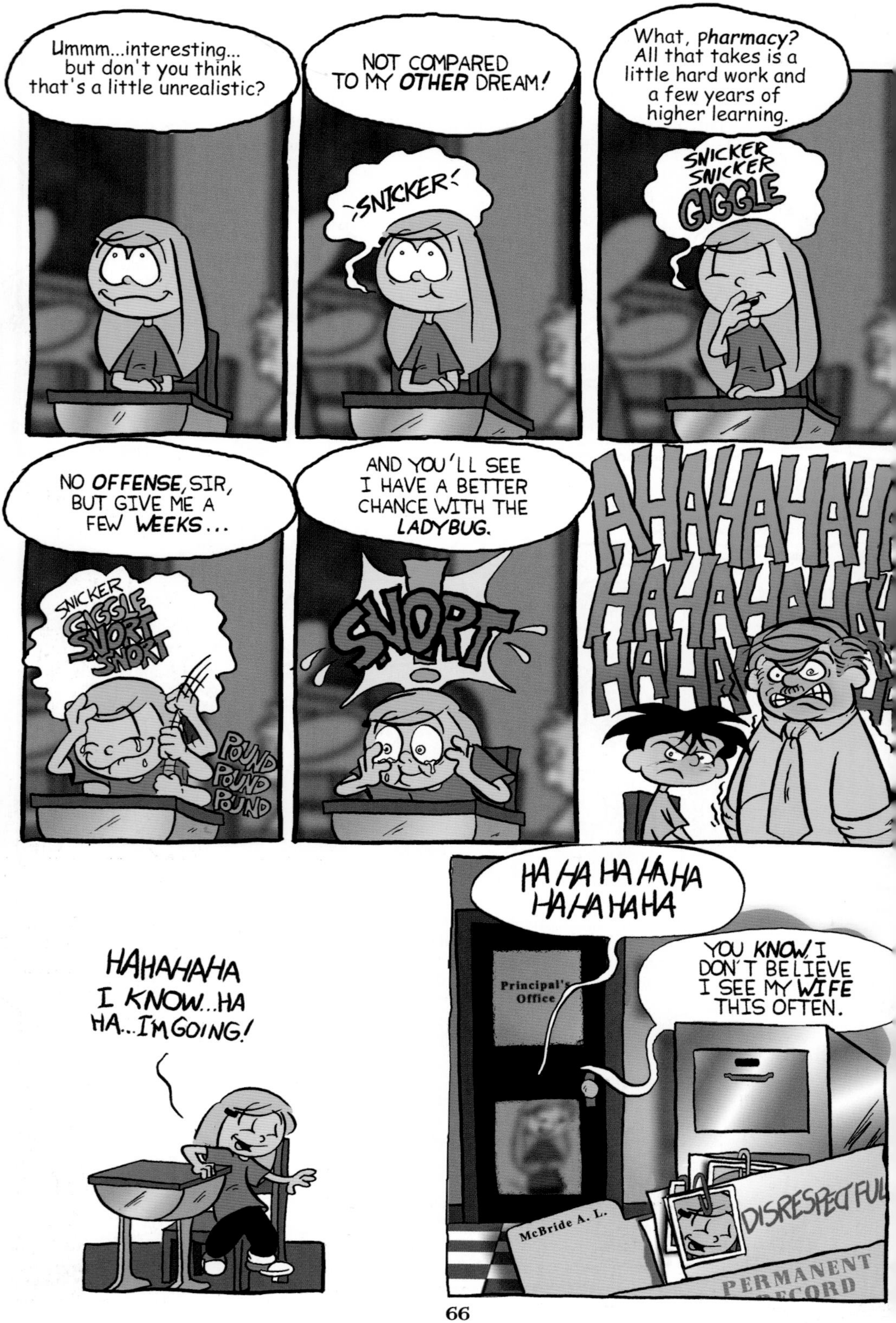
Ummm...interesting... but don't you think that's a little unrealistic?
NOT COMPARED TO MY OTHER DREAM!
SNICKER!
What, pharmacy? All that takes is a little hard work and a few years of higher learning.
SNICKER SNICKER GIGGLE
NO OFFENSE, SIR, BUT GIVE ME A FEW WEEKS...
SNICKER GIGGLE SNORT SNORT
POUND POUND POUND
AND YOU'LL SEE I HAVE A BETTER CHANCE WITH THE LADYBUG.
SNORT
AHAHAHAHA HAHAHAHA HAHA
HAHAHAHA I KNOW...HA HA...I'M GOING!
HA HA HA HA HA HA HA HA HA
YOU KNOW, I DON'T BELIEVE I SEE MY WIFE THIS OFTEN.
Principal's Office
McBride A. L.
DISRESPECTFUL
PERMANENT RECORD

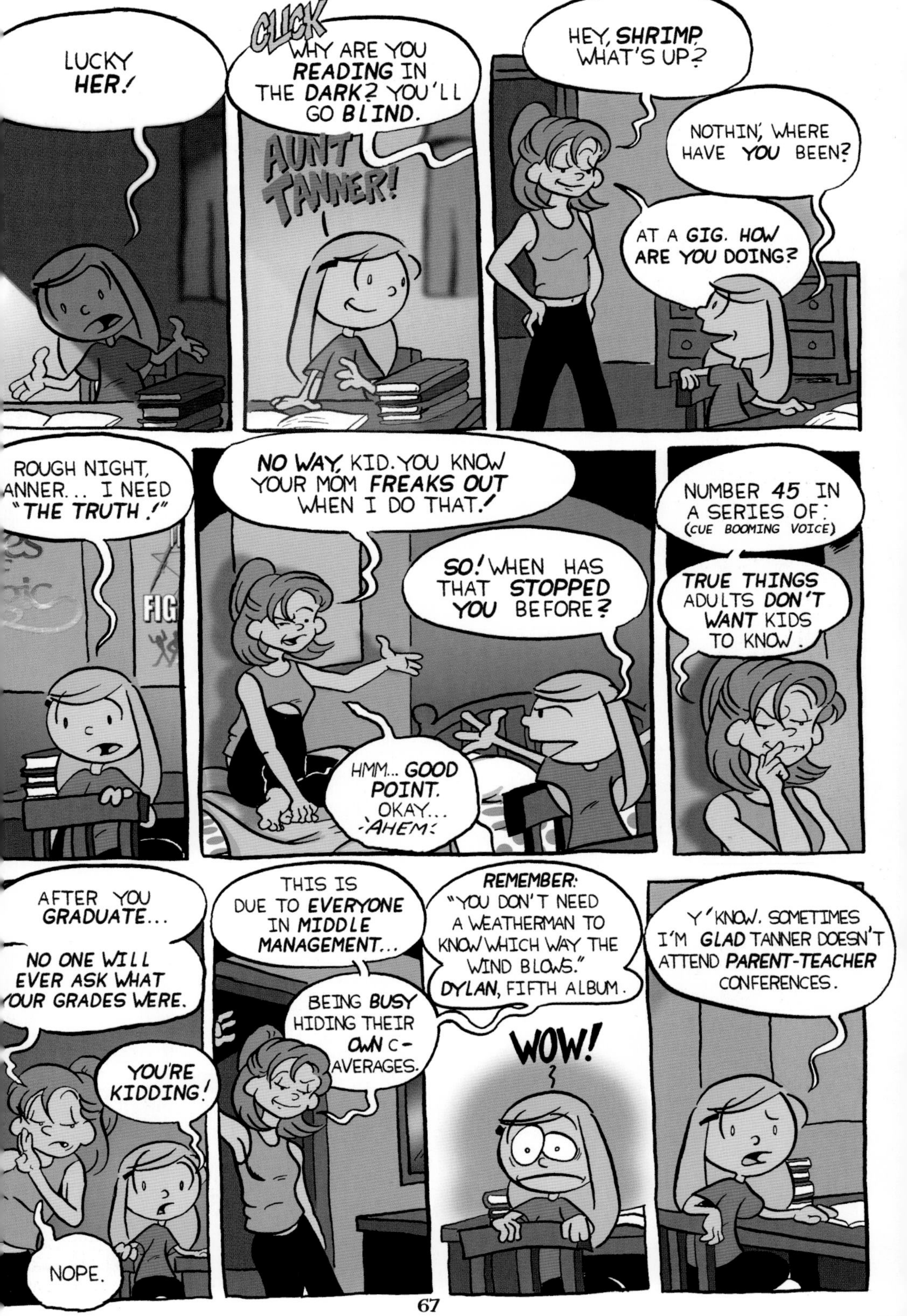
LUCKY HER.!
CLICK
WHY ARE YOU READING IN THE DARK? YOU'LL GO BLIND.
AUNT TANNER!
HEY, SHRIMP. WHAT'S UP?
NOTHIN', WHERE HAVE YOU BEEN?
AT A GIG. HOW ARE YOU DOING?
ROUGH NIGHT, ANNER... I NEED "THE TRUTH!"
NO WAY, KID. YOU KNOW YOUR MOM FREAKS OUT WHEN I DO THAT.!
SO! WHEN HAS THAT STOPPED YOU BEFORE?
HMM... GOOD POINT. OKAY... AHEM
NUMBER 45 IN A SERIES OF: (CUE BOOMING VOICE)
TRUE THINGS ADULTS DON'T WANT KIDS TO KNOW.
AFTER YOU GRADUATE...
NO ONE WILL EVER ASK WHAT YOUR GRADES WERE.
YOU'RE KIDDING!
NOPE.
THIS IS DUE TO EVERYONE IN MIDDLE MANAGEMENT...
BEING BUSY HIDING THEIR OWN C-AVERAGES.
REMEMBER: "YOU DON'T NEED A WEATHERMAN TO KNOW WHICH WAY THE WIND BLOWS." DYLAN, FIFTH ALBUM.
WOW!
Y'KNOW, SOMETIMES I'M GLAD TANNER DOESN'T ATTEND PARENT-TEACHER CONFERENCES.

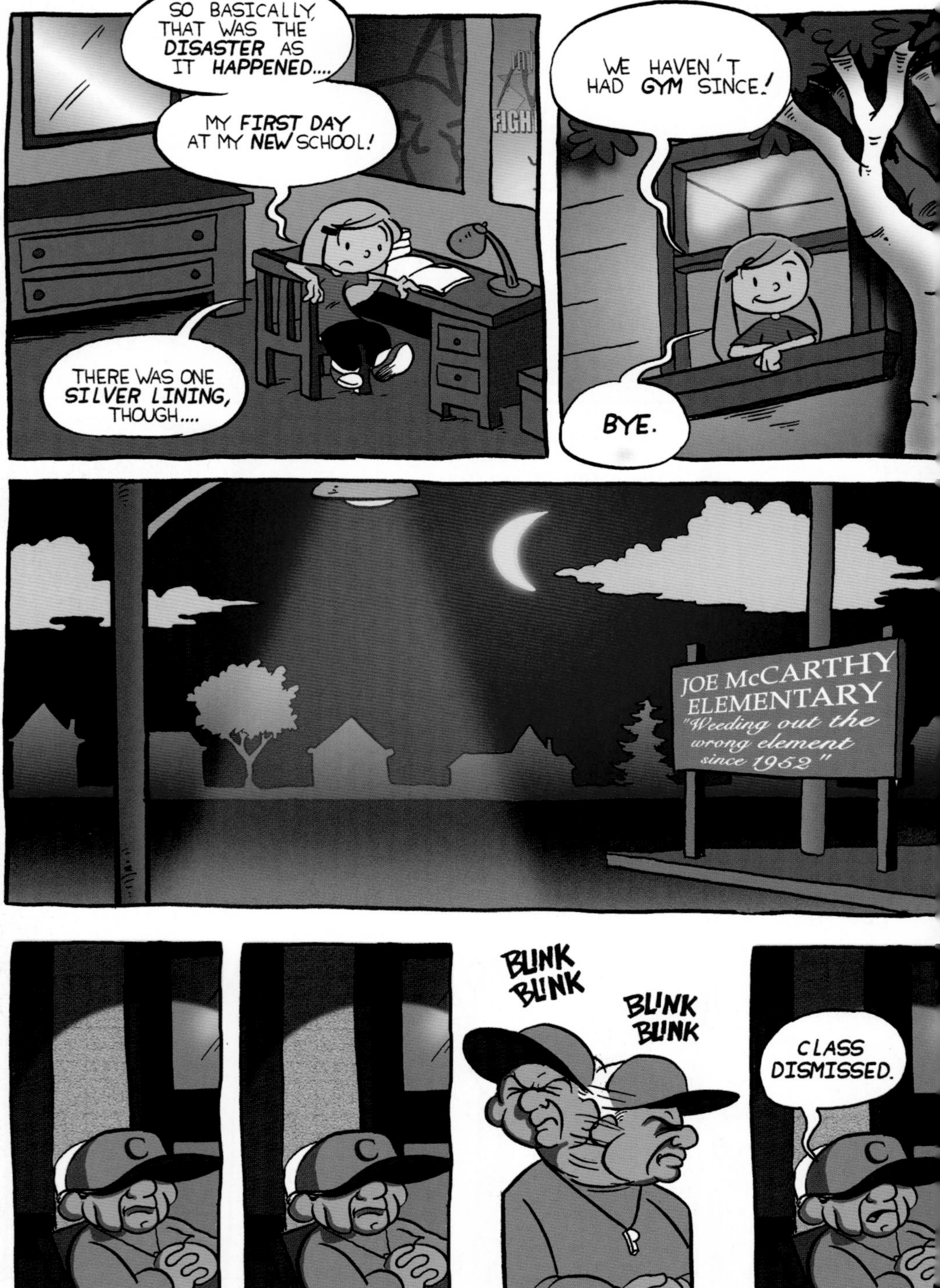
SO BASICALLY, THAT WAS THE DISASTER AS IT HAPPENED....
MY FIRST DAY AT MY NEW SCHOOL!
THERE WAS ONE SILVER LINING, THOUGH....
WE HAVEN'T HAD GYM SINCE!
BYE.
JOE McCARTHY ELEMENTARY "Weeding out the wrong element since 1952"
BLINK BLINK
BLINK BLINK
CLASS DISMISSED.

Loosely in Disguise, and Frightened

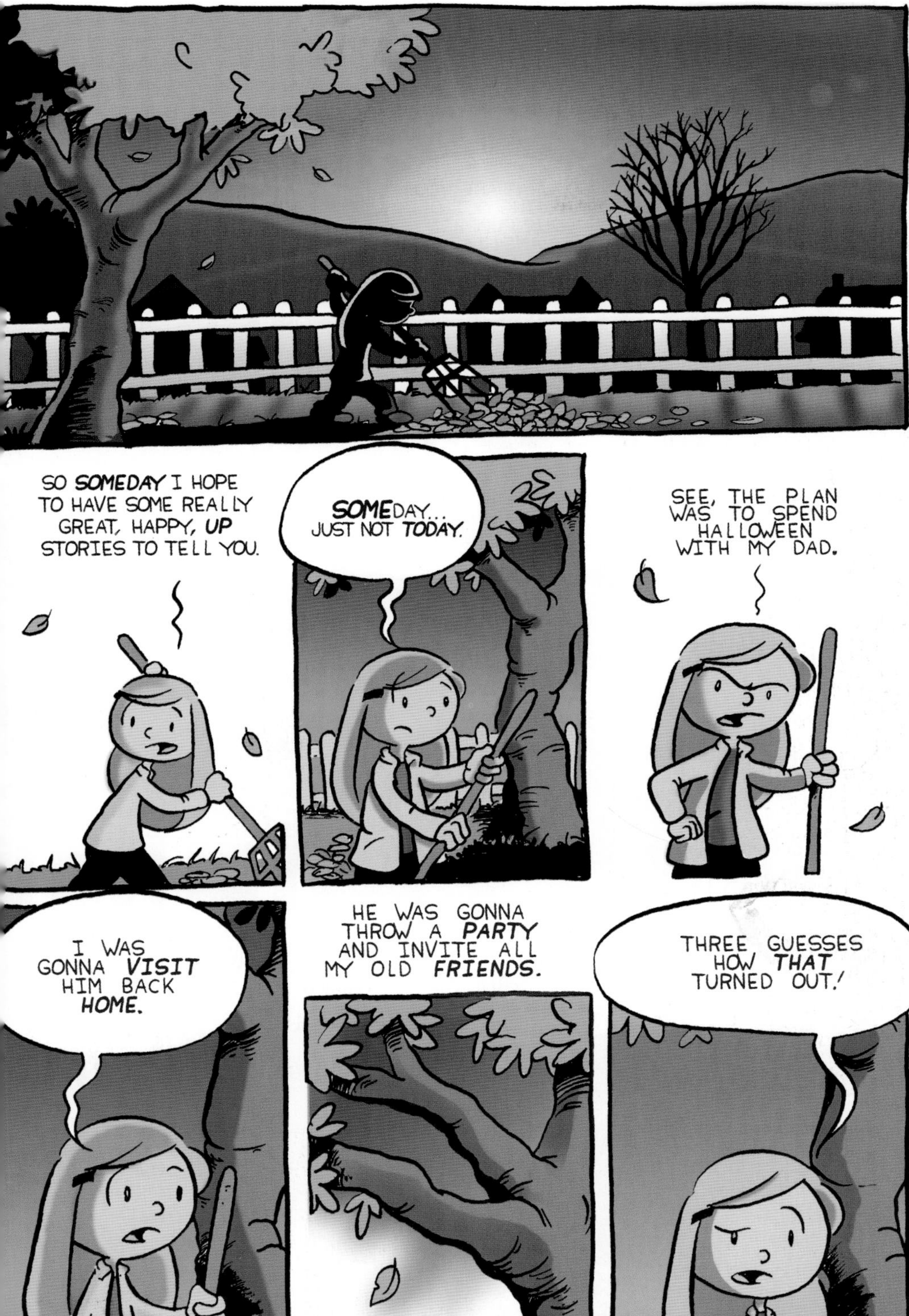
SO SOMEDAY I HOPE TO HAVE SOME REALLY GREAT, HAPPY, UP STORIES TO TELL YOU.
SOMEDAY... JUST NOT TODAY.
SEE, THE PLAN WAS TO SPEND HALLOWEEN WITH MY DAD.
I WAS GONNA VISIT HIM BACK HOME.
HE WAS GONNA THROW A PARTY AND INVITE ALL MY OLD FRIENDS.
THAT WAS THE PLAN, ANYWAY.
THREE GUESSES HOW THAT TURNED OUT!

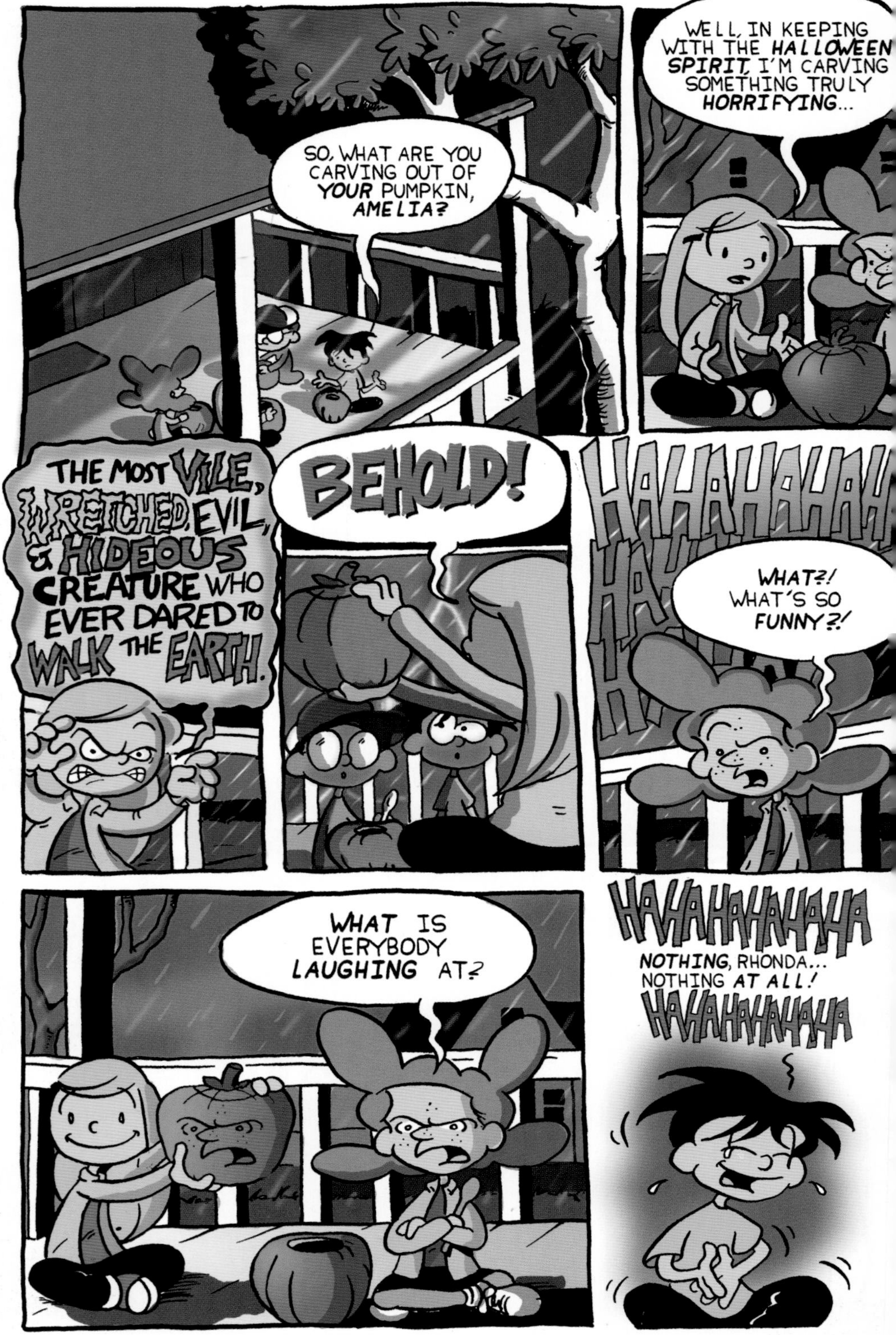
SO, WHAT ARE YOU CARVING OUT OF YOUR PUMPKIN, AMELIA?
WELL, IN KEEPING WITH THE HALLOWEEN SPIRIT, I'M CARVING SOMETHING TRULY HORRIFYING...
THE MOST VILE, WRETCHED, EVIL, & HIDEOUS CREATURE WHO EVER DARED TO WALK THE EARTH.
BEHOLD!
HAHAHAHAHAH HAHAHA
WHAT?! WHAT'S SO FUNNY?!
WHAT IS EVERYBODY LAUGHING AT?
HAHAHAHAHAHA
NOTHING, RHONDA... NOTHING AT ALL!
HAHAHAHAHAHA

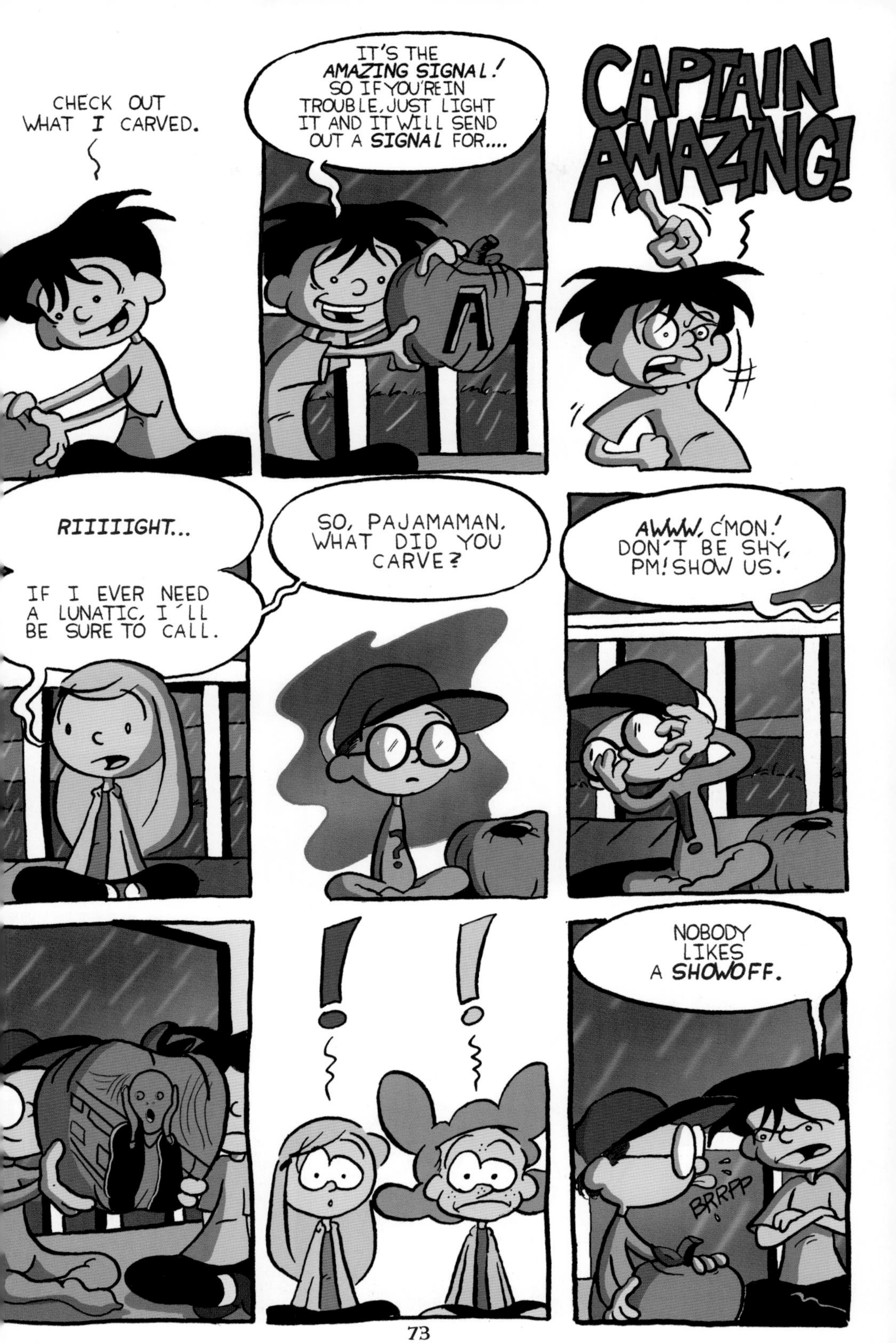
CHECK OUT WHAT I CARVED.
IT'S THE AMAZING SIGNAL! SO IF YOU'RE IN TROUBLE, JUST LIGHT IT AND IT WILL SEND OUT A SIGNAL FOR....
CAPTAIN AMAZING!
RIIIIIGHT...
IF I EVER NEED A LUNATIC, I'LL BE SURE TO CALL.
SO, PAJAMAMAN. WHAT DID YOU CARVE?
AWWW, C'MON! DON'T BE SHY, PM! SHOW US.
!
!
NOBODY LIKES A SHOWOFF.
BRRPP

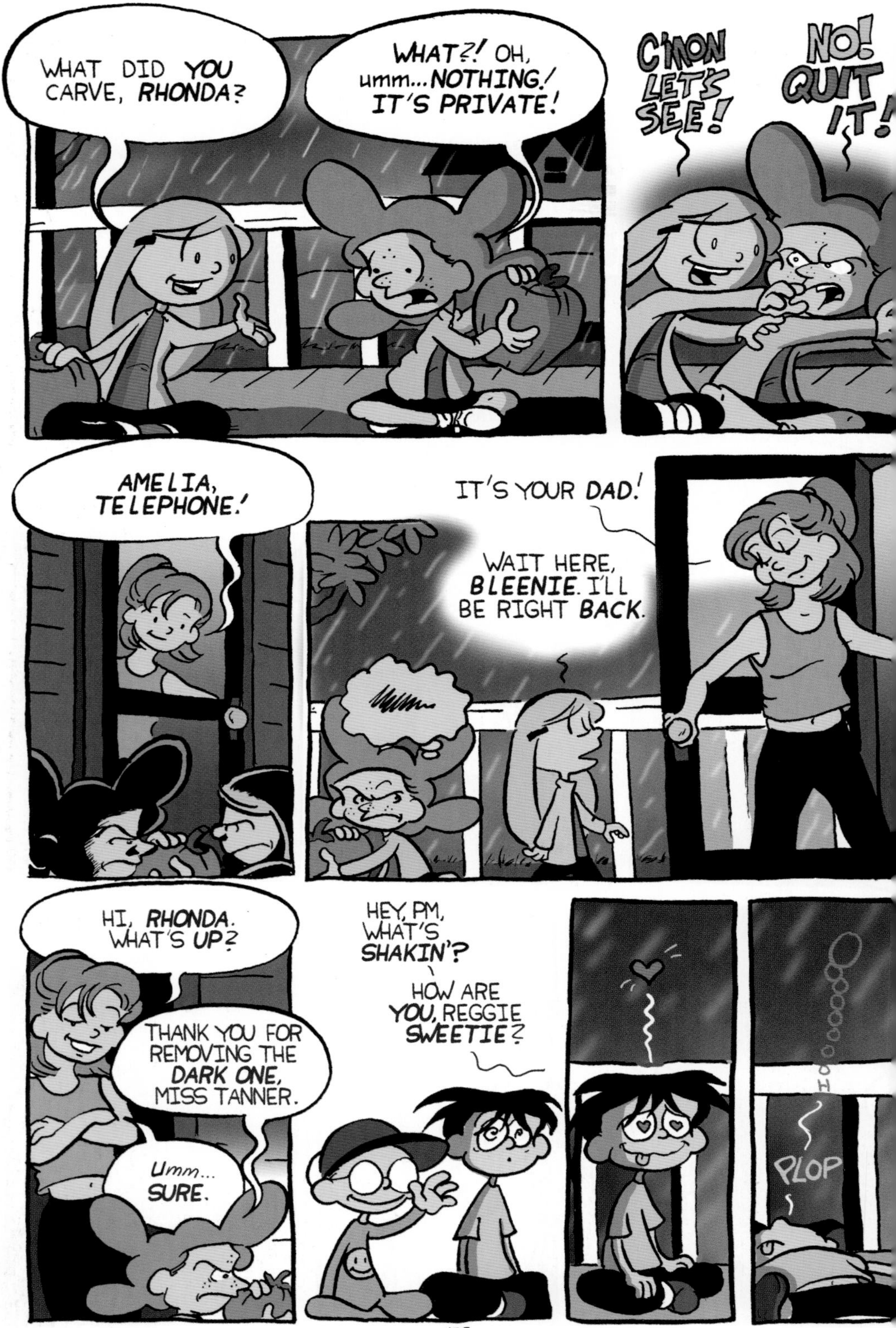
WHAT DID YOU CARVE, RHONDA?
WHAT?! OH, umm...NOTHING! IT'S PRIVATE!
C'MON LET'S SEE!
NO! QUIT IT!
AMELIA, TELEPHONE!
IT'S YOUR DAD!
WAIT HERE, BLEENIE. I'LL BE RIGHT BACK.
HI, RHONDA. WHAT'S UP?
THANK YOU FOR REMOVING THE DARK ONE, MISS TANNER.
Umm... SURE.
HEY, PM, WHAT'S SHAKIN'?
HOW ARE YOU, REGGIE SWEETIE?
PLOP

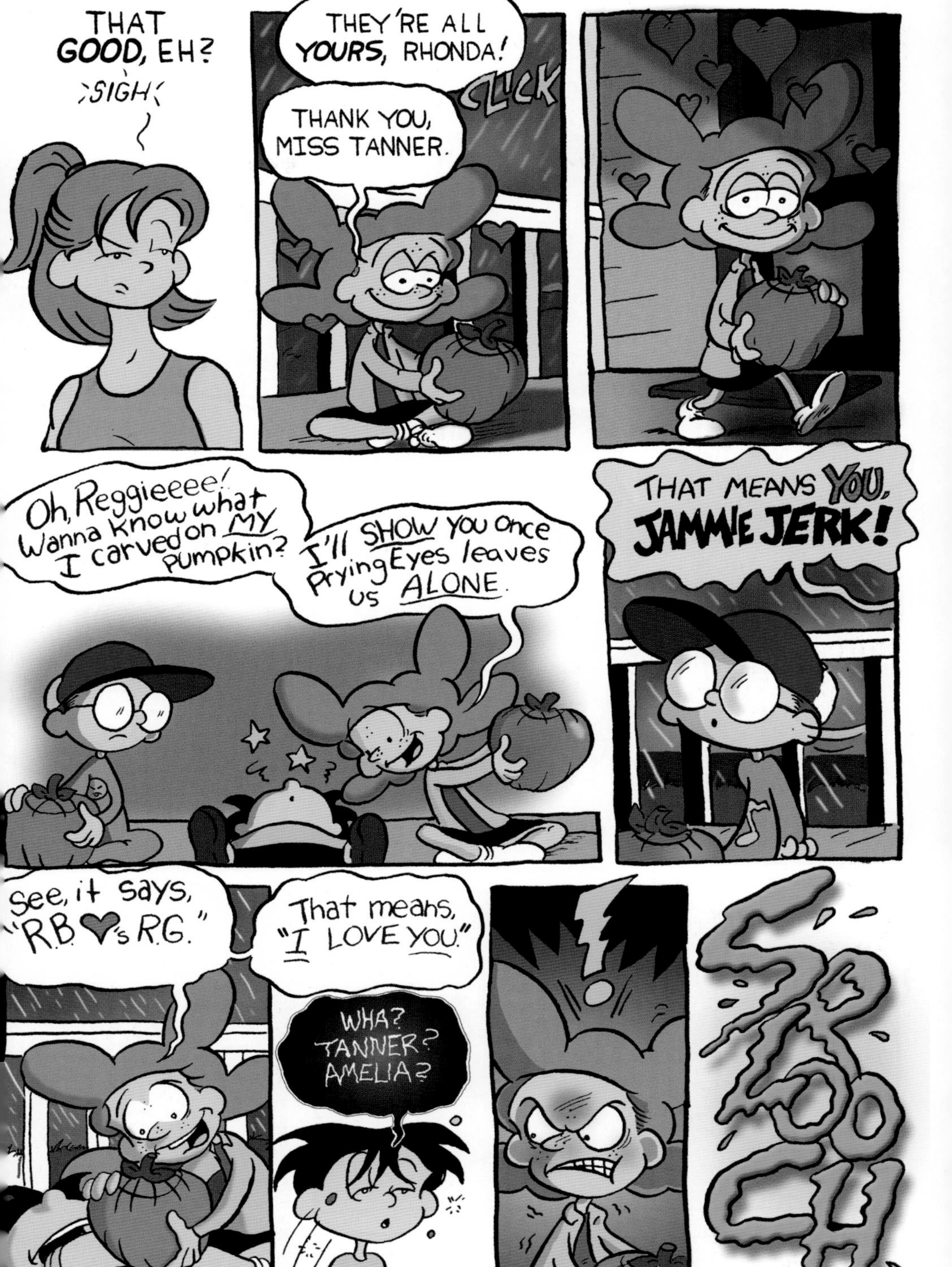
THAT GOOD, EH?
SIGH
THEY'RE ALL YOURS, RHONDA!
CLICK
THANK YOU, MISS TANNER.
Oh, Reggieeee! Wanna know what I carved on MY pumpkin?
I'll SHOW you once Prying Eyes leaves us ALONE.
THAT MEANS YOU, JAMMIE JERK!
See, it says, "R.B. ♥'s R.G."
That means, "I LOVE YOU."
WHA? TANNER? AMELIA?
SPLOOCH

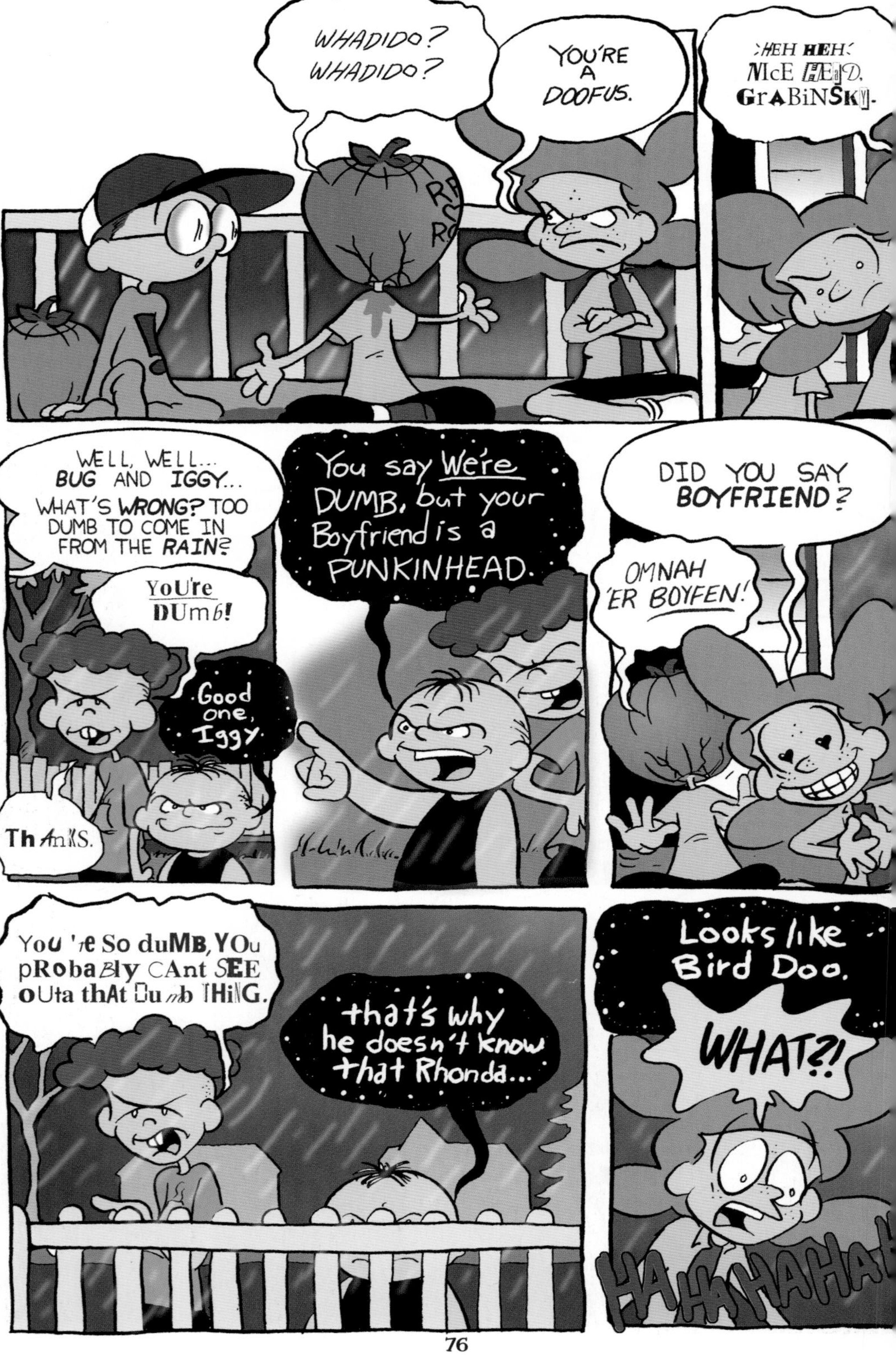
WHADIDO? WHADIDO?
YOU'RE A DOOFUS.
HEH HEH. NICE HEAD, GRABINSKY.
WELL, WELL... BUG AND IGGY... WHAT'S WRONG? TOO DUMB TO COME IN FROM THE RAIN?
YoU're DUmb!
Good one, Iggy.
ThAnKS.
You say We're DUMB, but your Boyfriend is a PUNKINHEAD.
DID YOU SAY BOYFRIEND?
OMNAH 'ER BOYFEN!
You're So duMB, YOu pRObaBly CAnt SEE oUta thAt Dumb THiNG.
that's why he doesn't know that Rhonda...
Looks like Bird Doo.
WHAT?!
HAHAHAHAHA

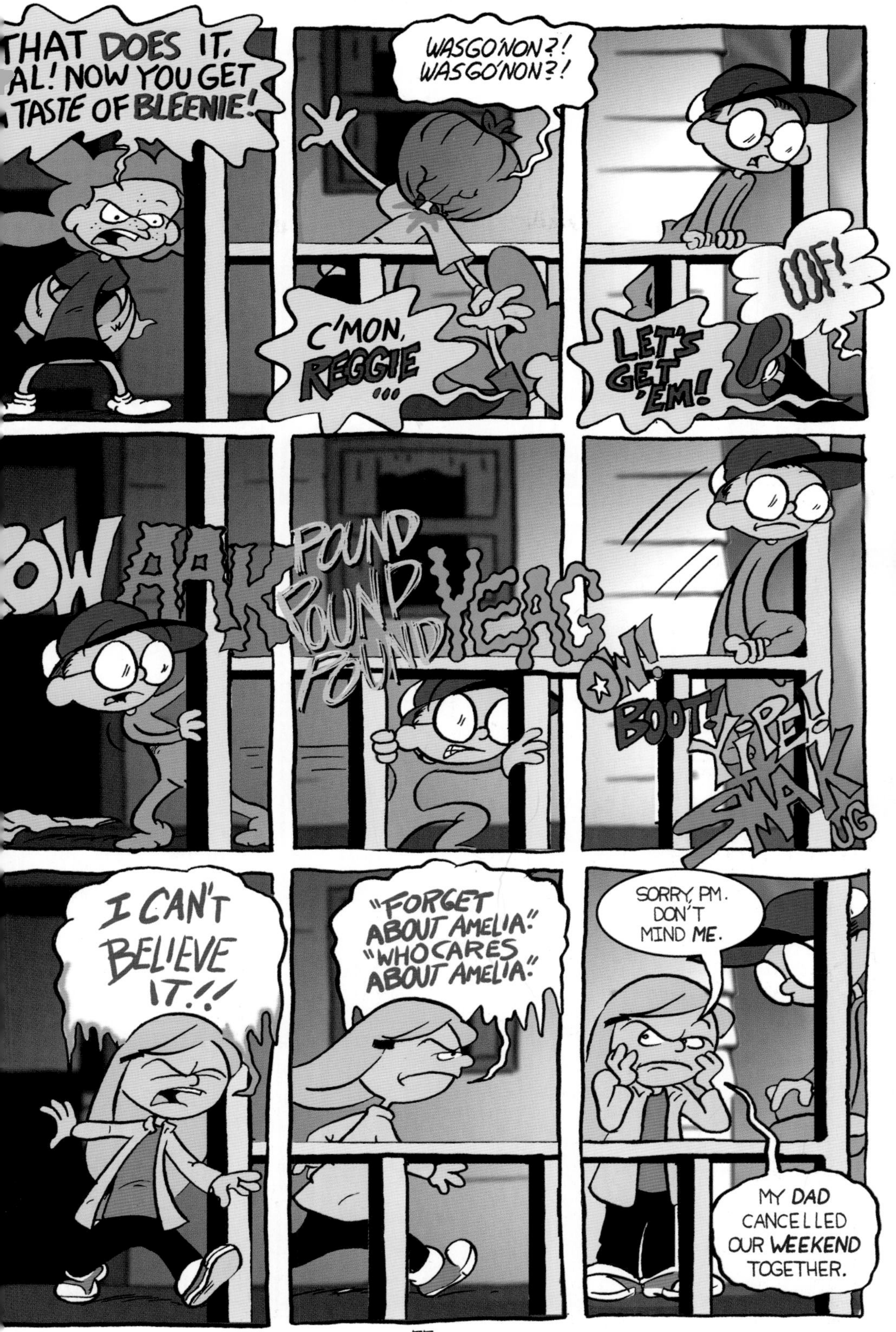
THAT DOES IT, AL! NOW YOU GET TASTE OF BLEENIE!
WASGO'NON?! WASGO'NON?!
C'MON, REGGIE ...
LET'S GET 'EM!
OOF!
OW
AAK
POUND POUND POUND POUND
YEAG
OW!
BOOT!
YIPE!
SMAK
UG
I CAN'T BELIEVE IT!!
"FORGET ABOUT AMELIA." "WHO CARES ABOUT AMELIA."
SORRY, PM. DON'T MIND ME.
MY DAD CANCELLED OUR WEEKEND TOGETHER.

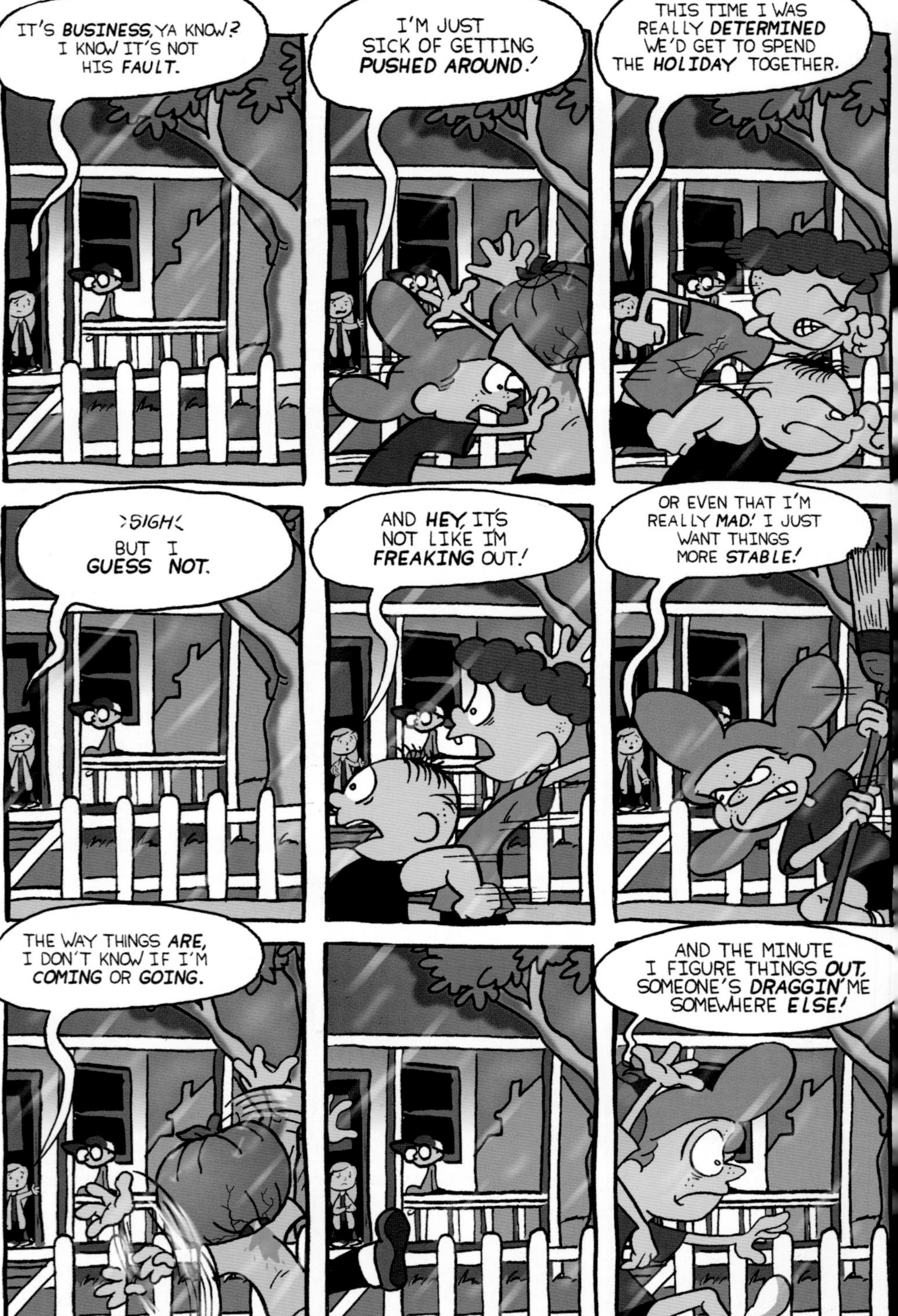
IT'S BUSINESS, YA KNOW? I KNOW IT'S NOT HIS FAULT.
I'M JUST SICK OF GETTING PUSHED AROUND!
THIS TIME I WAS REALLY DETERMINED WE'D GET TO SPEND THE HOLIDAY TOGETHER.
>SIGH< BUT I GUESS NOT.
AND HEY, IT'S NOT LIKE I'M FREAKING OUT!
OR EVEN THAT I'M REALLY MAD! I JUST WANT THINGS MORE STABLE!
THE WAY THINGS ARE, I DON'T KNOW IF I'M COMING OR GOING.
AND THE MINUTE I FIGURE THINGS OUT, SOMEONE'S DRAGGIN' ME SOMEWHERE ELSE!

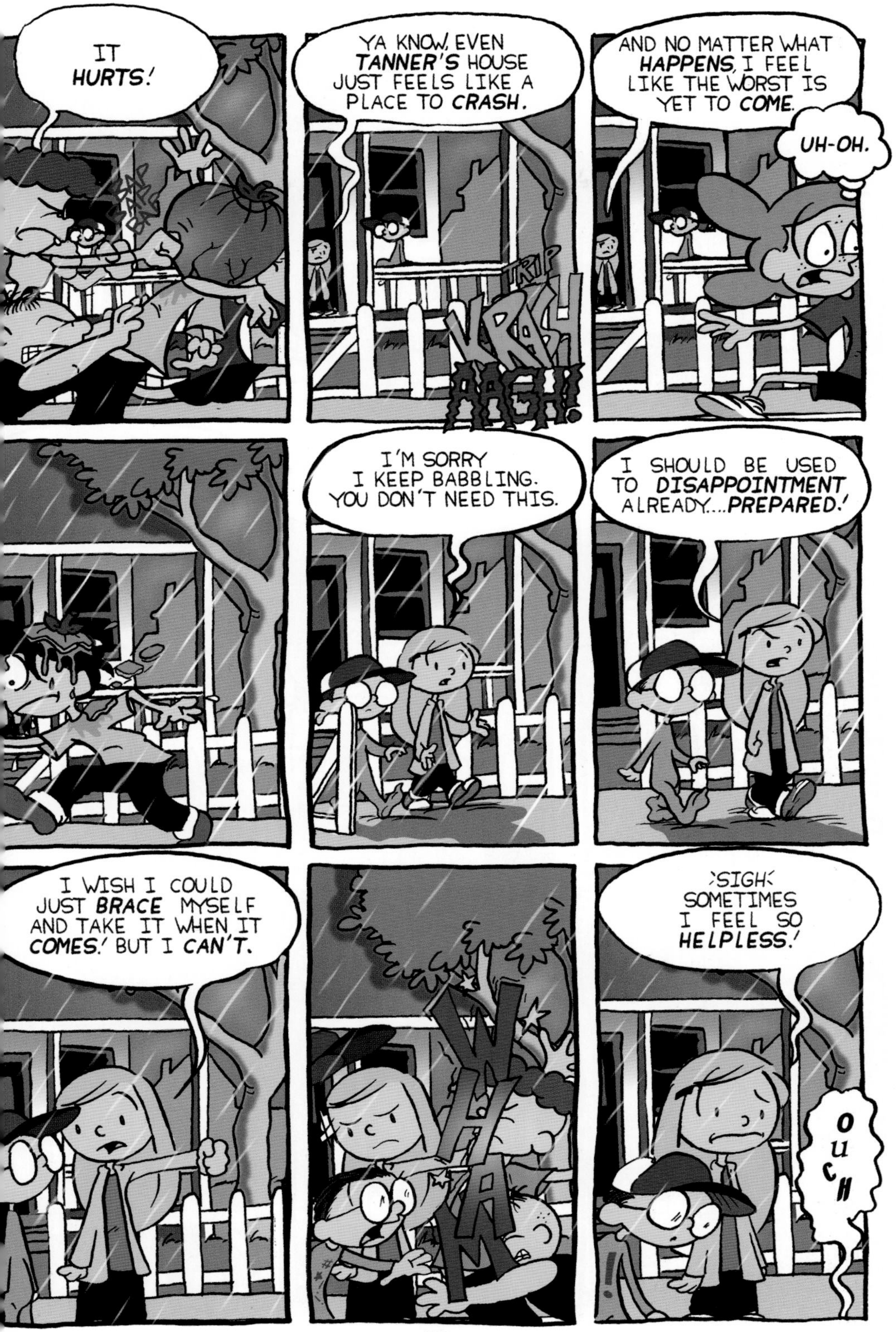
IT HURTS!
YA KNOW, EVEN TANNER'S HOUSE JUST FEELS LIKE A PLACE TO CRASH.
TRIP
KRASH
AAGH!
AND NO MATTER WHAT HAPPENS, I FEEL LIKE THE WORST IS YET TO COME.
UH-OH.
I'M SORRY I KEEP BABBLING. YOU DON'T NEED THIS.
I SHOULD BE USED TO DISAPPOINTMENT ALREADY....PREPARED!
I WISH I COULD JUST BRACE MYSELF AND TAKE IT WHEN IT COMES! BUT I CAN'T.
WHAM
SIGH
SOMETIMES I FEEL SO HELPLESS!
OUCH

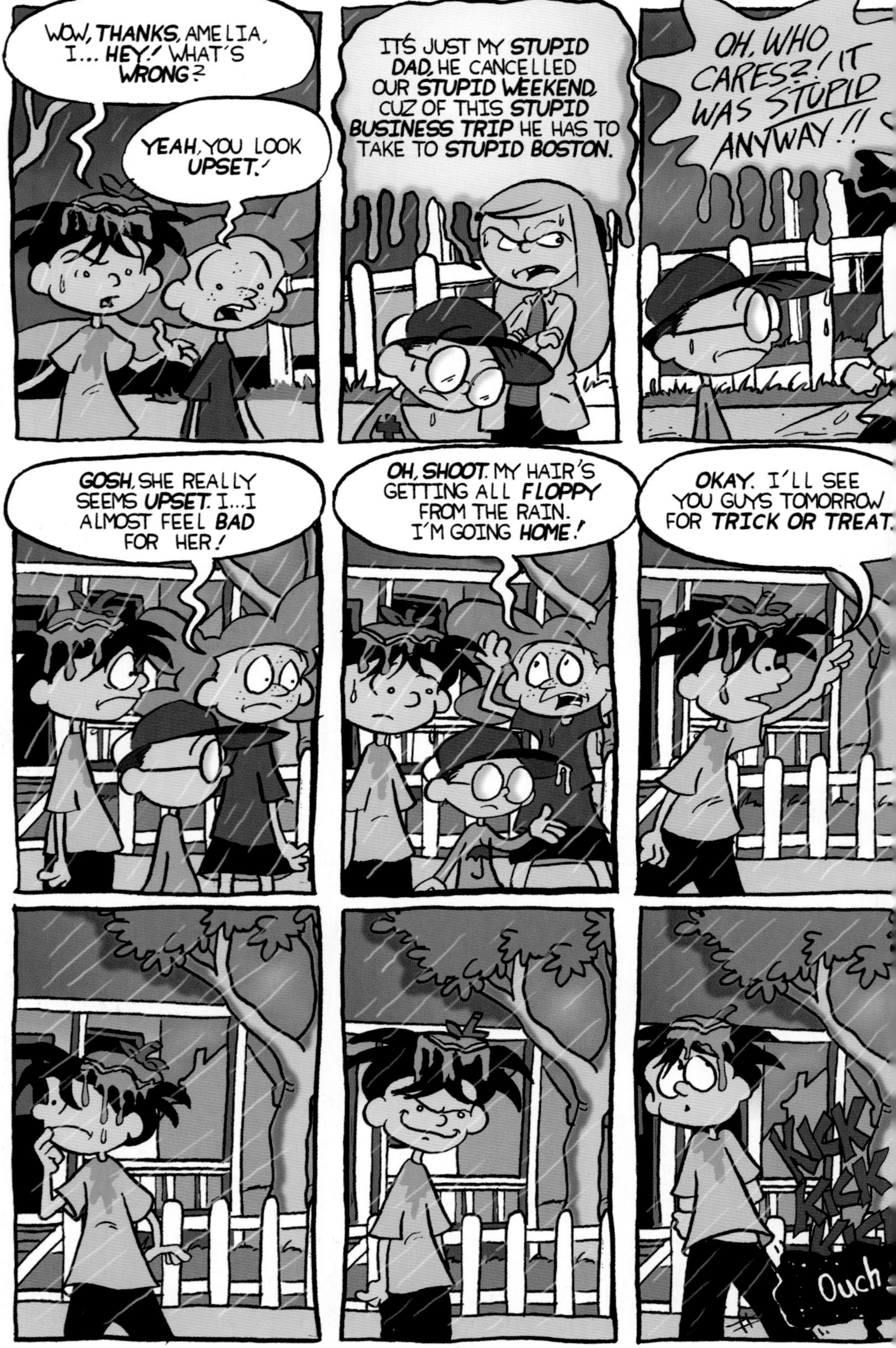

WOW, THANKS, AMELIA, I... HEY! WHAT'S WRONG?
YEAH, YOU LOOK UPSET!
IT'S JUST MY STUPID DAD, HE CANCELLED OUR STUPID WEEKEND CUZ OF THIS STUPID BUSINESS TRIP HE HAS TO TAKE TO STUPID BOSTON.
OH, WHO CARES?! IT WAS STUPID ANYWAY!!
GOSH, SHE REALLY SEEMS UPSET. I...I ALMOST FEEL BAD FOR HER!
OH, SHOOT. MY HAIR'S GETTING ALL FLOPPY FROM THE RAIN. I'M GOING HOME!
OKAY. I'LL SEE YOU GUYS TOMORROW FOR TRICK OR TREAT.
KICK KICK KICK
Ouch

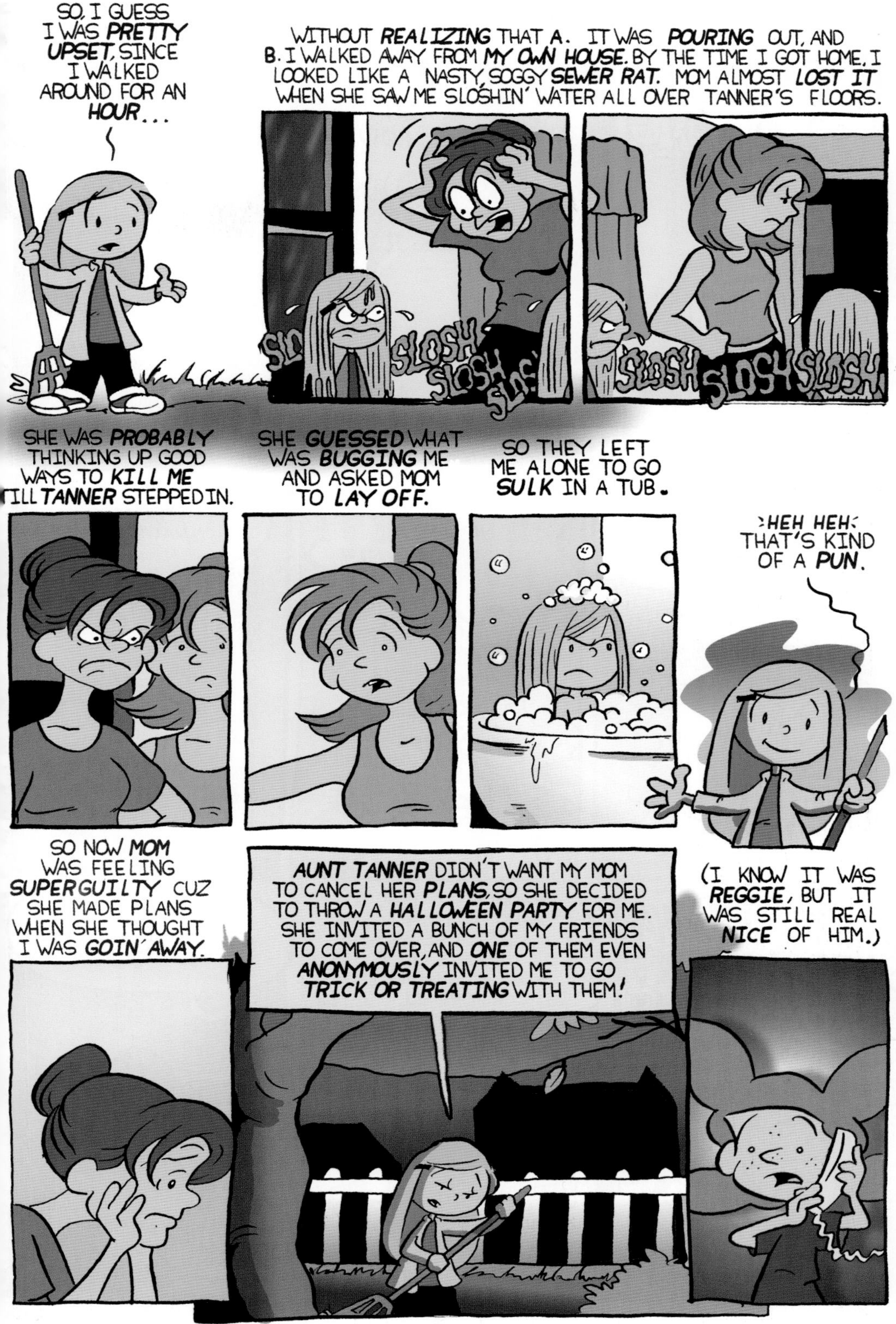
SO, I GUESS I WAS PRETTY UPSET, SINCE I WALKED AROUND FOR AN HOUR...
WITHOUT REALIZING THAT A. IT WAS POURING OUT, AND B. I WALKED AWAY FROM MY OWN HOUSE. BY THE TIME I GOT HOME, I LOOKED LIKE A NASTY, SOGGY SEWER RAT. MOM ALMOST LOST IT WHEN SHE SAW ME SLOSHIN' WATER ALL OVER TANNER'S FLOORS.
SLO
SLOSH
SLOSH
SLO
SLOSH
SLOSH
SLOSH
SHE WAS PROBABLY THINKING UP GOOD WAYS TO KILL ME TILL TANNER STEPPED IN.
SHE GUESSED WHAT WAS BUGGING ME AND ASKED MOM TO LAY OFF.
SO THEY LEFT ME ALONE TO GO SULK IN A TUB.
HEH HEH THAT'S KIND OF A PUN.
SO NOW MOM WAS FEELING SUPERGUILTY CUZ SHE MADE PLANS WHEN SHE THOUGHT I WAS GOIN' AWAY.
AUNT TANNER DIDN'T WANT MY MOM TO CANCEL HER PLANS, SO SHE DECIDED TO THROW A HALLOWEEN PARTY FOR ME. SHE INVITED A BUNCH OF MY FRIENDS TO COME OVER, AND ONE OF THEM EVEN ANONYMOUSLY INVITED ME TO GO TRICK OR TREATING WITH THEM!
(I KNOW IT WAS REGGIE, BUT IT WAS STILL REAL NICE OF HIM.)

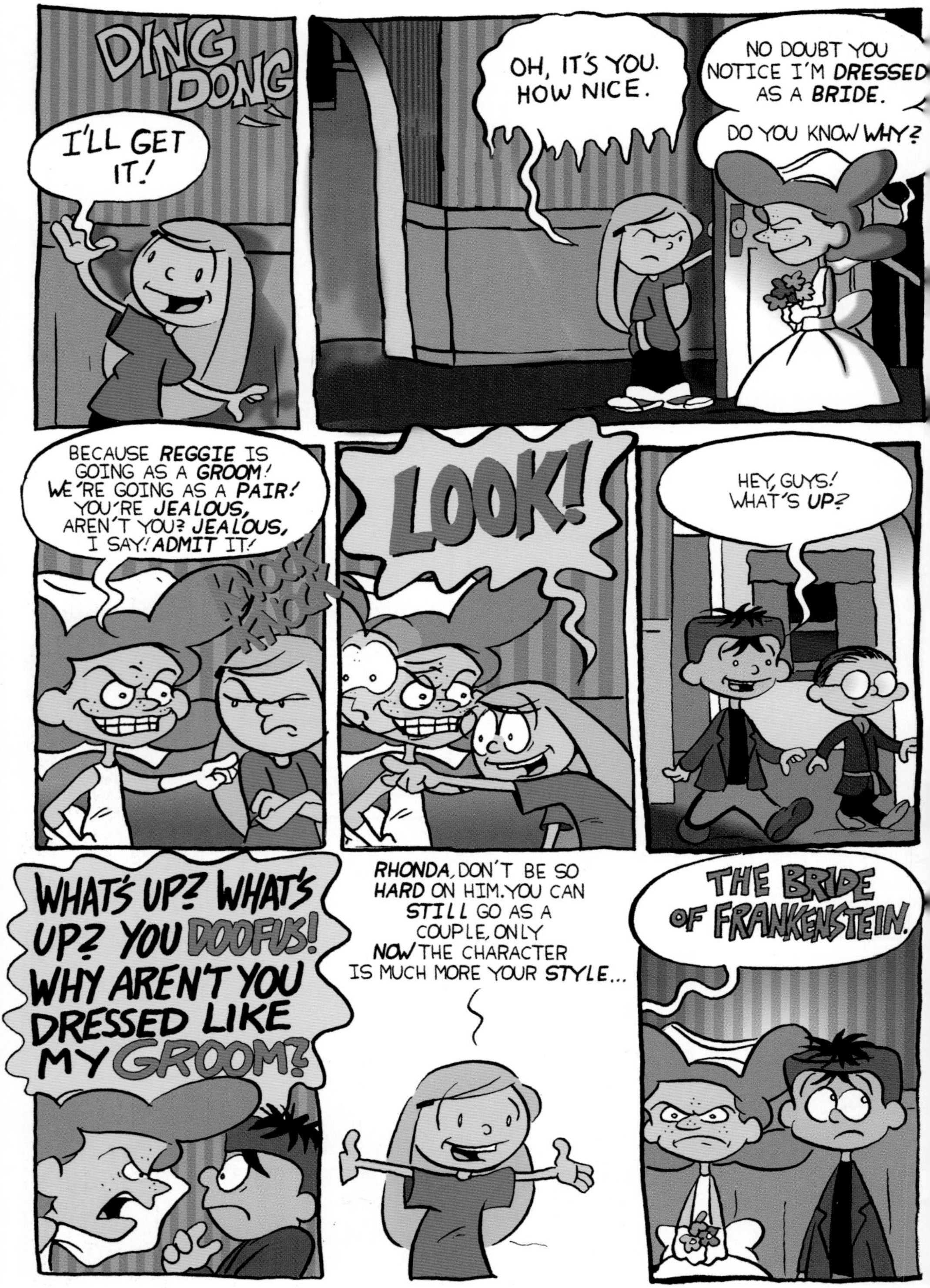
DING DONG
I'LL GET IT!
OH, IT'S YOU. HOW NICE.
NO DOUBT YOU NOTICE I'M **DRESSED** AS A **BRIDE**.
DO YOU KNOW **WHY**?
BECAUSE **REGGIE** IS GOING AS A **GROOM**! **WE'RE** GOING AS A **PAIR**! YOU'RE **JEALOUS**, AREN'T YOU? **JEALOUS**, I SAY! **ADMIT** IT!
LOOK!
HEY, GUYS! WHAT'S **UP**?
WHAT'S UP? WHAT'S UP? YOU DOOFUS! WHY AREN'T YOU DRESSED LIKE MY GROOM?
RHONDA, DON'T BE SO **HARD** ON HIM. YOU CAN **STILL** GO AS A COUPLE, ONLY **NOW** THE CHARACTER IS MUCH MORE YOUR **STYLE**...
THE BRIDE OF FRANKENSTEIN.

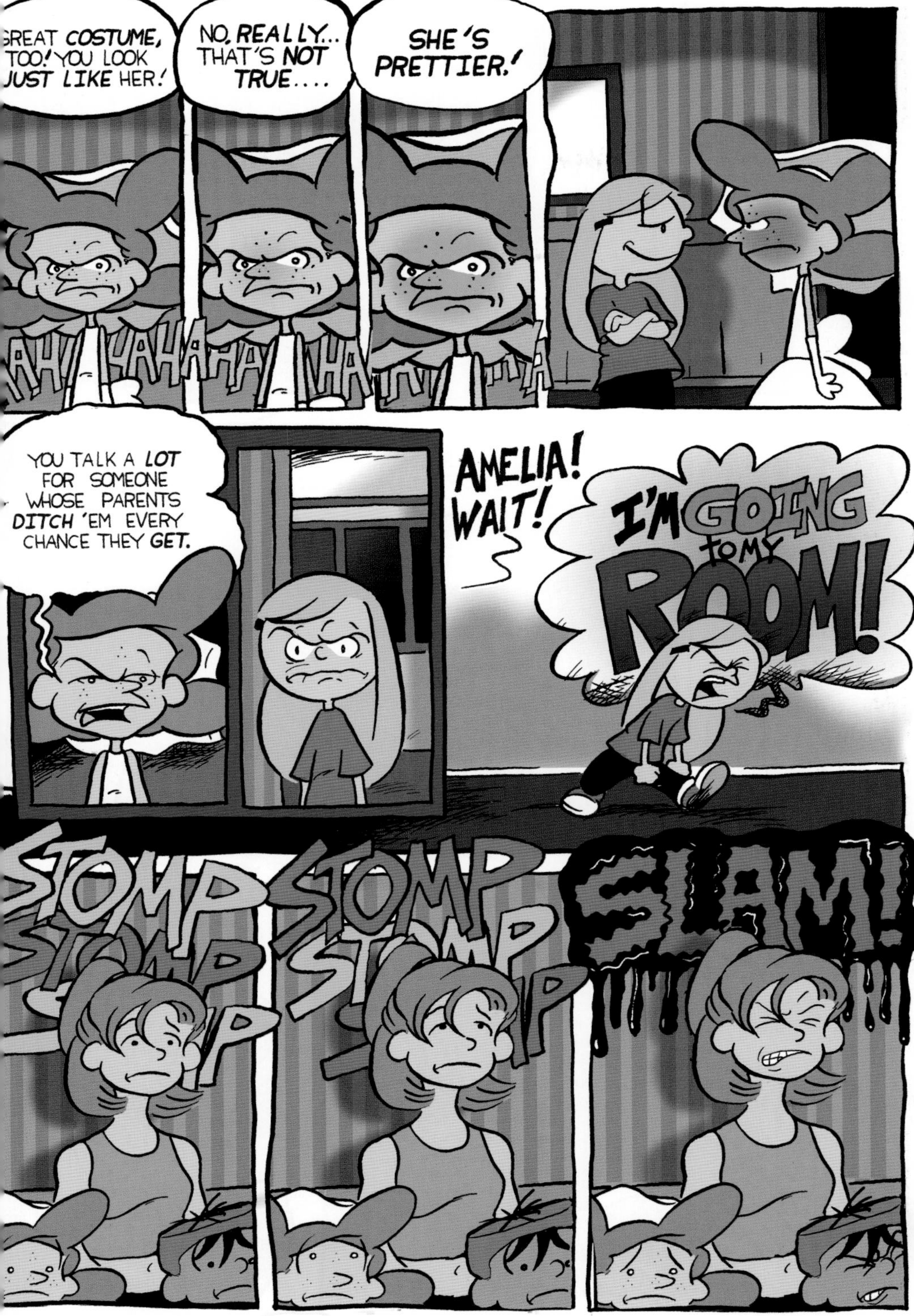
GREAT COSTUME, TOO! YOU LOOK JUST LIKE HER!
HAHAHAHA
NO, REALLY... THAT'S NOT TRUE....
SHE'S PRETTIER!
YOU TALK A LOT FOR SOMEONE WHOSE PARENTS DITCH 'EM EVERY CHANCE THEY GET.
AMELIA! WAIT!
I'M GOING TO MY ROOM!
STOMP STOMP
STOMP STOMP
SLAM!

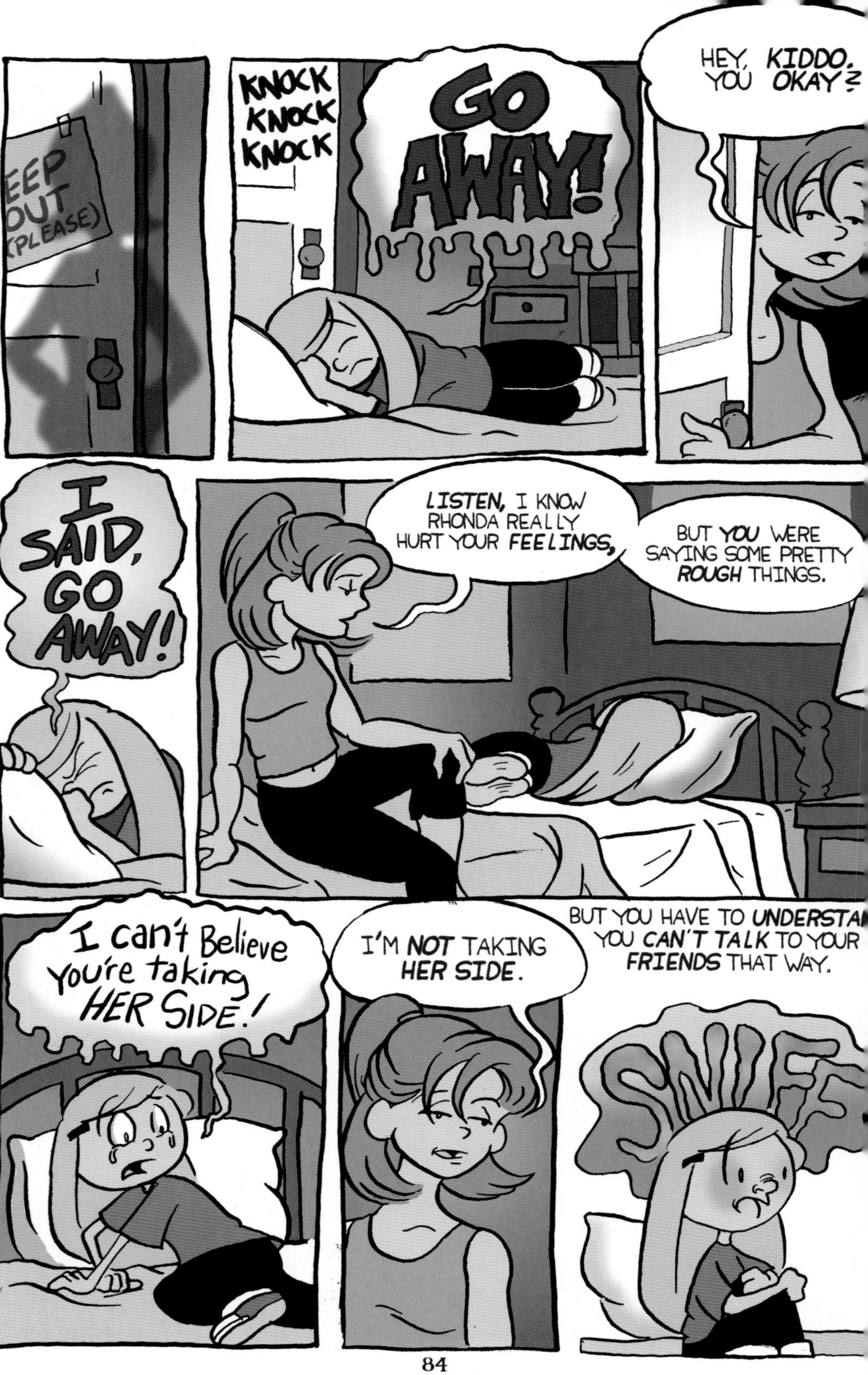
EEP
OUT
(PLEASE)
KNOCK
KNOCK
KNOCK
GO AWAY!
HEY, KIDDO. YOU OKAY?
I SAID, GO AWAY!
LISTEN, I KNOW RHONDA REALLY HURT YOUR FEELINGS,
BUT YOU WERE SAYING SOME PRETTY ROUGH THINGS.
I can't Believe you're taking HER SIDE!
I'M NOT TAKING HER SIDE.
BUT YOU HAVE TO UNDERSTA
YOU CAN'T TALK TO YOUR FRIENDS THAT WAY.

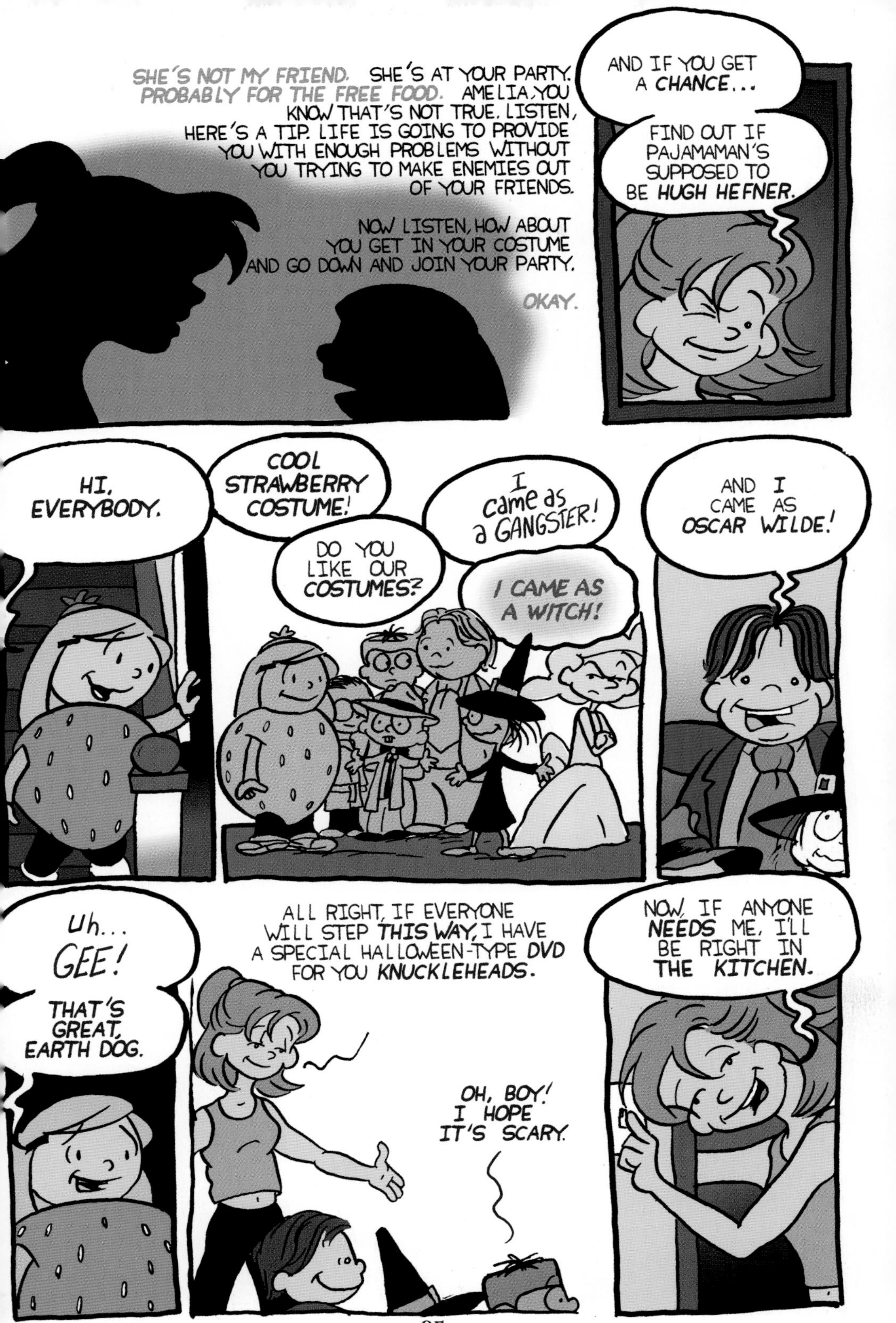

SHE'S NOT MY FRIEND.
SHE'S AT YOUR PARTY.
PROBABLY FOR THE FREE FOOD.
AMELIA, YOU KNOW THAT'S NOT TRUE. LISTEN, HERE'S A TIP. LIFE IS GOING TO PROVIDE YOU WITH ENOUGH PROBLEMS WITHOUT YOU TRYING TO MAKE ENEMIES OUT OF YOUR FRIENDS.
NOW LISTEN, HOW ABOUT YOU GET IN YOUR COSTUME AND GO DOWN AND JOIN YOUR PARTY.
OKAY.
AND IF YOU GET A CHANCE...
FIND OUT IF PAJAMAMAN'S SUPPOSED TO BE HUGH HEFNER.
HI, EVERYBODY.
COOL STRAWBERRY COSTUME!
DO YOU LIKE OUR COSTUMES?
I came as a GANGSTER!
I CAME AS A WITCH!
AND I CAME AS OSCAR WILDE!
Uh... GEE!
THAT'S GREAT, EARTH DOG.
ALL RIGHT, IF EVERYONE WILL STEP THIS WAY, I HAVE A SPECIAL HALLOWEEN-TYPE DVD FOR YOU KNUCKLEHEADS.
OH, BOY! I HOPE IT'S SCARY.
NOW, IF ANYONE NEEDS ME, I'LL BE RIGHT IN THE KITCHEN.

OH DEAR. I HOPE THIS ISN'T TOO SCARY!

T'sk- Dames!

I CAN *BARELY* SEE OVER MY *BERRY!*

SHH! IT'S ON!

ZOMBIE GORE PART 2!

SAY, *BABY*, YOU DON'T MIND IF WE WALK THROUGH THIS OLD *CEMETERY*, DO YA?

YOU HAVE *SOME* NERVE, *NOT* COMING AS MY *GROOM!*

I JUST THOUGHT IT WAS A *STUPID IDEA!* *BESIDES*, EVERYONE WOULD MAKE *FUN* OF ME!

WHY IF I DIDN'T KNOW *BETTER* I'D THINK THAT YOU WERE—

SOMEDAY, YOU'RE GONNA *LOSE ME, REGGIE GRABINSKY!*

WILL YOU *SHUT UP!* WE'RE *TRYING* TO WATCH THE *MOVIE!*

GROAN

NOW, BABY... WHY WOULD...? WAIT! LOOK OUT BEHIND YOU!

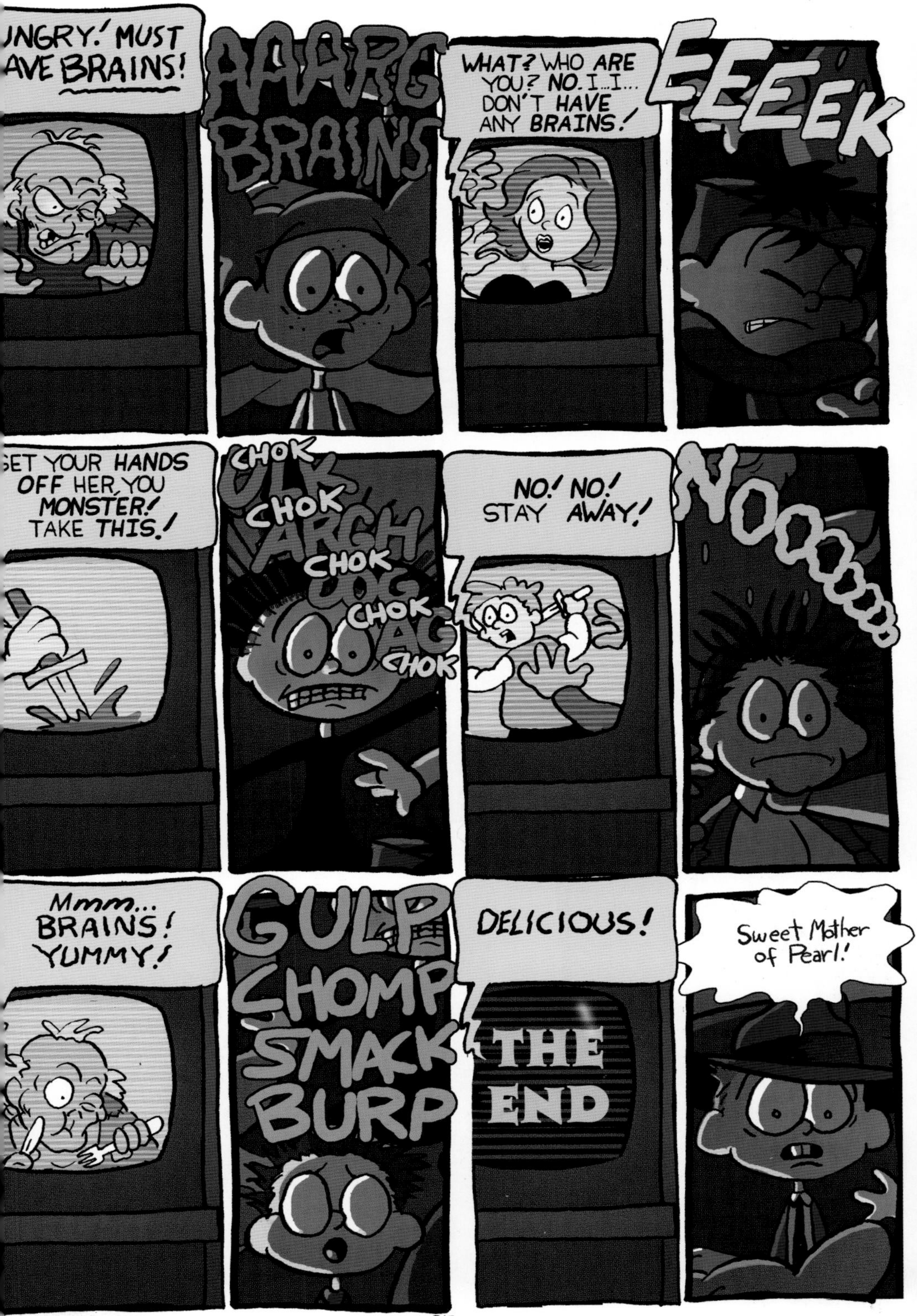
UNGRY! MUST
AVE BRAINS!
AAARG
BRAINS
WHAT? WHO ARE YOU? NO. I...I... DON'T HAVE ANY BRAINS!
EEEEK
GET YOUR HANDS OFF HER, YOU MONSTER! TAKE THIS!
CHOK
ULK
CHOK
ARGH
CHOK
UGG
CHOK
AG
CHOK
NO! NO! STAY AWAY!
NOOOOOO
Mmm... BRAINS! YUMMY!
GULP
CHOMP
SMACK
BURP
DELICIOUS!
THE END
Sweet Mother of Pearl!

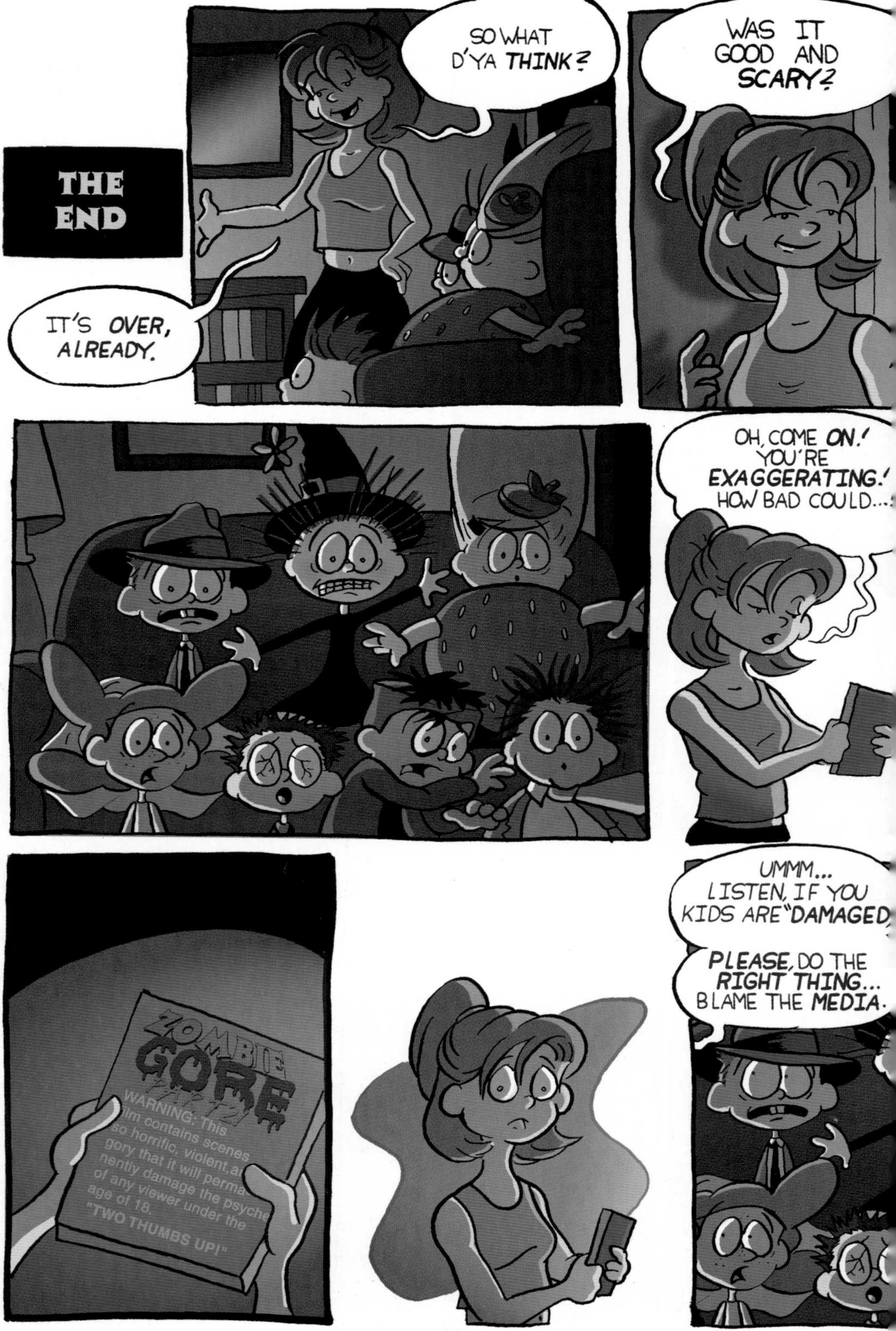
THE END
IT'S OVER, ALREADY.
SO WHAT D'YA THINK?
WAS IT GOOD AND SCARY?
OH, COME ON! YOU'RE EXAGGERATING! HOW BAD COULD...
ZOMBIE GORE
WARNING: This
ilm contains scenes
so horrific, violent, a
gory that it will perma
nently damage the psyche
of any viewer under the
age of 18.
"TWO THUMBS UP!"
UMMM... LISTEN, IF YOU KIDS ARE "DAMAGED,"
PLEASE, DO THE RIGHT THING... BLAME THE MEDIA.

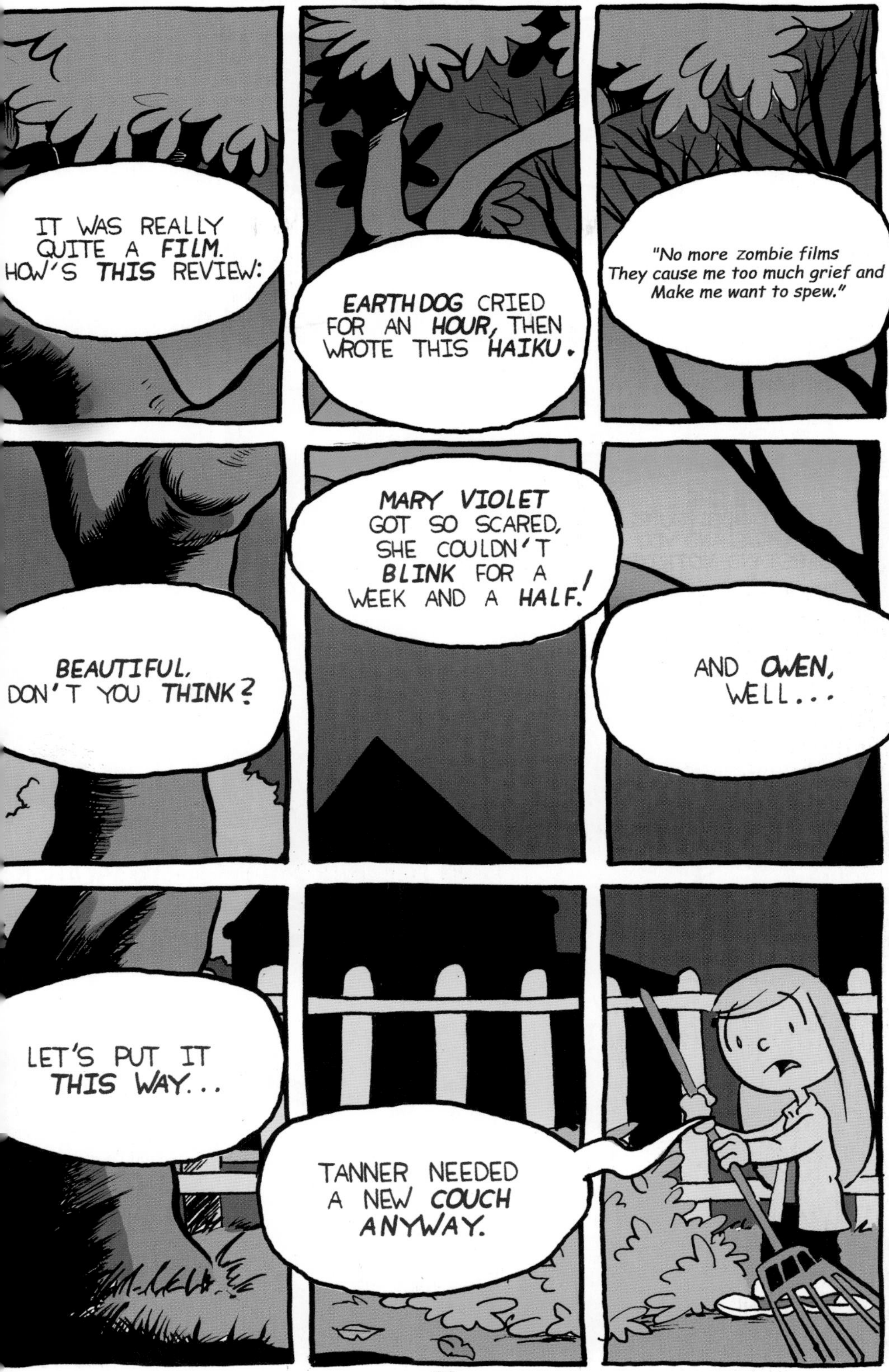
IT WAS REALLY QUITE A FILM. HOW'S THIS REVIEW:
EARTHDOG CRIED FOR AN HOUR, THEN WROTE THIS HAIKU.
"No more zombie films
They cause me too much grief and
Make me want to spew."
BEAUTIFUL, DON'T YOU THINK?
MARY VIOLET GOT SO SCARED, SHE COULDN'T BLINK FOR A WEEK AND A HALF!
AND OWEN, WELL...
LET'S PUT IT THIS WAY...
TANNER NEEDED A NEW COUCH ANYWAY.

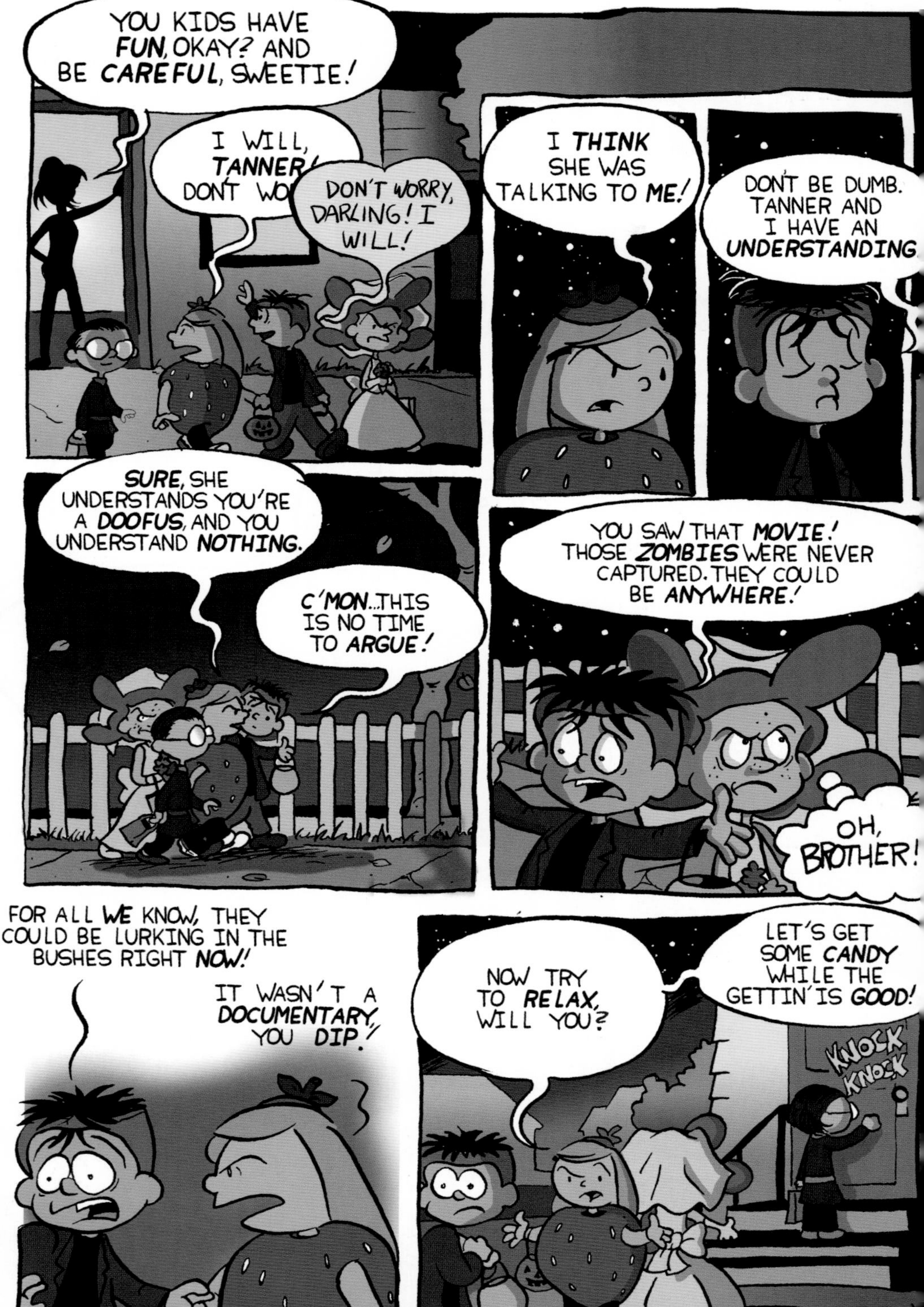
YOU KIDS HAVE FUN, OKAY? AND BE CAREFUL, SWEETIE!
I WILL, TANNER! DON'T WO
DON'T WORRY, DARLING! I WILL!
I THINK SHE WAS TALKING TO ME!
DON'T BE DUMB. TANNER AND I HAVE AN UNDERSTANDING.
SURE, SHE UNDERSTANDS YOU'RE A DOOFUS, AND YOU UNDERSTAND NOTHING.
C'MON...THIS IS NO TIME TO ARGUE!
YOU SAW THAT MOVIE! THOSE ZOMBIES WERE NEVER CAPTURED. THEY COULD BE ANYWHERE!
OH, BROTHER!
FOR ALL WE KNOW, THEY COULD BE LURKING IN THE BUSHES RIGHT NOW!
IT WASN'T A DOCUMENTARY, YOU DIP!
NOW TRY TO RELAX, WILL YOU?
LET'S GET SOME CANDY WHILE THE GETTIN' IS GOOD!
KNOCK KNOCK

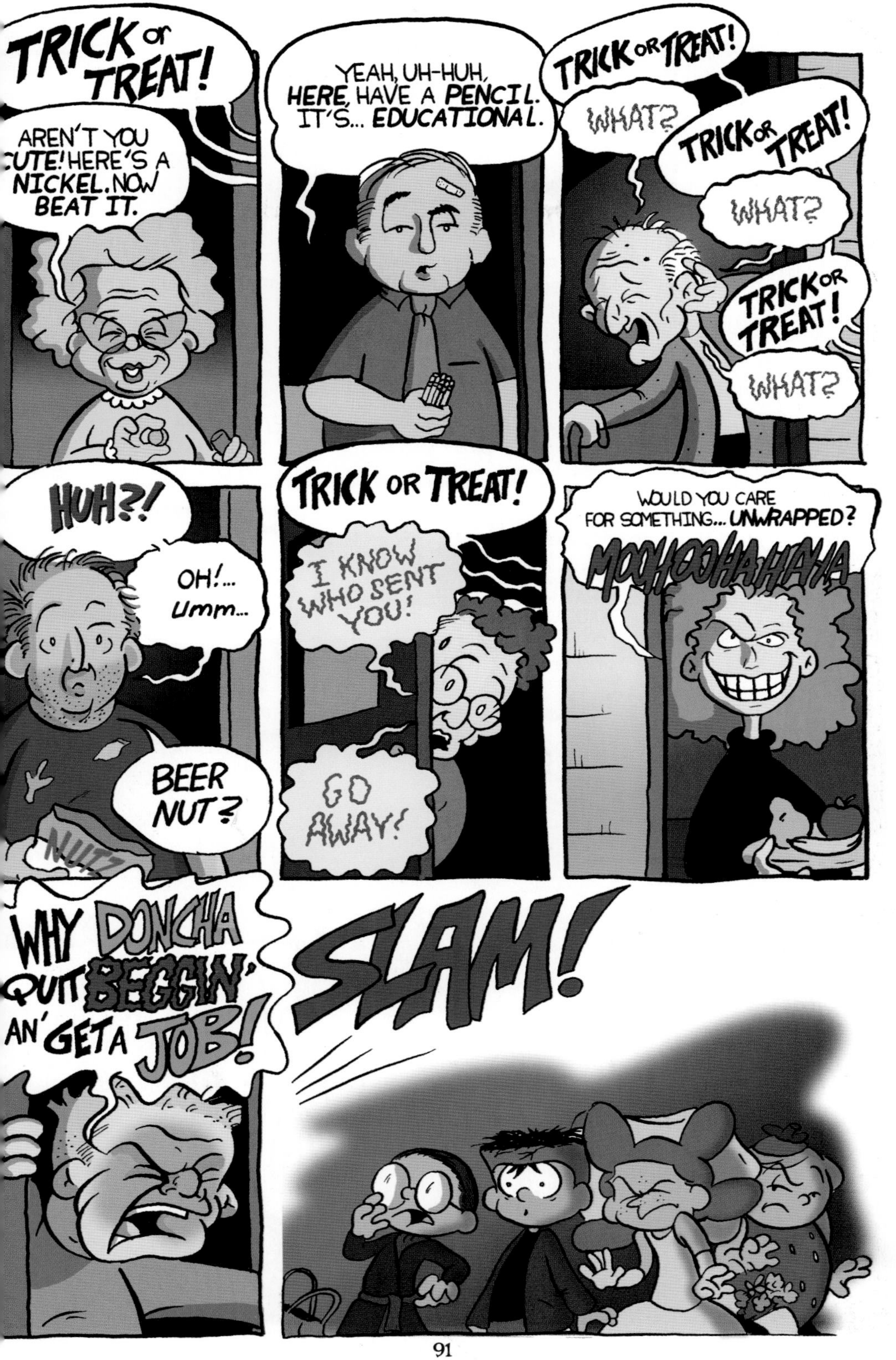
TRICK or TREAT!
AREN'T YOU CUTE! HERE'S A NICKEL. NOW BEAT IT.
YEAH, UH-HUH, HERE, HAVE A PENCIL. IT'S... EDUCATIONAL.
TRICK OR TREAT!
WHAT?
TRICK OR TREAT!
WHAT?
TRICK OR TREAT!
WHAT?
HUH?!
OH!... Umm...
BEER NUT?
NUTZ
TRICK OR TREAT!
I KNOW WHO SENT YOU!
GO AWAY!
WOULD YOU CARE FOR SOMETHING... UNWRAPPED?
MOOHOOHAHAHA
WHY DONCHA QUIT BEGGIN' AN' GET A JOB!
SLAM!

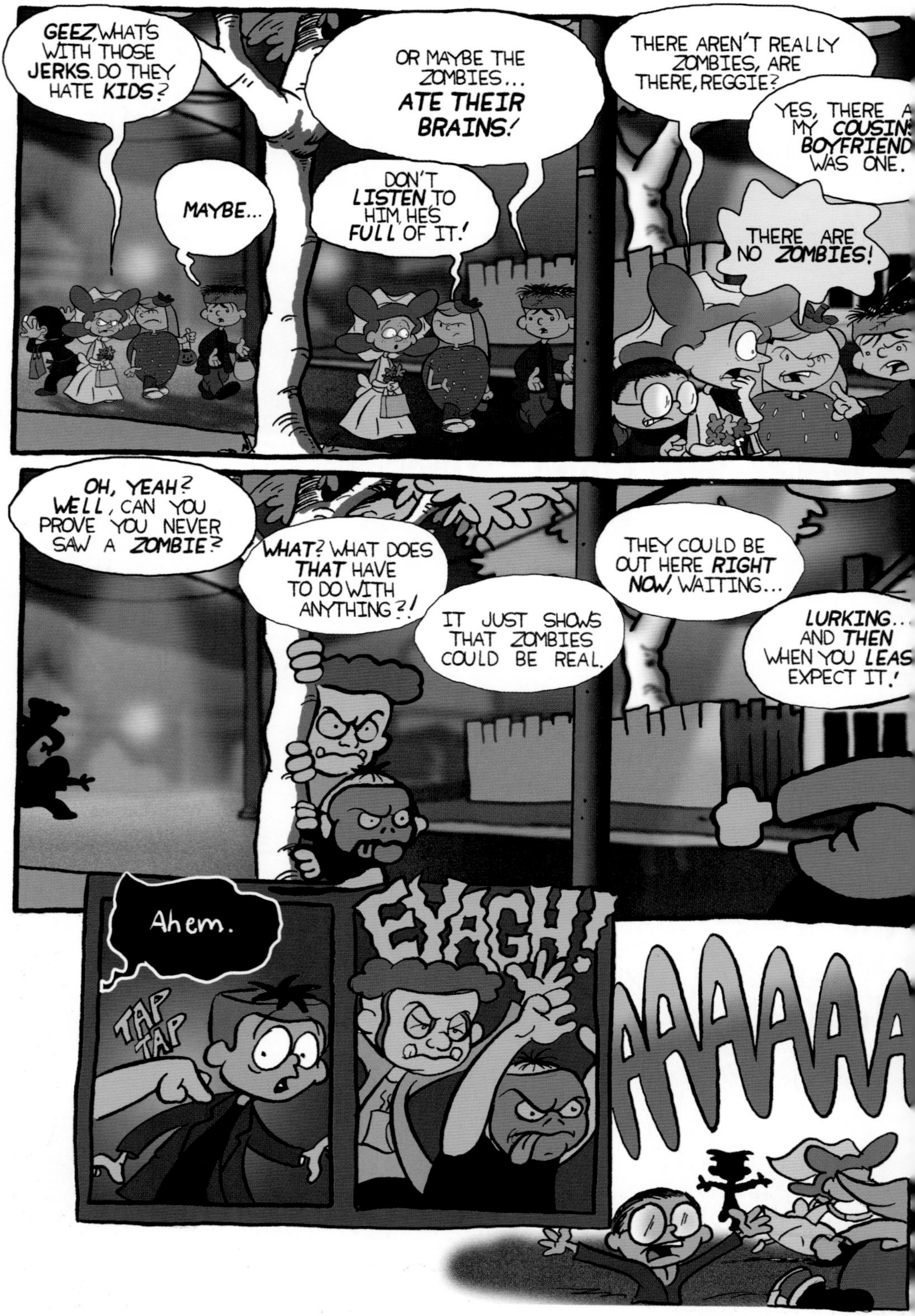
GEEZ, WHAT'S WITH THOSE JERKS. DO THEY HATE KIDS?
MAYBE...
OR MAYBE THE ZOMBIES... ATE THEIR BRAINS!
DON'T LISTEN TO HIM, HE'S FULL OF IT!
THERE AREN'T REALLY ZOMBIES, ARE THERE, REGGIE?
YES, THERE A MY COUSIN BOYFRIEND WAS ONE.
THERE ARE NO ZOMBIES!
OH, YEAH? WELL, CAN YOU PROVE YOU NEVER SAW A ZOMBIE?
WHAT? WHAT DOES THAT HAVE TO DO WITH ANYTHING?!
IT JUST SHOWS THAT ZOMBIES COULD BE REAL.
THEY COULD BE OUT HERE RIGHT NOW, WAITING...
LURKING... AND THEN WHEN YOU LEAS EXPECT IT!
Ahem.
TAP TAP
EYAGH!
AAAAAA

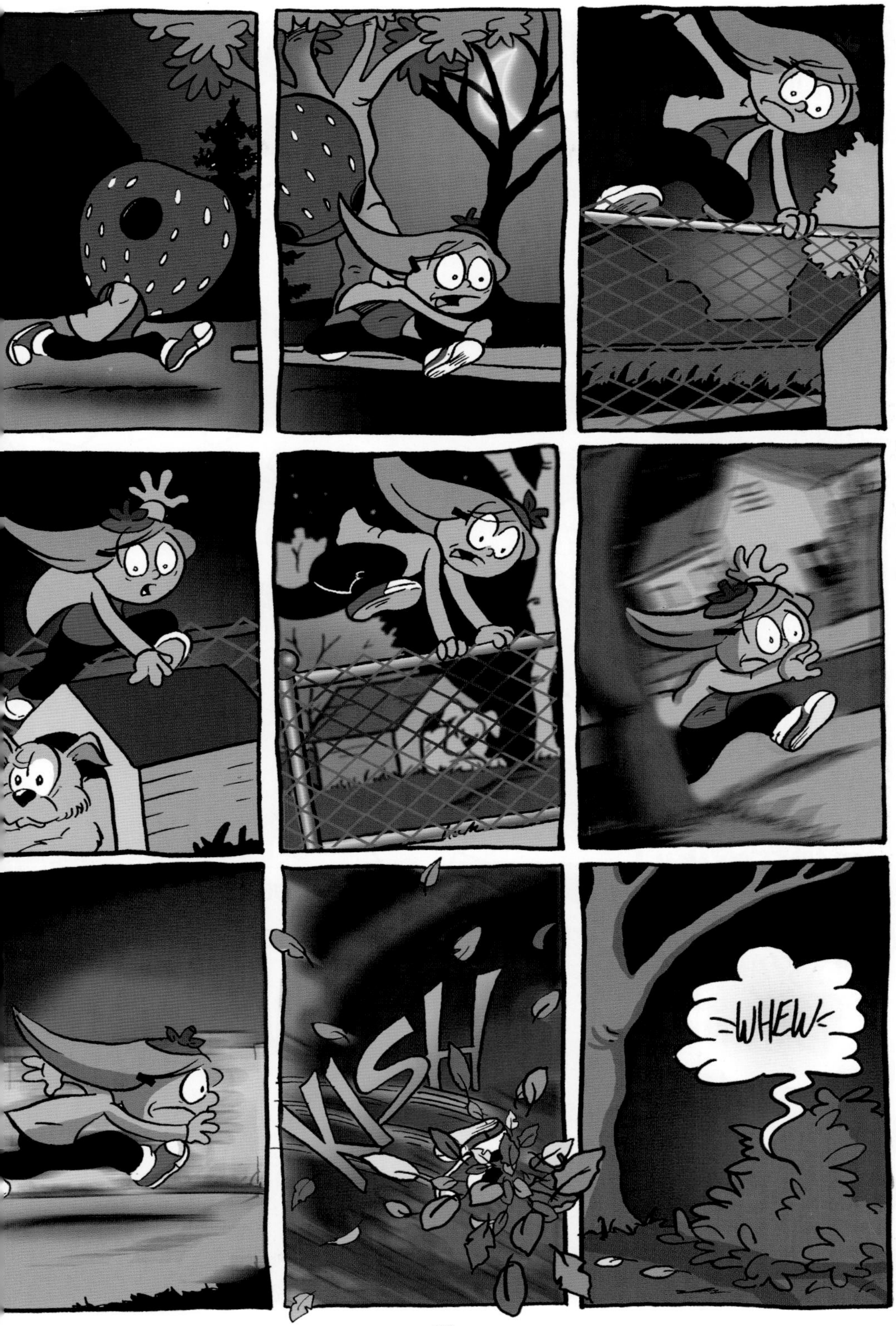
KISH!
WHEW

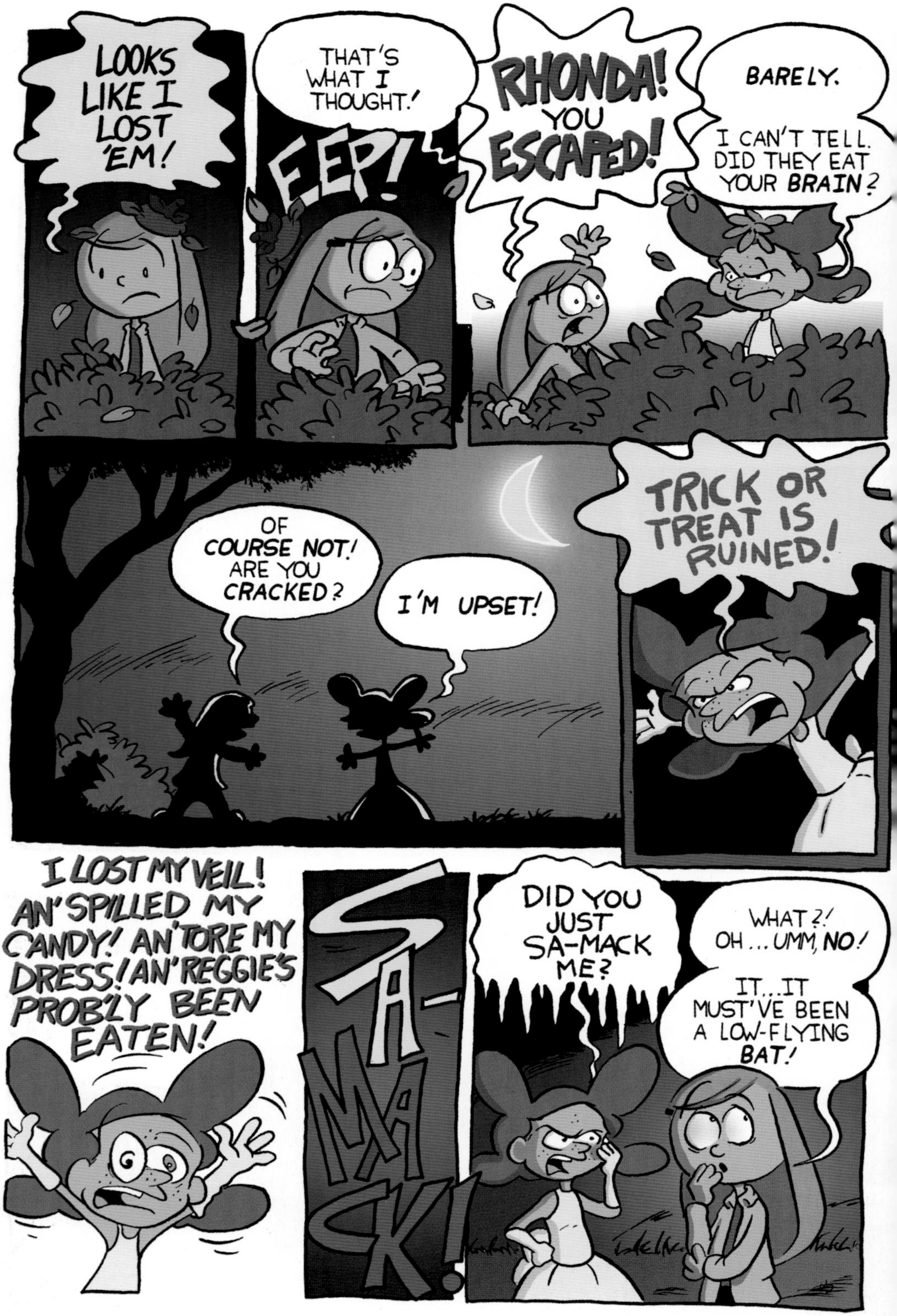
LOOKS LIKE I LOST 'EM!
THAT'S WHAT I THOUGHT!
EEP!
RHONDA! YOU ESCAPED!
BARELY.
I CAN'T TELL. DID THEY EAT YOUR BRAIN?
OF COURSE NOT! ARE YOU CRACKED?
I'M UPSET!
TRICK OR TREAT IS RUINED!
I LOST MY VEIL! AN' SPILLED MY CANDY! AN' TORE MY DRESS! AN' REGGIE'S PROB'LY BEEN EATEN!
SA-MA-CK!
DID YOU JUST SA-MACK ME?
WHAT?! OH ... UMM, NO!
IT...IT MUST'VE BEEN A LOW-FLYING BAT!

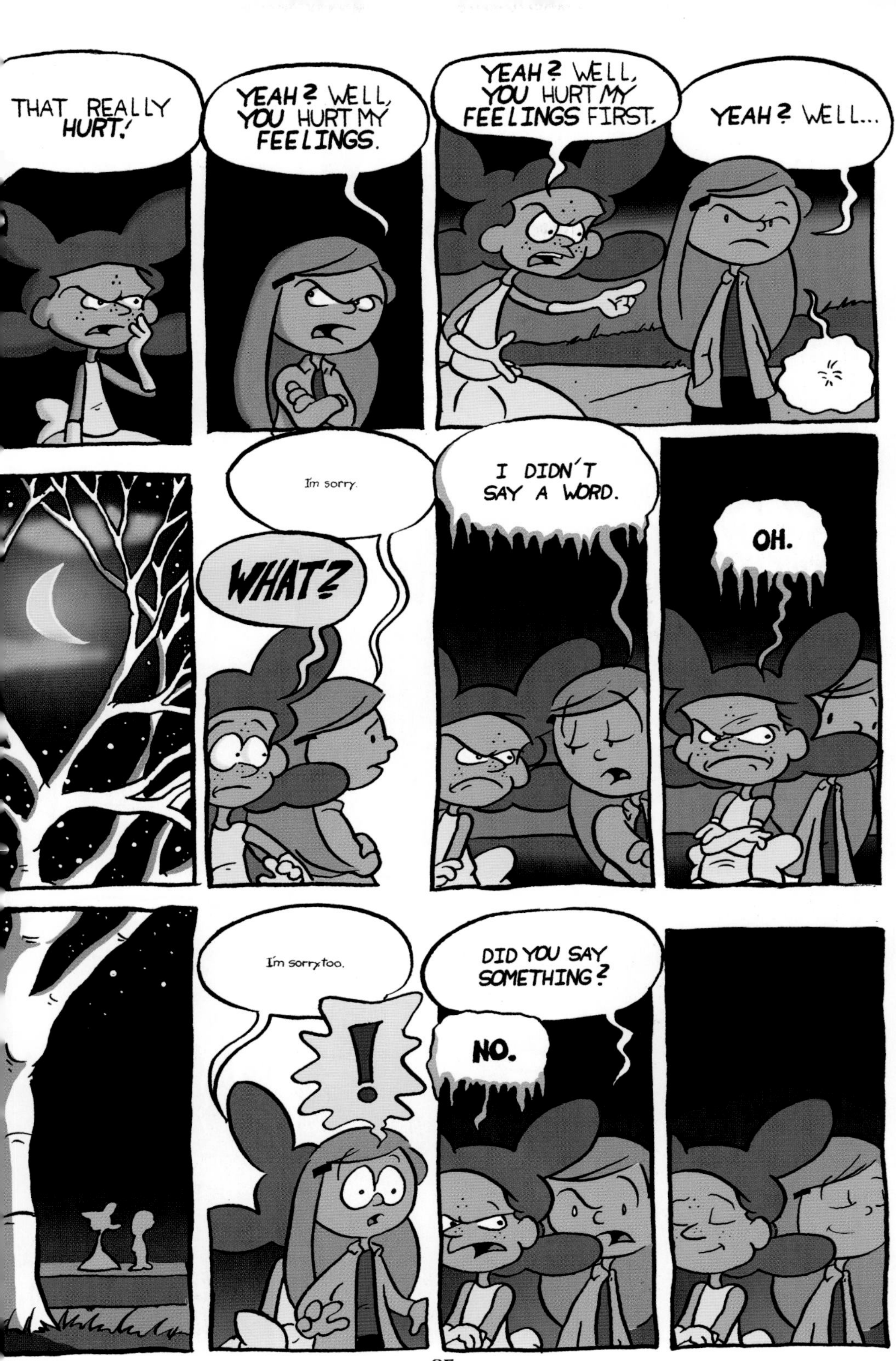
THAT REALLY HURT!
YEAH? WELL, YOU HURT MY FEELINGS.
YEAH? WELL, YOU HURT MY FEELINGS FIRST.
YEAH? WELL...
I'm sorry.
WHAT?
I DIDN'T SAY A WORD.
OH.
I'm sorry, too.
!
DID YOU SAY SOMETHING?
NO.

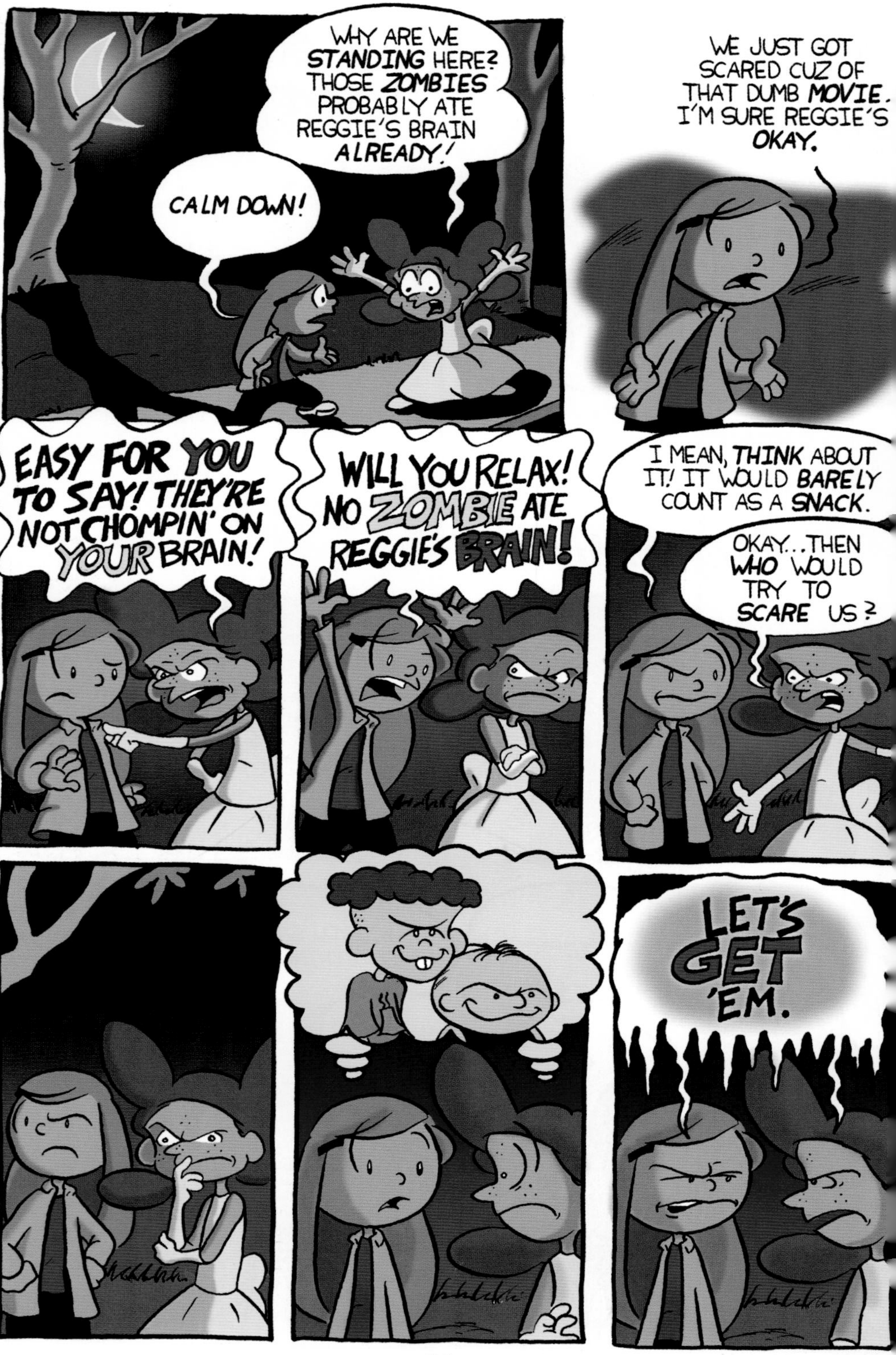

WHY ARE WE STANDING HERE? THOSE ZOMBIES PROBABLY ATE REGGIE'S BRAIN ALREADY!
CALM DOWN!
WE JUST GOT SCARED CUZ OF THAT DUMB MOVIE. I'M SURE REGGIE'S OKAY.
EASY FOR YOU TO SAY! THEY'RE NOT CHOMPIN' ON YOUR BRAIN!
WILL YOU RELAX! NO ZOMBIE ATE REGGIE'S BRAIN!
I MEAN, THINK ABOUT IT! IT WOULD BARELY COUNT AS A SNACK.
OKAY...THEN WHO WOULD TRY TO SCARE US?
LET'S GET 'EM.

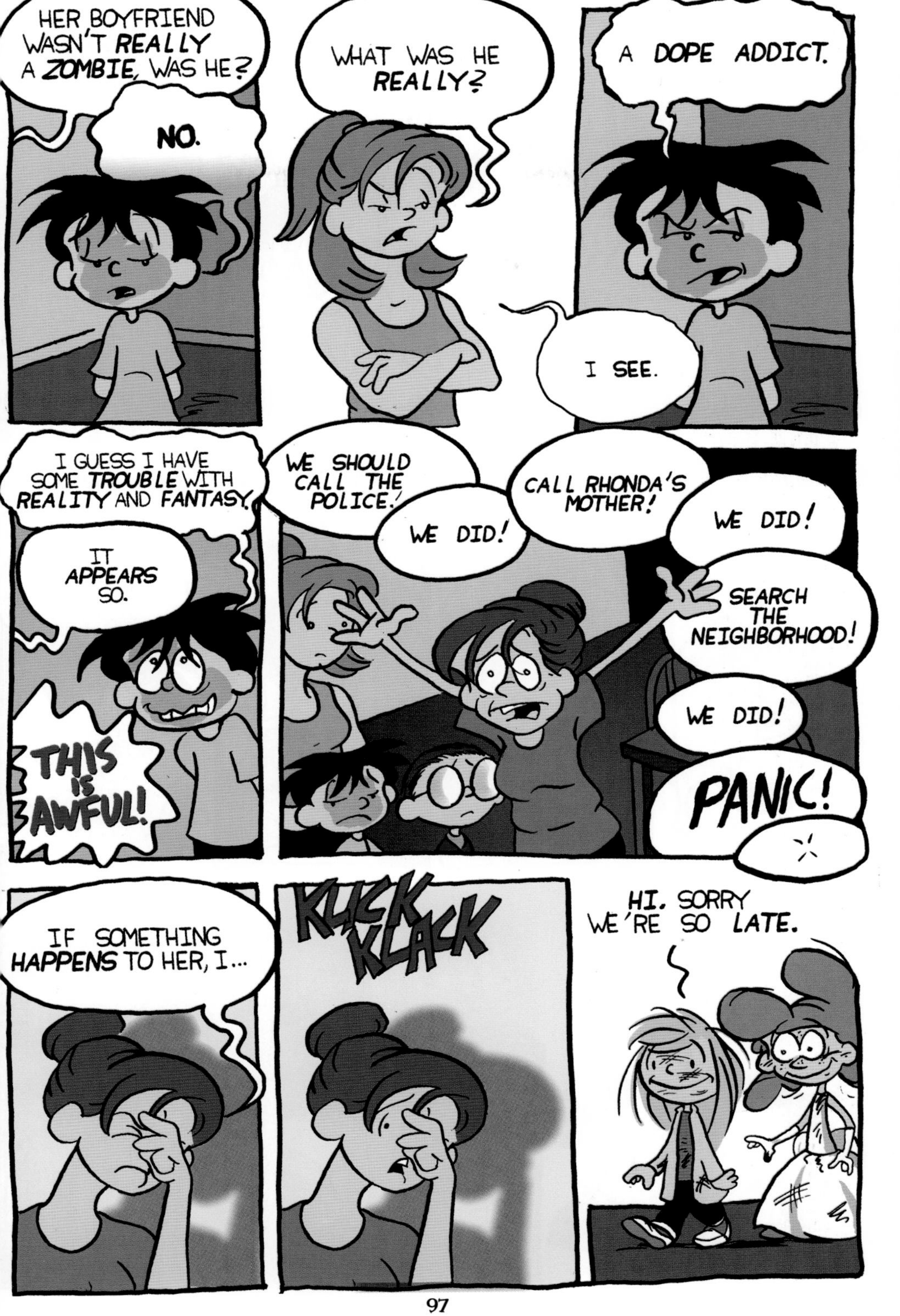
HER BOYFRIEND WASN'T REALLY A ZOMBIE, WAS HE?
NO.
WHAT WAS HE REALLY?
A DOPE ADDICT.
I SEE.
I GUESS I HAVE SOME TROUBLE WITH REALITY AND FANTASY.
IT APPEARS SO.
THIS IS AWFUL!
WE SHOULD CALL THE POLICE!
WE DID!
CALL RHONDA'S MOTHER!
WE DID!
SEARCH THE NEIGHBORHOOD!
WE DID!
PANIC!
IF SOMETHING HAPPENS TO HER, I...
KLICK KLACK
HI. SORRY WE'RE SO LATE.

OHSWEETHEARTWE WERESOWORRIEDABOUT YOUANDWHENYOUDIDNT COMEHOMEANDREGGIE [...]THAPPENED [...] GODYOURESAFE

¡SHEESH!

WHO WAS IT? WHO SCARED US?

WHO? DON'T YOU MEAN WHAT?

 WH-WH-WHAT? ¡GLP!

ZOMBIES, REGGIE! ZOMBIES!

NASTY, UGLY, EVIL ZOMBIES!

HOLY COW!

WHERE ARE THEY NOW?

I IMAGINE, RIGHT WHERE WE LEFT 'EM.

HA HA HA HA HA HA

98

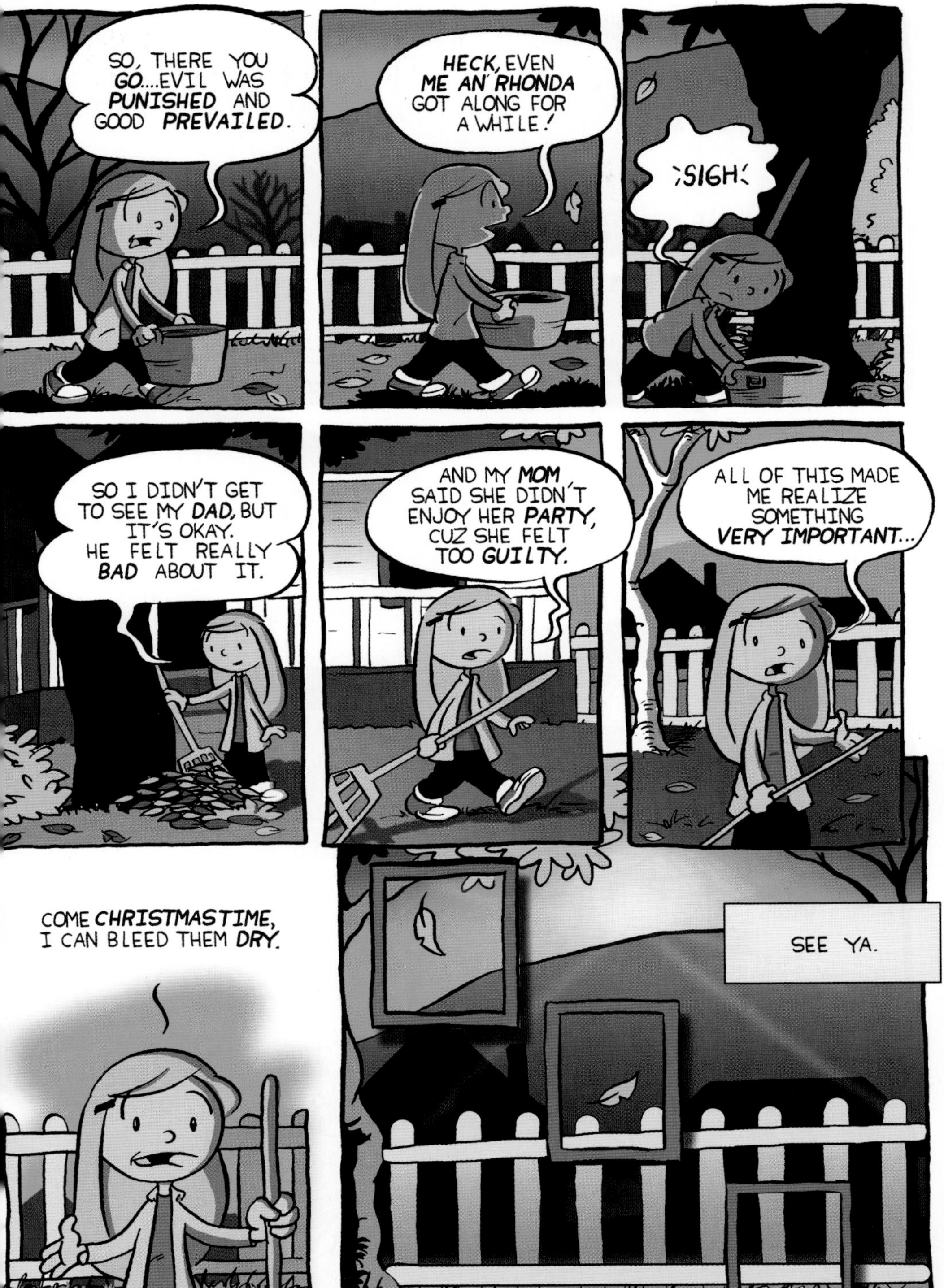
SO, THERE YOU GO....EVIL WAS PUNISHED AND GOOD PREVAILED.
HECK, EVEN ME AN' RHONDA GOT ALONG FOR A WHILE!
;SIGH;
SO I DIDN'T GET TO SEE MY DAD, BUT IT'S OKAY. HE FELT REALLY BAD ABOUT IT.
AND MY MOM SAID SHE DIDN'T ENJOY HER PARTY, CUZ SHE FELT TOO GUILTY.
ALL OF THIS MADE ME REALIZE SOMETHING VERY IMPORTANT...
COME CHRISTMASTIME, I CAN BLEED THEM DRY.
SEE YA.

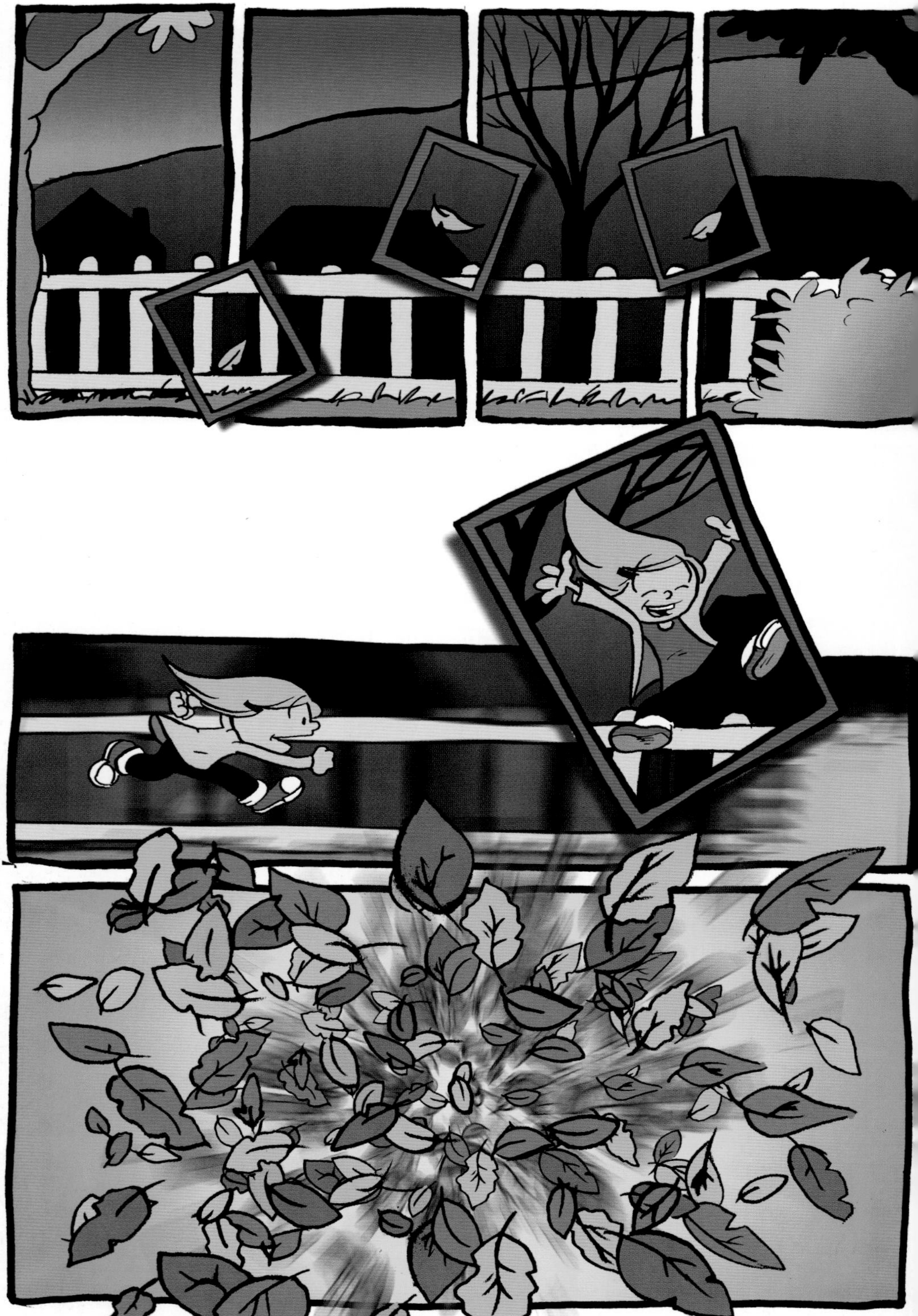

Amelia McBride and the Other Side of Yuletide

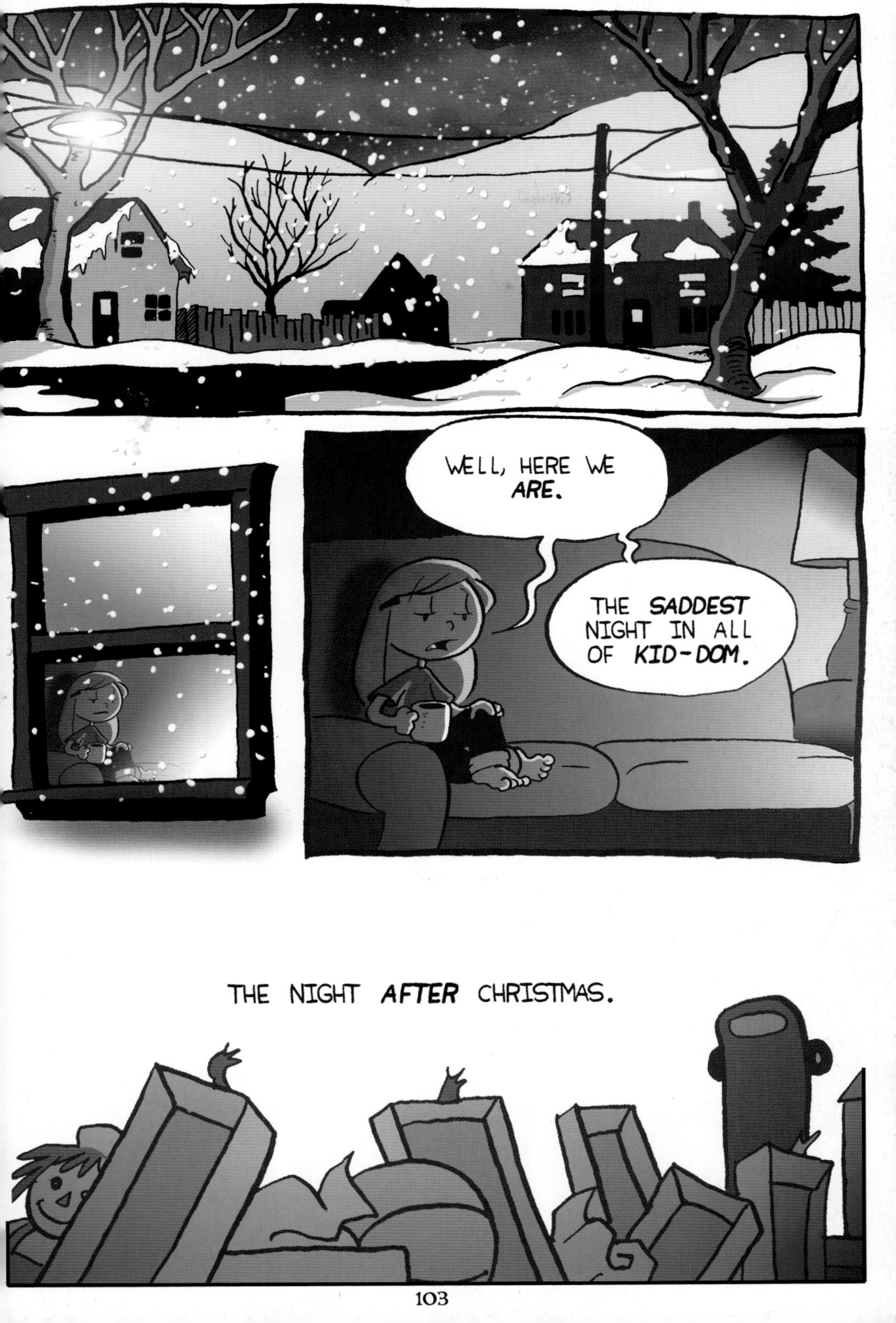
WELL, HERE WE **ARE.**
THE **SADDEST** NIGHT IN ALL OF **KID-DOM.**
THE NIGHT **AFTER** CHRISTMAS.

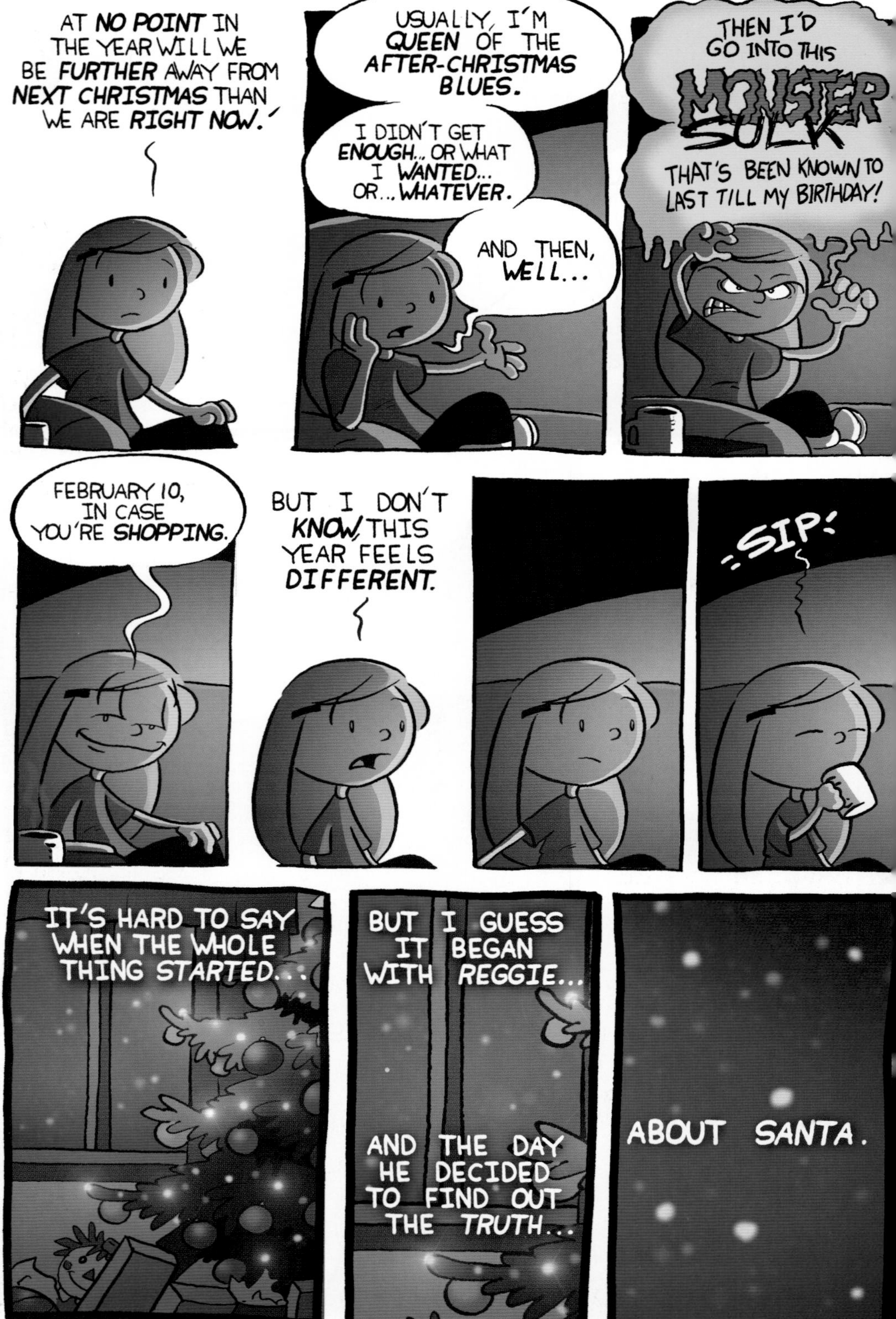
AT NO POINT IN THE YEAR WILL WE BE FURTHER AWAY FROM NEXT CHRISTMAS THAN WE ARE RIGHT NOW.
USUALLY, I'M QUEEN OF THE AFTER-CHRISTMAS BLUES.
I DIDN'T GET ENOUGH... OR WHAT I WANTED... OR... WHATEVER.
AND THEN, WELL...
THEN I'D GO INTO THIS
MONSTER SULK
THAT'S BEEN KNOWN TO LAST TILL MY BIRTHDAY!
FEBRUARY 10, IN CASE YOU'RE SHOPPING.
BUT I DON'T KNOW, THIS YEAR FEELS DIFFERENT.
SIP
IT'S HARD TO SAY WHEN THE WHOLE THING STARTED...
BUT I GUESS IT BEGAN WITH REGGIE...
AND THE DAY HE DECIDED TO FIND OUT THE TRUTH...
ABOUT SANTA.

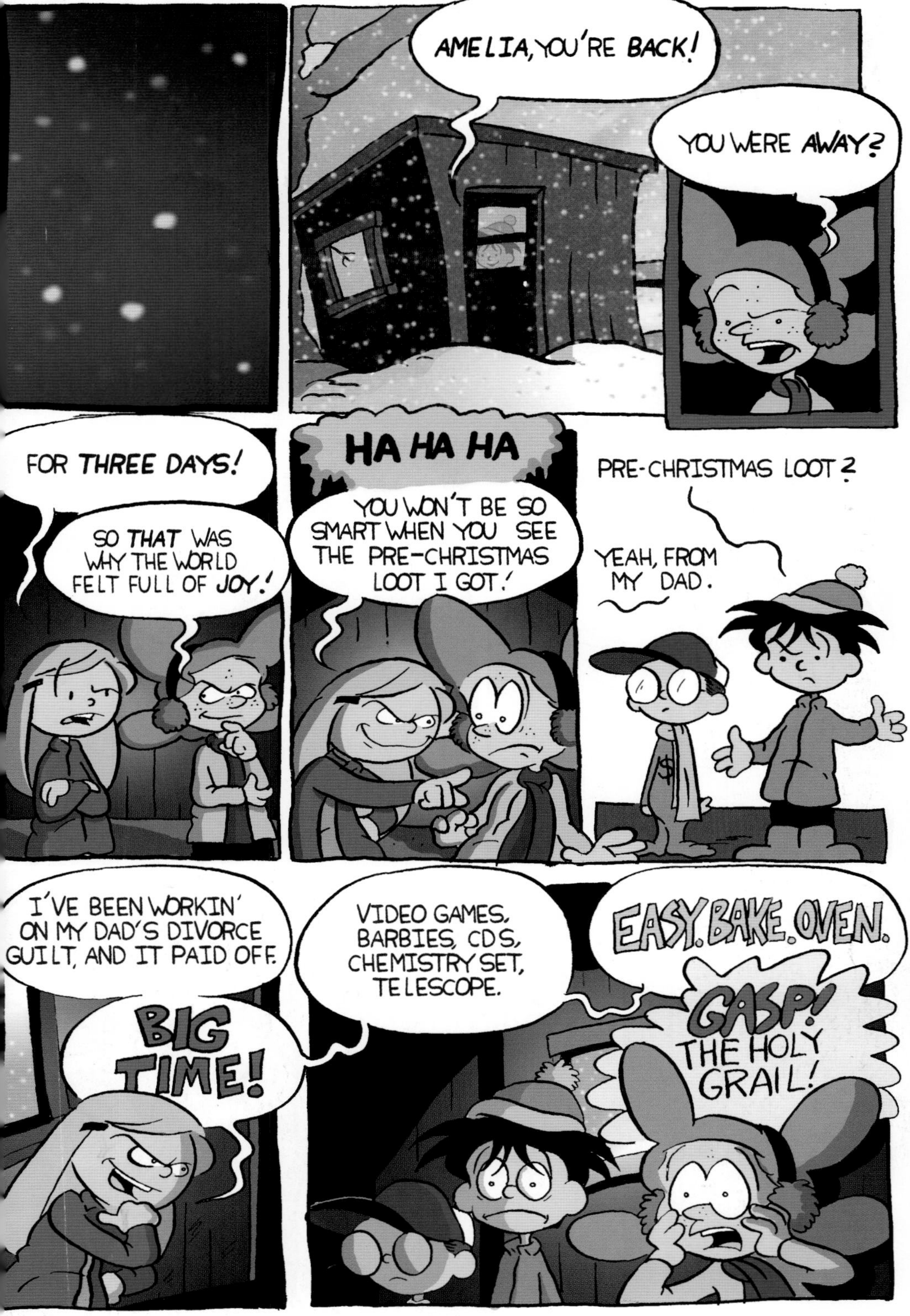
AMELIA, YOU'RE BACK!
YOU WERE AWAY?
FOR THREE DAYS!
SO THAT WAS WHY THE WORLD FELT FULL OF JOY!
HA HA HA
YOU WON'T BE SO SMART WHEN YOU SEE THE PRE-CHRISTMAS LOOT I GOT!
PRE-CHRISTMAS LOOT?
YEAH, FROM MY DAD.
I'VE BEEN WORKIN' ON MY DAD'S DIVORCE GUILT, AND IT PAID OFF.
BIG TIME!
VIDEO GAMES, BARBIES, CDS, CHEMISTRY SET, TELESCOPE.
EASY. BAKE. OVEN.
GASP! THE HOLY GRAIL!

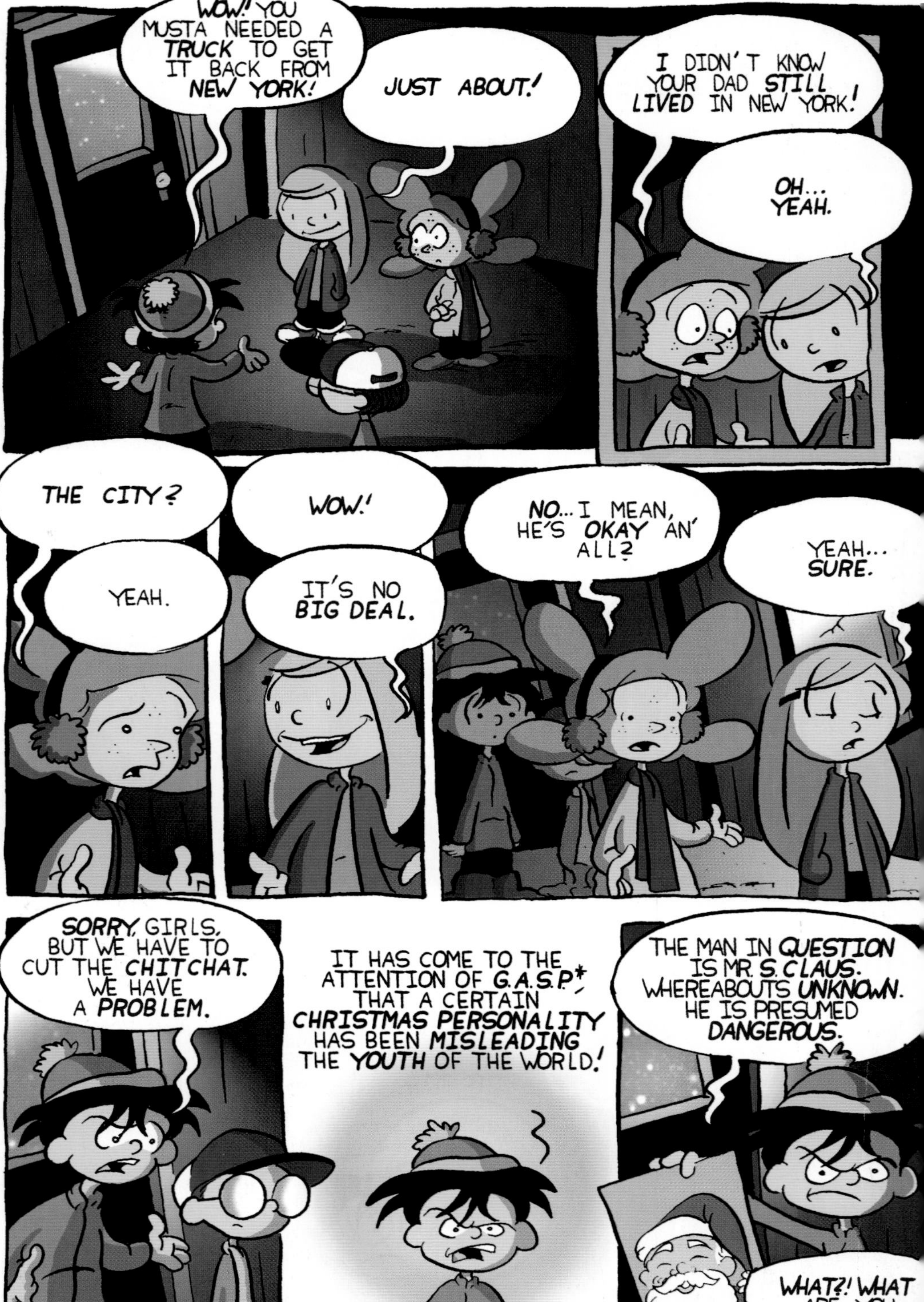
WOW! YOU MUSTA NEEDED A TRUCK TO GET IT BACK FROM NEW YORK!
JUST ABOUT!
I DIDN'T KNOW YOUR DAD STILL LIVED IN NEW YORK!
OH... YEAH.
THE CITY?
YEAH.
WOW!
IT'S NO BIG DEAL.
NO... I MEAN, HE'S OKAY AN' ALL?
YEAH... SURE.
SORRY, GIRLS, BUT WE HAVE TO CUT THE CHITCHAT. WE HAVE A PROBLEM.
IT HAS COME TO THE ATTENTION OF G.A.S.P.* THAT A CERTAIN CHRISTMAS PERSONALITY HAS BEEN MISLEADING THE YOUTH OF THE WORLD!
*GATHERING OF AWESOME SUPER PALS
THE MAN IN QUESTION IS MR. S. CLAUS. WHEREABOUTS UNKNOWN. HE IS PRESUMED DANGEROUS.
WHAT?! WHAT ARE YOU TALKING ABOUT

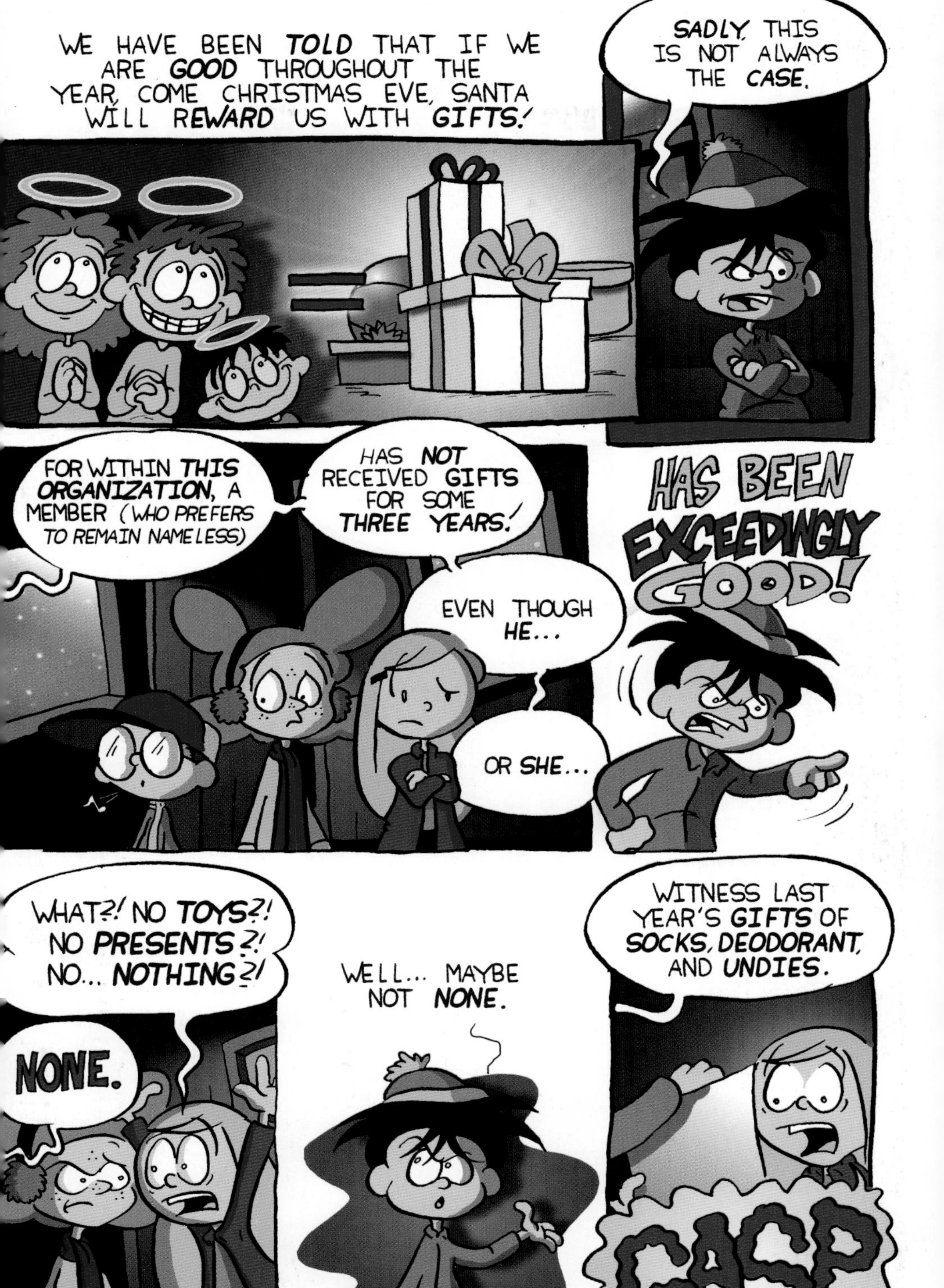
WE HAVE BEEN TOLD THAT IF WE ARE GOOD THROUGHOUT THE YEAR, COME CHRISTMAS EVE, SANTA WILL REWARD US WITH GIFTS!
SADLY, THIS IS NOT ALWAYS THE CASE.
FOR WITHIN THIS ORGANIZATION, A MEMBER (WHO PREFERS TO REMAIN NAMELESS)
HAS NOT RECEIVED GIFTS FOR SOME THREE YEARS!
EVEN THOUGH HE...
OR SHE...
HAS BEEN EXCEEDINGLY GOOD!
WHAT?! NO TOYS?! NO PRESENTS?! NO... NOTHING?!
NONE.
WELL... MAYBE NOT NONE.
WITNESS LAST YEAR'S GIFTS OF SOCKS, DEODORANT, AND UNDIES.
GASP

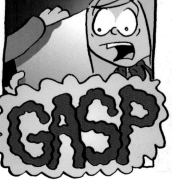

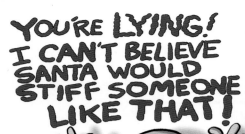

YOU'RE **LYING!** I CAN'T BELIEVE SANTA WOULD STIFF SOMEONE LIKE **THAT!**

I DON'T BELIEVE IN SANTA AT **ALL!** I THINK HE'S A SHILL FOR **SEARS.**

SHHH!

WHAT IF HE **HEARS** YOU?!

ARE YOU **KIDDING?**

THIS IS OUR **MISSION:** TO DISCOVER WHY **SANTA** IS BEING **UNFAIR.**

FURTHER, WHO IS BEHIND HIS **FUNDING?** **DOES** HE EVEN **EXIST?** AND IF **SO,** CAN WE **SUE** HIM?

YOU'RE A **DISTURBED** LITTLE BOY, DO YOU **KNOW** THAT?

I **PRIDE** MYSELF ON IT.

SO WHO'S **IN?** RHONDA? PAJAMAMAN? WHAT ABOUT **YOU,** AMELIA, ARE YOU **WITH** US?

OOOH... I **HATE** PEER PRESSURE!

GREAT.

WATCH OUT, **FAT MAN...**

YOU'RE GOING **DOWN!**

108

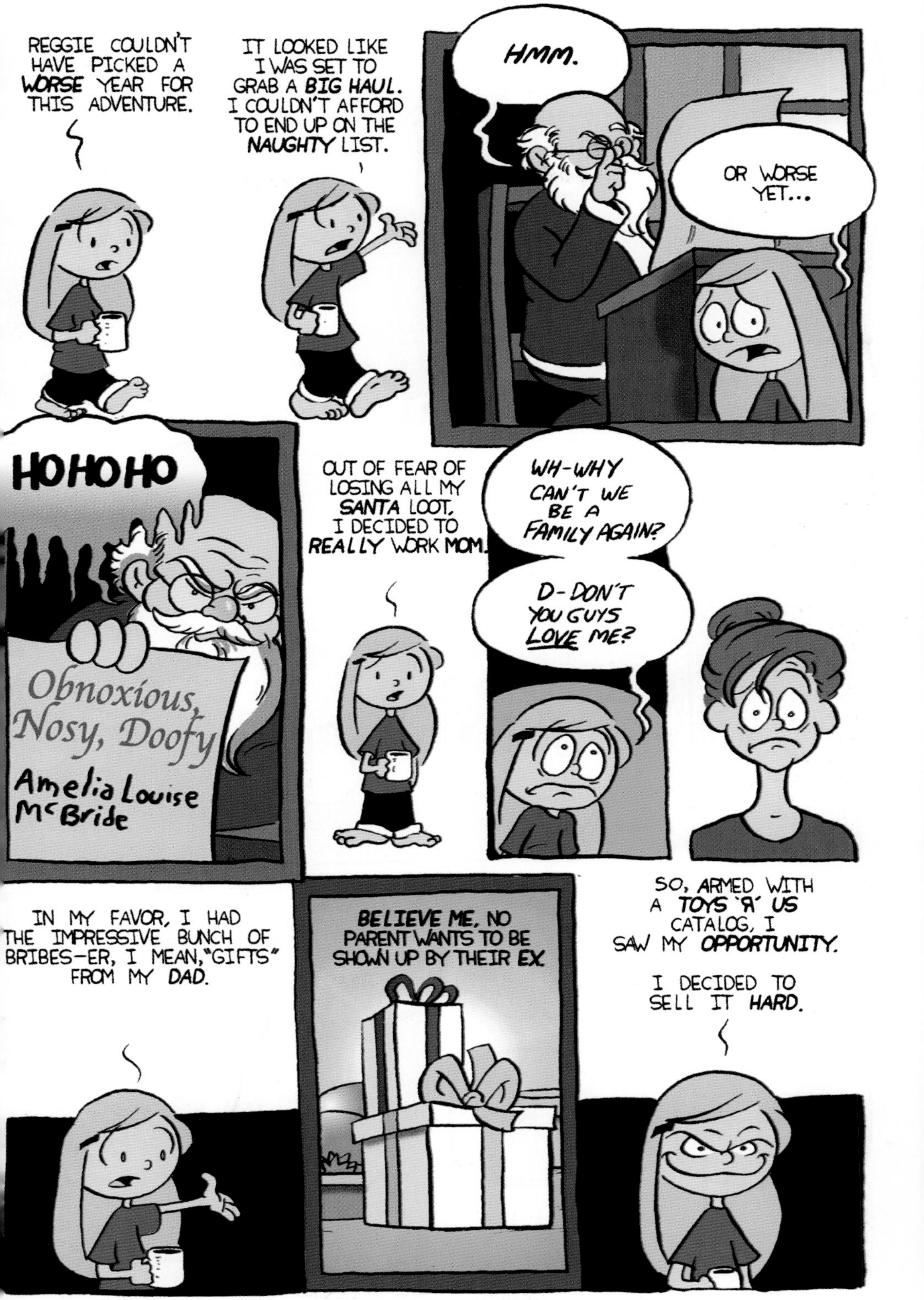
REGGIE COULDN'T HAVE PICKED A WORSE YEAR FOR THIS ADVENTURE.
IT LOOKED LIKE I WAS SET TO GRAB A BIG HAUL. I COULDN'T AFFORD TO END UP ON THE NAUGHTY LIST.
HMM.
OR WORSE YET...
HOHOHO
Obnoxious, Nosy, Doofy
Amelia Louise McBride
OUT OF FEAR OF LOSING ALL MY SANTA LOOT, I DECIDED TO REALLY WORK MOM.
WH-WHY CAN'T WE BE A FAMILY AGAIN?
D-DON'T YOU GUYS LOVE ME?
IN MY FAVOR, I HAD THE IMPRESSIVE BUNCH OF BRIBES—ER, I MEAN, "GIFTS" FROM MY DAD.
BELIEVE ME, NO PARENT WANTS TO BE SHOWN UP BY THEIR EX.
SO, ARMED WITH A TOYS 'R' US CATALOG, I SAW MY OPPORTUNITY.
I DECIDED TO SELL IT HARD.

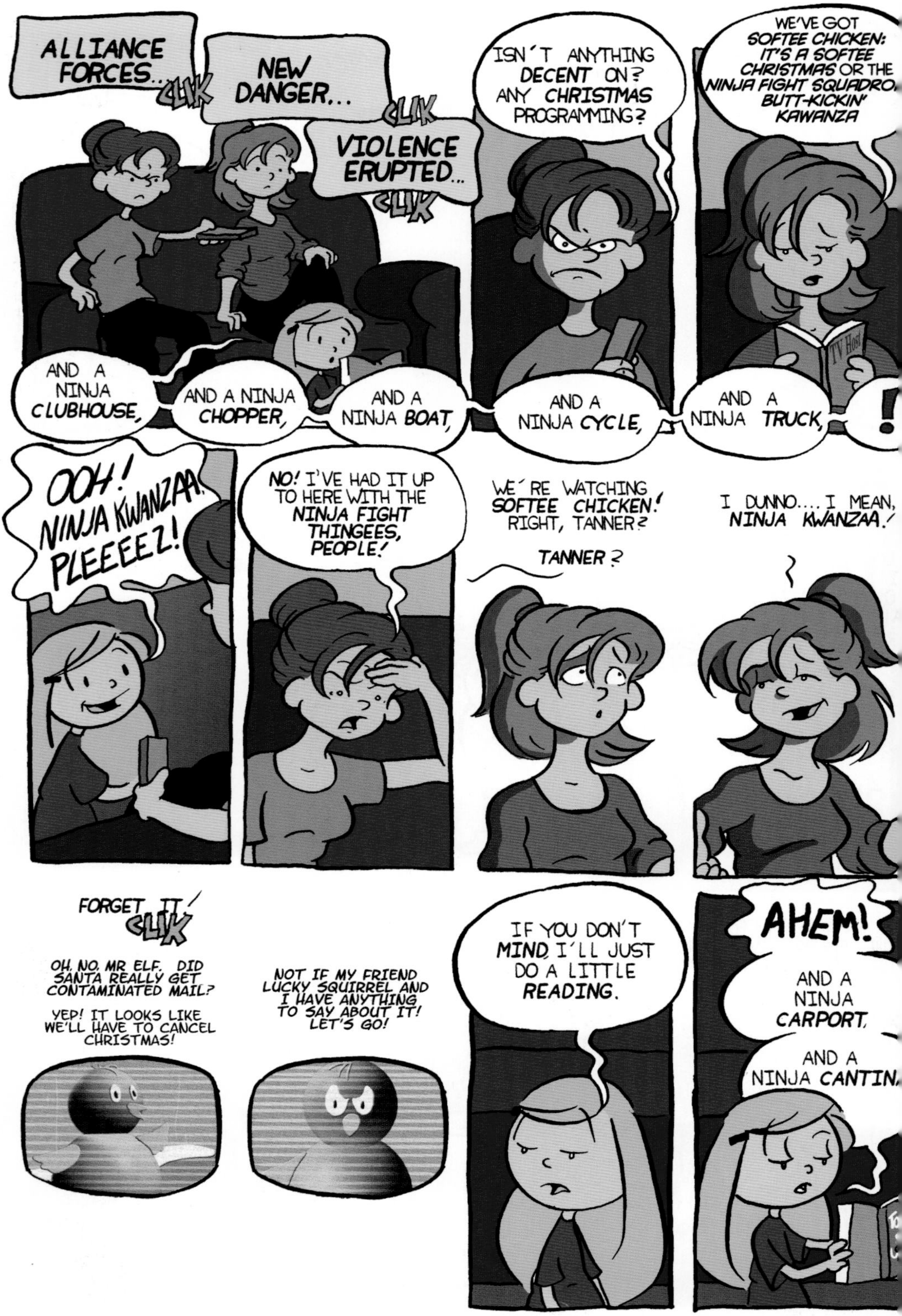
ALLIANCE FORCES...
CLIK
NEW DANGER...
CLIK
VIOLENCE ERUPTED...
CLIK
ISN'T ANYTHING DECENT ON? ANY CHRISTMAS PROGRAMMING?
WE'VE GOT SOFTEE CHICKEN: IT'S A SOFTEE CHRISTMAS OR THE NINJA FIGHT SQUADRO BUTT-KICKIN' KAWANZA
AND A NINJA CLUBHOUSE,
AND A NINJA CHOPPER,
AND A NINJA BOAT,
AND A NINJA CYCLE,
AND A NINJA TRUCK,
!
OOH! NINJA KWANZAA! PLEEEEZ!
NO! I'VE HAD IT UP TO HERE WITH THE NINJA FIGHT THINGEES, PEOPLE!
WE'RE WATCHING SOFTEE CHICKEN! RIGHT, TANNER?
TANNER?
I DUNNO.... I MEAN, NINJA KWANZAA!
FORGET IT!
CLIK
OH, NO, MR ELF. DID SANTA REALLY GET CONTAMINATED MAIL?
YEP! IT LOOKS LIKE WE'LL HAVE TO CANCEL CHRISTMAS!
NOT IF MY FRIEND LUCKY SQUIRREL AND I HAVE ANYTHING TO SAY ABOUT IT! LET'S GO!
IF YOU DON'T MIND, I'LL JUST DO A LITTLE READING.
AHEM!
AND A NINJA CARPORT,
AND A NINJA CANTIN

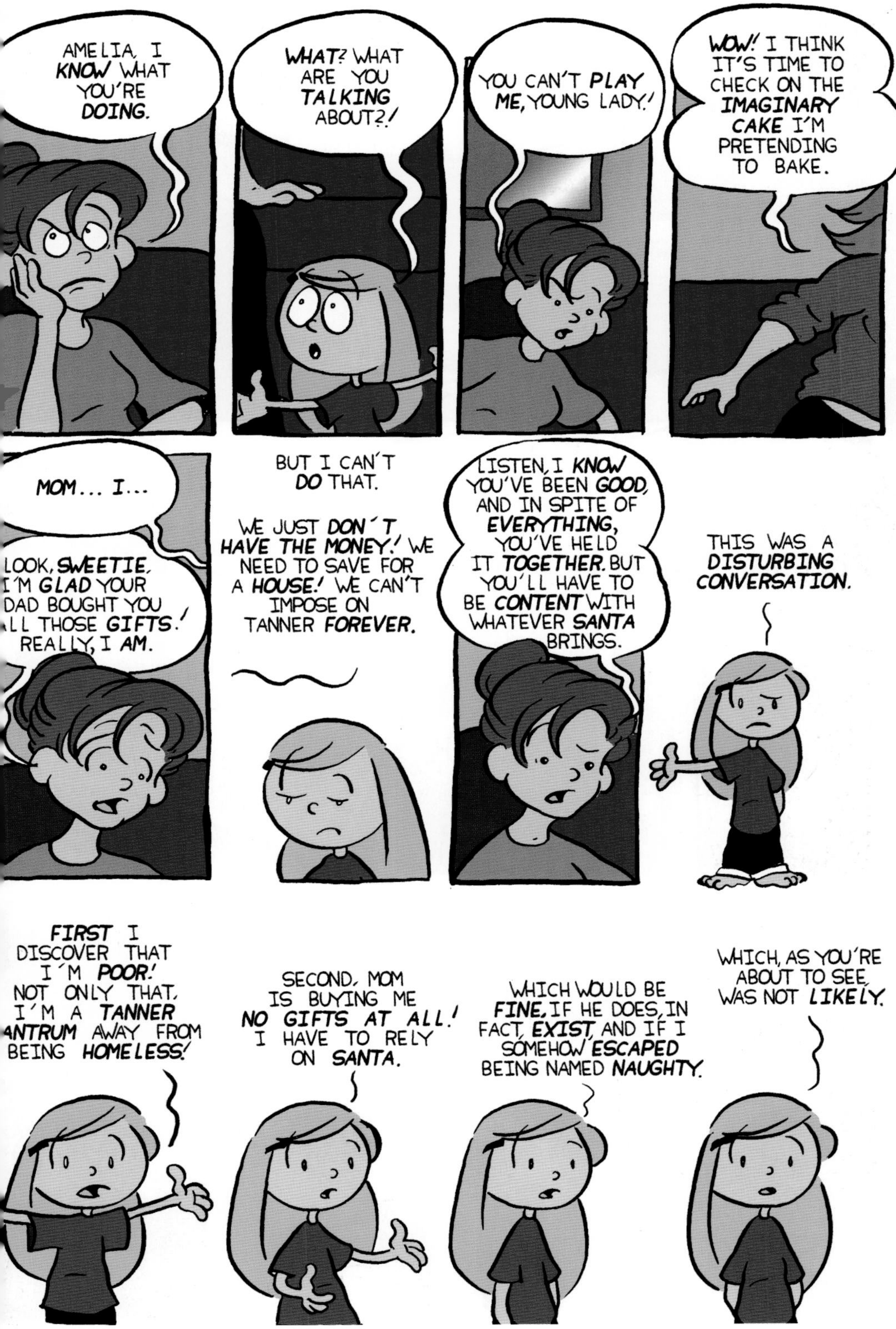
AMELIA, I KNOW WHAT YOU'RE DOING.
WHAT? WHAT ARE YOU TALKING ABOUT?!
YOU CAN'T PLAY ME, YOUNG LADY!
WOW! I THINK IT'S TIME TO CHECK ON THE IMAGINARY CAKE I'M PRETENDING TO BAKE.
MOM... I...
LOOK, SWEETIE, I'M GLAD YOUR DAD BOUGHT YOU ALL THOSE GIFTS! REALLY, I AM.
BUT I CAN'T DO THAT.
WE JUST DON'T HAVE THE MONEY! WE NEED TO SAVE FOR A HOUSE! WE CAN'T IMPOSE ON TANNER FOREVER.
LISTEN, I KNOW YOU'VE BEEN GOOD, AND IN SPITE OF EVERYTHING, YOU'VE HELD IT TOGETHER. BUT YOU'LL HAVE TO BE CONTENT WITH WHATEVER SANTA BRINGS.
THIS WAS A DISTURBING CONVERSATION.
FIRST I DISCOVER THAT I'M POOR! NOT ONLY THAT, I'M A TANNER TANTRUM AWAY FROM BEING HOMELESS!
SECOND, MOM IS BUYING ME NO GIFTS AT ALL! I HAVE TO RELY ON SANTA.
WHICH WOULD BE FINE, IF HE DOES, IN FACT, EXIST, AND IF I SOMEHOW ESCAPED BEING NAMED NAUGHTY.
WHICH, AS YOU'RE ABOUT TO SEE, WAS NOT LIKELY.

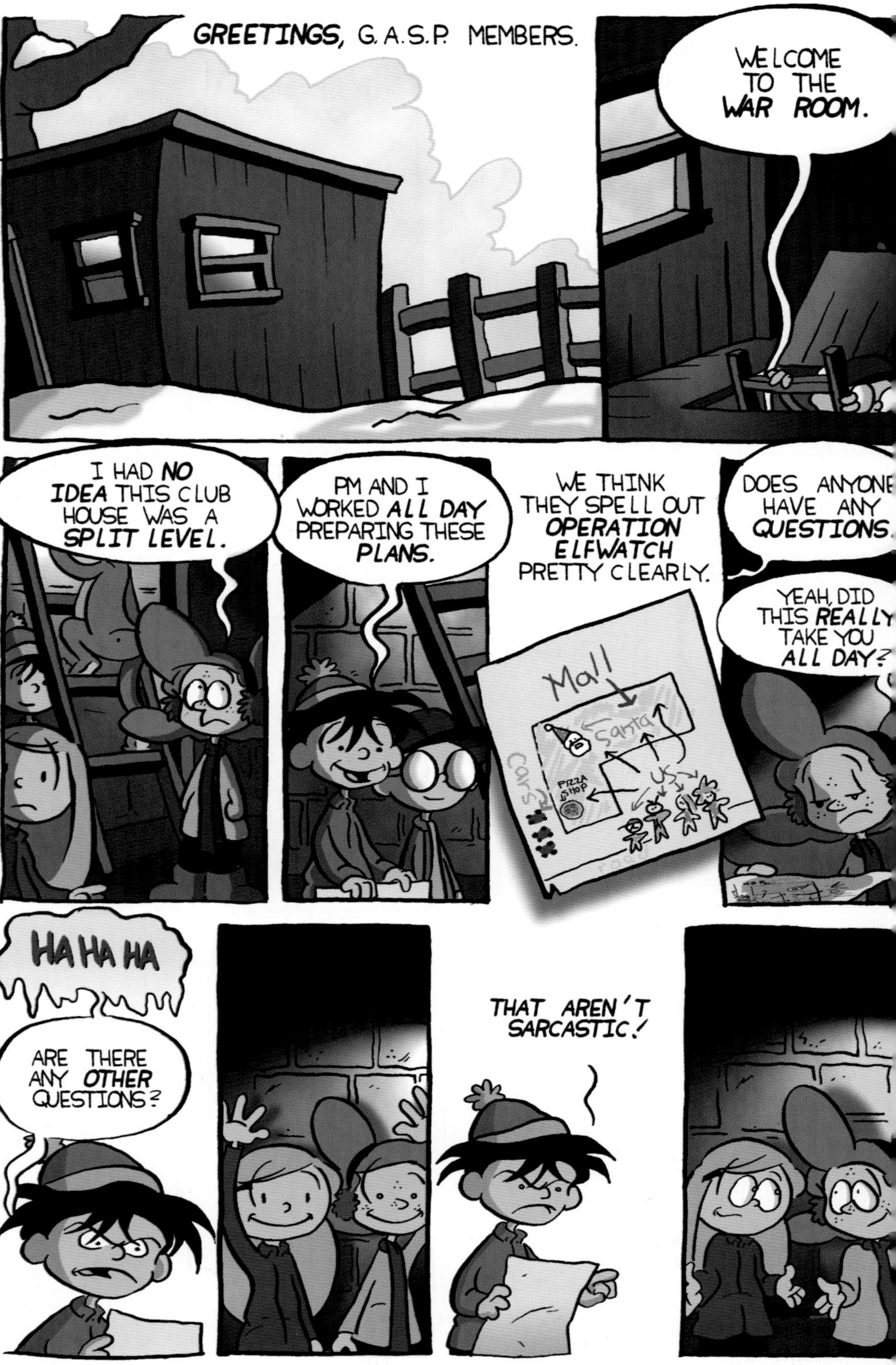
GREETINGS, G.A.S.P. MEMBERS.
WELCOME TO THE WAR ROOM.
I HAD NO IDEA THIS CLUB HOUSE WAS A SPLIT LEVEL.
PM AND I WORKED ALL DAY PREPARING THESE PLANS.
WE THINK THEY SPELL OUT OPERATION ELFWATCH PRETTY CLEARLY.
Mall
Santa
Cars
PIZZA SHOP
US
DOES ANYONE HAVE ANY QUESTIONS.
YEAH, DID THIS REALLY TAKE YOU ALL DAY?
HA HA HA
ARE THERE ANY OTHER QUESTIONS?
THAT AREN'T SARCASTIC!

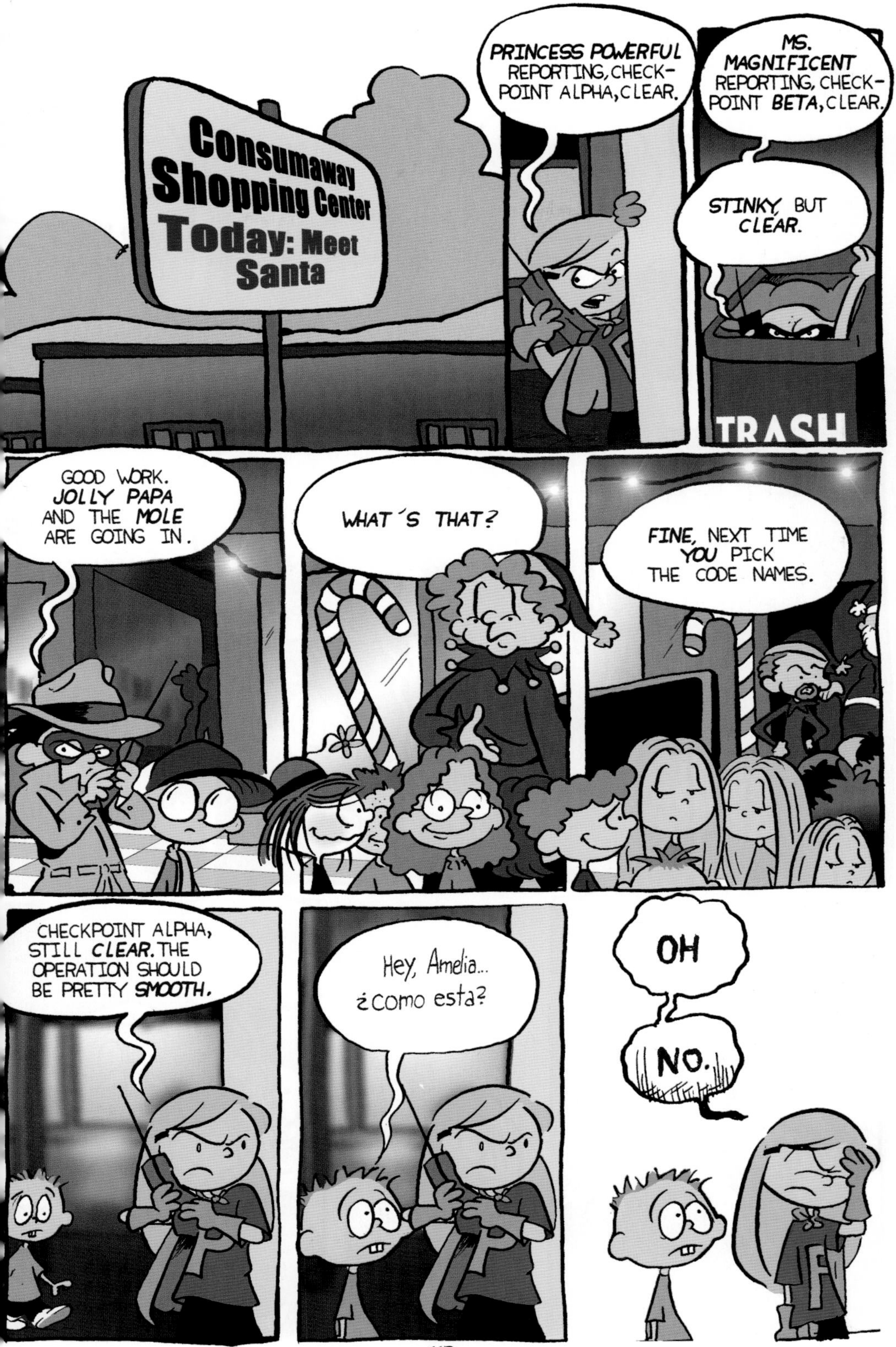
Consumaway Shopping Center Today: Meet Santa
PRINCESS POWERFUL REPORTING, CHECKPOINT ALPHA, CLEAR.
MS. MAGNIFICENT REPORTING, CHECKPOINT BETA, CLEAR.
STINKY, BUT CLEAR.
TRASH
GOOD WORK. JOLLY PAPA AND THE MOLE ARE GOING IN.
WHAT'S THAT?
FINE, NEXT TIME YOU PICK THE CODE NAMES.
CHECKPOINT ALPHA, STILL CLEAR. THE OPERATION SHOULD BE PRETTY SMOOTH.
Hey, Amelia... ¿como esta?
OH
NO.

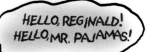

HELLO, REGINALD! HELLO, MR. PAJAMAS!

HELLO, MARY VIOLET.

Are you boys here to see santa?

UMMM... SORTA.

me, too, I have a very IMPORTANT question for him

HO HO HO HELLO, LITTLE GIRL. WHAT CAN SANTA DO FOR YOU?

I just have a QUESTION.

Why do you allow so much PAIN and SUFFERING to happen to PEOPLE who are GOOD and DECENT and PURE of HEART?

OH, I'M SORRY, DEAR.. I...I'M ONLY SANTA CLAUS. I...I'M NOT GO

I SEE....

What mall is HE at?

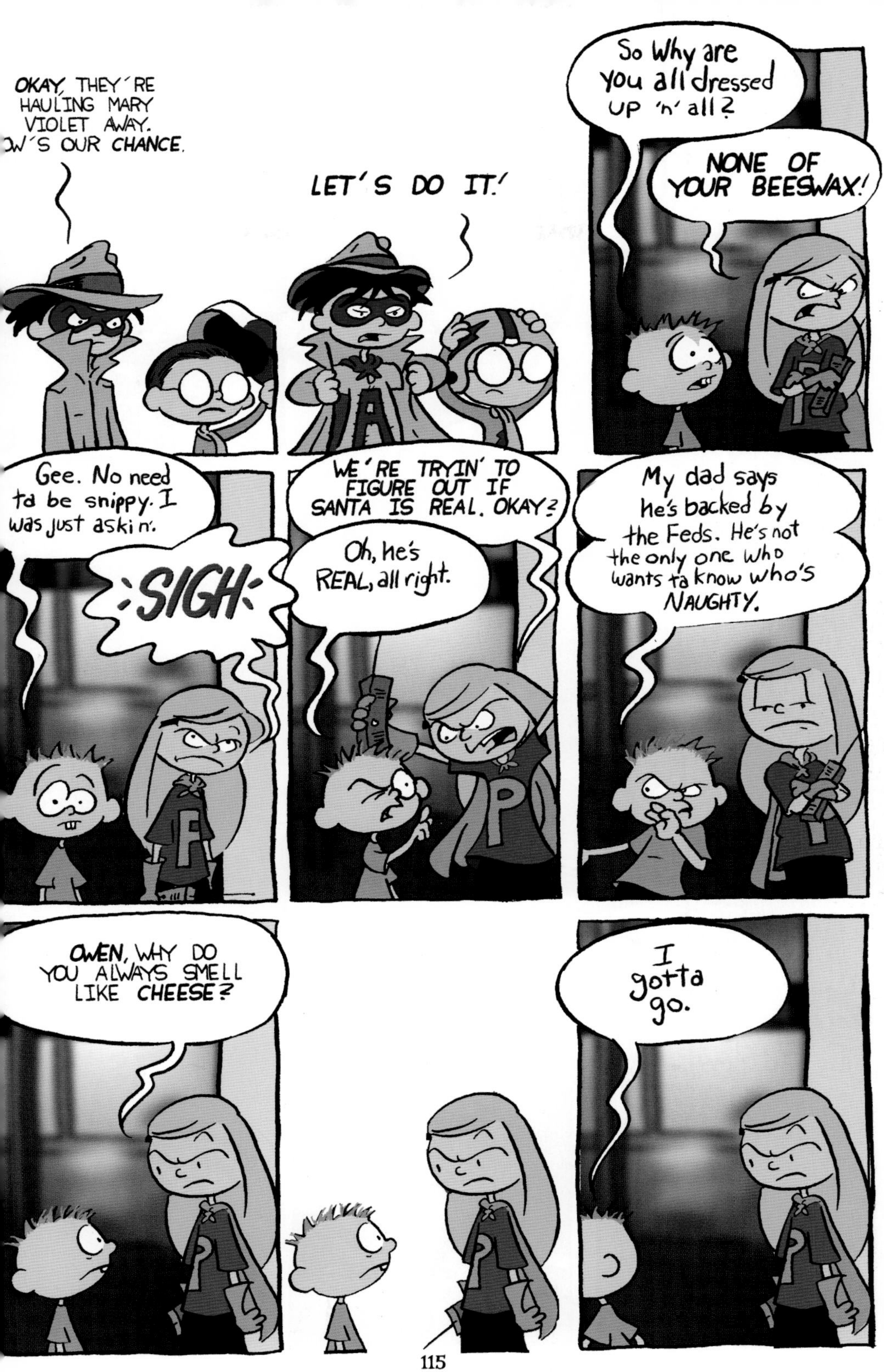

OKAY, THEY'RE HAULING MARY VIOLET AWAY. ...W'S OUR CHANCE.
LET'S DO IT!
So why are you all dressed up 'n' all?
NONE OF YOUR BEESWAX!
Gee. No need ta be snippy. I was just askin'.
SIGH
WE'RE TRYIN' TO FIGURE OUT IF SANTA IS REAL. OKAY?
Oh, he's REAL, all right.
My dad says he's backed by the Feds. He's not the only one who wants ta know who's NAUGHTY.
OWEN, WHY DO YOU ALWAYS SMELL LIKE CHEESE?
I gotta go.

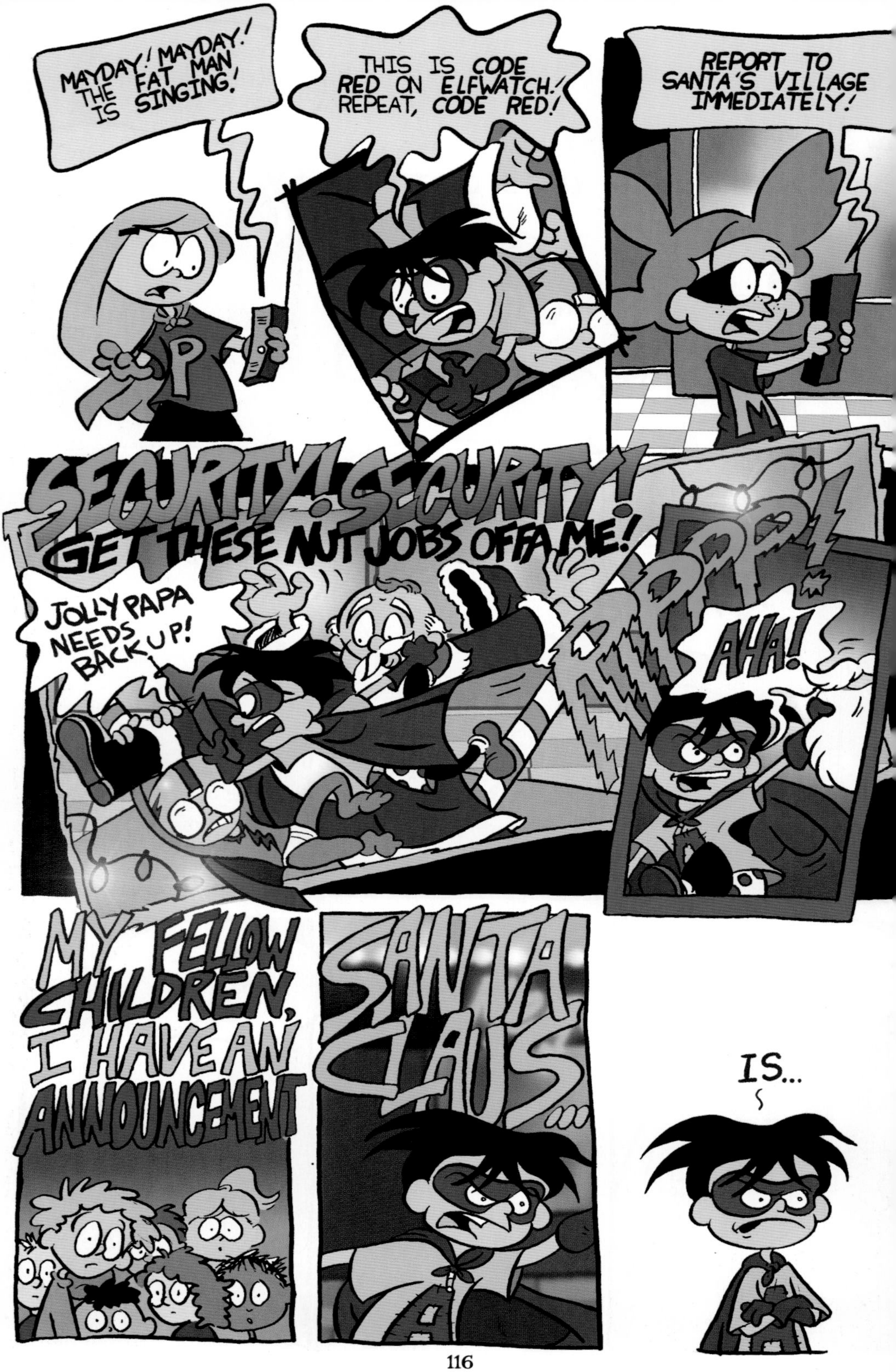
MAYDAY! MAYDAY! THE FAT MAN IS SINGING!
THIS IS CODE RED ON ELFWATCH! REPEAT, CODE RED!
REPORT TO SANTA'S VILLAGE IMMEDIATELY!
SECURITY! SECURITY! GET THESE NUT JOBS OFFA ME!
JOLLY PAPA NEEDS BACKUP!
RIPPP!
AHA!
MY FELLOW CHILDREN, I HAVE AN ANNOUNCEMENT
SANTA CLAUS...
IS...

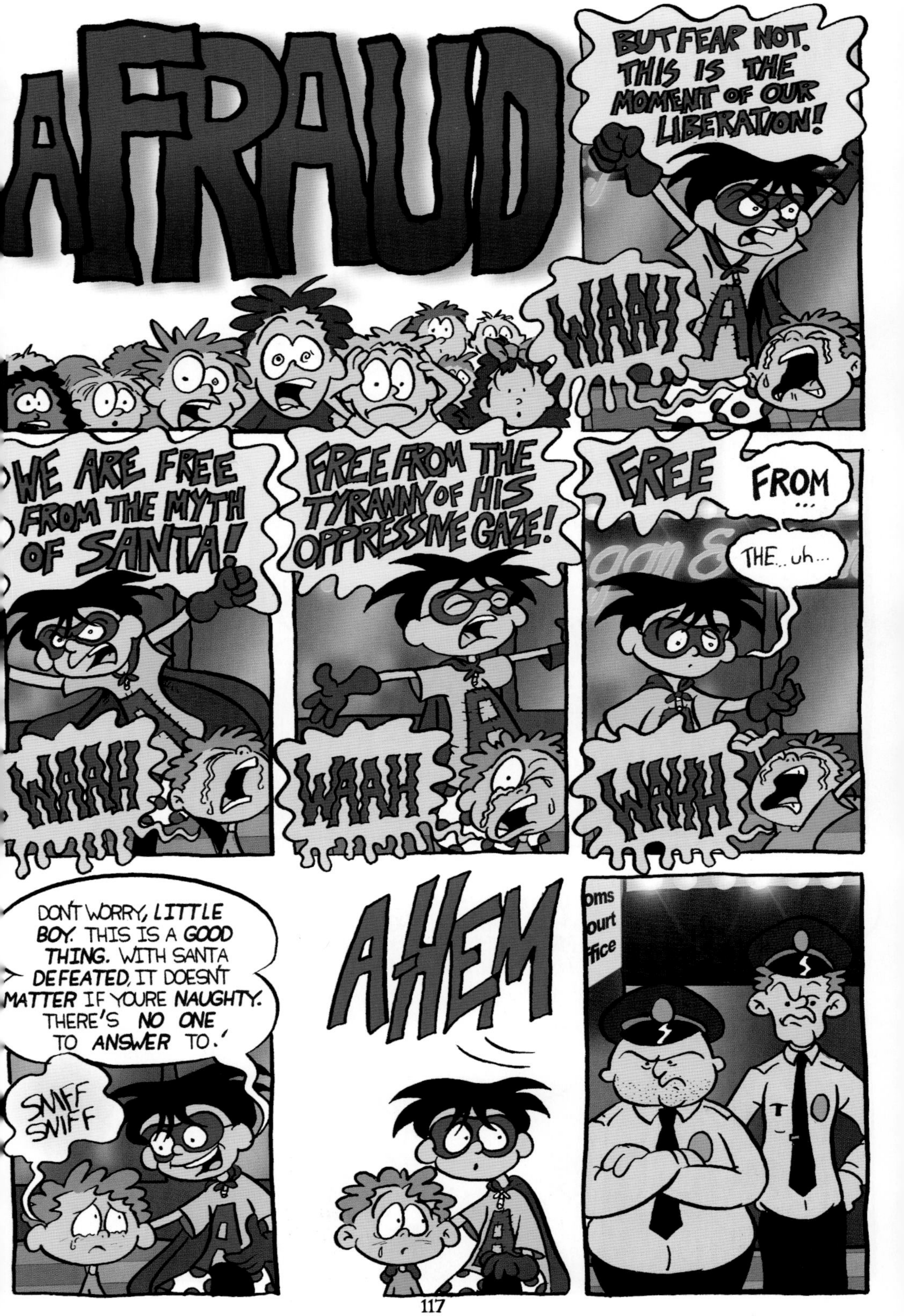
A FRAUD
BUT FEAR NOT. THIS IS THE MOMENT OF OUR LIBERATION!
WAAH
WE ARE FREE FROM THE MYTH OF SANTA!
WAAH
FREE FROM THE TYRANNY OF HIS OPPRESSIVE GAZE!
WAAH
FREE
FROM...
THE... uh...
WAHH
DON'T WORRY, LITTLE BOY. THIS IS A GOOD THING. WITH SANTA DEFEATED, IT DOESN'T MATTER IF YOU'RE NAUGHTY. THERE'S NO ONE TO ANSWER TO.
SNIFF SNIFF
AHEM

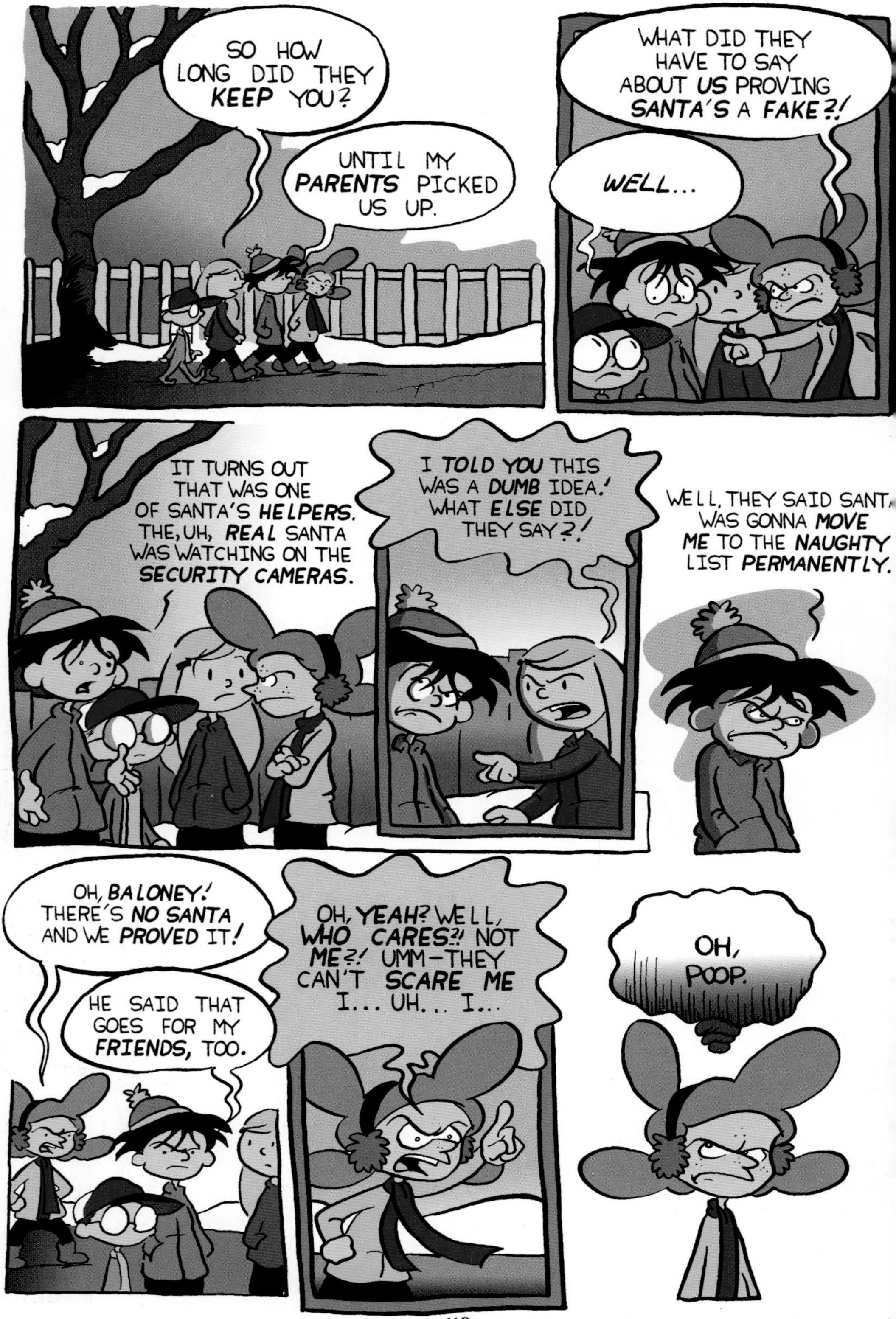
SO HOW LONG DID THEY KEEP YOU?
UNTIL MY PARENTS PICKED US UP.
WHAT DID THEY HAVE TO SAY ABOUT US PROVING SANTA'S A FAKE?!
WELL...
IT TURNS OUT THAT WAS ONE OF SANTA'S HELPERS. THE, UH, REAL SANTA WAS WATCHING ON THE SECURITY CAMERAS.
I TOLD YOU THIS WAS A DUMB IDEA! WHAT ELSE DID THEY SAY?!
WELL, THEY SAID SANTA WAS GONNA MOVE ME TO THE NAUGHTY LIST PERMANENTLY.
OH, BALONEY! THERE'S NO SANTA AND WE PROVED IT!
HE SAID THAT GOES FOR MY FRIENDS, TOO.
OH, YEAH? WELL, WHO CARES?! NOT ME?! UMM—THEY CAN'T SCARE ME I... UH... I...
OH, POOP.

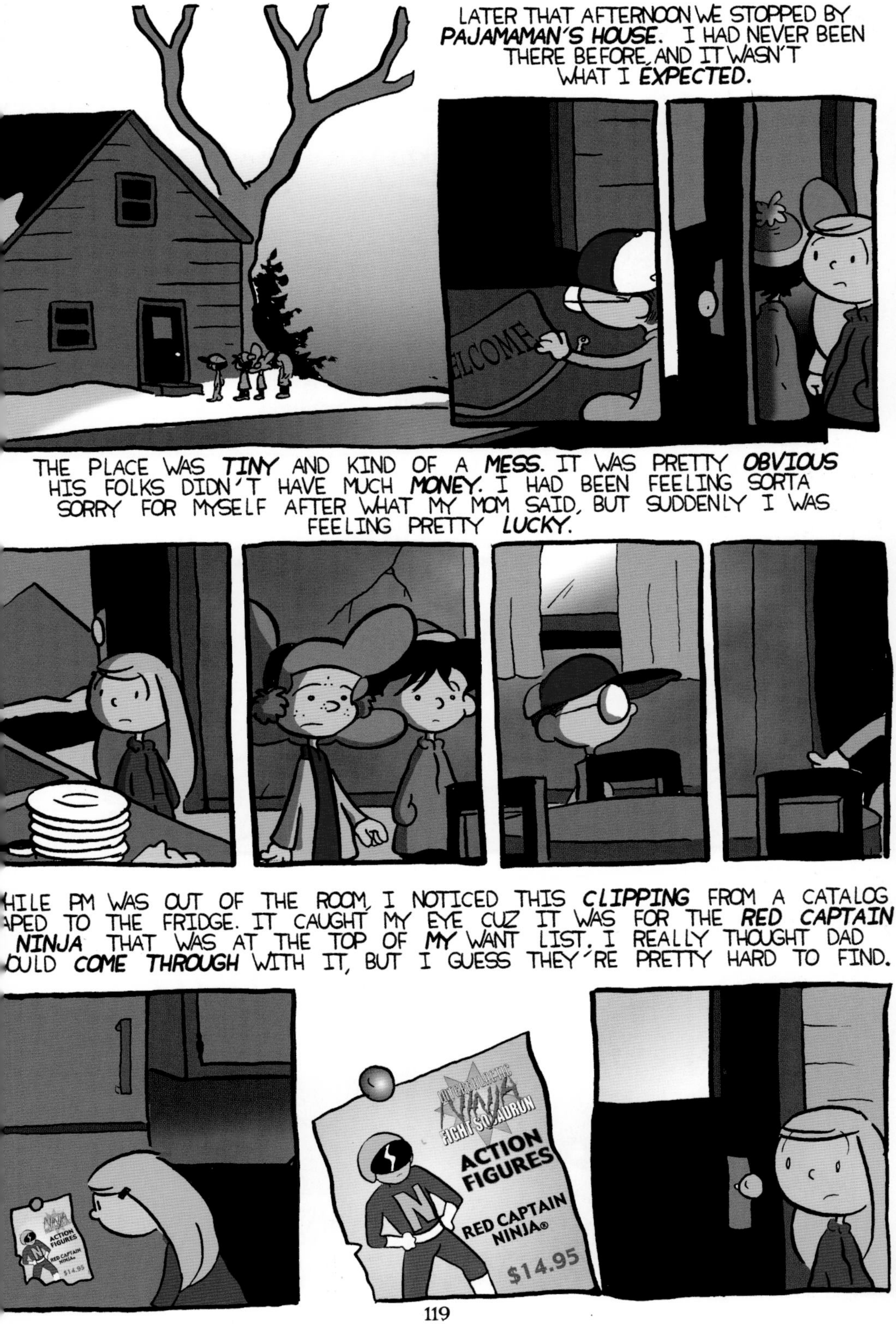
LATER THAT AFTERNOON WE STOPPED BY **PAJAMAMAN'S HOUSE**. I HAD NEVER BEEN THERE BEFORE, AND IT WASN'T WHAT I **EXPECTED**.
LCOME
THE PLACE WAS **TINY** AND KIND OF A **MESS**. IT WAS PRETTY **OBVIOUS** HIS FOLKS DIDN'T HAVE MUCH **MONEY**. I HAD BEEN FEELING SORTA SORRY FOR MYSELF AFTER WHAT MY MOM SAID, BUT SUDDENLY I WAS FEELING PRETTY **LUCKY**.
HILE PM WAS OUT OF THE ROOM, I NOTICED THIS **CLIPPING** FROM A CATALOG APED TO THE FRIDGE. IT CAUGHT MY EYE CUZ IT WAS FOR THE **RED CAPTAIN NINJA** THAT WAS AT THE TOP OF **MY** WANT LIST. I REALLY THOUGHT DAD OULD **COME THROUGH** WITH IT, BUT I GUESS THEY'RE PRETTY HARD TO FIND.
INTERGALACTIC
NINJA
FIGHT SQUADRON
ACTION FIGURES
RED CAPTAIN NINJA®
$14.95

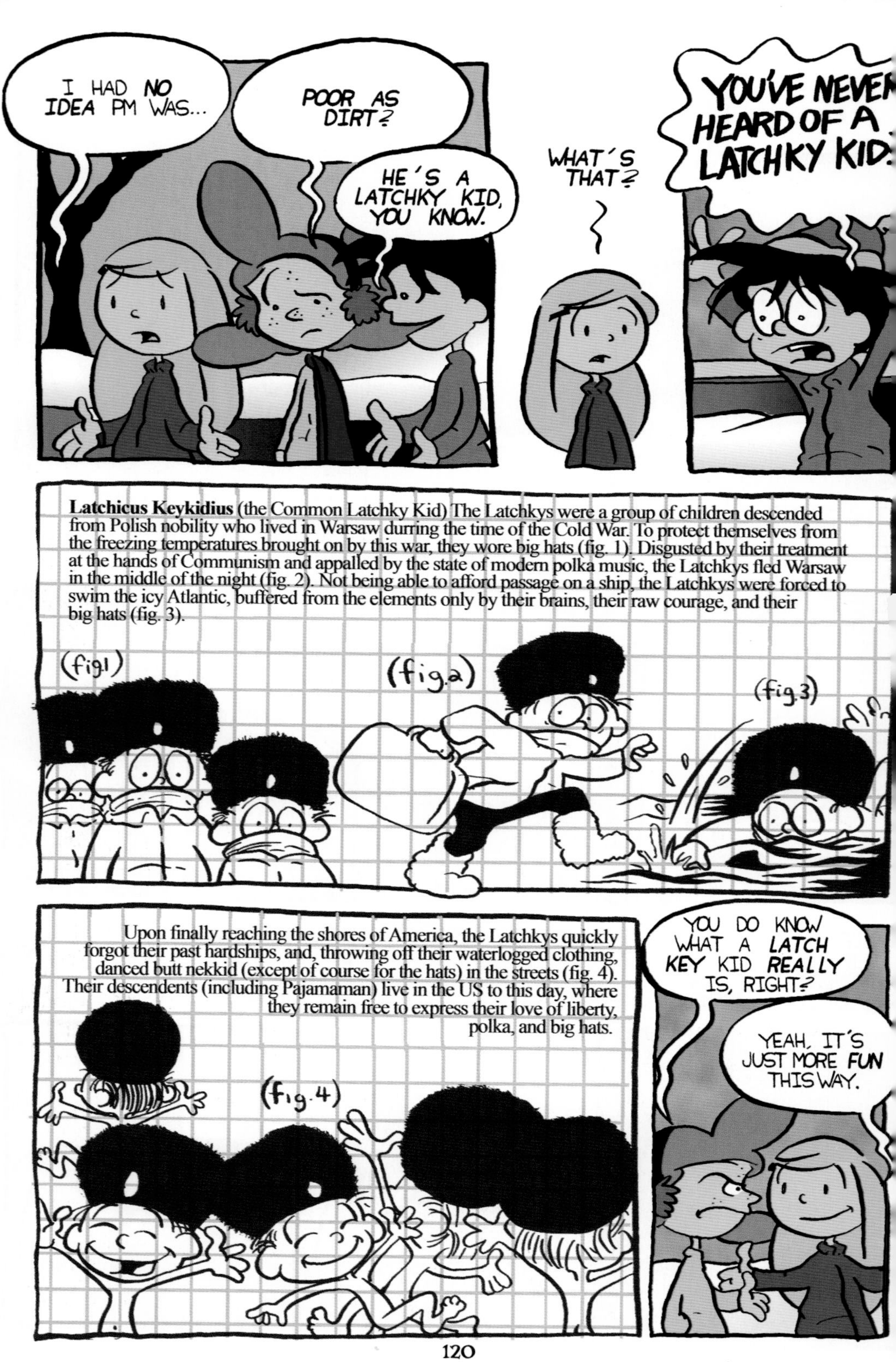
I HAD NO IDEA PM WAS...
POOR AS DIRT?
HE'S A LATCHKY KID, YOU KNOW.
WHAT'S THAT?
YOU'VE NEVER HEARD OF A LATCHKY KID?
Latchicus Keykidius (the Common Latchky Kid) The Latchkys were a group of children descended from Polish nobility who lived in Warsaw durring the time of the Cold War. To protect themselves from the freezing temperatures brought on by this war, they wore big hats (fig. 1). Disgusted by their treatment at the hands of Communism and appalled by the state of modern polka music, the Latchkys fled Warsaw in the middle of the night (fig. 2). Not being able to afford passage on a ship, the Latchkys were forced to swim the icy Atlantic, buffered from the elements only by their brains, their raw courage, and their big hats (fig. 3).
(fig.1)
(fig.2)
(fig.3)
Upon finally reaching the shores of America, the Latchkys quickly forgot their past hardships, and, throwing off their waterlogged clothing, danced butt nekkid (except of course for the hats) in the streets (fig. 4). Their descendents (including Pajamaman) live in the US to this day, where they remain free to express their love of liberty, polka, and big hats.
(fig.4)
YOU DO KNOW WHAT A LATCH KEY KID REALLY IS, RIGHT?
YEAH, IT'S JUST MORE FUN THIS WAY.

THINGS WENT ON AS USUAL, AND CHRISTMAS KEPT GETTING *CLOSER.*

BUT NO MATTER *WHAT,* I COULDN'T STOP THINKING ABOUT *PAJAMAMAN'S HOUSE* AND THAT STUPID CLIPPING.

I ASKED *REGGIE* ABOUT IT, AND HE ID PM WAS PROBABLY *HINTING* THAT HE WANTED IT FOR *CHRISTMAS*...

BUT THERE WAS NO CHANCE HE WOULD GET IT.

ULTIMATE ULTIMATE
NINJA
FIGHT SQUADRON

ACTION
FIGURES

RED CAPTAIN
NINJA®

$14.9

IT WAS WEIRD.

I WAS JUST USED TO THESE GUYS BEING MY FRIENDS. I NEVER THOUGHT ABOUT WHO WAS RICH OR POOR.

AND EVEN THOUGH I FELT *BAD* FOR PM, I STILL *REALLY WANTED* A MOUNTAIN OF PRESENTS FOR *ME.* WHICH PROBABLY PUT ME AT THE TOP OF A *NEW LIST*....

Whiny Self-Centered Jerks
AMELIA LOUISE McBRIDE
CELINE DION
P. DIDDY

ADD TO THIS THE NAGGING QUESTION OF WHY SANTA WOULD IGNORE SOMEONE LIKE PAJAMAMAN, AND THERE WAS ONLY ONE THING I COULD DO....

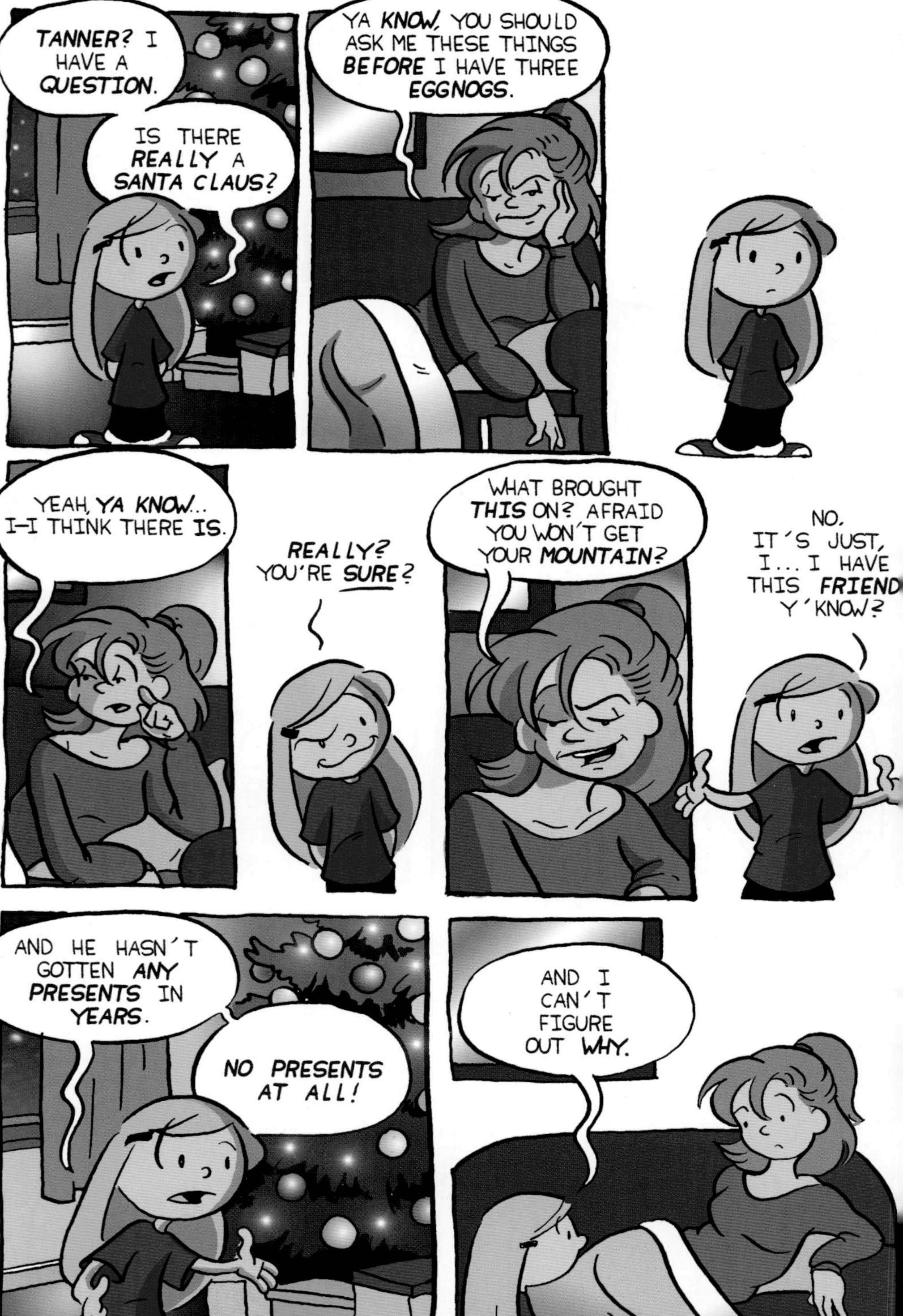
TANNER? I HAVE A QUESTION.
IS THERE REALLY A SANTA CLAUS?
YA KNOW, YOU SHOULD ASK ME THESE THINGS BEFORE I HAVE THREE EGGNOGS.
YEAH, YA KNOW... I-I THINK THERE IS.
REALLY? YOU'RE SURE?
WHAT BROUGHT THIS ON? AFRAID YOU WON'T GET YOUR MOUNTAIN?
NO. IT'S JUST, I... I HAVE THIS FRIEND Y'KNOW?
AND HE HASN'T GOTTEN ANY PRESENTS IN YEARS.
NO PRESENTS AT ALL!
AND I CAN'T FIGURE OUT WHY.

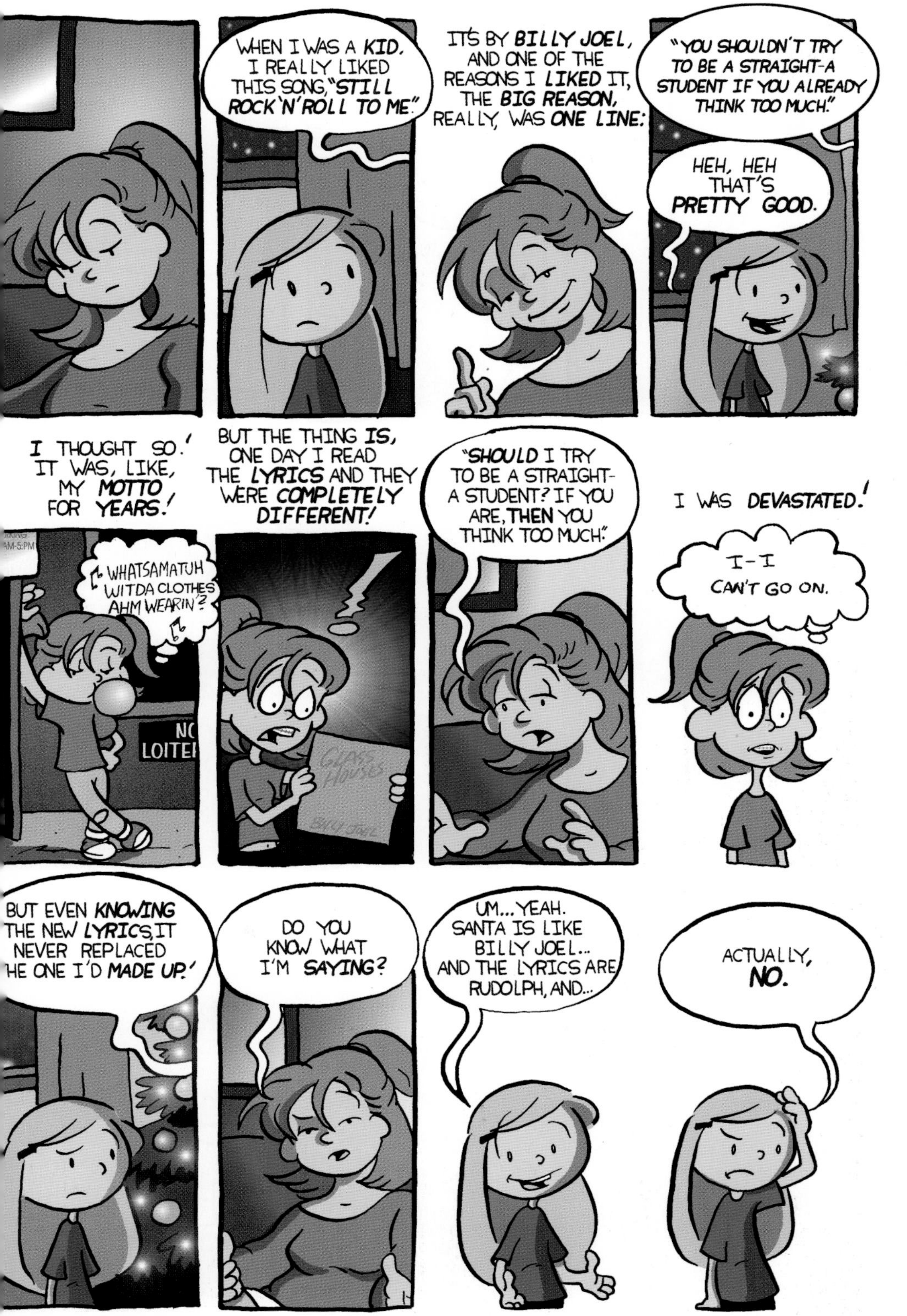

WHEN I WAS A KID, I REALLY LIKED THIS SONG, "STILL ROCK 'N' ROLL TO ME."
IT'S BY BILLY JOEL, AND ONE OF THE REASONS I LIKED IT, THE BIG REASON, REALLY, WAS ONE LINE:
"YOU SHOULDN'T TRY TO BE A STRAIGHT-A STUDENT IF YOU ALREADY THINK TOO MUCH."
HEH, HEH THAT'S PRETTY GOOD.
I THOUGHT SO! IT WAS, LIKE, MY MOTTO FOR YEARS!
WHATSAMATUH WITDA CLOTHES AHM WEARIN'?
NO LOITER
BUT THE THING IS, ONE DAY I READ THE LYRICS AND THEY WERE COMPLETELY DIFFERENT!
GLASS HOUSES
BILLY JOEL
"SHOULD I TRY TO BE A STRAIGHT-A STUDENT? IF YOU ARE, THEN YOU THINK TOO MUCH."
I WAS DEVASTATED!
I-I CAN'T GO ON.
BUT EVEN KNOWING THE NEW LYRICS, IT NEVER REPLACED HE ONE I'D MADE UP!
DO YOU KNOW WHAT I'M SAYING?
UM... YEAH. SANTA IS LIKE BILLY JOEL... AND THE LYRICS ARE RUDOLPH, AND...
ACTUALLY, NO.

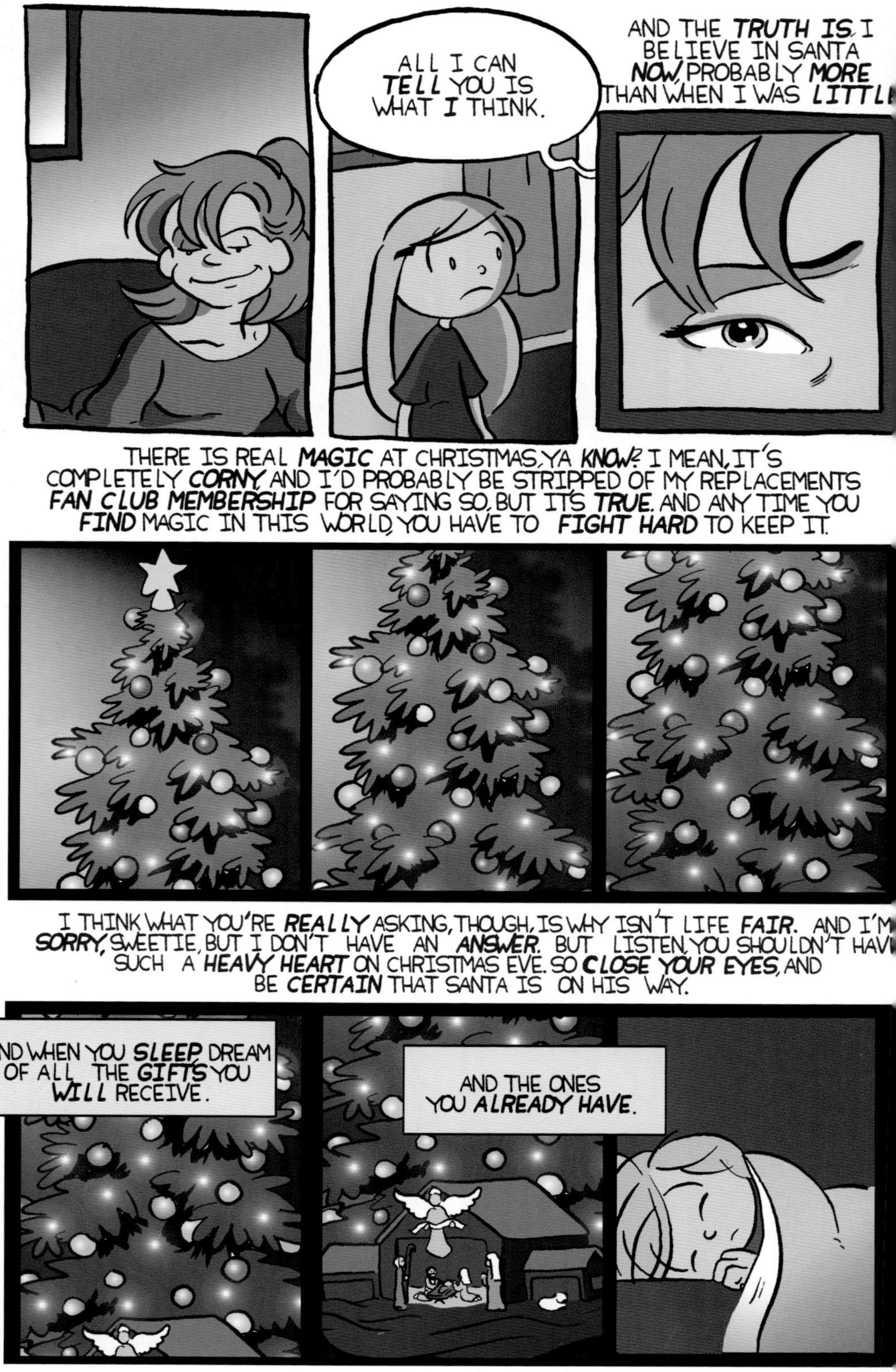
ALL I CAN TELL YOU IS WHAT I THINK.
AND THE TRUTH IS, I BELIEVE IN SANTA NOW, PROBABLY MORE THAN WHEN I WAS LITTL
THERE IS REAL MAGIC AT CHRISTMAS, YA KNOW? I MEAN, IT'S COMPLETELY CORNY, AND I'D PROBABLY BE STRIPPED OF MY REPLACEMENTS FAN CLUB MEMBERSHIP FOR SAYING SO, BUT IT'S TRUE. AND ANY TIME YOU FIND MAGIC IN THIS WORLD, YOU HAVE TO FIGHT HARD TO KEEP IT.
I THINK WHAT YOU'RE REALLY ASKING, THOUGH, IS WHY ISN'T LIFE FAIR. AND I'M SORRY, SWEETIE, BUT I DON'T HAVE AN ANSWER. BUT LISTEN, YOU SHOULDN'T HAV SUCH A HEAVY HEART ON CHRISTMAS EVE. SO CLOSE YOUR EYES, AND BE CERTAIN THAT SANTA IS ON HIS WAY.
AND WHEN YOU SLEEP, DREAM OF ALL THE GIFTS YOU WILL RECEIVE.
AND THE ONES YOU ALREADY HAVE.

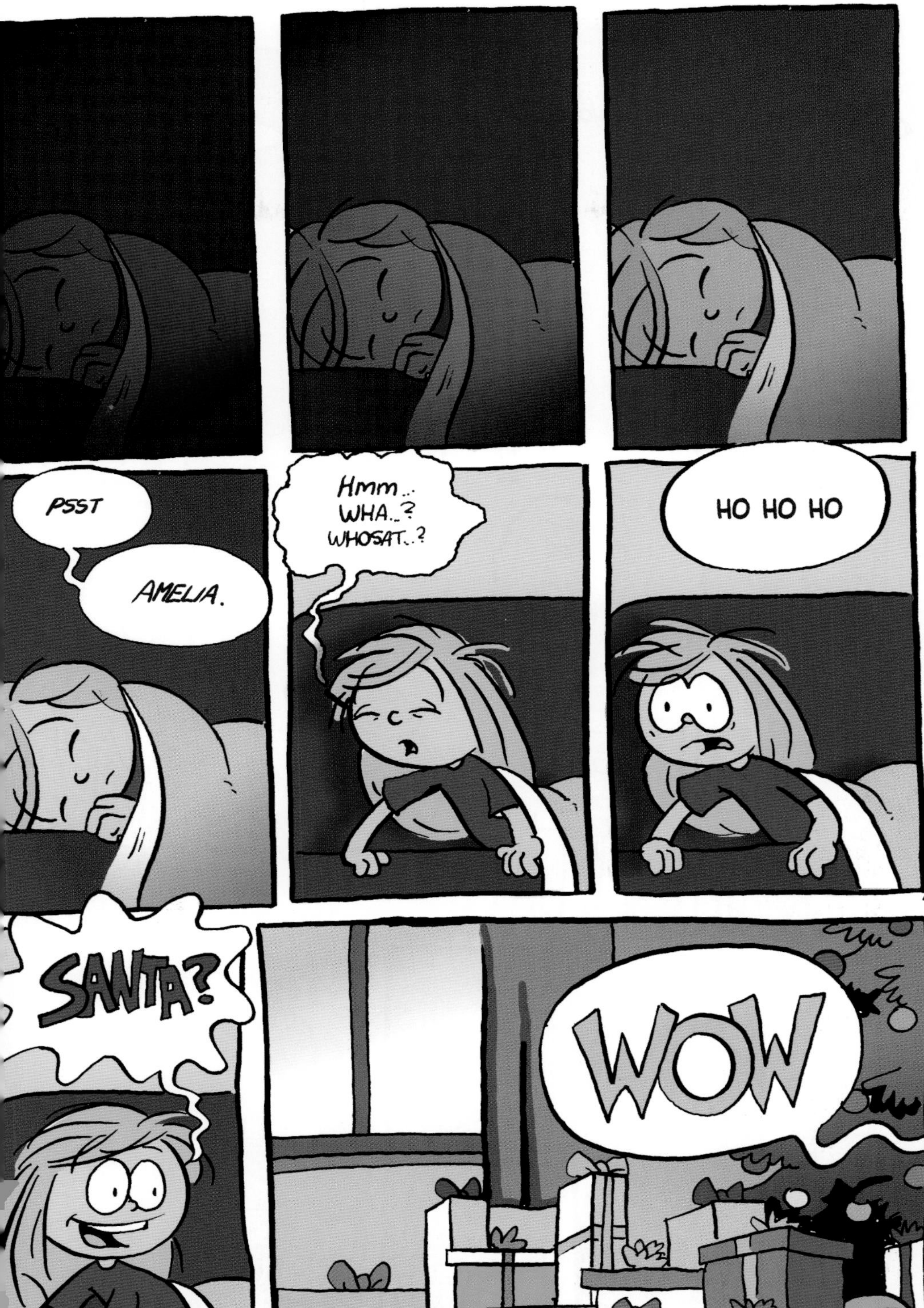
PSST
AMELIA.
Hmm... WHA..? WHOSAT..?
HO HO HO
SANTA?
WOW

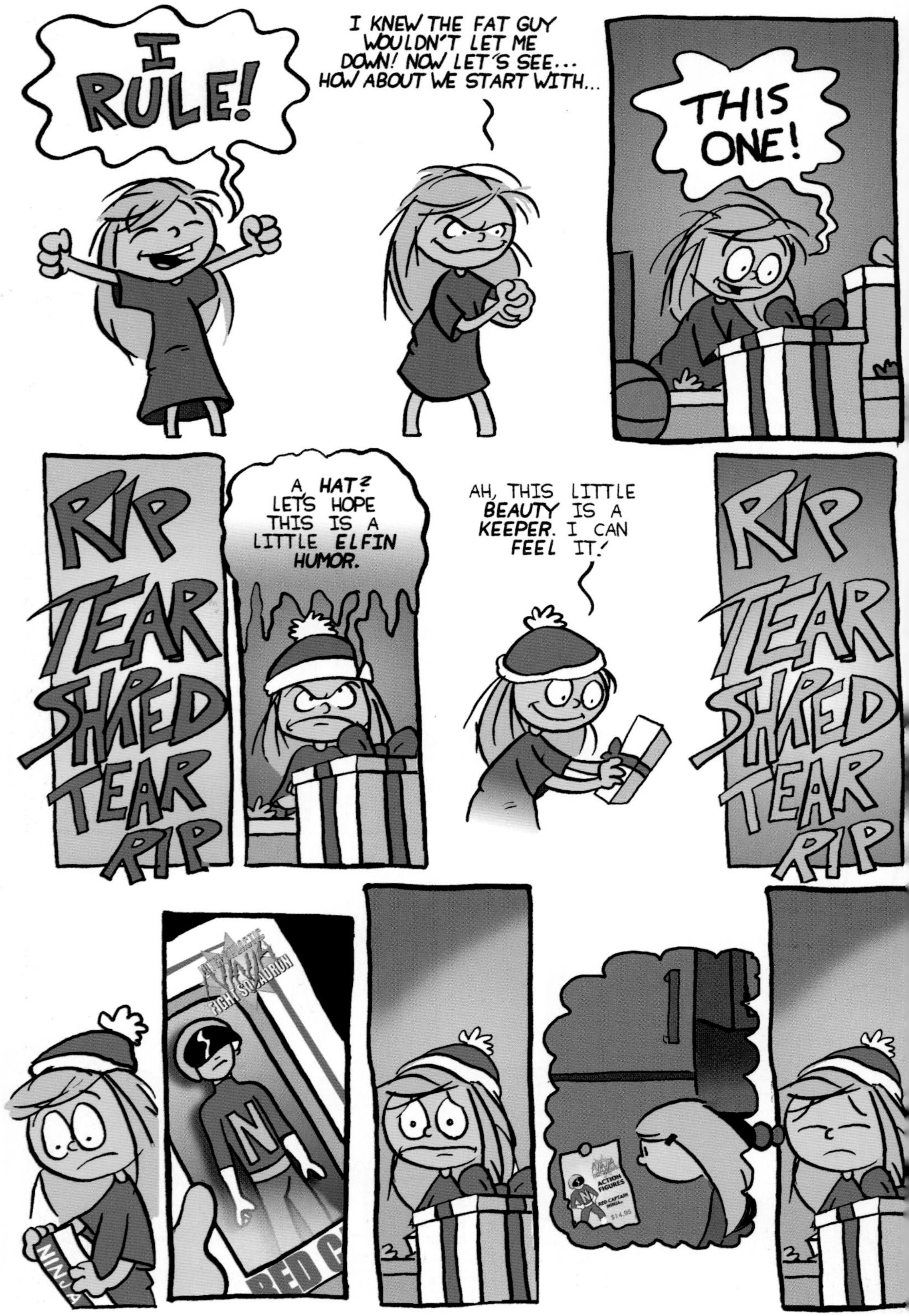
I RULE!
I KNEW THE FAT GUY WOULDN'T LET ME DOWN! NOW LET'S SEE... HOW ABOUT WE START WITH...
THIS ONE!
RIP TEAR SHRED TEAR RIP
A HAT? LET'S HOPE THIS IS A LITTLE ELFIN HUMOR.
AH, THIS LITTLE BEAUTY IS A KEEPER. I CAN FEEL IT!
RIP TEAR SHRED TEAR RIP
NINJA
FIGHT SQUADRON
RED C
ACTION FIGURES
RED CAPTAIN NINJA
$14.95

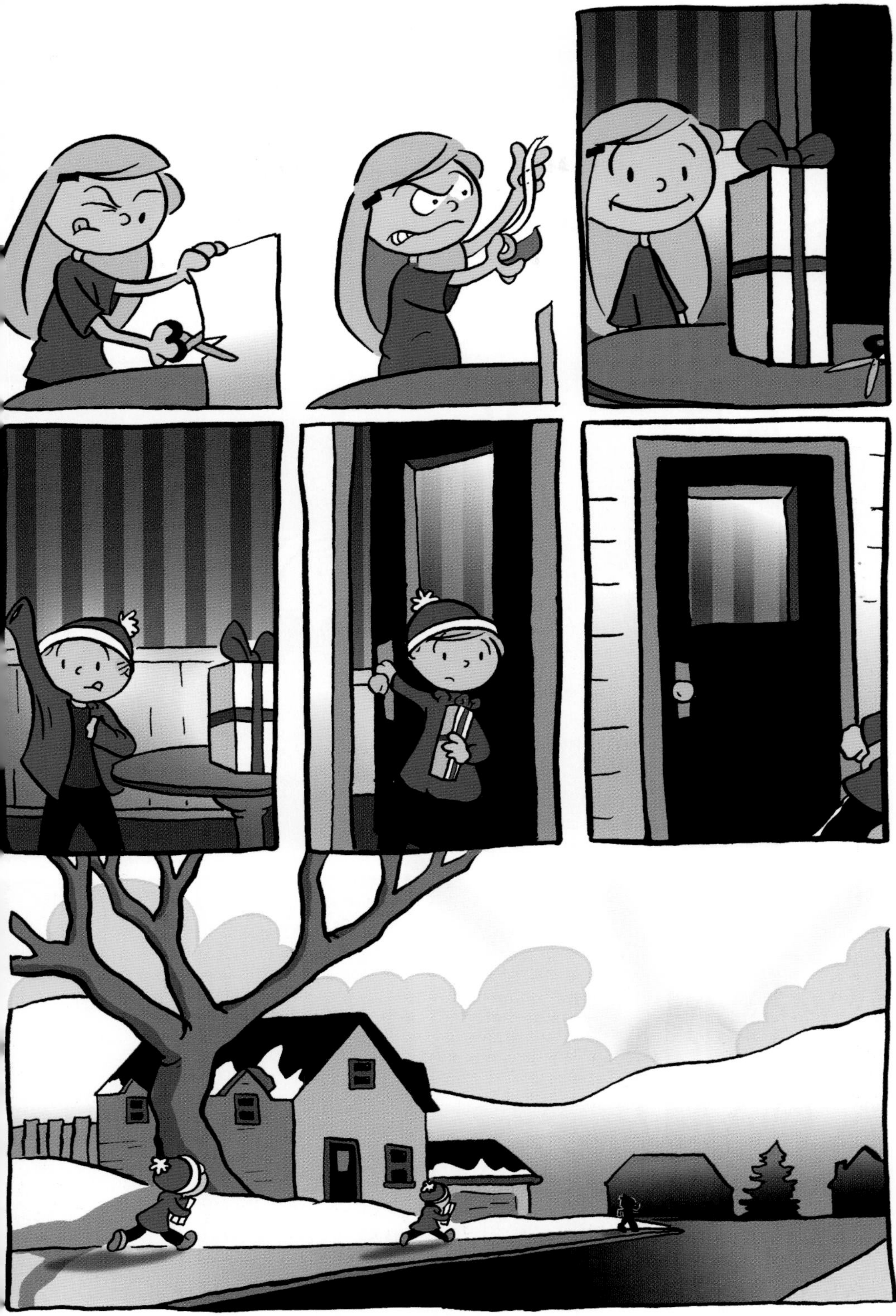

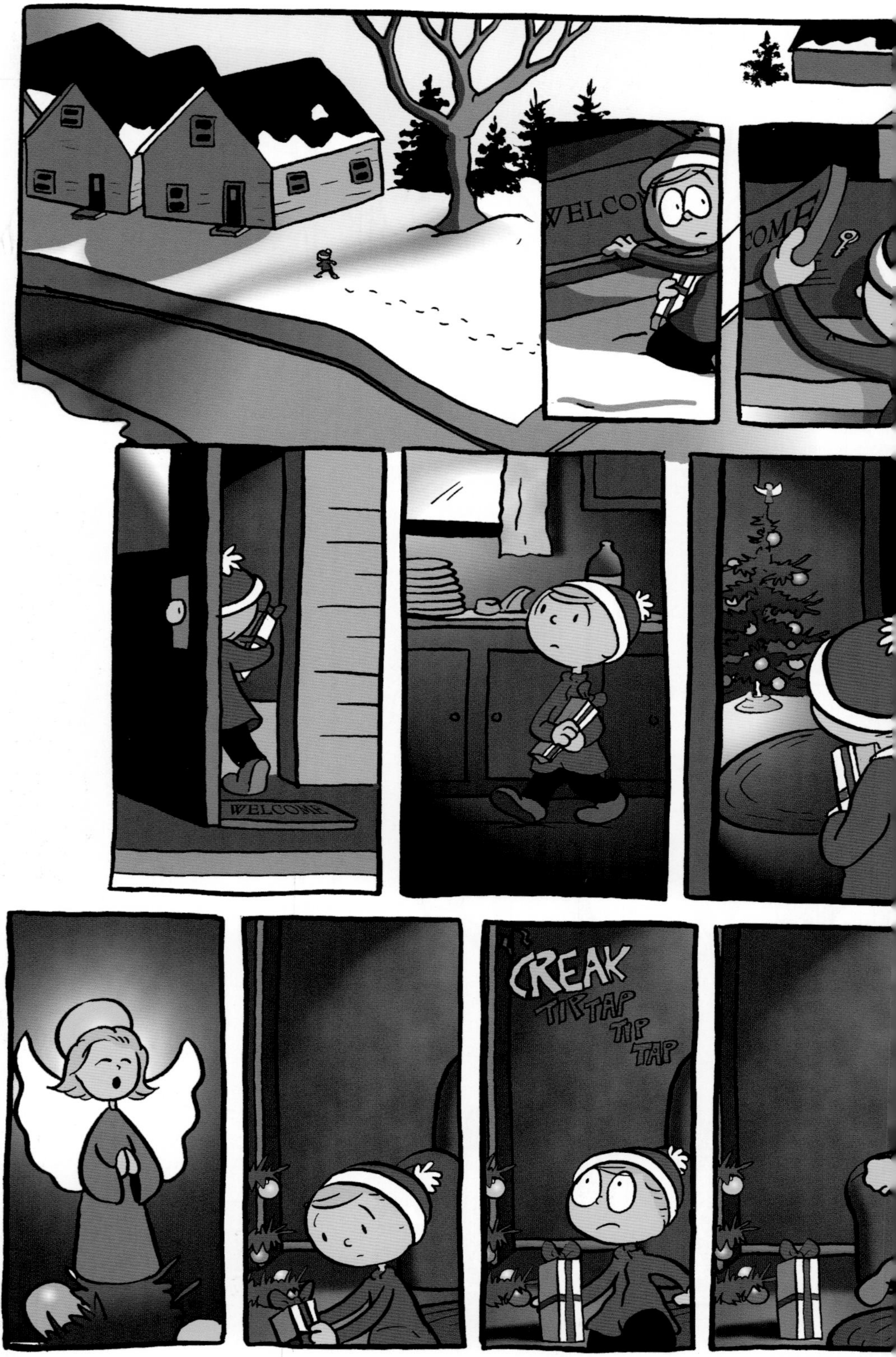
WELCOME
COME
WELCOME
CREAK
TIP TAP
TIP
TAP

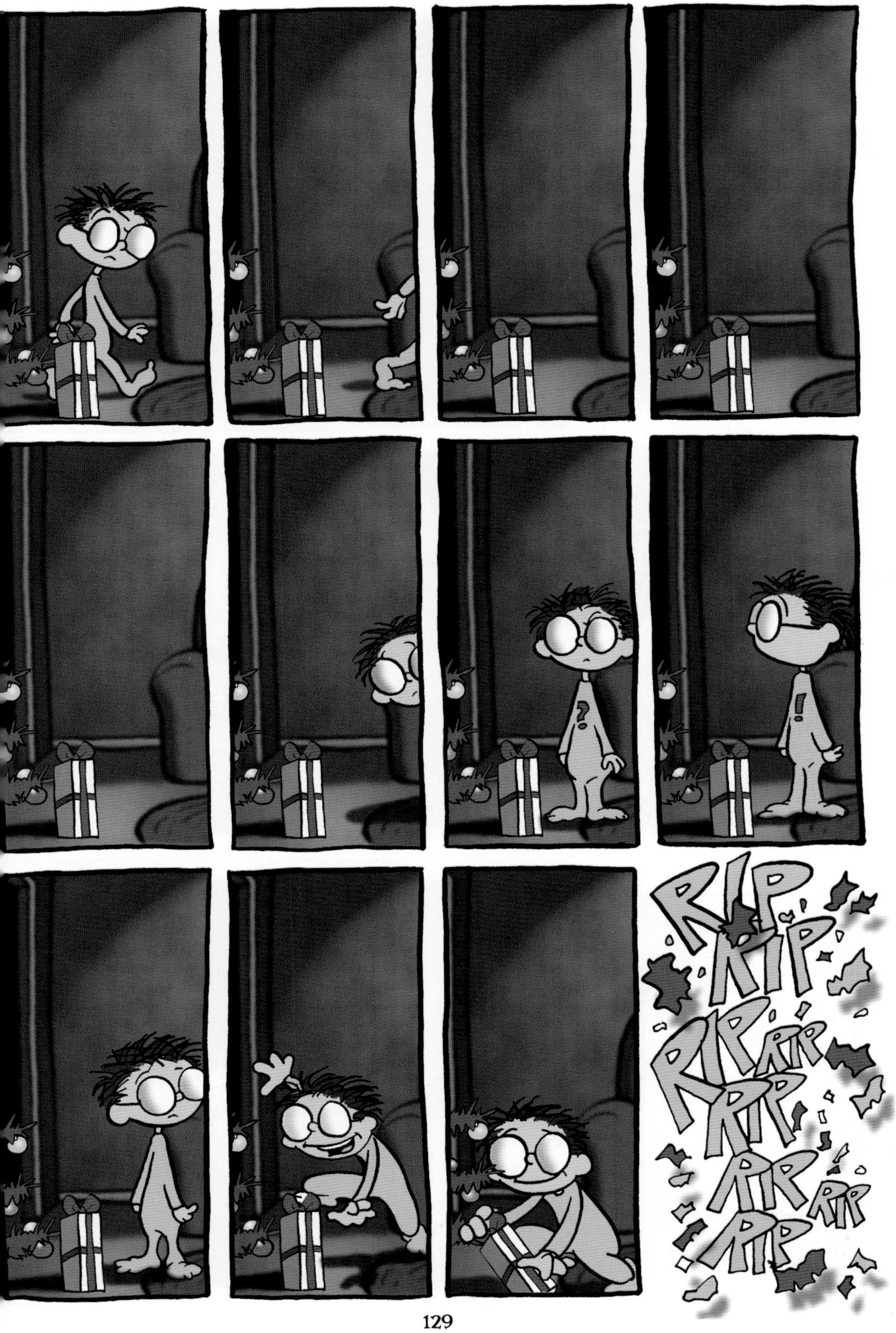
RIP
RIP
RIP
RIP
RIP
RIP
RIP
RIP
RIP

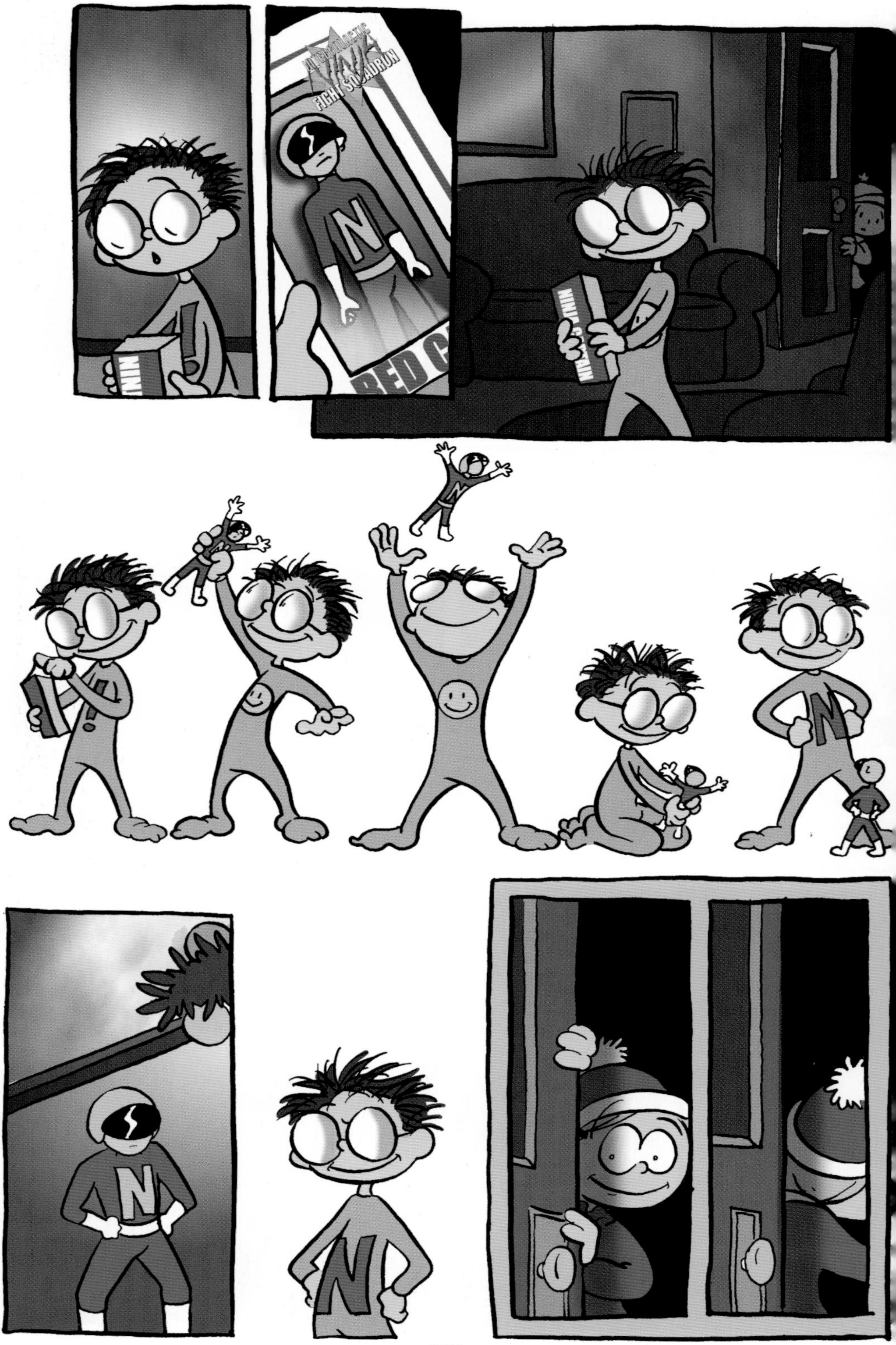
FIGHT SQUADRON

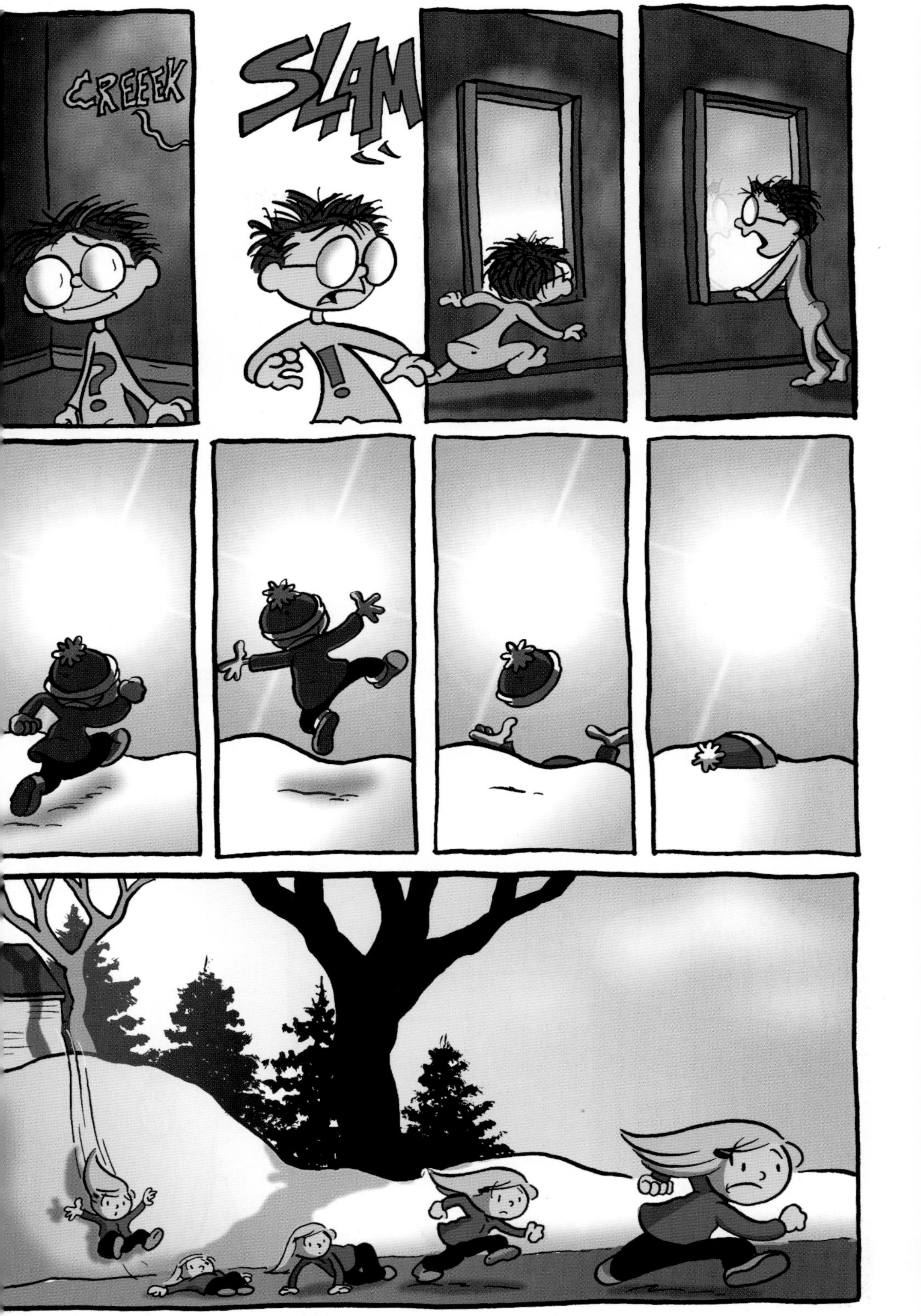
CREEEK
SLAM

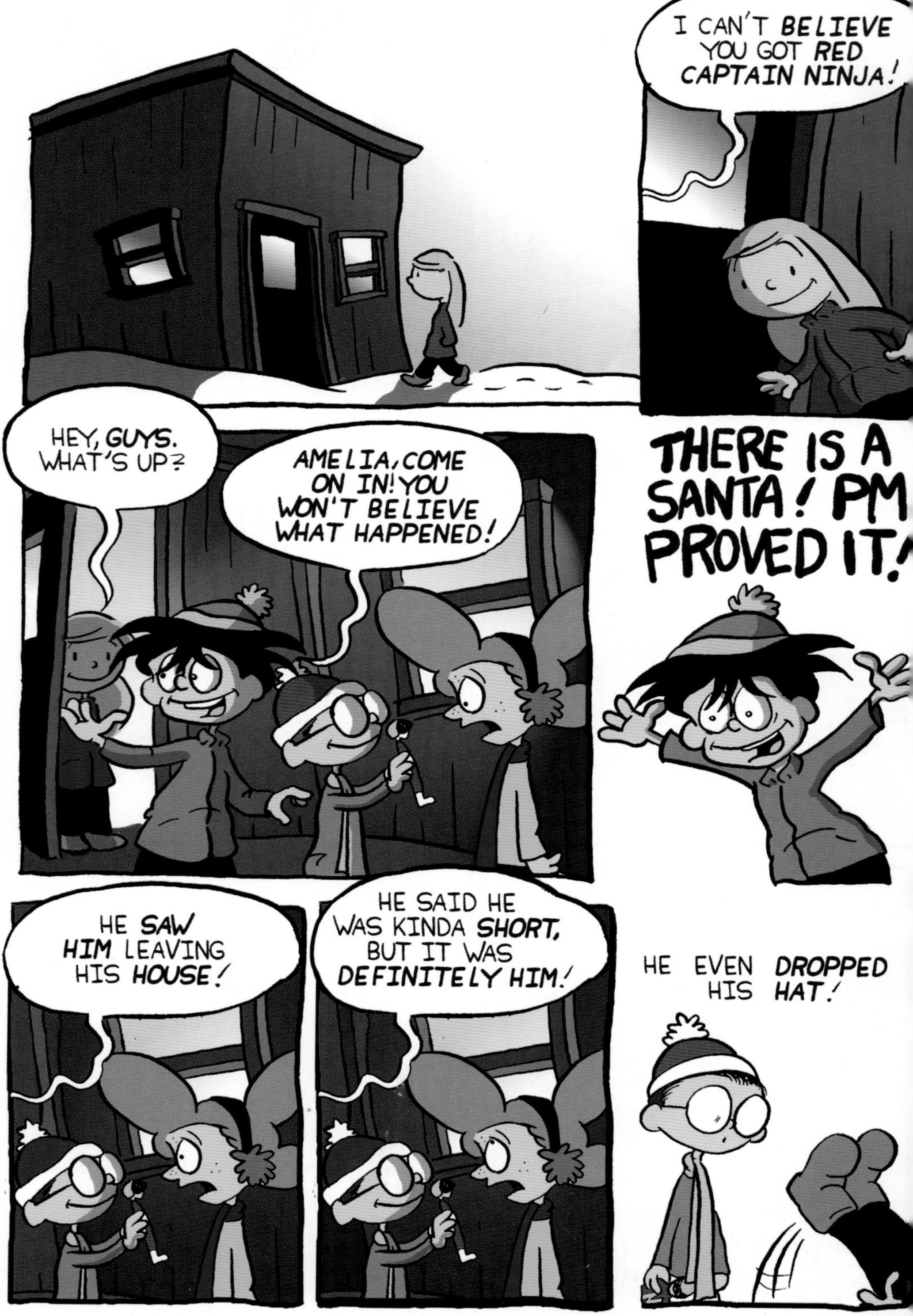
I CAN'T BELIEVE YOU GOT RED CAPTAIN NINJA!
HEY, GUYS. WHAT'S UP?
AMELIA, COME ON IN! YOU WON'T BELIEVE WHAT HAPPENED!
THERE IS A SANTA! PM PROVED IT!
HE SAW HIM LEAVING HIS HOUSE!
HE SAID HE WAS KINDA SHORT, BUT IT WAS DEFINITELY HIM!
HE EVEN DROPPED HIS HAT!

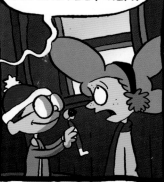

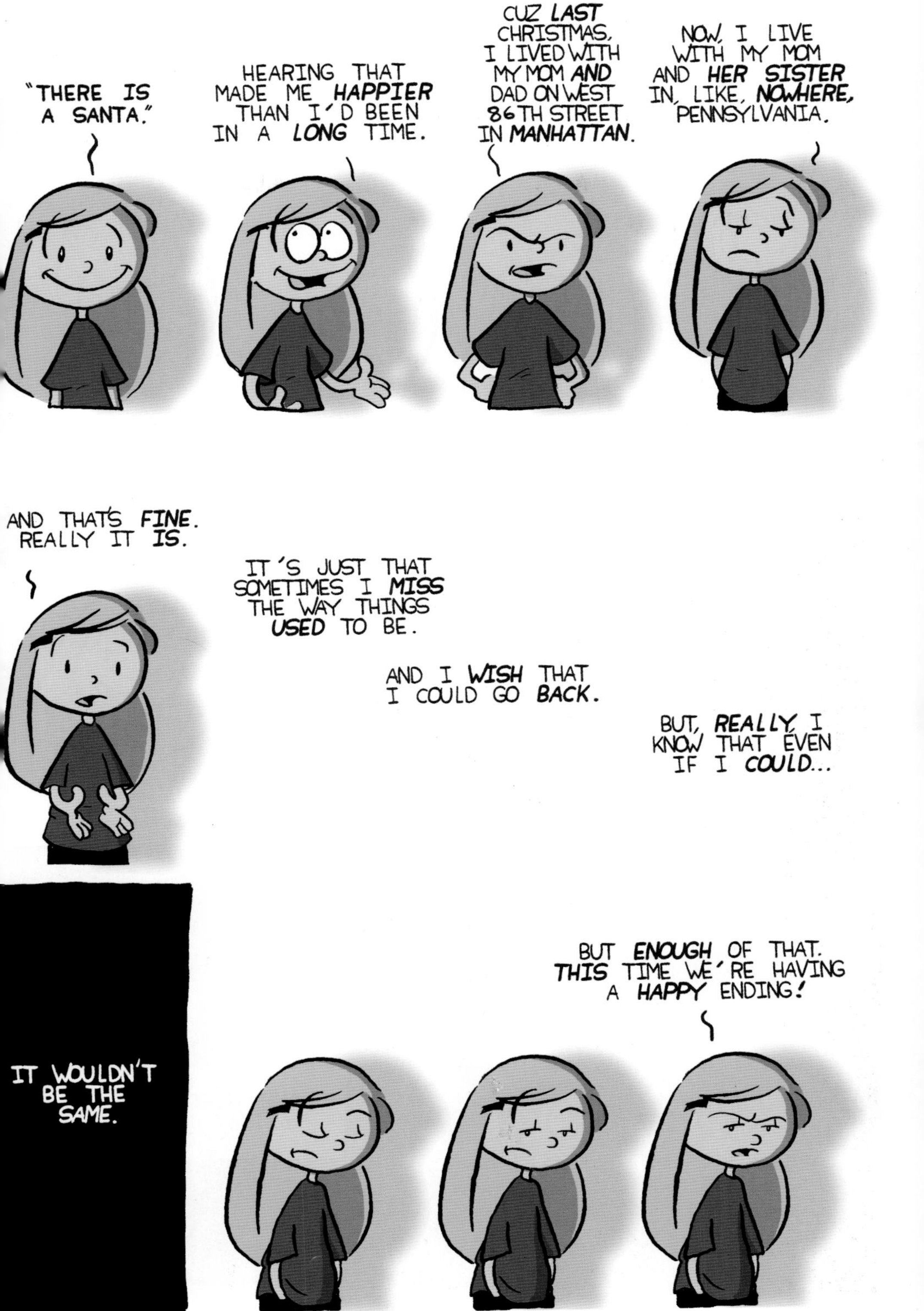

"THERE IS A SANTA."
HEARING THAT MADE ME HAPPIER THAN I'D BEEN IN A LONG TIME.
CUZ LAST CHRISTMAS, I LIVED WITH MY MOM AND DAD ON WEST 86TH STREET IN MANHATTAN.
NOW, I LIVE WITH MY MOM AND HER SISTER IN, LIKE, NOWHERE, PENNSYLVANIA.
AND THAT'S FINE. REALLY IT IS.
IT'S JUST THAT SOMETIMES I MISS THE WAY THINGS USED TO BE.
AND I WISH THAT I COULD GO BACK.
BUT, REALLY, I KNOW THAT EVEN IF I COULD...
IT WOULDN'T BE THE SAME.
BUT ENOUGH OF THAT. THIS TIME WE'RE HAVING A HAPPY ENDING!

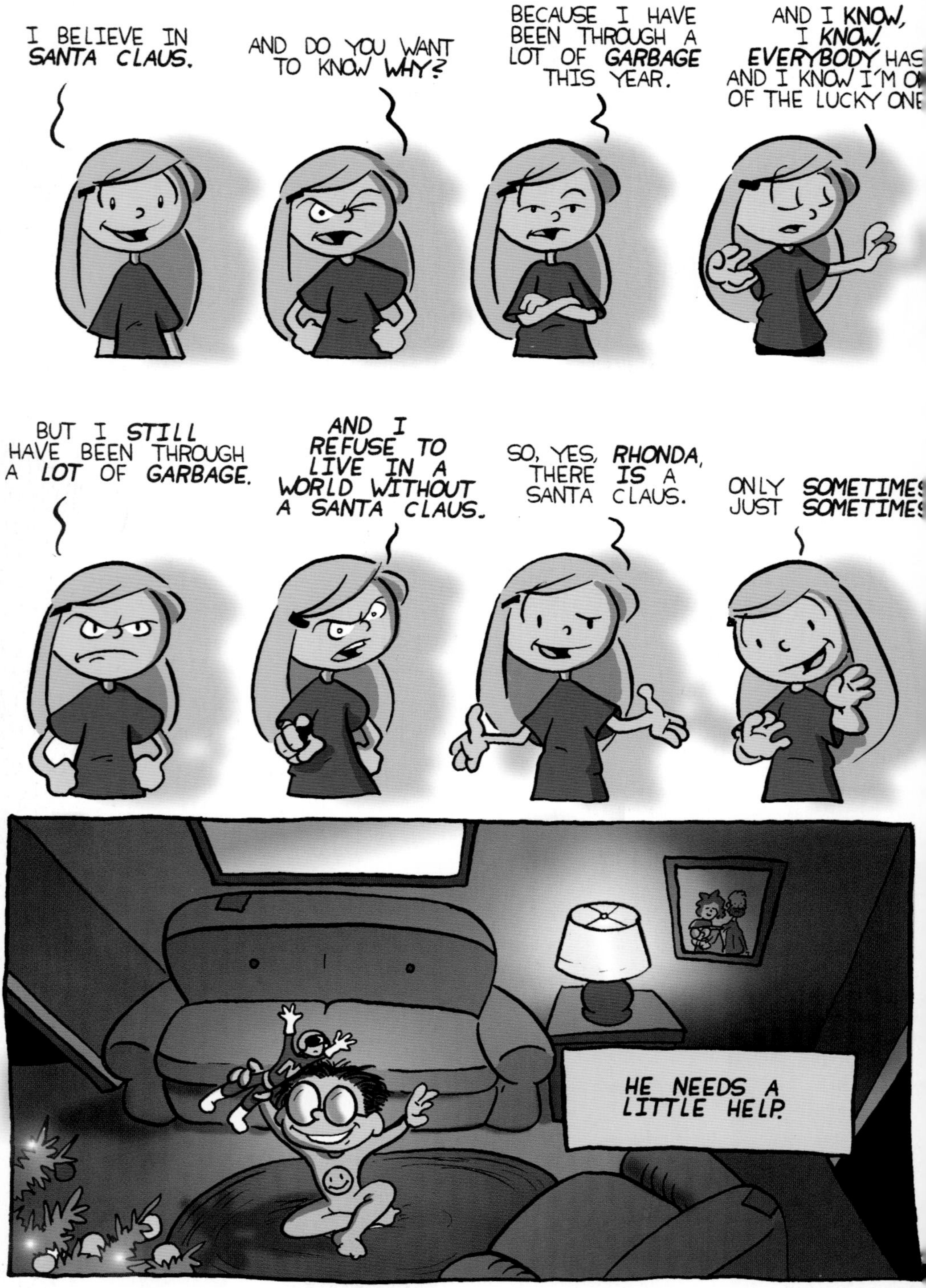
I BELIEVE IN SANTA CLAUS.
AND DO YOU WANT TO KNOW WHY?
BECAUSE I HAVE BEEN THROUGH A LOT OF GARBAGE THIS YEAR.
AND I KNOW, I KNOW, EVERYBODY HAS AND I KNOW I'M O OF THE LUCKY ONE
BUT I STILL HAVE BEEN THROUGH A LOT OF GARBAGE.
AND I REFUSE TO LIVE IN A WORLD WITHOUT A SANTA CLAUS.
SO, YES, RHONDA, THERE IS A SANTA CLAUS.
ONLY SOMETIMES JUST SOMETIMES
HE NEEDS A LITTLE HELP.

Speak Softee
to Me

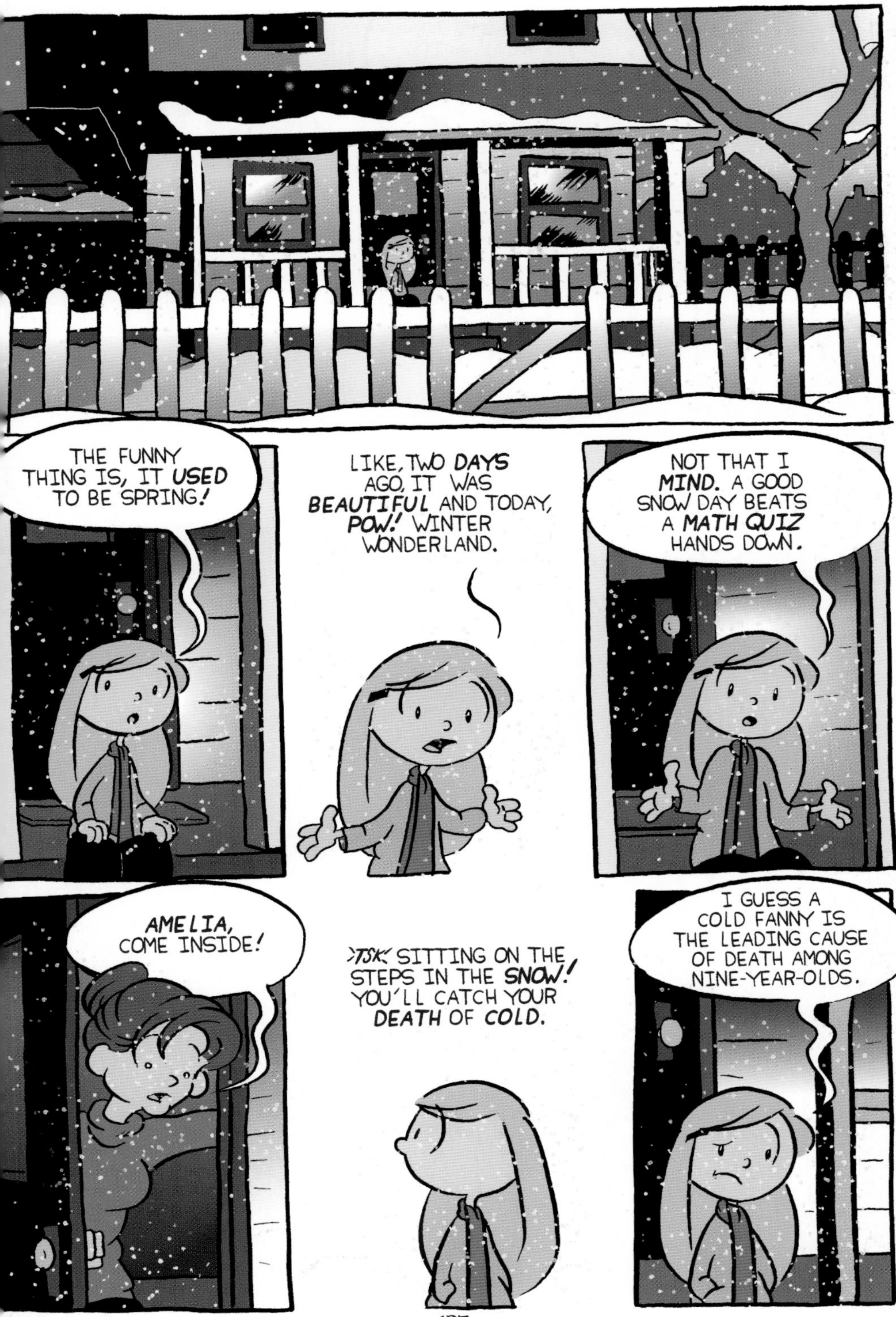
THE FUNNY THING IS, IT USED TO BE SPRING!
LIKE, TWO DAYS AGO, IT WAS BEAUTIFUL AND TODAY, POW! WINTER WONDERLAND.
NOT THAT I MIND. A GOOD SNOW DAY BEATS A MATH QUIZ HANDS DOWN.
AMELIA, COME INSIDE!
TSK! SITTING ON THE STEPS IN THE SNOW! YOU'LL CATCH YOUR DEATH OF COLD.
I GUESS A COLD FANNY IS THE LEADING CAUSE OF DEATH AMONG NINE-YEAR-OLDS.

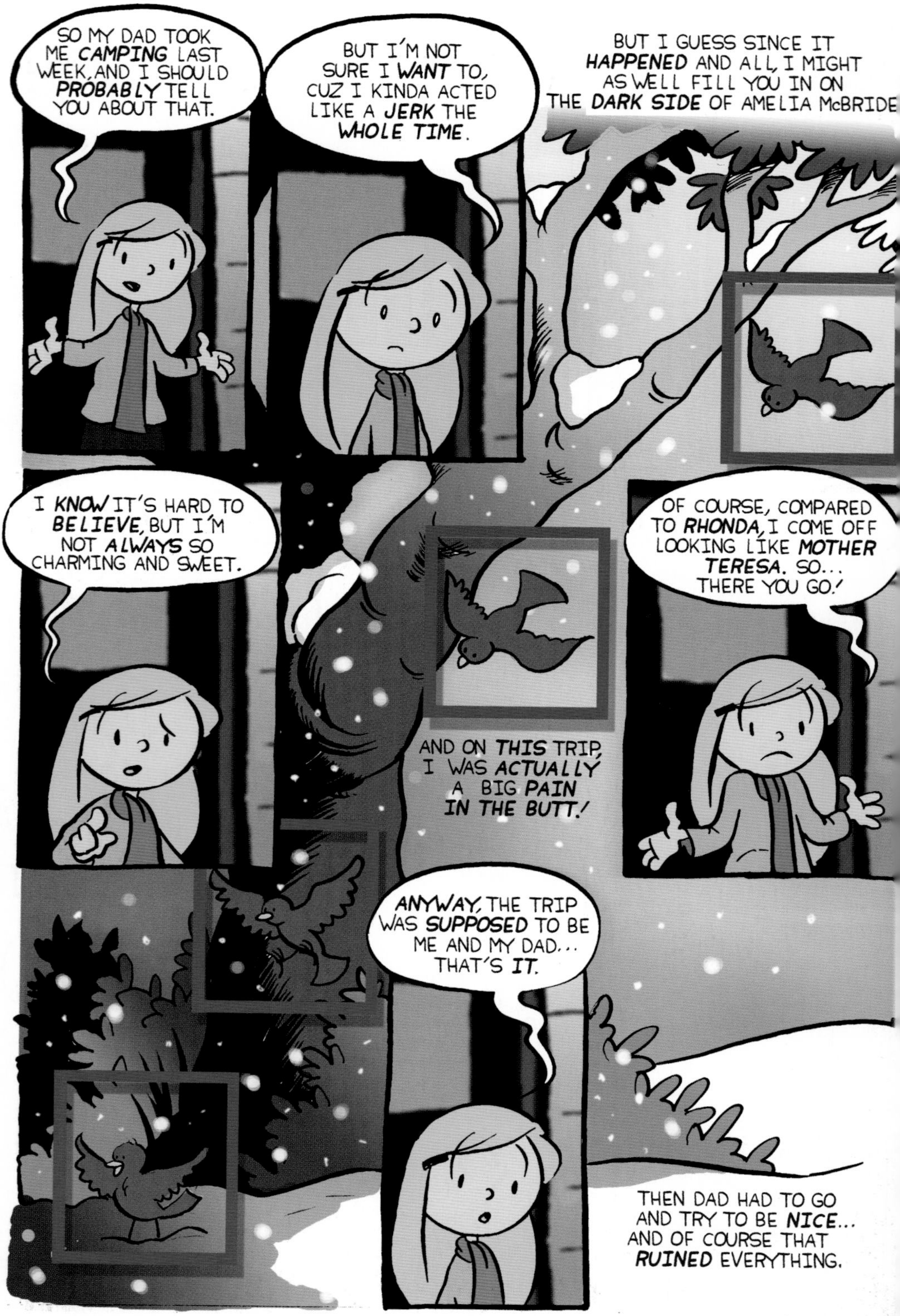

SO MY DAD TOOK ME CAMPING LAST WEEK, AND I SHOULD PROBABLY TELL YOU ABOUT THAT.
BUT I'M NOT SURE I WANT TO, CUZ I KINDA ACTED LIKE A JERK THE WHOLE TIME.
BUT I GUESS SINCE IT HAPPENED AND ALL, I MIGHT AS WELL FILL YOU IN ON THE DARK SIDE OF AMELIA McBRIDE.
I KNOW IT'S HARD TO BELIEVE, BUT I'M NOT ALWAYS SO CHARMING AND SWEET.
AND ON THIS TRIP, I WAS ACTUALLY A BIG PAIN IN THE BUTT!
OF COURSE, COMPARED TO RHONDA, I COME OFF LOOKING LIKE MOTHER TERESA. SO... THERE YOU GO!
ANYWAY, THE TRIP WAS SUPPOSED TO BE ME AND MY DAD... THAT'S IT.
THEN DAD HAD TO GO AND TRY TO BE NICE... AND OF COURSE THAT RUINED EVERYTHING.

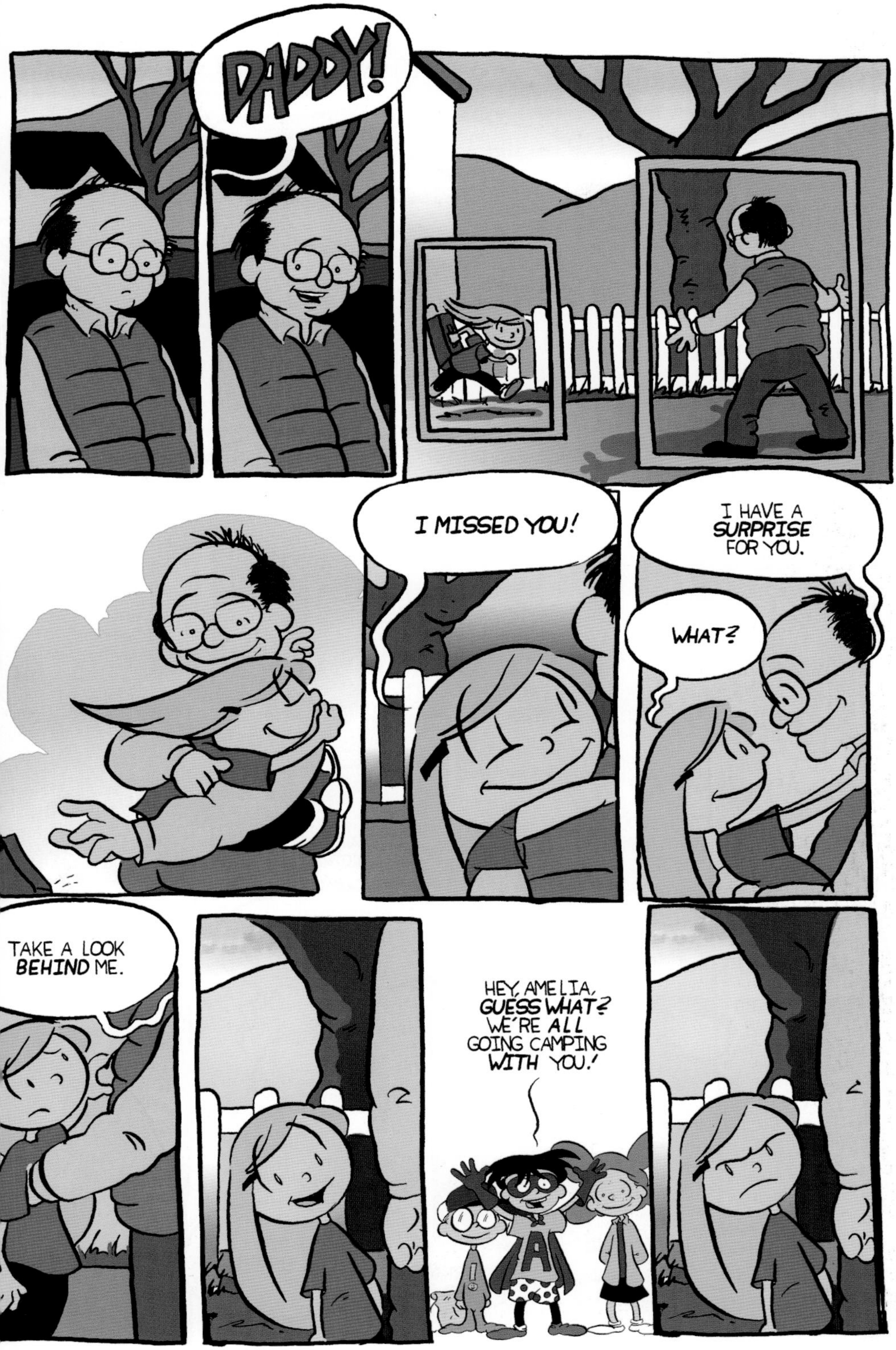
DADDY!
I MISSED YOU!
I HAVE A SURPRISE FOR YOU.
WHAT?
TAKE A LOOK BEHIND ME.
HEY, AMELIA, GUESS WHAT? WE'RE ALL GOING CAMPING WITH YOU!

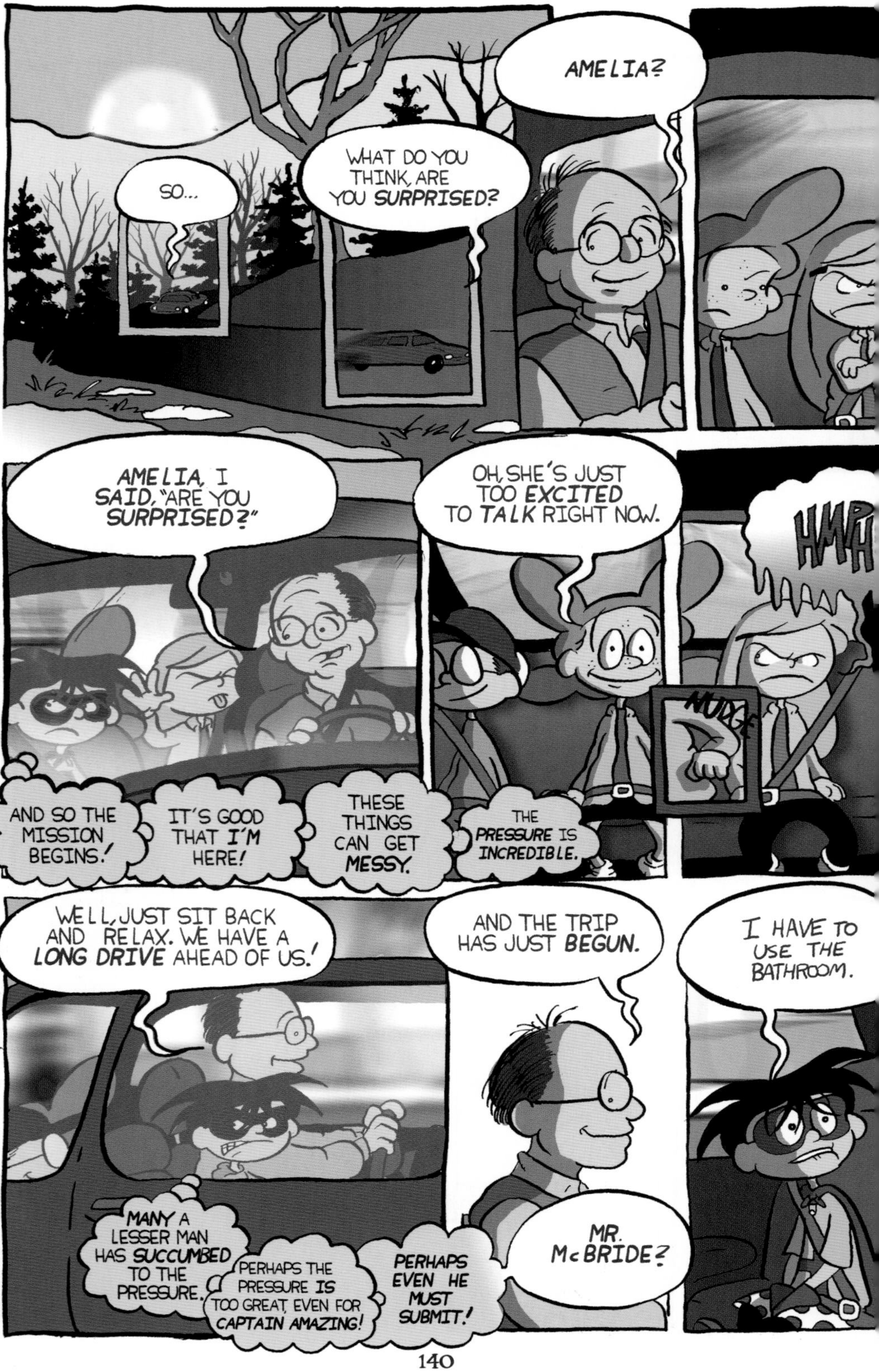
SO...
WHAT DO YOU THINK, ARE YOU SURPRISED?
AMELIA?
AMELIA, I SAID, "ARE YOU SURPRISED?"
OH, SHE'S JUST TOO EXCITED TO TALK RIGHT NOW.
HMPH
MUDGE
AND SO THE MISSION BEGINS!
IT'S GOOD THAT I'M HERE!
THESE THINGS CAN GET MESSY.
THE PRESSURE IS INCREDIBLE.
WELL, JUST SIT BACK AND RELAX. WE HAVE A LONG DRIVE AHEAD OF US!
AND THE TRIP HAS JUST BEGUN.
I HAVE TO USE THE BATHROOM.
MANY A LESSER MAN HAS SUCCUMBED TO THE PRESSURE.
PERHAPS THE PRESSURE IS TOO GREAT, EVEN FOR CAPTAIN AMAZING!
PERHAPS EVEN HE MUST SUBMIT!
MR. McBRIDE?

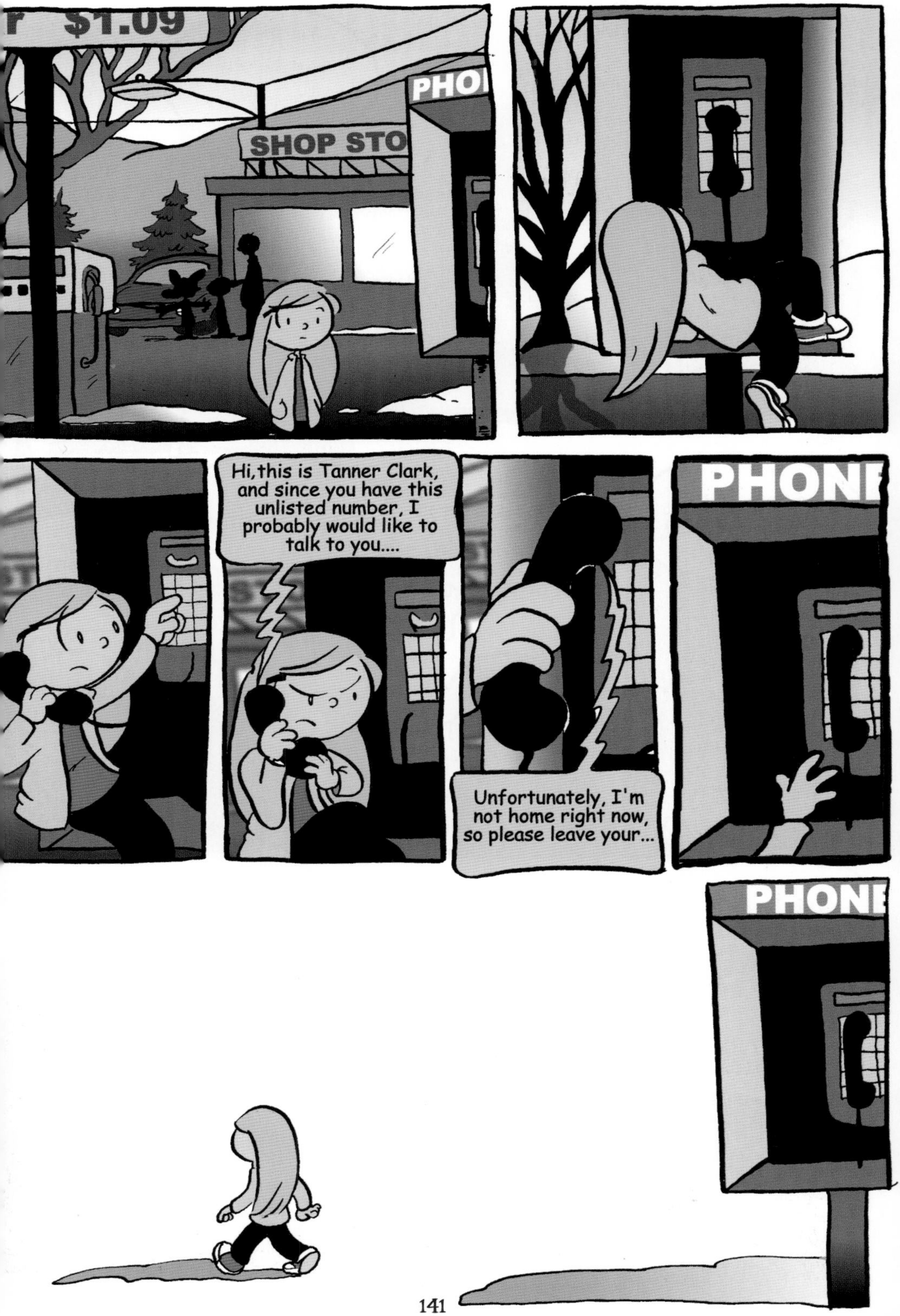
$1.09
PHO
SHOP STO
Hi, this is Tanner Clark, and since you have this unlisted number, I probably would like to talk to you....
Unfortunately, I'm not home right now, so please leave your...
PHONE
PHONE

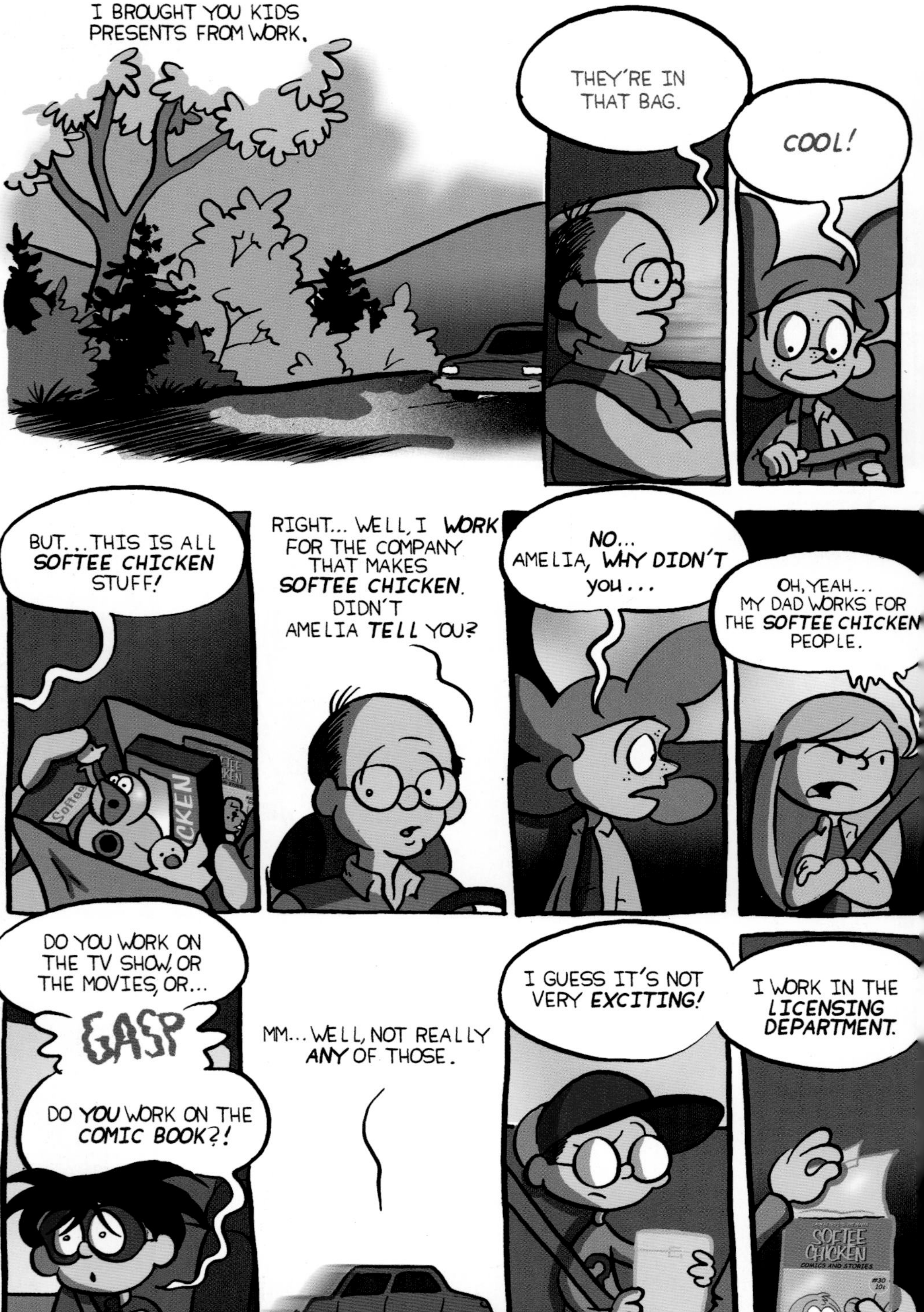
I BROUGHT YOU KIDS PRESENTS FROM WORK.
THEY'RE IN THAT BAG.
COOL!
BUT... THIS IS ALL SOFTEE CHICKEN STUFF!
RIGHT... WELL, I WORK FOR THE COMPANY THAT MAKES SOFTEE CHICKEN. DIDN'T AMELIA TELL YOU?
NO... AMELIA, WHY DIDN'T YOU...
OH, YEAH... MY DAD WORKS FOR THE SOFTEE CHICKEN PEOPLE.
DO YOU WORK ON THE TV SHOW, OR THE MOVIES, OR...
GASP
DO YOU WORK ON THE COMIC BOOK?!
MM... WELL, NOT REALLY ANY OF THOSE.
I GUESS IT'S NOT VERY EXCITING!
I WORK IN THE LICENSING DEPARTMENT.
SOFTEE CHICKEN
COMICS AND STORIES

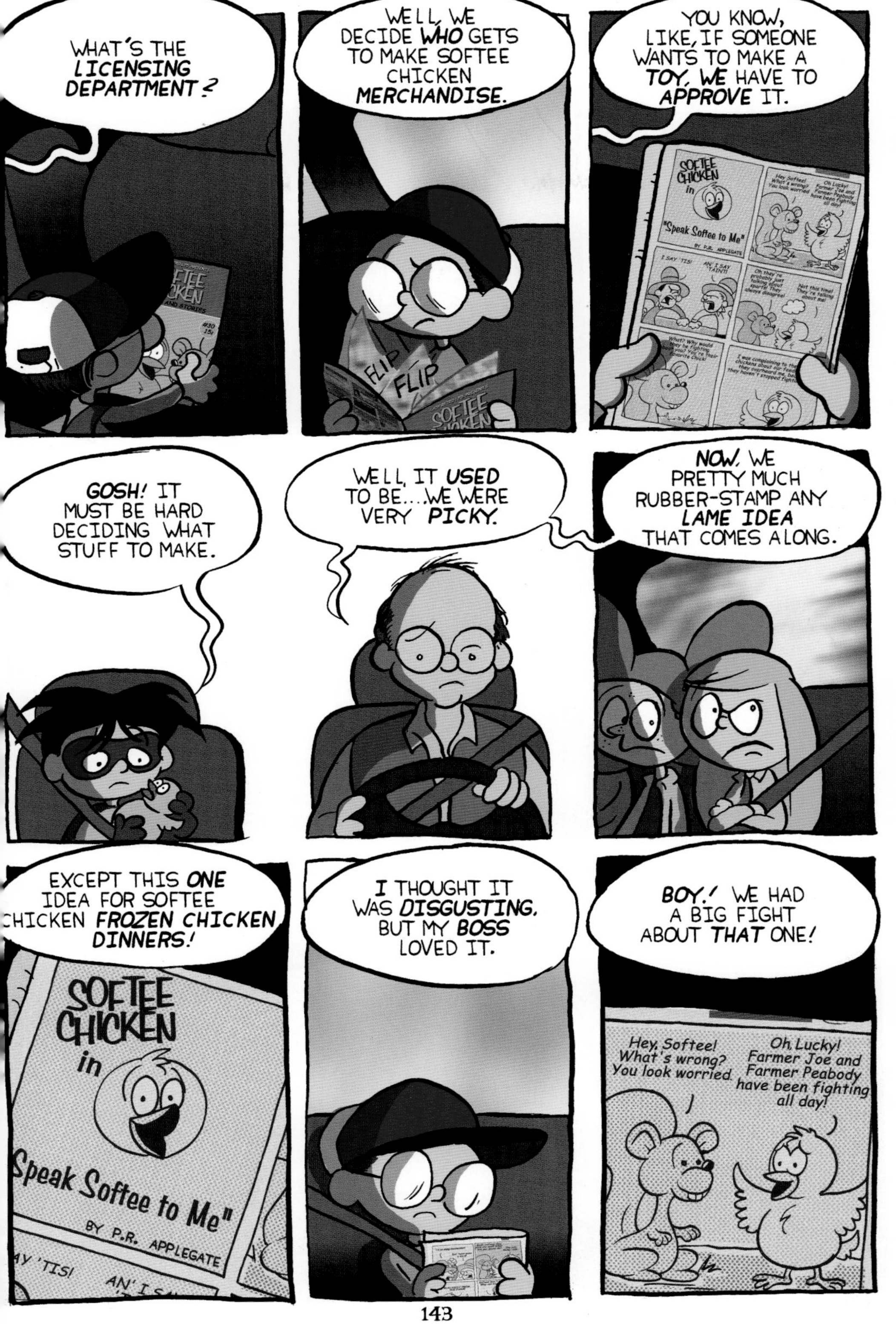
WHAT'S THE LICENSING DEPARTMENT?
SOFTEE CHICKEN
WELL, WE DECIDE WHO GETS TO MAKE SOFTEE CHICKEN MERCHANDISE.
FLIP
FLIP
YOU KNOW, LIKE, IF SOMEONE WANTS TO MAKE A TOY, WE HAVE TO APPROVE IT.
SOFTEE CHICKEN in
"Speak Softee to Me"
BY P.R. APPLEGATE
GOSH! IT MUST BE HARD DECIDING WHAT STUFF TO MAKE.
WELL, IT USED TO BE... WE WERE VERY PICKY.
NOW, WE PRETTY MUCH RUBBER-STAMP ANY LAME IDEA THAT COMES ALONG.
EXCEPT THIS ONE IDEA FOR SOFTEE CHICKEN FROZEN CHICKEN DINNERS!
SOFTEE CHICKEN in
"Speak Softee to Me"
BY P.R. APPLEGATE
I THOUGHT IT WAS DISGUSTING, BUT MY BOSS LOVED IT.
BOY! WE HAD A BIG FIGHT ABOUT THAT ONE!
Hey, Softee! What's wrong? You look worried.
Oh, Lucky! Farmer Joe and Farmer Peabody have been fighting all day!

>HEH HEH< WE MUST'VE GONE BACK AND FORTH FOR *MONTHS.*

I SAY 'TIS!

AN' I SAY 'TAINT!

What? Why w— they be figh— about you? You— favorite C—

REMEMBER *THAT,* AMELIA? *AMELIA?*

OH, *IGNORE* HER, MR. McBRIDE. SHE'S ALWAYS *GROUCHY* IN THE *MORNING.*

Oh, they're probably just talking about sports! They always disagree!

Not this time! They're talking about me!

YEAH, I... I GUESS *THAT'S* IT.

What? Why would they be fighting about you? You're their favorite Chick!

WHAT'S *THIS* TOY?

HMMM? OH...THAT'S THE *SOFTEE TALKIE.*

I was complaining to the other chickens about our feed! I bet they overheard me, because they haven't stopped fighting since!

WE THOUGHT *WALKIE-TALKIES* WOULD BE A BIG *HIT* WITH KIDS.

FLIP

TILL WE REALIZED MOST OF 'EM HAVE *CELL PHONES.*

'Tis ya dang Ronkwaller!

Dat 'taint even a word!

UN AWAY FROM THE FARM!

Sof— Wh—

l Don't be suc— t t—

WALKIE-TALKIES, EH? THEY COULD COME IN HANDY WITH MY *CRIME FIGHTING.*

Gosh Softee! They sure are mad! What are you gonna do?

The only thing I can...

MY *LAST* SET WAS CONFISCATE— BY *SANTA CLAUS* WHEN I TRIED TO *BUST* HIM.

144

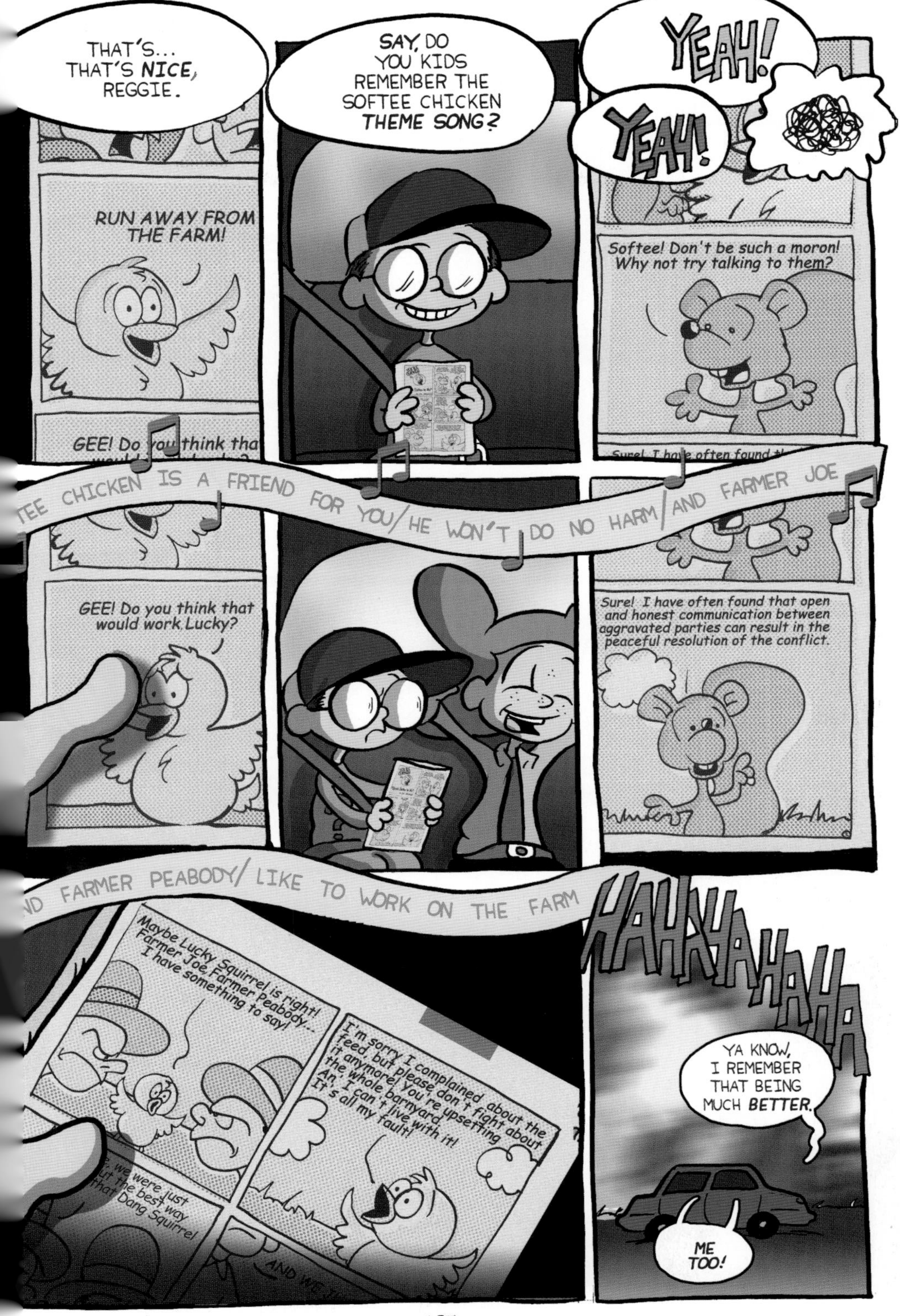
THAT'S... THAT'S **NICE,** REGGIE.
RUN AWAY FROM THE FARM!
SAY, DO YOU KIDS REMEMBER THE SOFTEE CHICKEN **THEME SONG?**
YEAH!
YEAH!
Softee! Don't be such a moron! Why not try talking to them?
TEE CHICKEN IS A FRIEND FOR YOU/ HE WON'T DO NO HARM/ AND FARMER JOE
GEE! Do you think that would work,Lucky?
Sure! I have often found that open and honest communication between aggravated parties can result in the peaceful resolution of the conflict.
ND FARMER PEABODY/ LIKE TO WORK ON THE FARM
Maybe Lucky Squirrel is right! Farmer Joe, Farmer Peabody... I have something to say!
I'm sorry I complained about the feed, but please don't fight about it anymore! You're upsetting the whole barnyard. An' I can't live with it! It's all my fault!
HAHAHAHAHAHA
YA KNOW, I REMEMBER THAT BEING MUCH **BETTER.**
ME TOO!

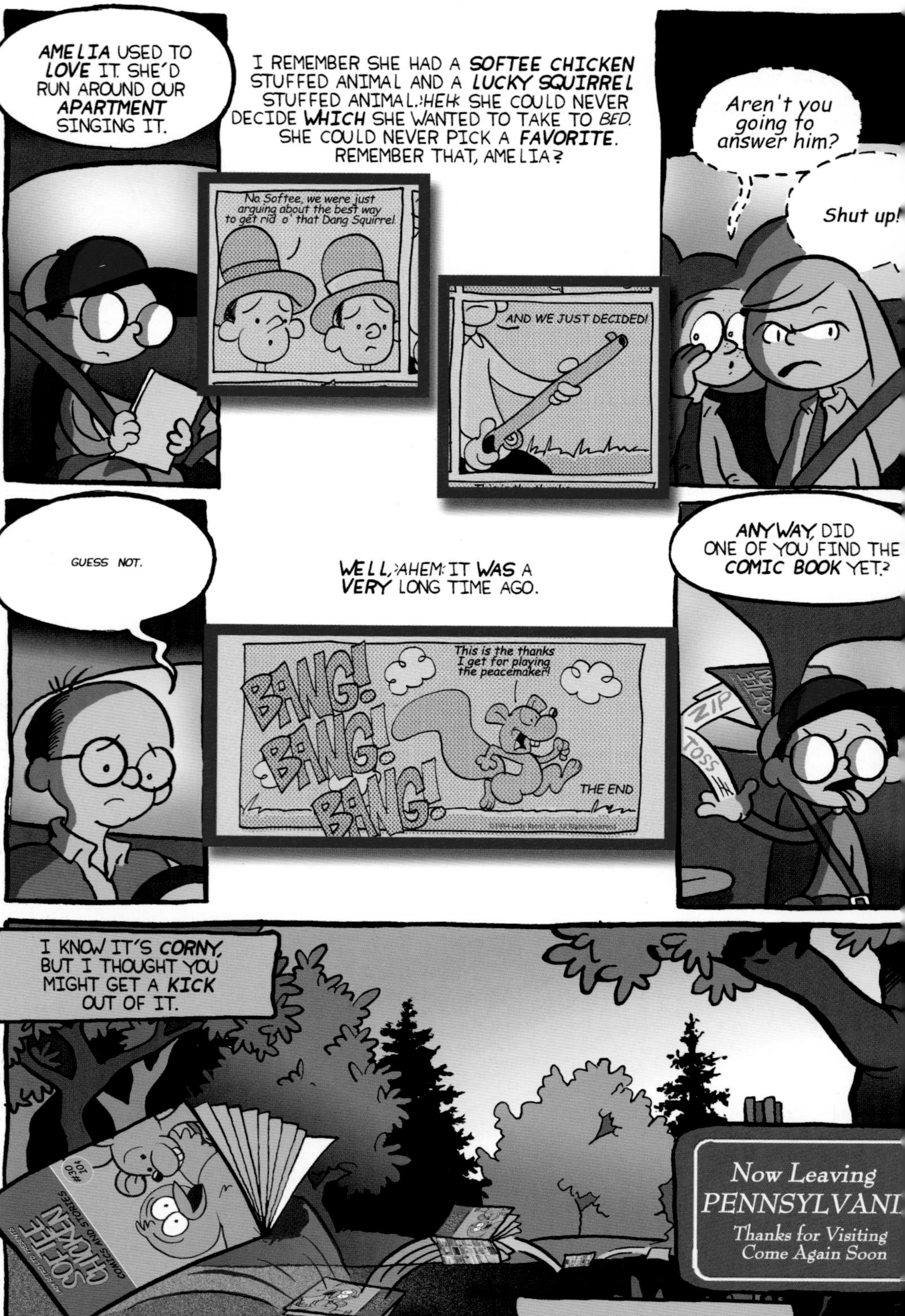
AMELIA USED TO LOVE IT. SHE'D RUN AROUND OUR APARTMENT SINGING IT.
I REMEMBER SHE HAD A SOFTEE CHICKEN STUFFED ANIMAL AND A LUCKY SQUIRREL STUFFED ANIMAL. :HEH: SHE COULD NEVER DECIDE WHICH SHE WANTED TO TAKE TO BED. SHE COULD NEVER PICK A FAVORITE. REMEMBER THAT, AMELIA?
No, Softee, we were just arguing about the best way to get rid o' that Dang Squirrel.
AND WE JUST DECIDED!
Aren't you going to answer him?
Shut up!
GUESS NOT.
WELL, :AHEM: IT WAS A VERY LONG TIME AGO.
BANG! BANG! BANG!
This is the thanks I get for playing the peacemaker!
THE END
ANYWAY, DID ONE OF YOU FIND THE COMIC BOOK YET?
ZIP
TOSS
I KNOW IT'S CORNY, BUT I THOUGHT YOU MIGHT GET A KICK OUT OF IT.
Now Leaving PENNSYLVANI
Thanks for Visiting
Come Again Soon
IT'S NOT EVERY DAY YOU SEE A $400 COMIC BOOK.

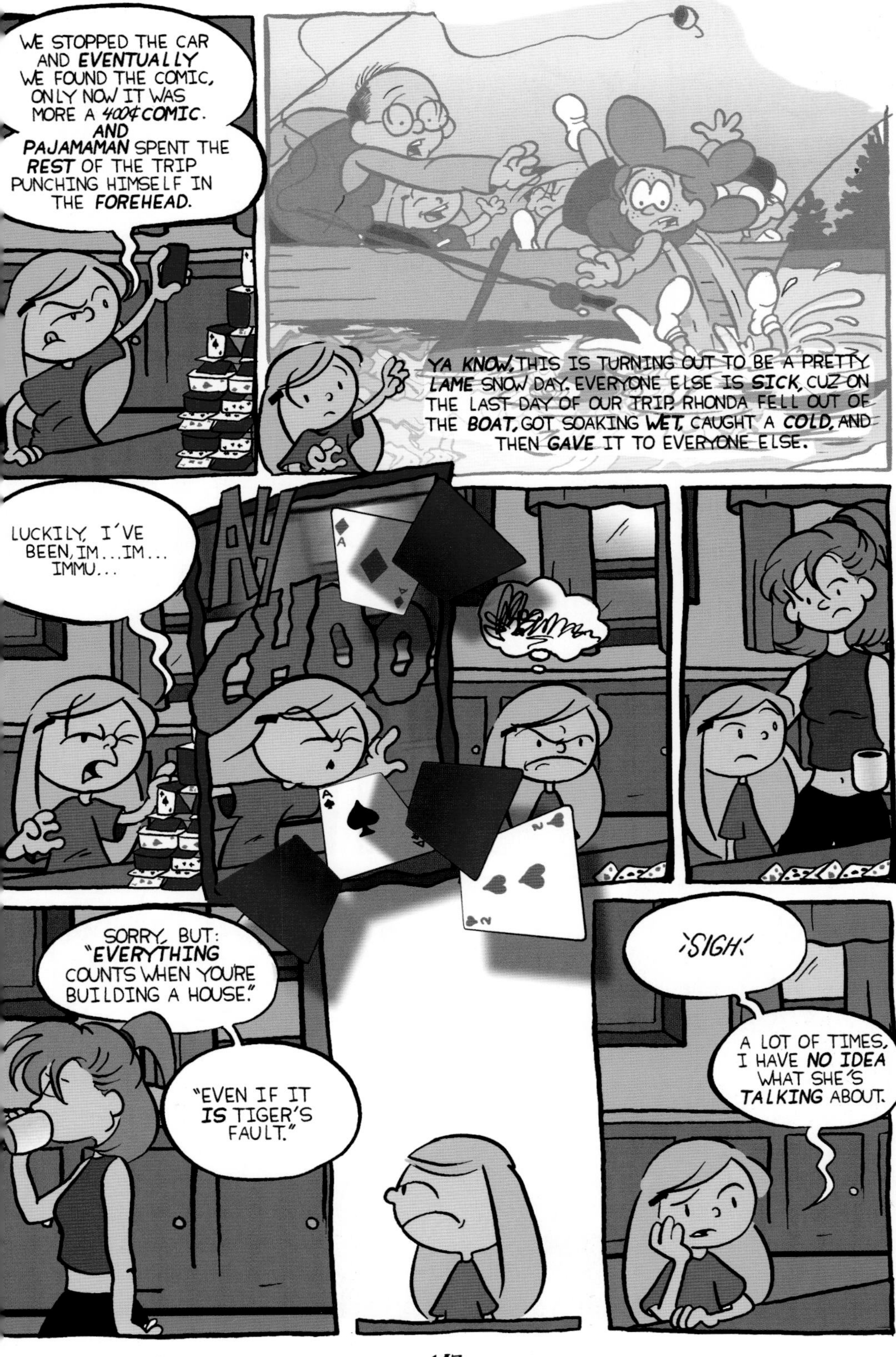
WE STOPPED THE CAR AND EVENTUALLY WE FOUND THE COMIC, ONLY NOW IT WAS MORE A 400¢ COMIC.
AND PAJAMAMAN SPENT THE REST OF THE TRIP PUNCHING HIMSELF IN THE FOREHEAD.
YA KNOW, THIS IS TURNING OUT TO BE A PRETTY LAME SNOW DAY. EVERYONE ELSE IS SICK, CUZ ON THE LAST DAY OF OUR TRIP RHONDA FELL OUT OF THE BOAT, GOT SOAKING WET, CAUGHT A COLD, AND THEN GAVE IT TO EVERYONE ELSE.
LUCKILY, I'VE BEEN, IM...IM... IMMU...
AH CHOO
SORRY, BUT: "EVERYTHING COUNTS WHEN YOU'RE BUILDING A HOUSE."
"EVEN IF IT IS TIGER'S FAULT."
¡SIGH!
A LOT OF TIMES, I HAVE NO IDEA WHAT SHE'S TALKING ABOUT.

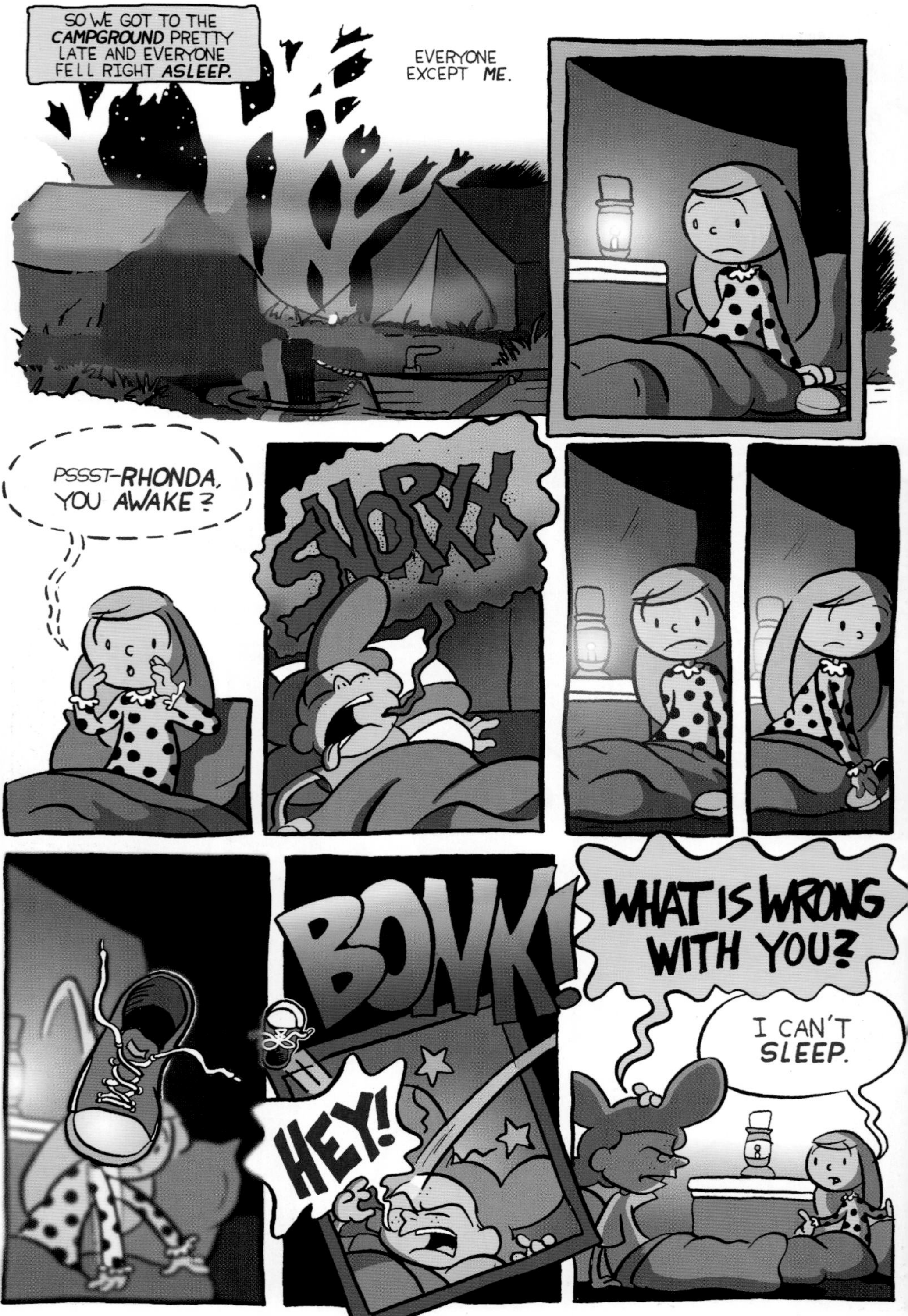
SO WE GOT TO THE CAMPGROUND PRETTY LATE AND EVERYONE FELL RIGHT ASLEEP.
EVERYONE EXCEPT ME.
PSSST-RHONDA, YOU AWAKE?
SNORKK
BONK!
HEY!
WHAT IS WRONG WITH YOU?
I CAN'T SLEEP.

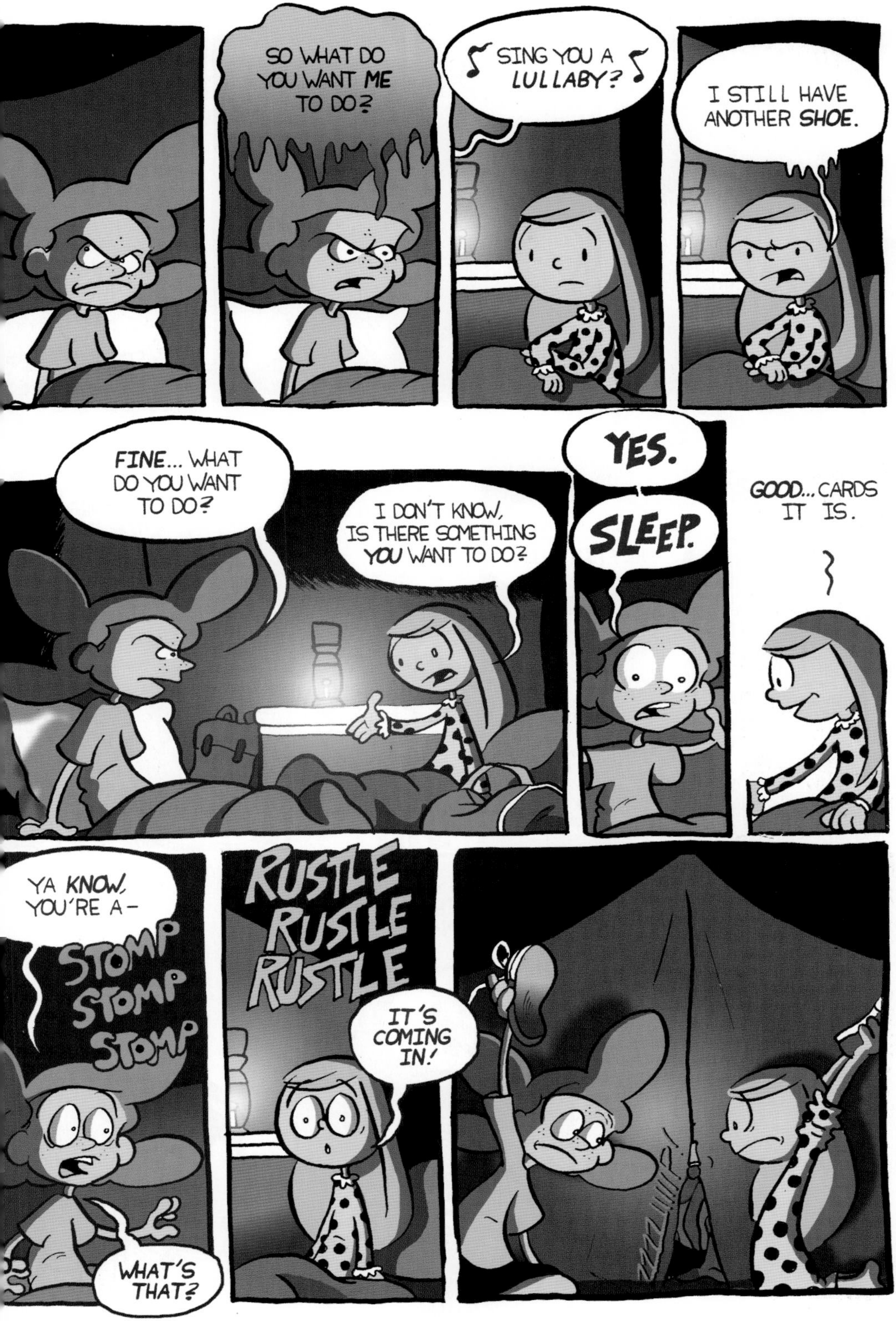
SO WHAT DO YOU WANT ME TO DO?
SING YOU A LULLABY?
I STILL HAVE ANOTHER SHOE.
FINE... WHAT DO YOU WANT TO DO?
I DON'T KNOW, IS THERE SOMETHING YOU WANT TO DO?
YES.
SLEEP.
GOOD... CARDS IT IS.
YA KNOW, YOU'RE A–
STOMP STOMP STOMP
WHAT'S THAT?
RUSTLE RUSTLE RUSTLE
IT'S COMING IN!
ZZZZIIIIIIIP!

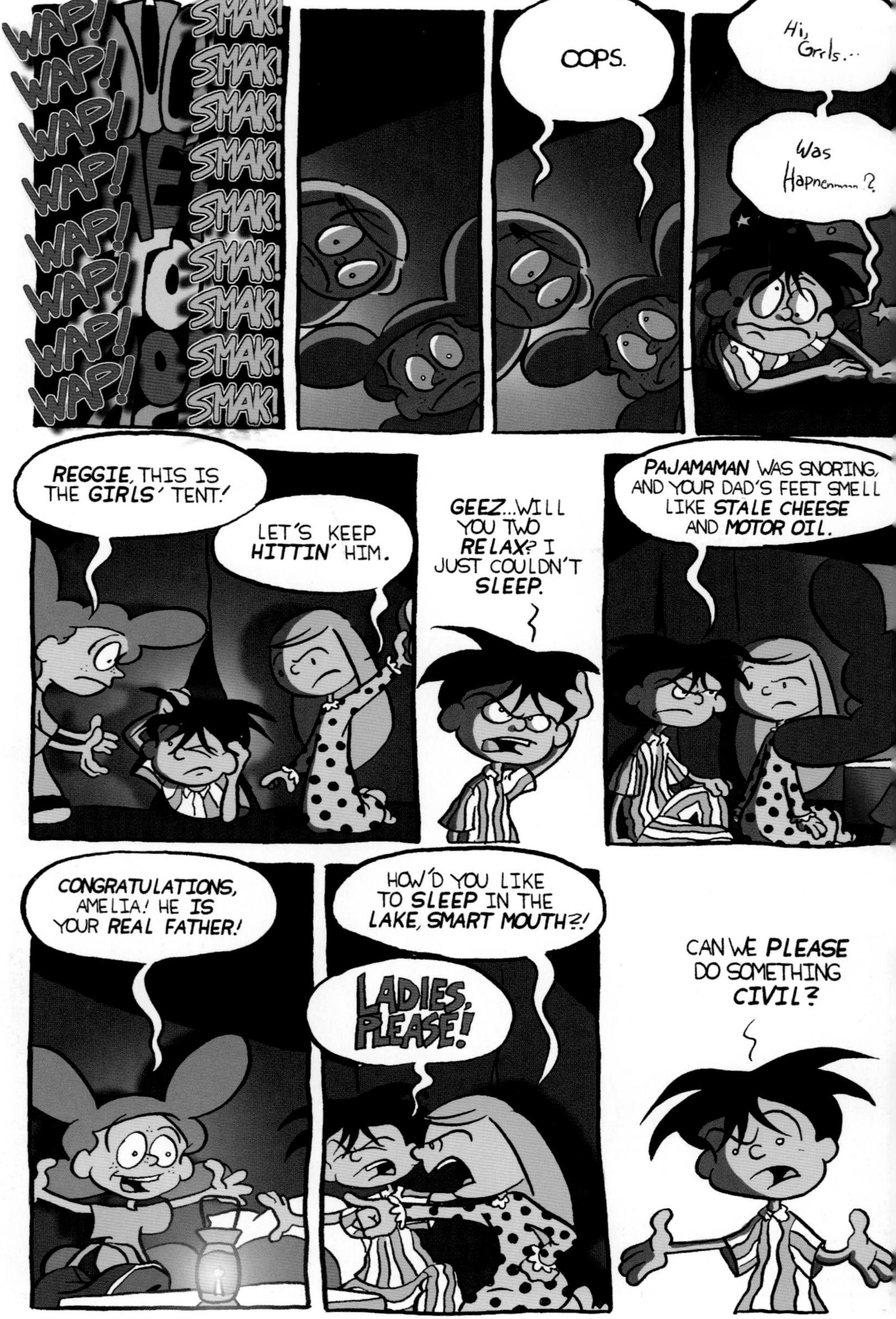
WAP! WAP! WAP! WAP! WAP! WAP! WAP! WAP!
SMAK! SMAK! SMAK! SMAK! SMAK! SMAK! SMAK! SMAK! SMAK!
OOPS.
Hi, Grrls...
Was Hapnennnn..?
REGGIE, THIS IS THE GIRLS' TENT!
LET'S KEEP HITTIN' HIM.
GEEZ...WILL YOU TWO RELAX? I JUST COULDN'T SLEEP.
PAJAMAMAN WAS SNORING, AND YOUR DAD'S FEET SMELL LIKE STALE CHEESE AND MOTOR OIL.
CONGRATULATIONS, AMELIA! HE IS YOUR REAL FATHER!
HOW'D YOU LIKE TO SLEEP IN THE LAKE, SMART MOUTH?!
LADIES, PLEASE!
CAN WE PLEASE DO SOMETHING CIVIL?

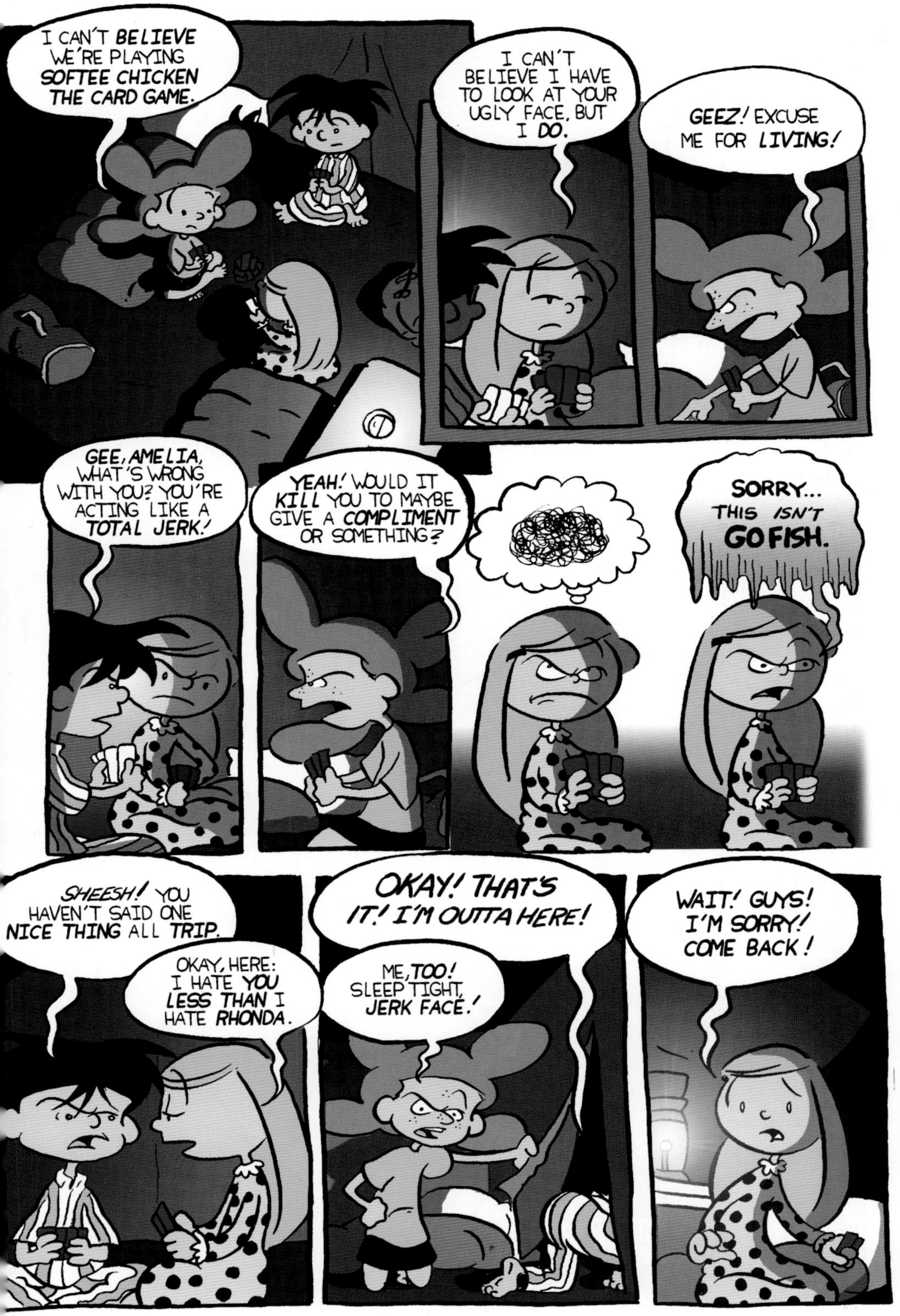

I CAN'T BELIEVE WE'RE PLAYING SOFTEE CHICKEN THE CARD GAME.
I CAN'T BELIEVE I HAVE TO LOOK AT YOUR UGLY FACE, BUT I DO.
GEEZ! EXCUSE ME FOR LIVING!
GEE, AMELIA, WHAT'S WRONG WITH YOU? YOU'RE ACTING LIKE A TOTAL JERK!
YEAH! WOULD IT KILL YOU TO MAYBE GIVE A COMPLIMENT OR SOMETHING?
SORRY... THIS ISN'T GO FISH.
SHEESH! YOU HAVEN'T SAID ONE NICE THING ALL TRIP.
OKAY, HERE: I HATE YOU LESS THAN I HATE RHONDA.
OKAY! THAT'S IT! I'M OUTTA HERE!
ME, TOO! SLEEP TIGHT, JERK FACE!
WAIT! GUYS! I'M SORRY! COME BACK!

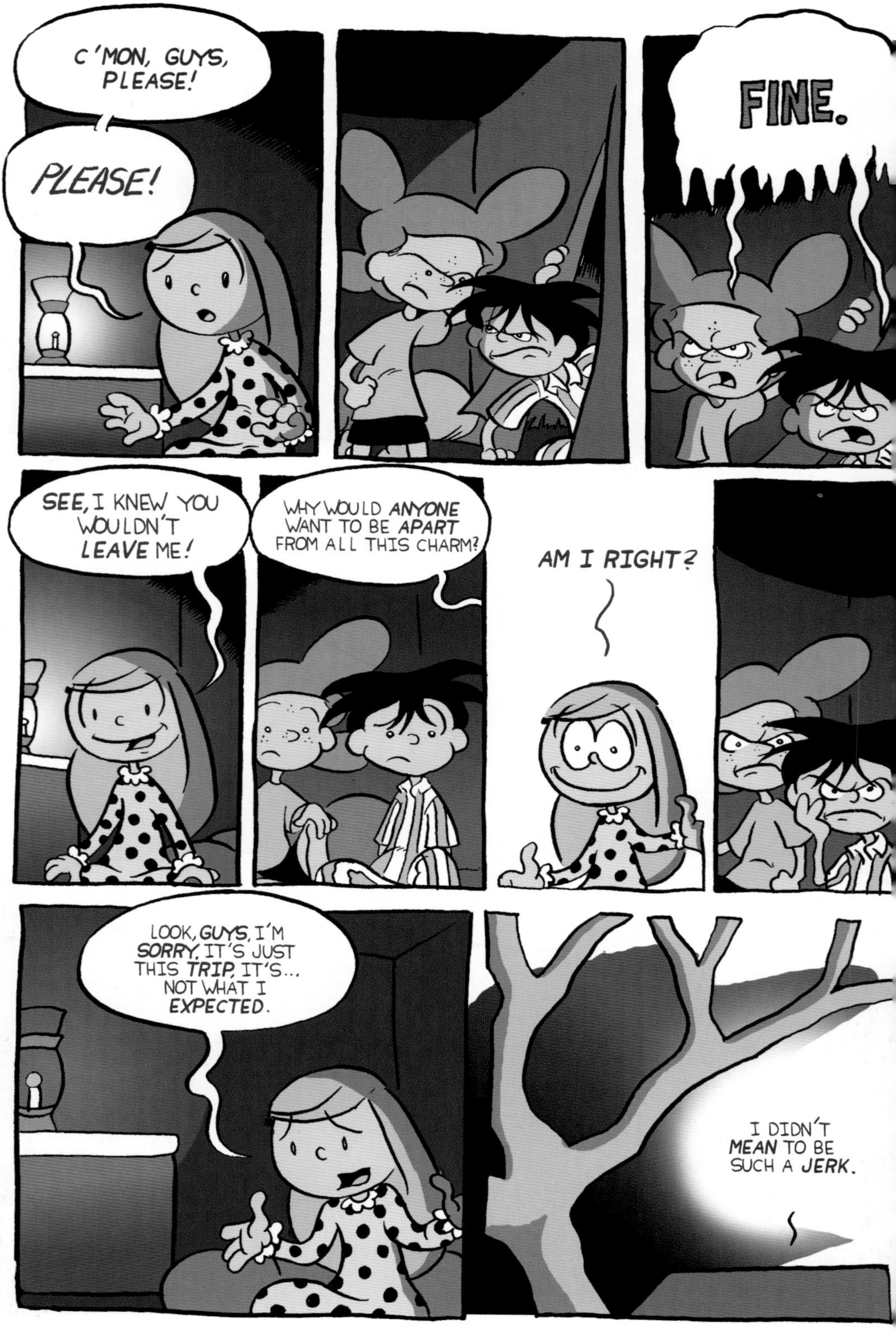
C'MON, GUYS, PLEASE!
PLEASE!
FINE.
SEE, I KNEW YOU WOULDN'T LEAVE ME!
WHY WOULD ANYONE WANT TO BE APART FROM ALL THIS CHARM?
AM I RIGHT?
LOOK, GUYS, I'M SORRY. IT'S JUST THIS TRIP, IT'S... NOT WHAT I EXPECTED.
I DIDN'T MEAN TO BE SUCH A JERK.

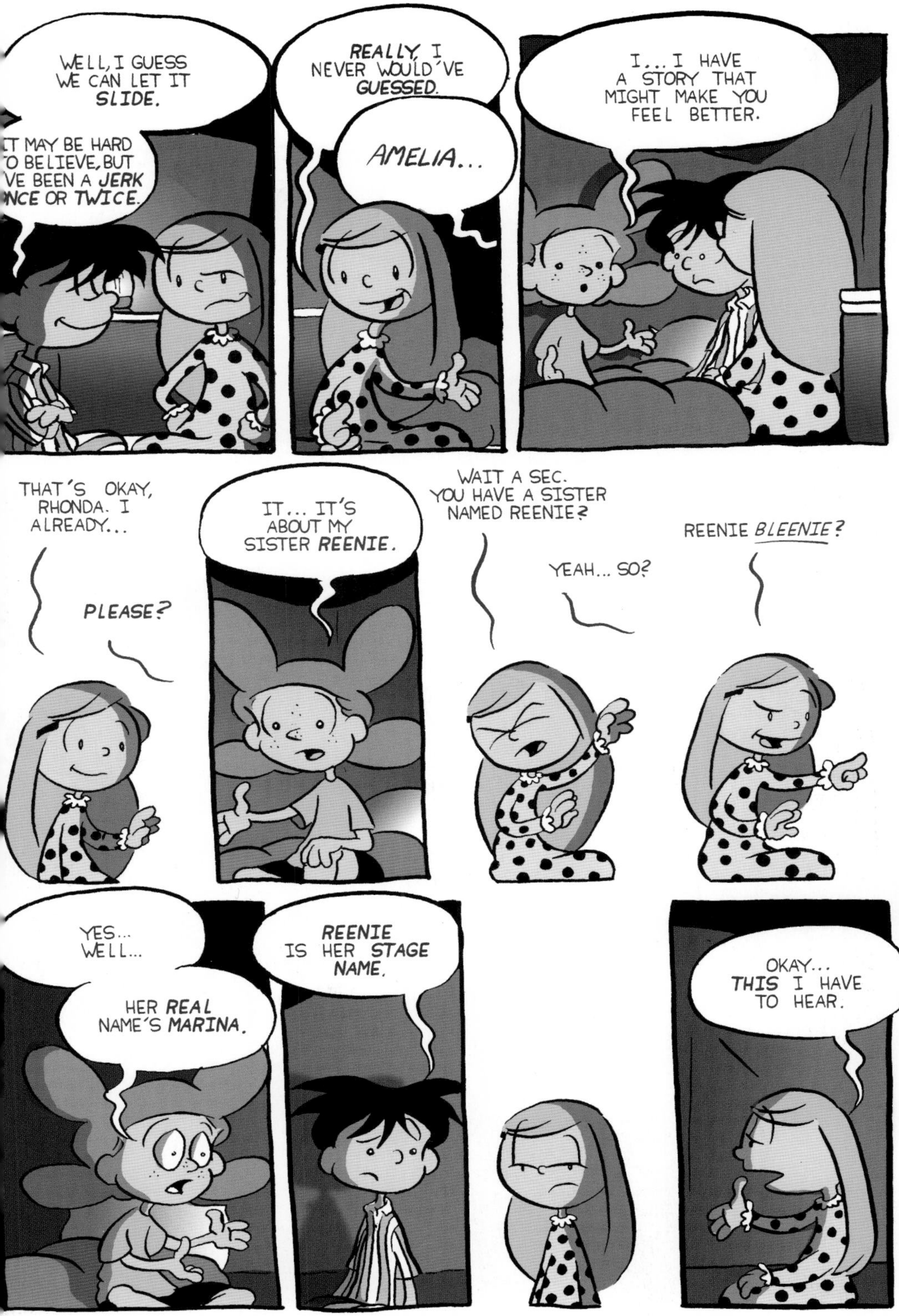
WELL, I GUESS WE CAN LET IT SLIDE.
IT MAY BE HARD TO BELIEVE, BUT I'VE BEEN A JERK ONCE OR TWICE.
REALLY, I NEVER WOULD'VE GUESSED.
AMELIA...
I... I HAVE A STORY THAT MIGHT MAKE YOU FEEL BETTER.
THAT'S OKAY, RHONDA. I ALREADY...
PLEASE?
IT... IT'S ABOUT MY SISTER REENIE.
WAIT A SEC. YOU HAVE A SISTER NAMED REENIE?
YEAH... SO?
REENIE BLEENIE?
YES... WELL...
HER REAL NAME'S MARINA.
REENIE IS HER STAGE NAME.
OKAY... THIS I HAVE TO HEAR.

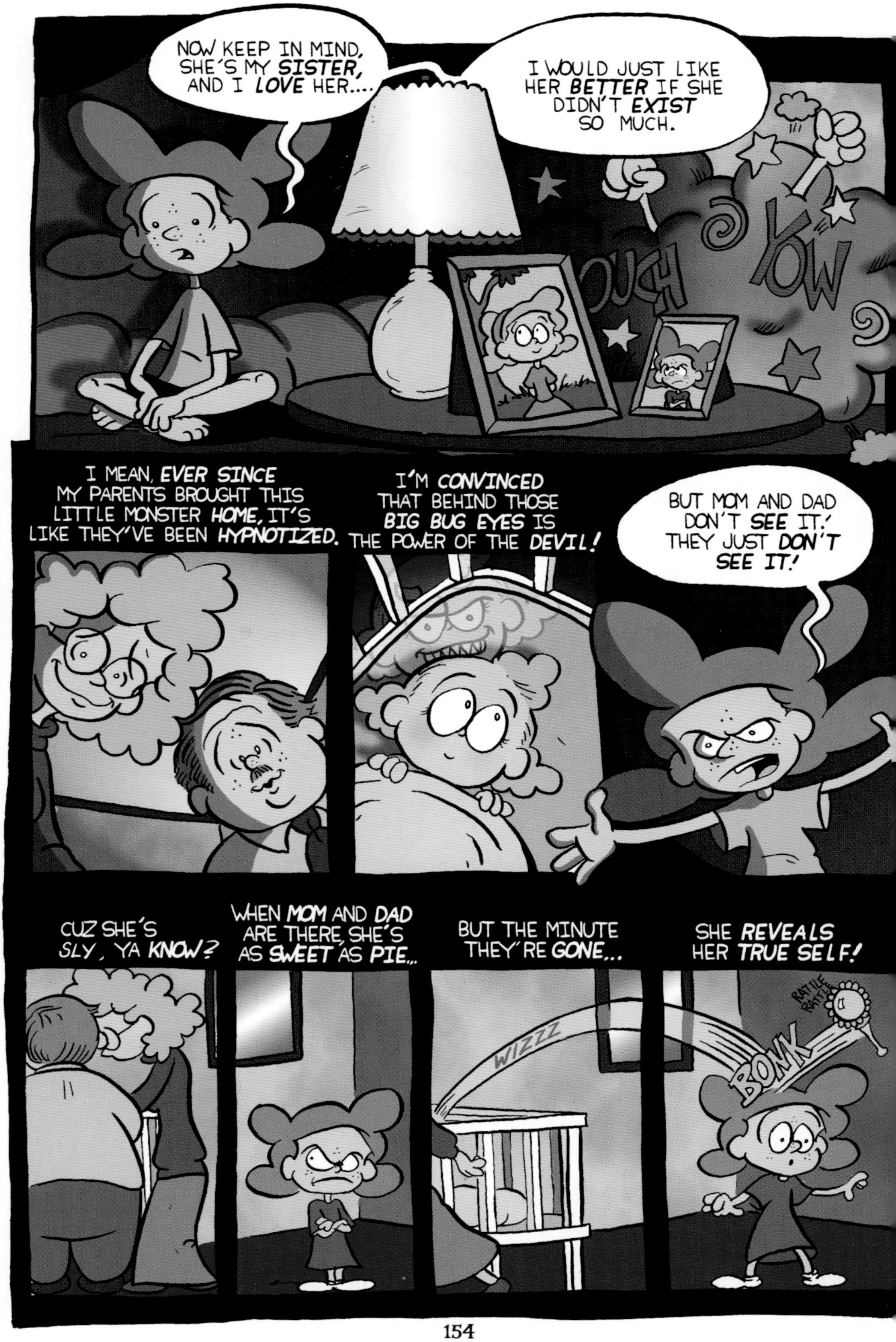
NOW KEEP IN MIND, SHE'S MY SISTER, AND I LOVE HER....
I WOULD JUST LIKE HER BETTER IF SHE DIDN'T EXIST SO MUCH.
OUCH
YOW
I MEAN, EVER SINCE MY PARENTS BROUGHT THIS LITTLE MONSTER HOME, IT'S LIKE THEY'VE BEEN HYPNOTIZED.
I'M CONVINCED THAT BEHIND THOSE BIG BUG EYES IS THE POWER OF THE DEVIL!
BUT MOM AND DAD DON'T SEE IT! THEY JUST DON'T SEE IT!
CUZ SHE'S SLY, YA KNOW?
WHEN MOM AND DAD ARE THERE, SHE'S AS SWEET AS PIE...
BUT THE MINUTE THEY'RE GONE...
WIZZZ
SHE REVEALS HER TRUE SELF!
RATTLE RATTLE
BONK

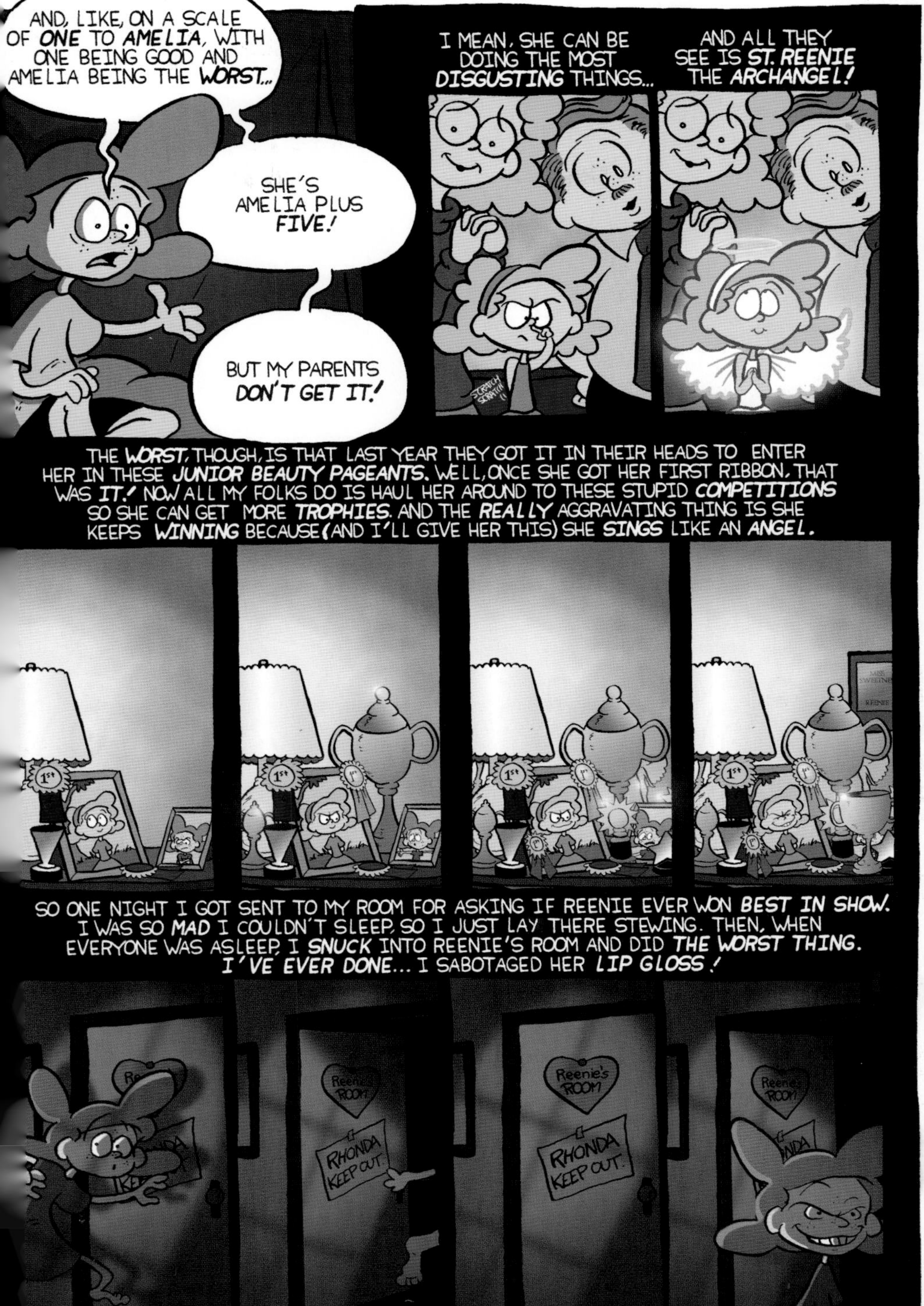
AND, LIKE, ON A SCALE OF ONE TO AMELIA, WITH ONE BEING GOOD AND AMELIA BEING THE WORST...
SHE'S AMELIA PLUS FIVE!
BUT MY PARENTS DON'T GET IT!
I MEAN, SHE CAN BE DOING THE MOST DISGUSTING THINGS...
SCRATCH SCRATCH
AND ALL THEY SEE IS ST. REENIE THE ARCHANGEL!
THE WORST, THOUGH, IS THAT LAST YEAR THEY GOT IT IN THEIR HEADS TO ENTER HER IN THESE JUNIOR BEAUTY PAGEANTS. WELL, ONCE SHE GOT HER FIRST RIBBON, THAT WAS IT! NOW ALL MY FOLKS DO IS HAUL HER AROUND TO THESE STUPID COMPETITIONS SO SHE CAN GET MORE TROPHIES. AND THE REALLY AGGRAVATING THING IS SHE KEEPS WINNING BECAUSE (AND I'LL GIVE HER THIS) SHE SINGS LIKE AN ANGEL.
SO ONE NIGHT I GOT SENT TO MY ROOM FOR ASKING IF REENIE EVER WON BEST IN SHOW. I WAS SO MAD I COULDN'T SLEEP, SO I JUST LAY THERE STEWING. THEN, WHEN EVERYONE WAS ASLEEP, I SNUCK INTO REENIE'S ROOM AND DID THE WORST THING. I'VE EVER DONE... I SABOTAGED HER LIP GLOSS!
Reenie's ROOM
RHONDA KEEP OUT

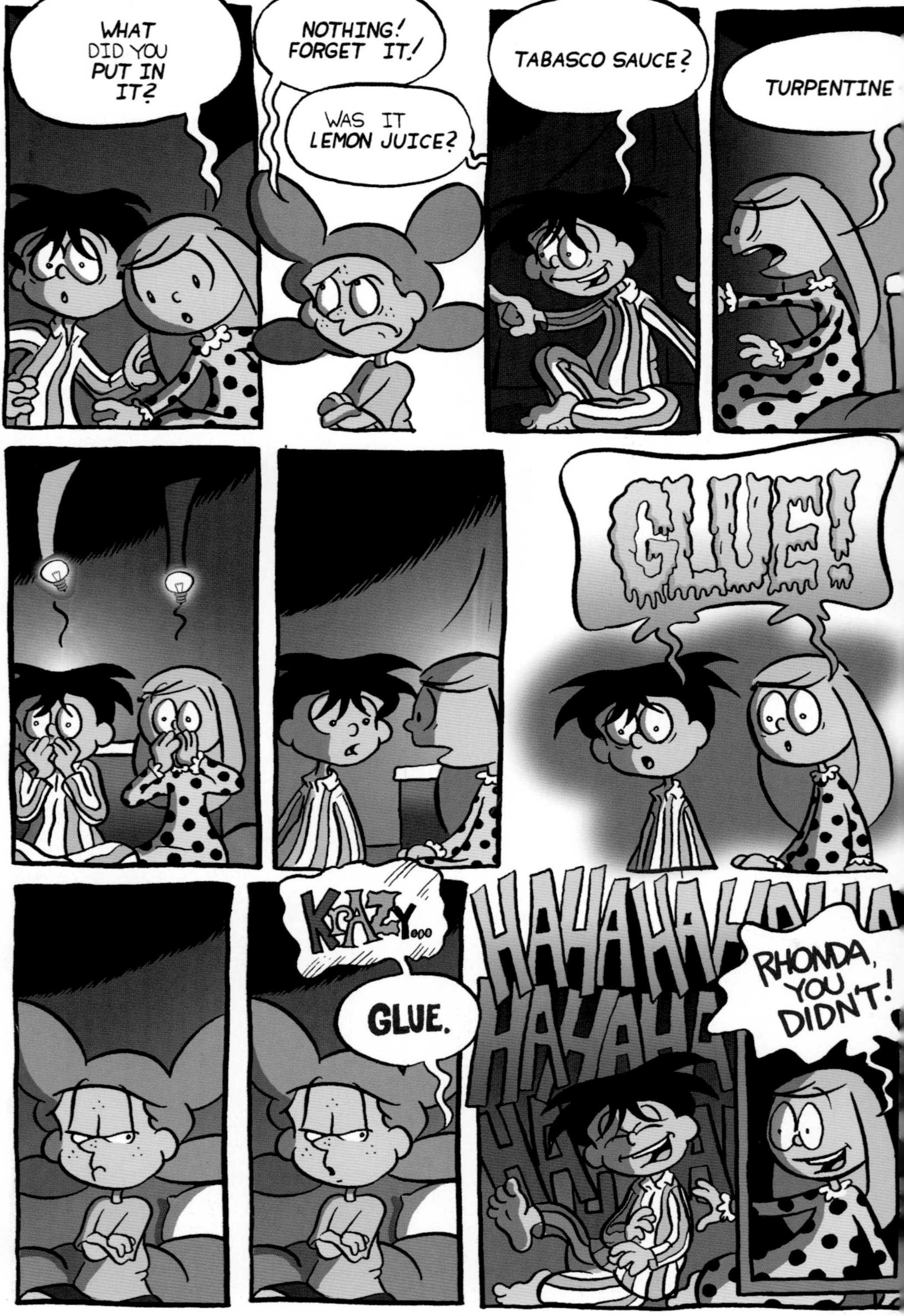

WHAT DID YOU PUT IN IT?
NOTHING! FORGET IT!
WAS IT LEMON JUICE?
TABASCO SAUCE?
TURPENTINE
GLUE!
KRAZY...
GLUE.
HAHAHAHA
HAHAHA
RHONDA, YOU DIDN'T!

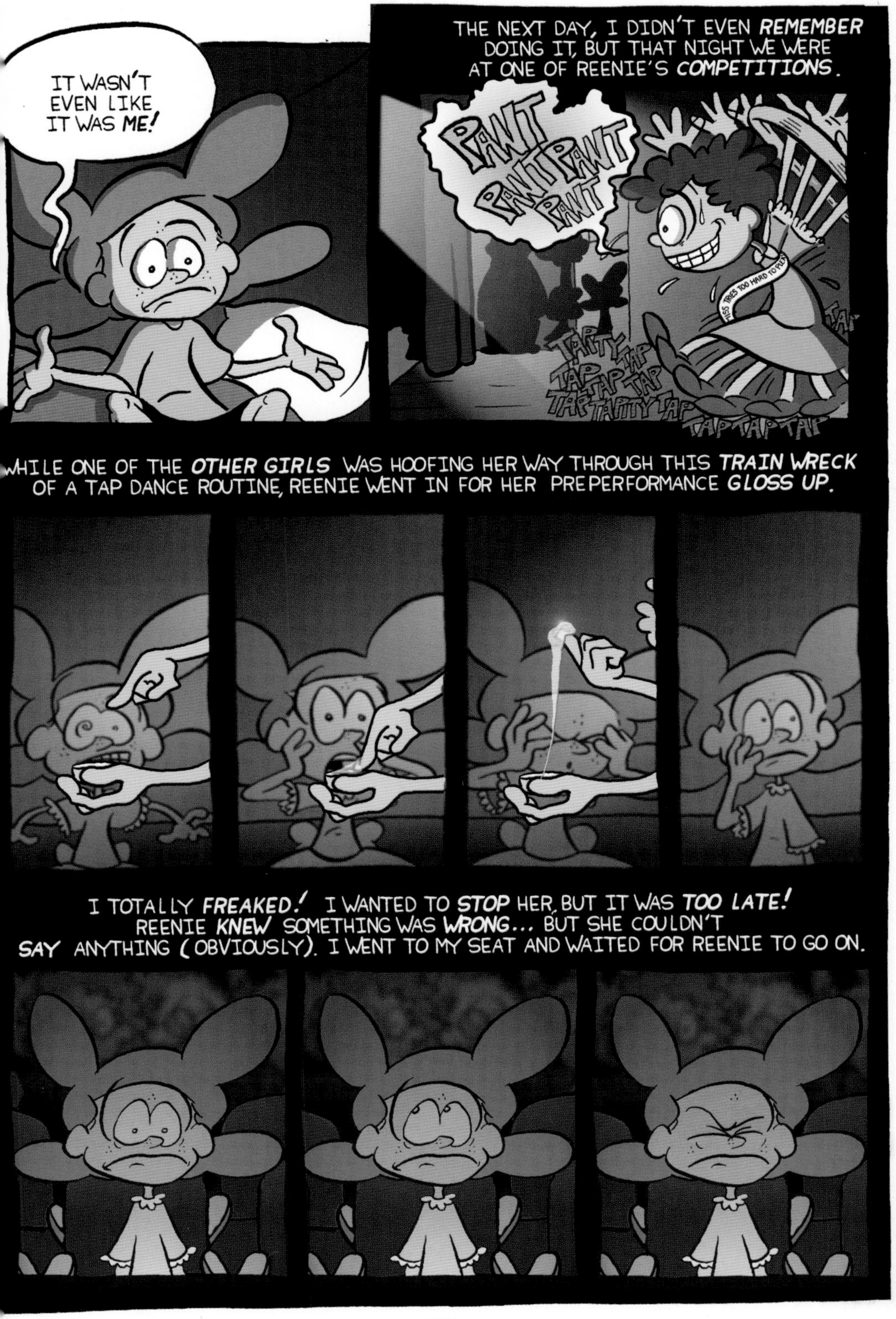
IT WASN'T EVEN LIKE IT WAS ME!
THE NEXT DAY, I DIDN'T EVEN REMEMBER DOING IT, BUT THAT NIGHT WE WERE AT ONE OF REENIE'S COMPETITIONS.
PANT PANT PANT PANT PANT
TAPPITY TAP TAP TAP TAP TAP TAP TAPPITY TAP TAP TAP TAP
WHILE ONE OF THE OTHER GIRLS WAS HOOFING HER WAY THROUGH THIS TRAIN WRECK OF A TAP DANCE ROUTINE, REENIE WENT IN FOR HER PREPERFORMANCE GLOSS UP.
I TOTALLY FREAKED! I WANTED TO STOP HER, BUT IT WAS TOO LATE! REENIE KNEW SOMETHING WAS WRONG... BUT SHE COULDN'T SAY ANYTHING (OBVIOUSLY). I WENT TO MY SEAT AND WAITED FOR REENIE TO GO ON.

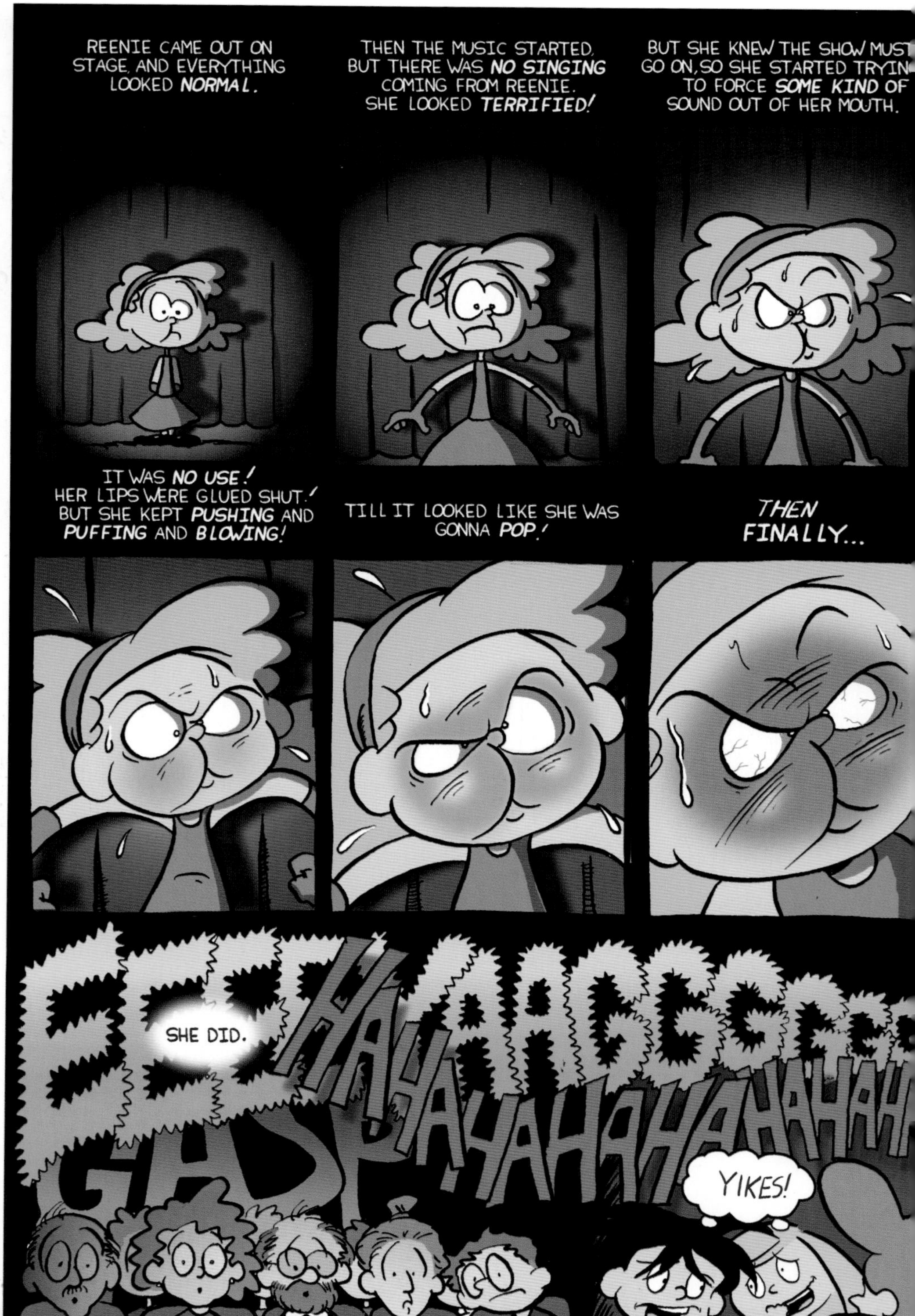
REENIE CAME OUT ON STAGE, AND EVERYTHING LOOKED **NORMAL.**
THEN THE MUSIC STARTED, BUT THERE WAS **NO SINGING** COMING FROM REENIE. SHE LOOKED **TERRIFIED!**
BUT SHE KNEW THE SHOW MUST GO ON, SO SHE STARTED TRYIN TO FORCE **SOME KIND OF** SOUND OUT OF HER MOUTH.
IT WAS **NO USE!** HER LIPS WERE GLUED SHUT! BUT SHE KEPT **PUSHING** AND **PUFFING** AND **BLOWING!**
TILL IT LOOKED LIKE SHE WAS GONNA **POP!**
THEN **FINALLY...**
SHE DID.
YIKES!

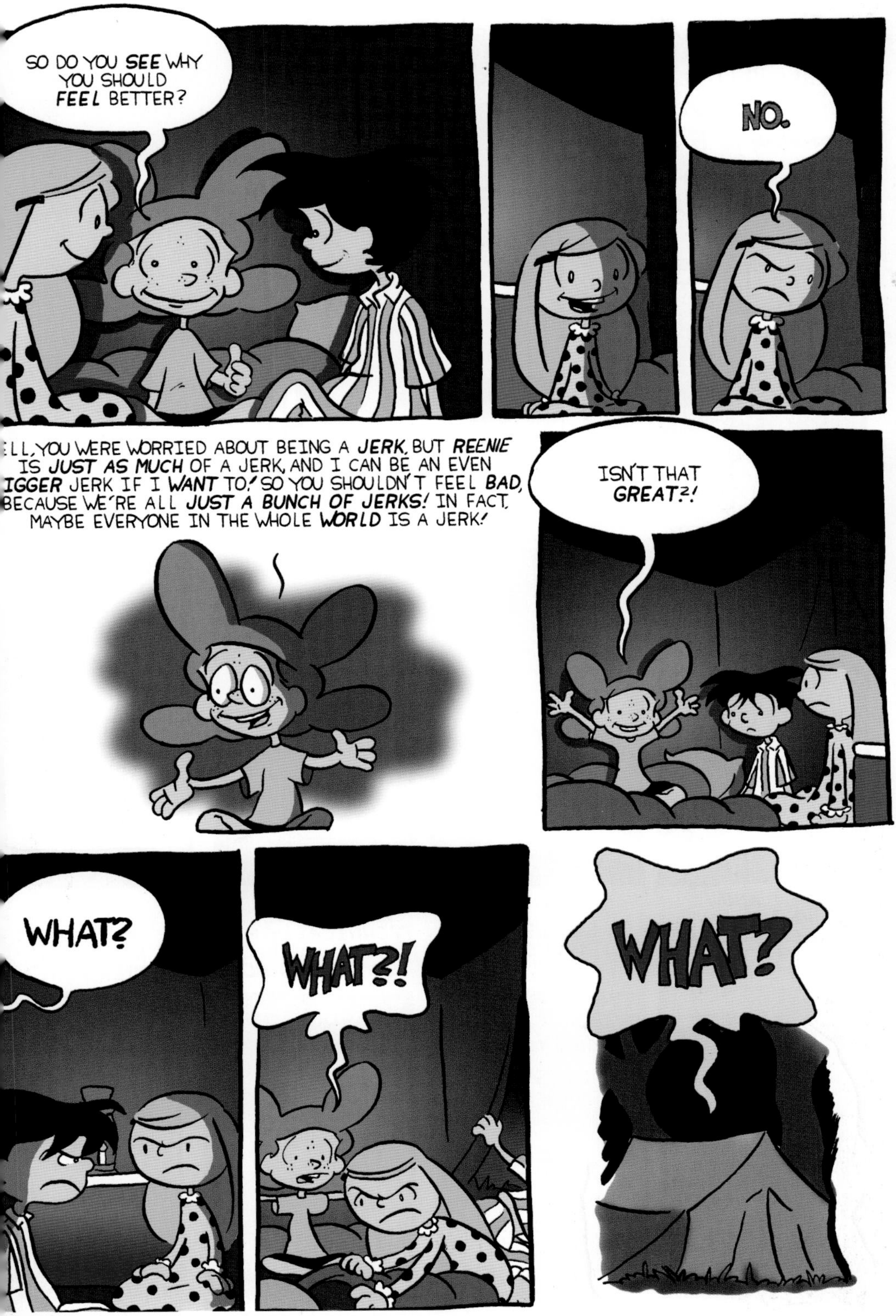

SO DO YOU SEE WHY YOU SHOULD FEEL BETTER?
NO.
ELL, YOU WERE WORRIED ABOUT BEING A JERK, BUT REENIE IS JUST AS MUCH OF A JERK, AND I CAN BE AN EVEN IGGER JERK IF I WANT TO! SO YOU SHOULDN'T FEEL BAD, BECAUSE WE'RE ALL JUST A BUNCH OF JERKS! IN FACT, MAYBE EVERYONE IN THE WHOLE WORLD IS A JERK!
ISN'T THAT GREAT?!
WHAT?
WHAT?!
WHAT?

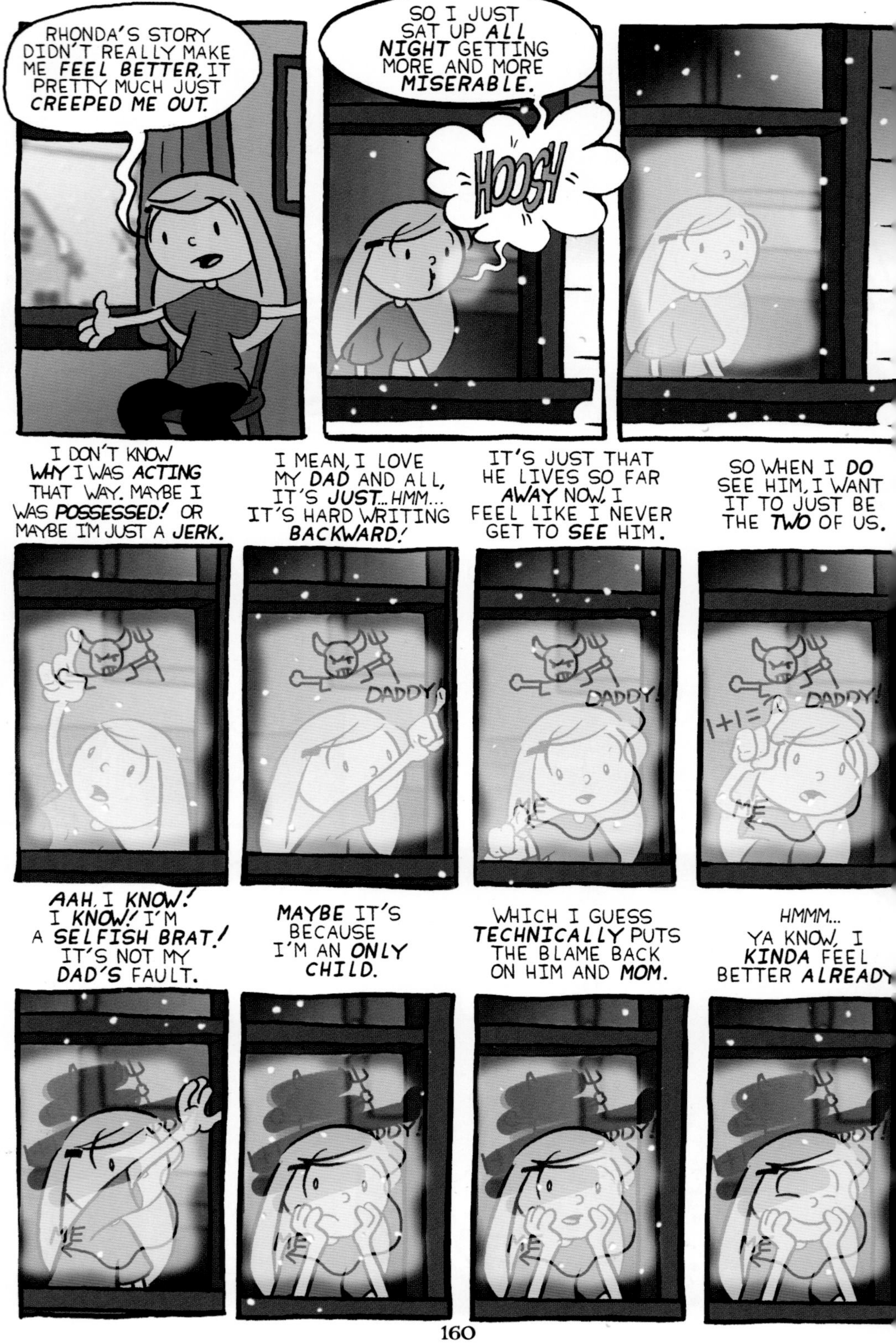

RHONDA'S STORY DIDN'T REALLY MAKE ME FEEL BETTER, IT PRETTY MUCH JUST CREEPED ME OUT.
SO I JUST SAT UP ALL NIGHT GETTING MORE AND MORE MISERABLE.
HOOSH
I DON'T KNOW WHY I WAS ACTING THAT WAY. MAYBE I WAS POSSESSED! OR MAYBE I'M JUST A JERK.
I MEAN, I LOVE MY DAD AND ALL, IT'S JUST... HMM... IT'S HARD WRITING BACKWARD!
DADDY!
IT'S JUST THAT HE LIVES SO FAR AWAY NOW, I FEEL LIKE I NEVER GET TO SEE HIM.
DADDY!
ME
SO WHEN I DO SEE HIM, I WANT IT TO JUST BE THE TWO OF US.
1+1=
DADDY!
ME
AAH, I KNOW! I KNOW! I'M A SELFISH BRAT! IT'S NOT MY DAD'S FAULT.
MAYBE IT'S BECAUSE I'M AN ONLY CHILD.
WHICH I GUESS TECHNICALLY PUTS THE BLAME BACK ON HIM AND MOM.
HMMM... YA KNOW, I KINDA FEEL BETTER ALREADY

I WOKE UP THE NEXT MORNING, AND MY DAD WAS UP AND WAITING FOR ME. WE WENT FOR A WALK WHILE THE OTHERS WERE SLEEPING.

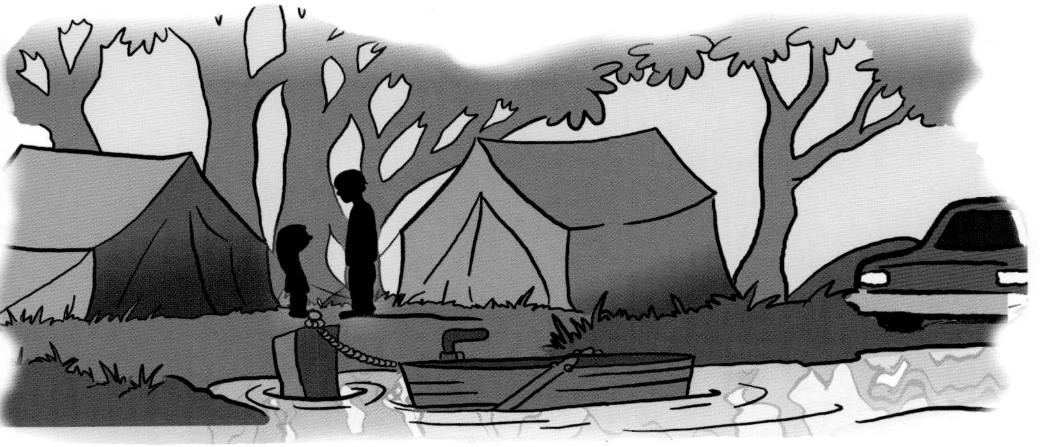

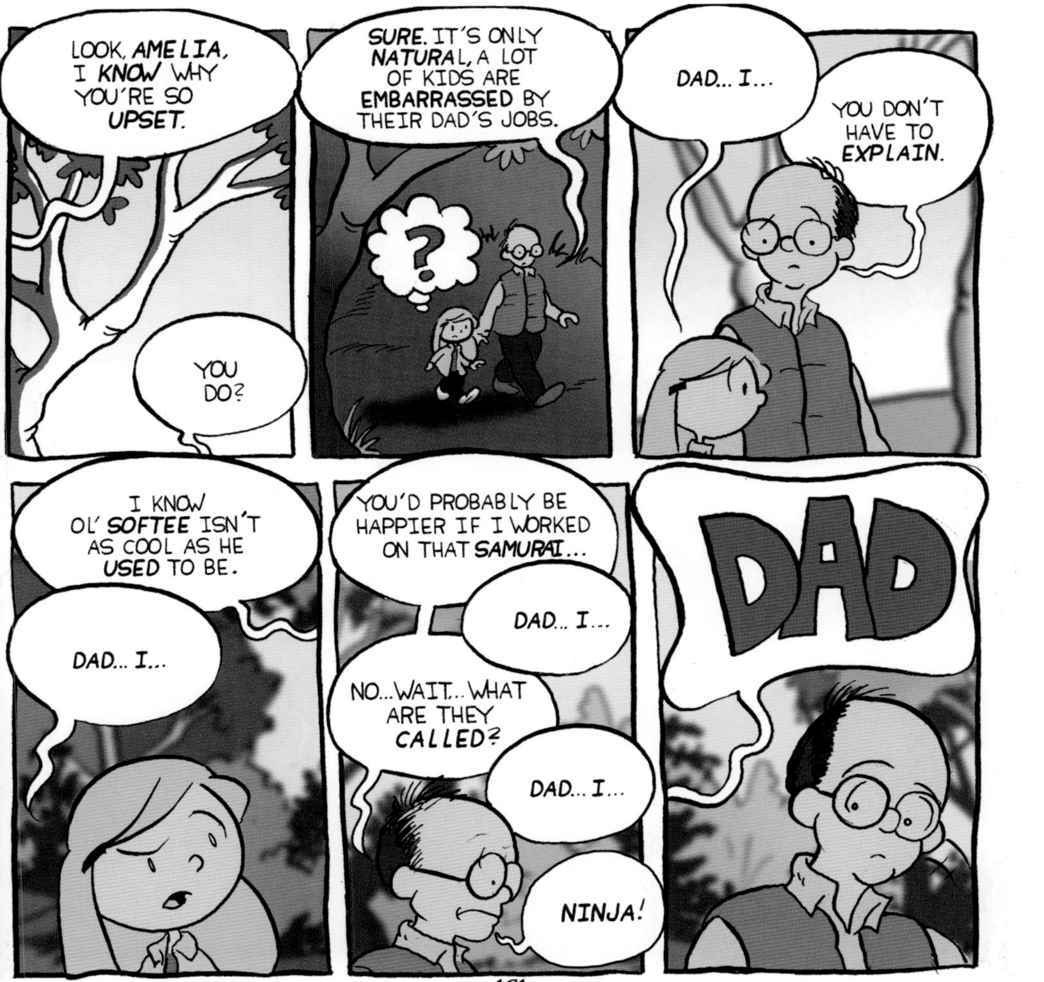
LOOK, AMELIA, I KNOW WHY YOU'RE SO UPSET.
YOU DO?
SURE. IT'S ONLY NATURAL, A LOT OF KIDS ARE EMBARRASSED BY THEIR DAD'S JOBS.
?
DAD... I...
YOU DON'T HAVE TO EXPLAIN.
I KNOW OL' SOFTEE ISN'T AS COOL AS HE USED TO BE.
DAD... I...
YOU'D PROBABLY BE HAPPIER IF I WORKED ON THAT SAMURAI...
DAD... I...
NO...WAIT...WHAT ARE THEY CALLED?
DAD... I...
NINJA!
DAD

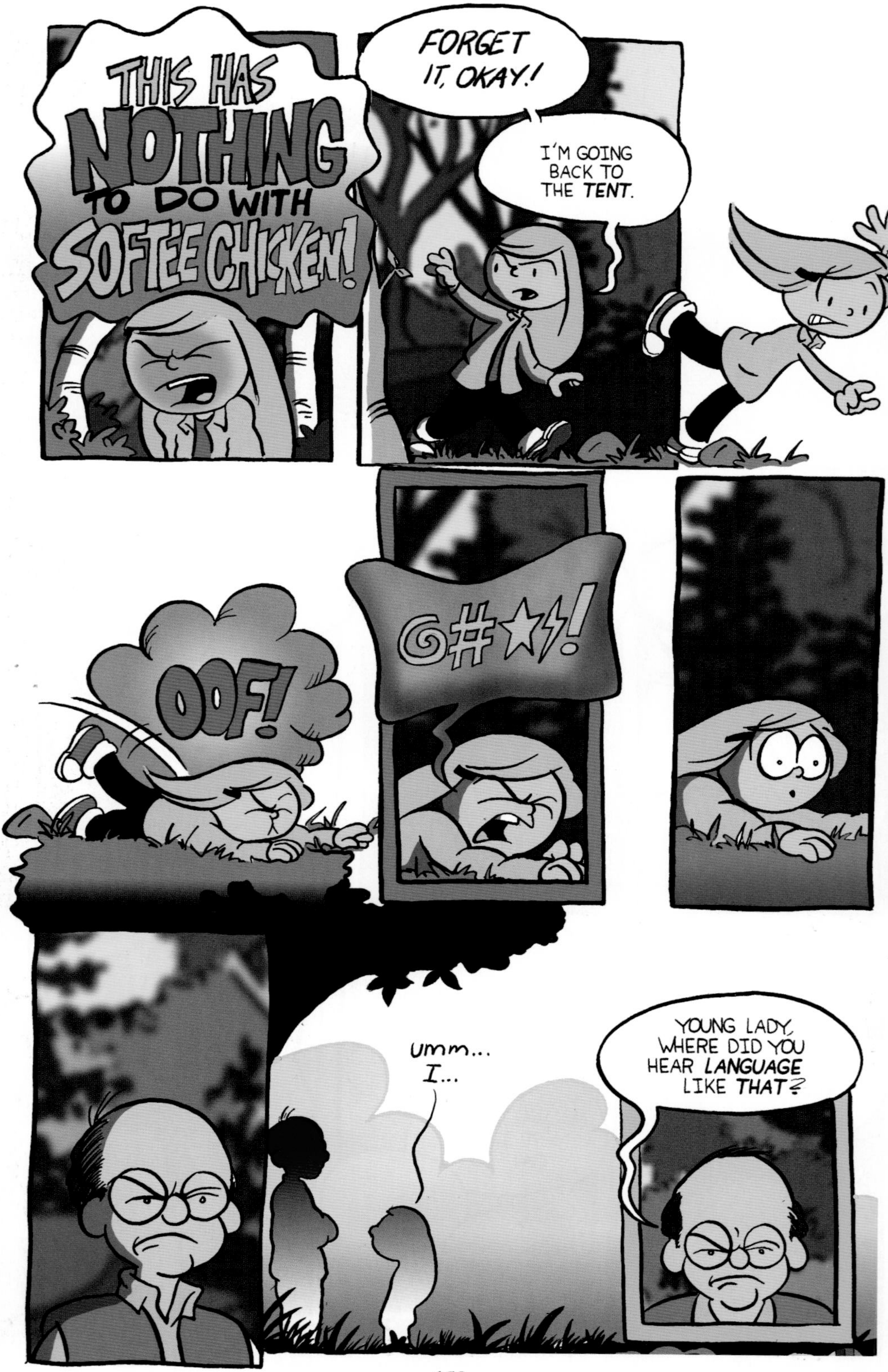
THIS HAS NOTHING TO DO WITH SOFTEE CHICKEN!
FORGET IT, OKAY!
I'M GOING BACK TO THE TENT.
OOF!
@#★ϟ!
umm... I...
YOUNG LADY, WHERE DID YOU HEAR LANGUAGE LIKE THAT?

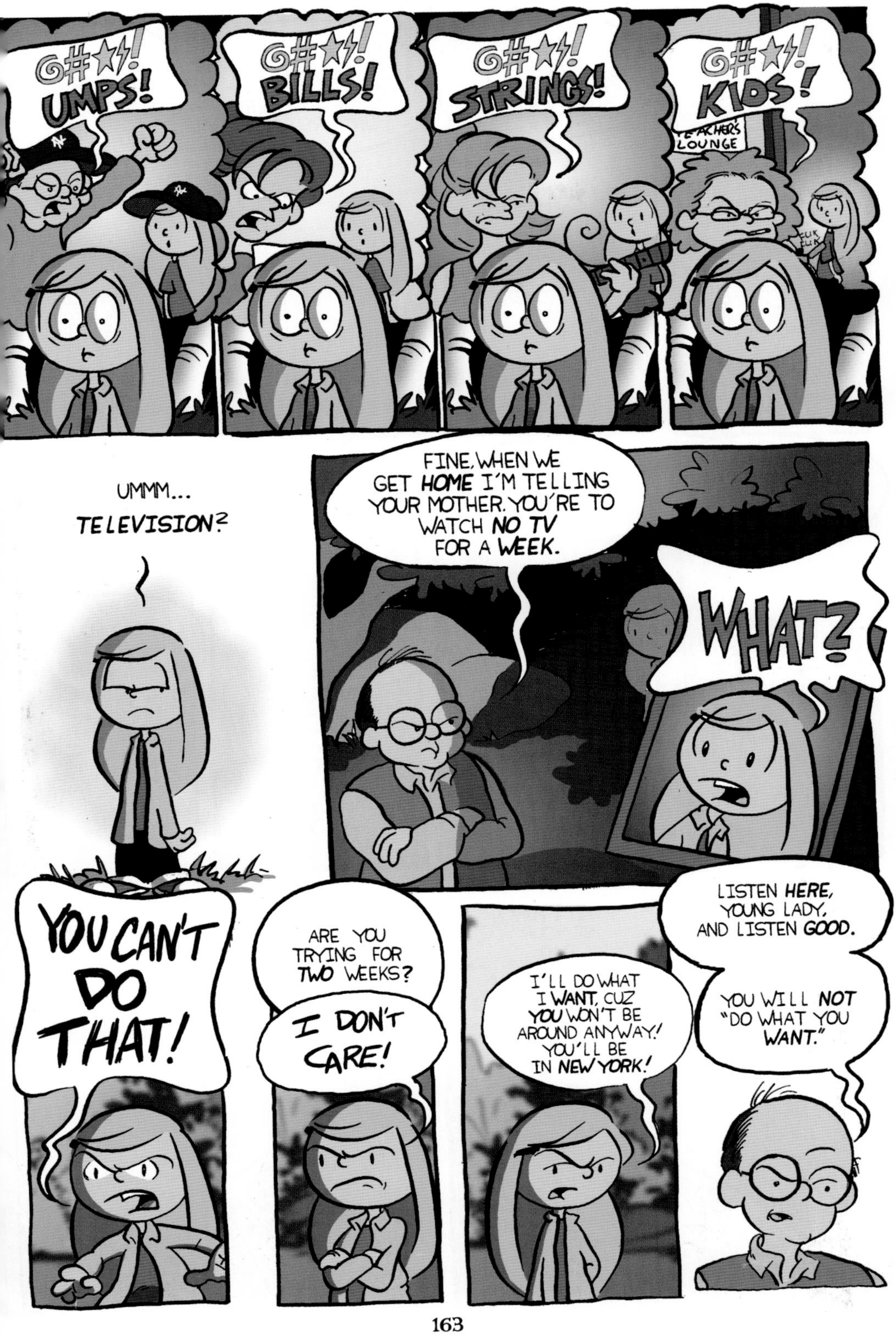
G#★ϟ! UMPS!
G#★ϟ! BILLS!
G#★ϟ! STRINGS!
G#★ϟ! KIDS!
TEACHER'S LOUNGE
UMMM... TELEVISION?
FINE, WHEN WE GET HOME I'M TELLING YOUR MOTHER. YOU'RE TO WATCH NO TV FOR A WEEK.
WHAT?
YOU CAN'T DO THAT!
ARE YOU TRYING FOR TWO WEEKS?
I DON'T CARE!
I'LL DO WHAT I WANT, CUZ YOU WON'T BE AROUND ANYWAY! YOU'LL BE IN NEW YORK!
LISTEN HERE, YOUNG LADY, AND LISTEN GOOD.
YOU WILL NOT "DO WHAT YOU WANT."

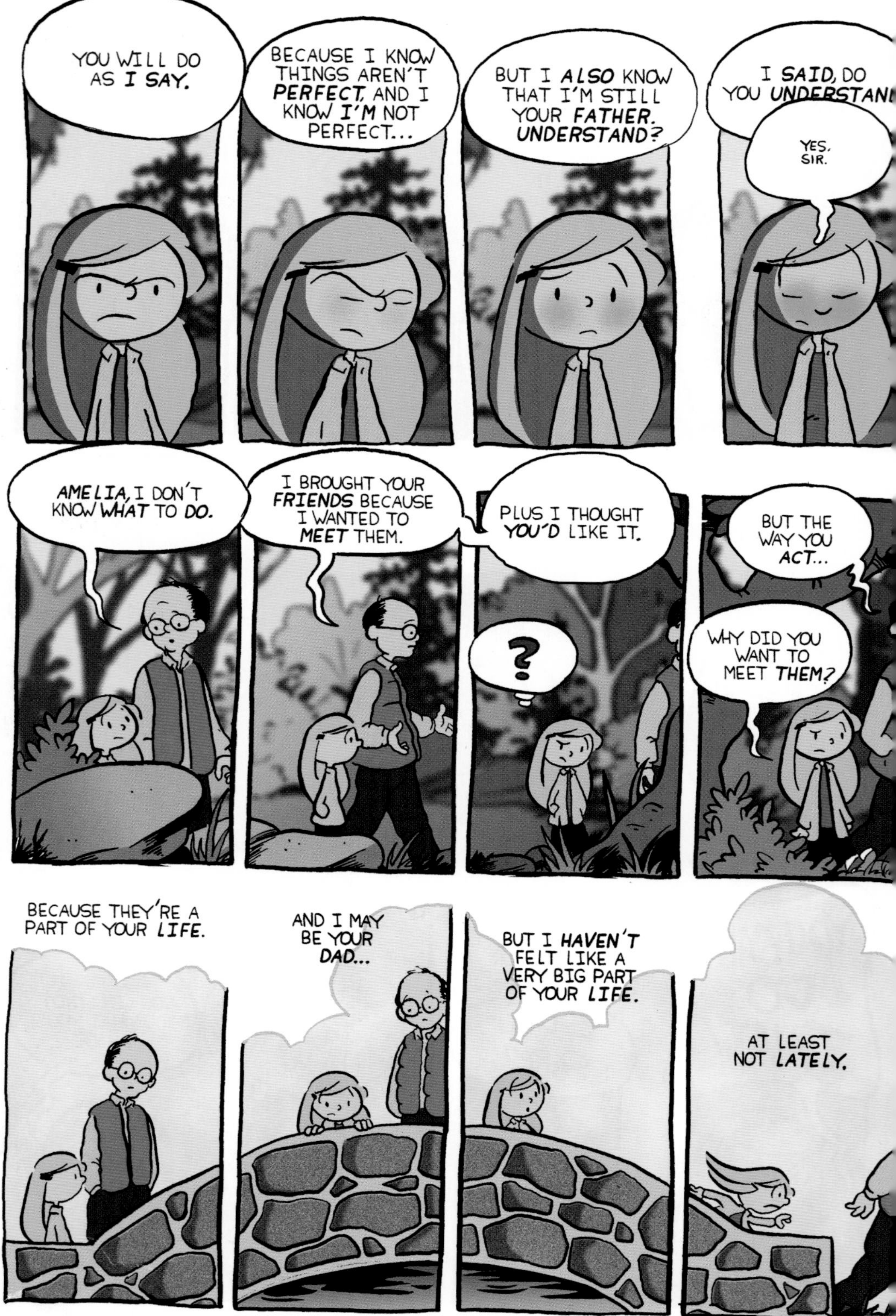
YOU WILL DO AS I SAY.
BECAUSE I KNOW THINGS AREN'T PERFECT, AND I KNOW I'M NOT PERFECT...
BUT I ALSO KNOW THAT I'M STILL YOUR FATHER. UNDERSTAND?
I SAID, DO YOU UNDERSTAN
YES, SIR.
AMELIA, I DON'T KNOW WHAT TO DO.
I BROUGHT YOUR FRIENDS BECAUSE I WANTED TO MEET THEM.
PLUS I THOUGHT YOU'D LIKE IT.
?
BUT THE WAY YOU ACT...
WHY DID YOU WANT TO MEET THEM?
BECAUSE THEY'RE A PART OF YOUR LIFE.
AND I MAY BE YOUR DAD...
BUT I HAVEN'T FELT LIKE A VERY BIG PART OF YOUR LIFE.
AT LEAST NOT LATELY.

LOOK, DAD, I'M *SORRY*. I REALLY *AM*.

I GUESS... I GUESS I WAS SCARED.

CUZ I—I GUESS I SOMETIMES *WORRY*.

THAT MAYBE THE WHOLE *DIVORCE* THING...

WAS CUZ YOU DIDN'T WANT TO BE WITH *ME*.

AMELIA! YOU *KNOW* THAT'S NOT TRUE.

YEAH...WELL... I DON'T KNOW. IT SEEMED THAT WAY *SOMETIMES*.

I... I DON'T KNOW WHAT TO *SAY*, AMELIA.

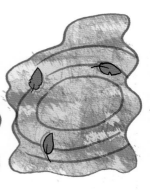

EXCEPT THAT IT'S NOT *TRUE*.

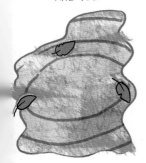

YOUR *MOM* AND I AREN'T TOGETHER FOR A *LOT* OF REASONS, BUT *NONE* OF THEM ARE YOU.

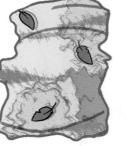

LOOK... I KNOW THINGS HAVEN'T BEEN THAT *GREAT*, BUT WE CAN *WORK* ON *THAT*. WHAT DO YOU *SAY*?

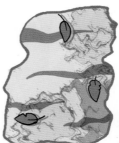

⟩SIGH⟨ YEAH. OKAY.

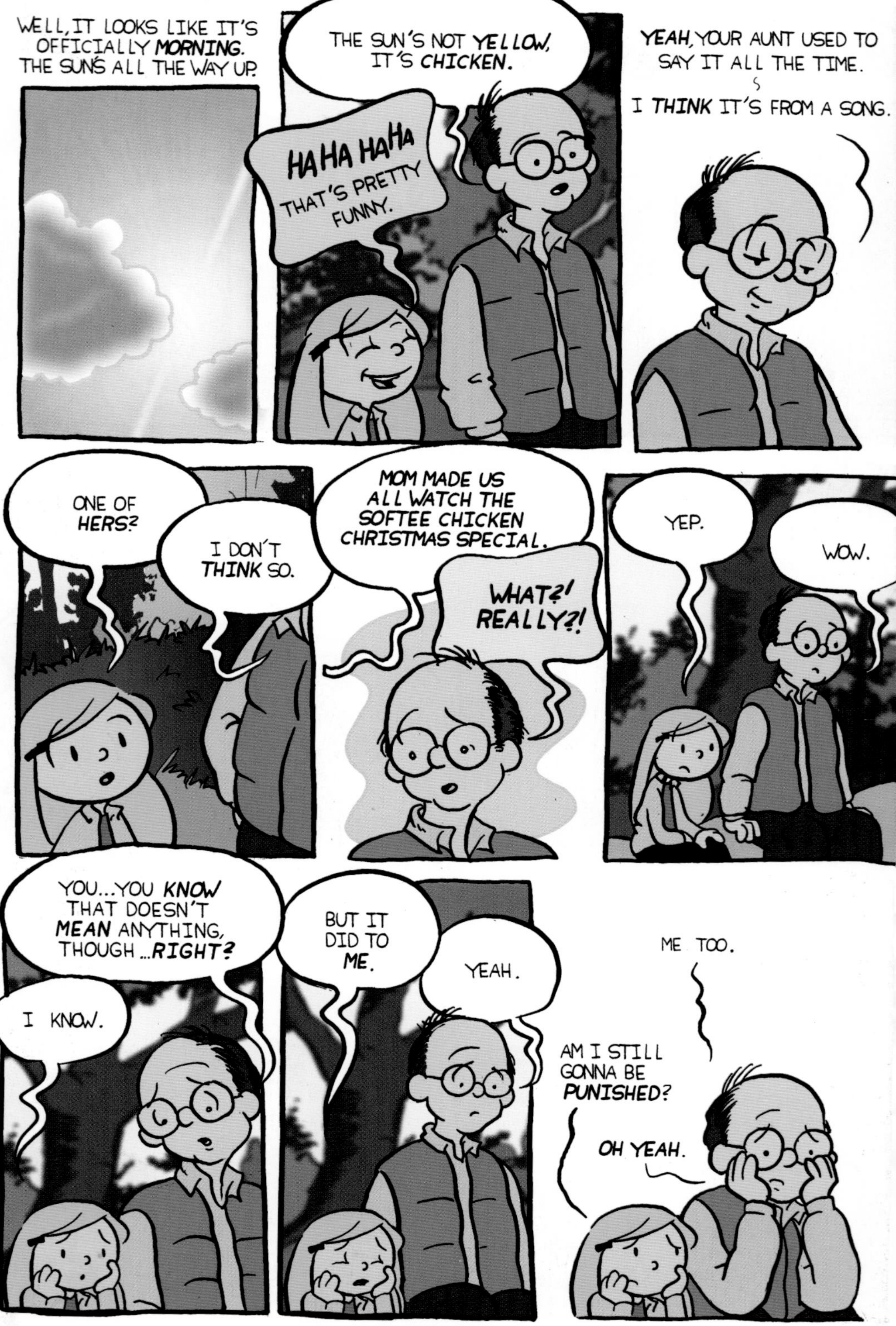
WELL, IT LOOKS LIKE IT'S OFFICIALLY MORNING. THE SUN'S ALL THE WAY UP.
THE SUN'S NOT YELLOW, IT'S CHICKEN.
HA HA HA HA THAT'S PRETTY FUNNY.
YEAH, YOUR AUNT USED TO SAY IT ALL THE TIME.
I THINK IT'S FROM A SONG.
ONE OF HERS?
I DON'T THINK SO.
MOM MADE US ALL WATCH THE SOFTEE CHICKEN CHRISTMAS SPECIAL.
WHAT?! REALLY?!
YEP.
WOW.
YOU...YOU KNOW THAT DOESN'T MEAN ANYTHING, THOUGH ...RIGHT?
I KNOW.
BUT IT DID TO ME.
YEAH.
ME TOO.
AM I STILL GONNA BE PUNISHED?
OH YEAH.

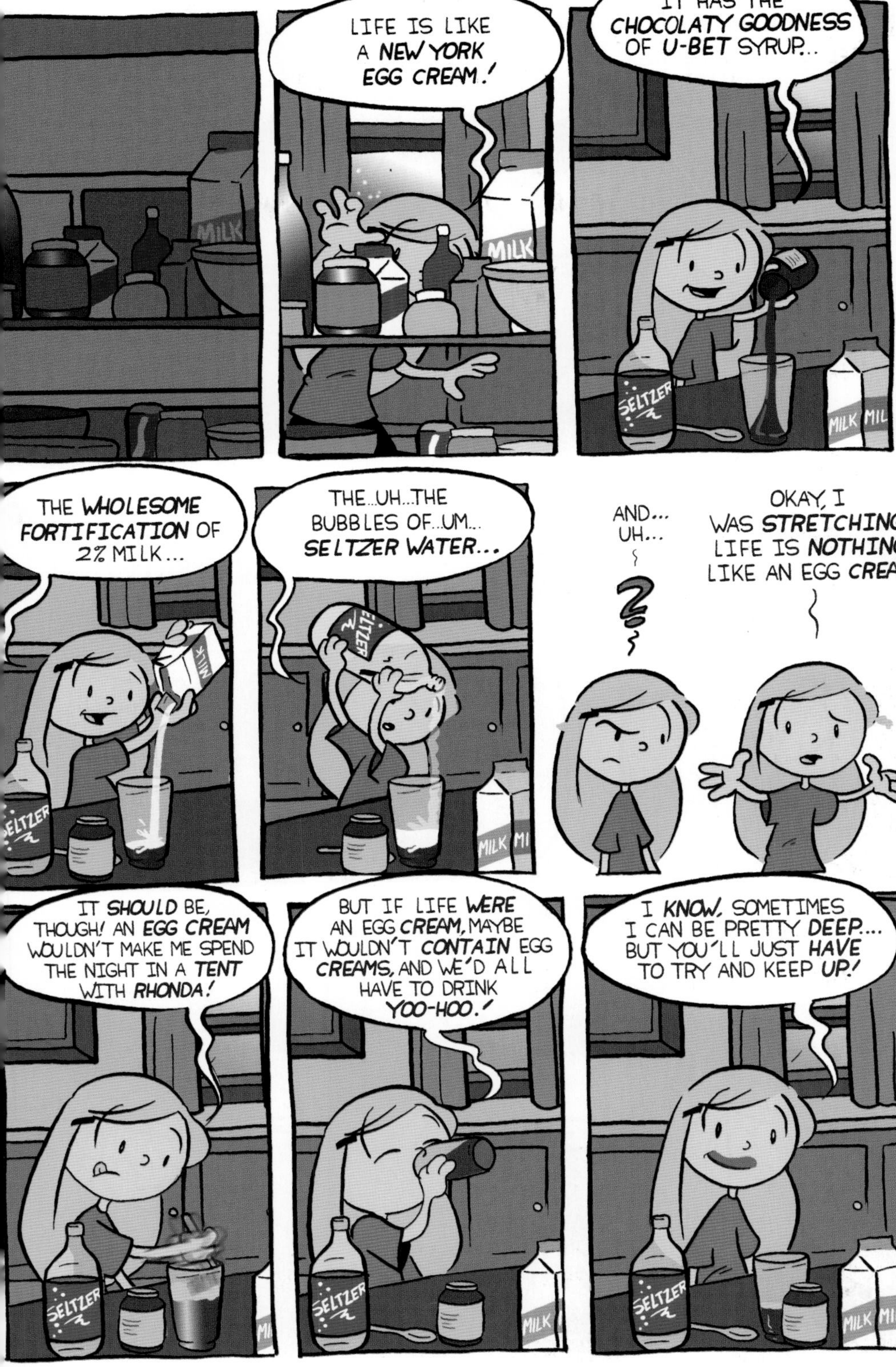
LIFE IS LIKE A NEW YORK EGG CREAM!
IT HAS THE CHOCOLATY GOODNESS OF U-BET SYRUP...
MILK
THE WHOLESOME FORTIFICATION OF 2% MILK...
THE...UH...THE BUBBLES OF...UM... SELTZER WATER...
SELTZER
AND... UH...
OKAY, I WAS STRETCHING. LIFE IS NOTHING LIKE AN EGG CREAM.
IT SHOULD BE, THOUGH! AN EGG CREAM WOULDN'T MAKE ME SPEND THE NIGHT IN A TENT WITH RHONDA!
BUT IF LIFE WERE AN EGG CREAM, MAYBE IT WOULDN'T CONTAIN EGG CREAMS, AND WE'D ALL HAVE TO DRINK YOO-HOO!
I KNOW. SOMETIMES I CAN BE PRETTY DEEP.... BUT YOU'LL JUST HAVE TO TRY AND KEEP UP!

ANYWAY, THAT'S THE STORY OF MY BIG CAMPING TRIP. I CHEERED UP AND WE EVEN MANAGED TO HAVE SOME FUN.
SELTZER
MILK MI
AND IT WAS REALLY GOOD TO TALK TO MY DAD LIKE THAT. I THINK THINGS ARE GONNA BE ALL RIGHT NOW.
LTZER
I MEAN, I KNOW IT'S GONNA BE HARD AND ALL, BUT I REALLY THINK...UH...I-I REALLY...UMM...
WHAT?
WHAT?
OH...
HAHAHA
SELTZER
MILK MIL
SO MATURE OF YOU!
SELTZER
MILK M
SELTZER
MILK M
SOOOOOOoo MATURE!
SELTZER
MILK M

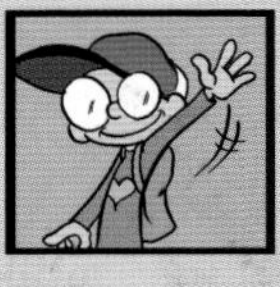

Jimmy Gownley's
AMELIA RULES!™

Join Amelia and the gang for
adventures, mishaps, and homework.

Collect them all!

☐ **#1:** *The Whole World's Crazy*
ISBN: 978-1-4169-8604-1

☐ **#2:** *What Makes You Happy*
Coming August 2009!
ISBN: 978-1-4169-8605-8

☐ **#3:** *Superheroes*
Coming January 2010!
ISBN: 978-1-4169-8606-5

☐ **#4:** *When the Past Is a Present*
Coming April 2010!
ISBN: 978-1-4169-8607-2

☐ *A Very Ninja Christmas*
Coming October 2009!
ISBN: 978-1-4169-8959-2

PER

10/9/21 - removed stained front pg.
JC-RIS